Where the River Flows Both Ways

Written by Stephen Densmore

First paperback edition April 2019

Book design Dee Densmore

ISBN 978-0-578-50199-4

Published by Stephen E. Densmore

This book is dedicated to:

My mother, Pauline Densmore

for bringing me into this world

My daughters, Ami & Aki Densmore

for inspiring me in myriad ways

My wife, Jacqueline Densmore

whose unbending love, partnership & encouragement

made this book a reality

Table of Contents

Prologue

At the beginning of time, the Mother of the World worked to shape the Earth. She worked until her fingers were raw and she was exhausted. Still, she was not pleased with what she had done. So she sat at the top of the highest place she could find, and felt sad. One tear came to her eye. It rolled down her cheek and collected in a dimple on the great mountain's face, a place the People would later call Lake Tear of the Clouds.

And so, when the clouds drop their rain and the little lake bubbles over, the water spills down the mountain side, tumbling around moss-covered rocks, through the cool shade of the hemlock forest, its mist making little rainbows in shafts of sunlight. The brook gurgles and bounces and laughs like a playful child bounding down the mountain. The brook gathers other brooks as it goes, becoming strong and swift and cocky.

It curls and hurls itself through the valleys, curving like a serpent, sucking in soil and felling great trees in its path. It carves the land, bringing dirt and small stones with it to other places. It is a river now. And it wants to change everything.

The young river slams against the sides of mountains like a buck into a thicket, roaring its displeasure at the hard, unyielding stone. But the river laughs, splashing wildly against the rocks. Because it knows that over time it will wear them all down. Over time, the river knows it will carve them into new shapes, create coves and secret places, break through walls and make waterfalls. It will, over time, bring everything down to the sea.

And the Mother of the World looked upon all of this and she smiled, because she knew that the river would make sure that the Earth would always be new. She blessed the river. It became the bringer of life to the People who lived in the world. For, as long as the river flowed, there would be water for them to drink and fish for them to eat. But, most of all, there would always be change and wonder in the world.

I: Two Boys Fishing

The great river flowed south out of the High Peaks of the Adirondacks, the ancient mountains that have defined Upstate New York for a billion years. The mountains had once soared as high as the Himalayas, but hundreds of millions of years of unrelenting erosion had brought them down, rounded them, and humbled them in the eyes of those who measure mountains. In the southern foothills of the Adirondacks, the Hudson River curled around the foot of Antone Mountain and made its way toward Corinth, a little village that clung to the river's western bank.

The river flowed under a substantial, but unremarkable steel and concrete bridge that spanned the Hudson between Corinth and the rural town of Hadley. It was here, about a third of the way across from the Corinth side on a rapidly warming summer morning, that two shirtless boys stared intently into the swirling water below. Draped like a couple of boney blankets over the bridge's silver-painted metal railing, they pointed their fishing poles downward as if genuflecting toward the water 20 feet below them and gazed, transfixed, at their bait—weighted wads of uncooked bacon skewered on treble-hooks—resting on the sandy bottom.

The boys were cousins and neighbors who often fished together in the streams and lakes around Corinth. They spoke occasionally, but mostly they just stared into the water, passing this blue-skied summer morning immersed in the hobby that had brought them together. Both had taken to fishing young and had found in it a way to escape the hubbub and unwanted drama that came with their large, unwieldy families.

And while they would often fish for wild brook trout in the tiny creeks that drained the mountains encircling their little Adirondack village, today they sought bigger, more impressive prey. Probably inspired by a recent episode of the American Sportsman, one of their favorite TV shows, where host Kurt Gowdy and some drawling southern-bred quarterback

6

grappled with blue marlin in the Caribbean, they had risen at dawn to go to the bridge armed with oversized hooks, smelly bait pilfered from their refridgerators, and trusty Zebco 202 rod and reel combos in hopes of landing a carp.

The bloated bottom-feeders—sometimes weighing as much as 25 pounds—were the truest test of a boy's line, reel, technique, and resolve, not at all finicky and delicate like a trout. For the most part, carp lived in the shallows of the river, basking and sucking in muck at the bottom. But their kind also flocked to this particular spot about a 100 yards from the bank, because this was where the village's sewage emptied into the river. Twenty-four hours a day an unmistakeable yellow-green cloud of untreated effluent billowed up from a pipe at the bottom of the Hudson. Submerged just a few feet north of the overhanging bridge, the sewage cloud started out dense and well-defined and then dissipated into the river in an ever-expanding-V, not unlike the steam that belches out of an old-time locomotive. This, the boys knew, was the best place to fish for carp.

As the morning heated up and the summer sun rose in the sky, the little village awakened with it and cars began driving across the bridge. Since almost everyone in Corinth knew everyone else, it wasn't uncommon for the boys to experience welcoming beeps and salutations coming from drivers passing with their windows rolled down.

"Morning boys!"

"How's the fishin boys?" (Some would holler without stopping to hear the answer.)

But one car—a yellow Gremlin with a dented fender—did stop, idling in the lane leading out of town. The driver's side window opened and a small cloud of smoke puffed out and upward. Along with the smoke, a song, unfamiliar to the boys and booming from the radio inside, burst out of the Gremlin, piercing the peace of the morning.

"...I'm going on down to Yasgur's farm
I'm going to join in a rock 'n' roll band
I'm going to camp out on the land
I'm going to try an' get my soul free
We are stardust
We are golden
And we've got to get ourselves
Back to the garden..."

The volume on the song lowered and the smoke cleared, revealing the broad, ear-to-ear grinning face of Johnny "Hog" Stevens. Already somewhat of a local legend at only 17, Johnny's gregariousness, athletic skills, and outrageous exploits at illicit beer swilling parties had endeared him to many in the small mill town. He was also the best friend of the bespectacled boy's oldest brother, Michael. And that, by the rules of engagement followed by all upstate teenagers, entitled him to pick on his friend's little brothers mercilessly.

"How's it going little Digger?" he said, invoking the hated nickname that haunted the sons of undertakers everywhere. "You still trying to learn how to fish?"

"Yeah, guess so, Hog . . ." the boy responded, mindful not to be too sassy in his response.

"Some day I'm gonna take you up to Stony Creek and show you how to fly fish, sonny . . .. Well, gotta blow this popcicle stand! See you in the funny papers, little Digger. See you later, Dougie,"he blurted out, finally acknowledging the boy's cousin, and then drove off toward Glens Falls.

"Okay. See ya Hog,"said the boy, not admitting that he had no idea what "fly fishing" was.

"He's such a weirdo!" the boy said to his cousin. And then they went back to their fishing.

Soon they were again gazing downward and becoming hypnotized by the water and their reflections in the glassy

8

surface, hoping that a carp would suck in their bait and start the mad scramble that comes with fighting a carp.

But it wasn't long before they were again interrupted, surprised actually.

"How's it goin' boys?"

The startled cousins banged their knees against the railing, reacting to the familiar voice that had broken their silence."Geez dad, don't do that! I almost lost my glasses in the river!"complained the 10-year-old while pushing up the perpetually broken glasses that always seemed to be sliding down his nose.

"Hello Uncle Irv, how's it goin'?"

"It's going pretty good Dougie, pretty good. Just starting my walk. You boys catching anything?"

A stocky, short man with a ruddy complexion, Irv Densmore was known far and wide as the "Walking Mayor" due to his obsessive daily hikes—which stretched 10-12 miles every day, regardless of the weather or season--across the Hudson and into the many trails that traversed the woods on the other side of the river. That, and the fact that he had long served as the village's chief elected official, made him the Walking Mayor and people who had business with the village or simply wanted to "give Irv a piece of their mind" knew they could intercept him, either coming or going, like clock work, on any given morning at the center of the bridge.

Although most of his hair was long gone, what remained was combed impeccably straight in parallel furrows back over his head, leaving him with an austere and somewhat aristocratic look. He spent a good deal of time before going out in the morning fussing and adjusting his hair and his clothing—much to the dismay of his wife and seven children, who often anxiously waited for him in the hunter green Bonneville station wagon prior to family trips, sending emissaries to hound and

9

cajole him into coming, usually to no avail. The result of all this daily fussing was a man with a consistently tucked and tidy appearance, an appearance that resolved to maintain itself throughout the day and night in spite of rain, snow, wind, small town political exigencies, or even death. Today he was wearing green, pressed shorts with a lemon-colored button-down shirt, tucked in of course, and a captain's cap (purchased on a family vacation to Maine), that was cocked slightly to the side. He wore unblemished brown walking shoes with black socks pulled tightly up as high as they could go over his calves.

Irv also served as the town's only undertaker, an occupation that distinguished him from practically 95% of Corinth's menfolk, who all tended to work in the International Paper Company's sprawling factory. The factory was situated at a point where the river roared over two dams and a series of cataracts and had provided power for this prolific paper mill for more than 100 years. IP or "the Mill" as it was simply called, provided reliable and substantial incomes for several hundred men (and some women) and their families, who lived comfortably in two story homes with broad front porches and picket fences; homes with ample yards that lined tidy streets in a village that could have been imagined and painted by Norman Rockwell. The company and the powerful union that represented the Mill's workers saw to it that the town and its people were well cared for with money for just about anything a happy, healthy town could ask for—public ice skating rinks; and youth basketball, softball, and boxing programs; well-tended parks; and regular parades, carnivals, and festivals—that many towns could only dream of.

For their part in this bargain, the men of Corinth toiled in the Mill from high school graduation until their funerals, working alongside each other inside the monstrous, inter-connected machines that ran around the clock, 365-days a year, in gigantic windowless buildings perched high above the Hudson. Trucks and trains brought a constant supply of logs, cut from the boundless timber tracts covering the mountains around Corinth and deep into the foothills of the Adirondacks, depositing them in mountainous piles that fed the factory day and night. Workers pulled the logs into the mouth of the Mill, commencing the violent physical and chemical processes that tranformed hard, unyielding wood into a homogeneous slurry that could be treated and coated and rolled onto massive spools to be turned into a particularly fine kind of glossy paper suitable for magazines like *Time, Vogue,* or, perhaps, preferably for the men of Corinth, *Field and Stream.*

And so, as he was about to set off on his daily trek across the river, a decaying black pickup truck slowed and then stopped next to Irv Densmore on the bridge.

"Morning Irvin," said a spidery-looking older man, lacking several teeth, who leaned purposefully out of his car window. "Terrible business, what happened to that Winslow boy, eh Irvin?"

The boy saw his father's expression dissolve from carefree—or at least Irv Densmore's version of carefree—to something more grave and guarded. In spite of his efforts to flee, however momentarily, from his many burdens, whether they were political, business, or family-related, they often found him nonetheless. And, as if on cue, as he stood tantalizingly close to his moment of peace and quiet in the woods over yonder, here was a member of the community, someone Irv hunted with every autumn at the Hadley Hunting Club, asking about a great tragedy that had unfolded just a day earlier, something that had yet to be fully understood, if ever it could be.

"Well, yes, Enos, it's about as tragic a situation as you could ever imagine," he said earnestly. "A father accidently killing his own son. And so young. Tragic."

"Indeed it is Irvin, but I hear'd the young man had been drinkin' afore he jumped in his car to drive off. Is that there true, Irvin?"

"Now Enos, who in God's name told you that? There's been a full investigation by the Sheriff's Department and nothing along those lines came out....Honestly, Enos, these poor young people have got enough to worry about without people making up stories, hurtful stories, about them."

"Well, I suppose yer right Irvin. 'Preciate yer taking the time to talk to me about it. Now go an have yerself a good walk and I'll see you up at the huntin' camp next weekend fer the clam bake."

"Alright Enos, I'm looking forward to it." And the man drove off, his ancient truck popping and wheezing from a litany of ailments, the boys suddenly intrigued by the conversation they couldn't have helped overhearing.

"What happened to the boy, dad?"

"Well, son, it's just an awful, terrible situation. I'd rather not even talk about it, but I suppose you'll be hearing things on the streets . . ..The Winslow boy, Tommy Winslow, was on his lunch break at the Mill and he wanted to go home for lunch, over at that house he and his young wife rent on Center Street...Well, he finished his lunch and realized that he was running late so I guess he was hurrying a little . . .. He got in his car and backed up and, well, he didn't realize that his little boy, his two-year-old son, had followed him out the screen door. I don't know any other way to say it. He backed over his son trying to get back to work. Killed his son. Tragic. Just tragic . . .. Now the little one is over at the funeral home and there'll be a service for him tomorrow."

"That's just awful dad,"said the boy, who couldn't quite comprehend how someone could back over his own son. And yet, being the son of a funeral director, several other tragedies had found their way into the parlor located one floor below where the boy lived with his parents, six siblings, a cat and a dog. The town's saddest occasions, it seemed, visited his house in one form or another, whether they were teenagers who died

12

in a fiery car crash while drag racing at Emmy's Flats or the time a man and two of his children went over the dam in their crippled motor boat two years earlier. Of course, the vast majority of his father's funerals were as expected as the seasons, usually when infirmed elderly folks, a friend's grandmother or grandfather, passed away, leading to a wake and service that served to gather family members, close and extended, for the first time in years. The grief at these times seemed measured and the people not altogether unhappy, and Irv would bring these elements together seamlessly, always appropriately somber, but also working assiduously to ensure that the many goals of a well run funeral—closure, being chief among them—were accomplished. Funerals like the one Irv was preparing for the Winslow child were anything but customary and they brought with them an entire community's angst and fear, when there could be no easy closure, only questions.

"Well boys, I'm going to see if I can finish my walk. I'll see you later."

"Bye dad."

"See you later Uncle Irv," said Dougie.

The boy in the broken spectacles and his cousin eventually gave in to the heat like so many others, leaving their perches on the bridge after the sun began to bake their backs and, fishless for the entire morning, they lost interest in the quest that had seemed so important the night before.

"This stinks . . ." said the boy, still staring down into the glassy-green water.

"Yep," said Dougie.

"Wanna go to the beach?"

"Sure." Dougie was a boy of few words. He enjoyed nature quietly, and that made him a good fishing companion.

They packed up their creels and the pilfered smelly bait and walked across the McKiernans' large lawn, climbed over the white picket fence into the Densmore Funeral Home back parking lot, and split up to go to their respective houses. The boy bounded through the wide back door, ran up the ramp that led both up to the funeral parlor and the home above it, as well as downward to an expansive underground garage and basement that housed the unseen infrastructure of the funeral business: an impressive slate gray Cadillac hearse complete with tail fins, an inventory of caskets (pine, maple, and aluminum primarily), and the "preparation room," a fascinating but forbidden place where the departed were brought for embalming, cosmetology and dressing prior to public viewing. Passing the door that led to the parlor on the first floor, the boy continued up another two flights of stairs and burst into the sprawling flat above the funeral parlor. As he ran to his room at the far end of the house, he heard his mother's voice from the kitchen.

"Excuse me young man. Get back in here this instant!"

Pauline Densmore stood in the expansive kitchen, wearing an apron and tending a large bubbling pot of something that would likely be cooking all day until they gathered for the family's evening meal. The kitchen was really more like a command center than a kitchen for, along with all the requisite appliances, counter space, and storage needed to support a small army, it also contained the family's washer and dryer—which, much like the Mill, seemed to be running day and night—and the enormous family dinner table. From here, she could see northward out a large bank of windows to the river and the bridge and could even see Irv as he returned home from his daily walk. To the west she could look out at the funeral home's front parking lot, where neighborhood children often played when no funerals were occurring, and she could see the backs of commercial establishments lining Main Street as well as the pretty mountains to the west. And she could, as she did today, cordon off an area of the kitchen that would serve as an easily observable play area for her two youngest children, Bobby and Shelly, keeping them close to her while she tended to the never-ending series of chores that came with her lot. The kitchen was a whirring epicenter of constant family activity and the boy's mother was always there.

Although slightly taller than his father and wearing dramatic, dark horn-rimmed glasses that were considered stylish at the time but looked slightly comical to him, the boy's mother nonetheless commanded obedience from every member of her brood. They came and went freely and with little supervision throughout the long undifferentiated days of the summer, but the children, the boys in particular, were attuned to the tones in their mother's voice and responded to certain intonations with the attention of a well-drilled private.

"I went to make bacon for breakfast this morning and half of it was gone. Do you have any idea where my bacon went?"

"Yeah," he responded, hanging his head in shame and pushing his glasses back up his sweaty nose. "I just took a little. Dougie and I went fishing and we needed some bait."

"Well," she said, softening somewhat. "Luckily I had some ham. Don't do that anymore without asking and why wouldn't you just use worms? Bacon?" She said, not expecting an answer she could comprehend and shaking her head, as she often did at the odd behavior and impulsivities that effervesced around her boys, especially during the summer.

"Okay mom. I'm sorry. It won't happen again . . .. Can I go down to the beach?"

"Okay, just be back in time for supper."

"Okay mom!"

Each boy re-emerged a short time later after shedding their dungarees in favor of shorts, cut-offs made from blue jeans that had long ago become unsalvageable. These ragged unhemmed shorts were standard issue for boys heading to the beach or any of the many unsupervised swimming holes that attracted overheated boys in the summer. They met at the front of the funeral home and walked barefoot down Sherman Avenue, a relatively short village street where virtually every house contained families—several, like the Towers, Densmores, and Saunders families had seven or more children—making it a compact neighborhood with a remarkably large concentration of children of all ages.

From Sherman Ave., the boys cut down Main Street, with its surprisingly diverse collection of commercial establishments, such as Jimmy Montello's Barber Shop, the Marine Midland Bank, Keyo's Restaurant, Eddy's Gas Station, Pike's Garage (where the boy would go to collect used and discarded auto parts when he was five), the News Room, the Grand Union Supermarket, the liquor store, the hardware store, Dottie's Ice Cream shop (just across from the beach) and of course, Clairman's, where the boy would often go to inspect and dream about the store's well stocked selection of rods, reels, lures, hunting, trapping and camping supplies. Norm Trudeau, the store's French-Canadian owner, would occasionally give him discounts on otherwise inaccessible sporting goods items that he had his eye on as well as impart advice about techniques and lures that the boy found valuable. But today, sweltering and focused on achieving relief, the shoeless boys hot-footed their way over the steaming sidewalks bound for the beach.

The village beach was where many Corinthians congregated on hot, sticky summer afternoons like this one. The river curled lovingly around a short bend above the bridge and slowed there, creating a lazy place before the Hudson picked up speed, went under the bridge and plunged over the Curtis Dam. It was a little half-bowl of sand, carted in some time before by village fathers seeking a place to cool their families while they sweated away their shifts at the Mill a few miles downstream.

Boys from all over town went there when the sun made other pursuits unbearable. Pick up baseball games at the recreation fields ended; fishing poles were set aside, and bikes were parked as boys began gathering at the little riverbank park next to the red-brick library on lower Main Street like sea birds returning to their roosts after a long morning of foraging.

On such days, whole families, except for the fathers, would take up positions on the sand or the narrow strip of grass between Main Street and the beach—where there were benches and a towering granite statue of an anonymous Civil War infantryman--spreading blankets and staking temporary claims for their clans. Matrons in horn-rimmed sunglasses and floppy straw hats sat on beach chairs at the center of the claim, often holding a baby beneath an umbrella, the rest of the brood let loose to splash and play in the shallows. Small packs of shirtless, itinerant, adolescent boys would chase each other through the beach, plunging into the water and sending toddlers scurrying and mothers hissing—all for the benefit of various teenaged girls lounging on towels and acting disinterested.

The boys, in that sparkling age somewhere between nine and twelve, neither watched nor worried about, still disinterested in girls, were free to simply have fun. Some would take their t-shirts or towels and use them as nets to catch minnows in the shallows, transferring their haul to the motes of recently-constructed sand castles. After a cooling dunk in the river, some would while away the afternoon on the beach, digging holes and covering toes, limbs, or their entire torsos in sand while chatting with their kindred.

Invariably a pack of boys would gather just off beach property to the north, where a rope with a prodigious knot tied at the bottom hung from the limb of an ancient willow tree that was rooted on a high bank, a good 10 feet above the water line. Here the boys would line up and take turns swinging out into space

17

over a deepened pool where Mill Creek flowed into the Hudson River. Upon releasing his grip from the gnarly knot at the bottom of the rope, each boy, now airborne, was expected to perform in some meaningful way for the rest of his peers, whether it be by emitting blood curdling screams or by creatively twirling, tumbling or cartwheeling, before smacking into the water.

This day was no different and when the call went up for those daring enough to participate in rope antics, the boy in the glasses made his way up the beach, past the families and the teenagers who couldn't be bothered, while "American Woman, stay away from me!" blasted out of one portable radio and "Like a Bridge Over Troubled Water..." trilled out of another. He walked past the benches, where three long haired, odd-looking characters, people he didn't know, dressed in colorful shirts and bell-bottom blue jeans lingered on a bench near the granite statue of the infantryman. A short distance north of the park's concrete bath house stood the old willow tree and the boys were already chanting the names—the nicknames that is—of each boy taking a hold of the rope.

"Lipper! Lipper! Lipper!!!"

"Meat-head! Meat-head! Meat-Head!!!"

"Fart! Fart! Fart!!!"

Over time, just about every boy would acquire a nickname that could haunt him well into adulthood. In Corinth, a boy's nickname was meant to be a badge of shame, a personalized brand seared into his hide for all to see. And he was expected to accept his particular brand without complaint, if only to keep the public ridicule from getting worse. Some nicknames evolved simply enough, highlighting a physical attribute, such as with Lipper. Others were just derogatory in nature, possibly due to past excesses, as with Fart, or a perceived lack of mental acuity, as with Meathead. Still others bordered upon brilliant, exhibiting a kind of group creativity that the boy would grudgingly admire later in life. For instance "Bino," a well-liked athletic boy, received his nickname because he was so blond and fair that he was deemed close enough in complexion to being an albino. One of the cruelest nicknames doled out to one young member of the pack was "Pearl Harbor," who was so named because his teeth were so distinctly ravaged by decay, either through poor nutrition or lack of dental attention or both, that they looked as if they'd been the target of a successful bombing mission. And then there was Chicken, Hog, Bones, Hole, Boner Bill, Scuz, Minnow, V-Head, Fat Harry, Spud, Tater Head, and many, many others.

The boy with the glasses took his turn and heard his nickname—Froggy, Froggy, Froggy (due to his pigeon-toed walk)—chanted as he swung out over the inky black waters, released, spun around and slapped into the river. As he swam back to shore, exhilarated and cooled down, he heard the boys from the bank above suddenly yelling and pointing to a spot not far from him.

"Snapping turtle! Get the hell out of the water! It's a snapper!"

Snapping turtles were the great white sharks of the river. Large, mysterious creatures that rose out of deep protected places along the bank, with ancient fierce expressions and jaws that could easily snap thick branches, snappers were misunderstood monsters that struck terror in the hearts of vulnerable boys swimming through their domain. The boy swam like he'd never swum before, plowing through the water at breakneck speed and pulling himself onto the shore, terrified but relieved. As he rose, a great roar of laughter and heckling went up from the collection of boys still up on the bank above him and he realized that he'd been duped. One of the older boys, a friend of his brothers, had conceived the ruse and others joined in for sport.

"Not funny, jerks!" he called up to them. "I hope you get your toe bit off, next time you swim."

"Get lost Froggy!"

"A-holes!" he muttered under his breath.

The boy walked back along the river to the beach and tried to shake the unpleasant experience. He ran into one of his older brothers, Davey, and a few of his friends on the grassy strip above the beach. They'd been swimming for a while and were contemplating whether they should go over to Doody's house to shoot some hoops or maybe ride their bikes up to the high school.

"I don't know, David, but I just saw Debbie and her friends heading over to Dottie's for ice cream. Whadya say Sir Lancelot?" asked Reed, Dave's best friend, in a mock serious tone that made everyone laugh. "She's been looking at you funny, pal."

"Yeah, okay, Reed, let's head over to Dottie's," Davey said, acknowledging that, unlike boys of 10, boys of 12 and 13 were becoming much more interested in the comings and goings of the opposite sex.

"Can I go too? I've got some of my allowance left," the boy asked his brother, who grimaced. Then Reed, sensing a problem, conceived an elaborate solution that, if handled properly, might just work.

"Listen buddy, we're going over to Dottie's to talk to some girls. You don't want to do anything as icky as that do you?"

"I don't know, s'pose not. But it's free country Reed, and I can go there if I want to."

"Of course you can! But I'm just saying maybe you'd rather go over to the statue and try to get the treasure."

"What treasure?"

"Everybody knows there's a treasure behind the speech. If you can read the speech—the Gettysburg Address—perfectly, three times, that whole big metal panel on the side of the statue will just fall off and you'll get the treasure inside. But you gotta read it perfectly!"

"That's the dumbest thing I've ever heard Reed."

"No, really, it's true."

"Yeah okay, I'll go give it a try. See you later Reed. See you at supper Davey."

"See you later lil' brother," said his brother before they headed across the street.

By now the boy had been up since sunrise and he was starting to feel the day tugging at his eyelids. Ten-year-old boys don't take naps so the boy walked over toward the statue that rose up out of the grass, casting a welcome shadow where he might find some relief from the heat. He sat on one of the bevels, carved like polished steps into the base of the statue. Above the bevels the statue had four faces, each with its own distinctive features: on one side, the phrase "Eternal Vigilance is the Price of Freedom" was carved in granite; another side listed the names of Corinth's honored dead from the Civil War; and on the eastern side, now shaded and cool, was a great bronze plaque, into which the Gettysburg Address had been molded, forming the words in sharp relief to the black painted background.

The boy adjusted his glasses and began to read, not to indulge or even embrace Reed's claims about a secret treasure, but rather, in his diminished state, woozy from a long trying day, he wanted to see if he could indeed read the address perfectly. He read through it once, but felt he had not done it perfectly and so began again in hopes of improving his pronunciation of the words and navigate its archaic grammar.

> *"Four score and seven years ago our fathers brought forth on this continent a new nation, conceived in liberty, and dedicated to the proposition that all men are created equal.*

"Now we are engaged in a great civil war, testing whether that nation, or any nation so conceived and so dedicated, can long endure. We are met on a great battlefield of that war. We have come to dedicate a portion of that field, as a final resting place for those who here gave their lives that that nation might live. It is altogether fitting and proper that we should do this.

"But, in a larger sense, we can not dedicate, we can not consecrate, we can not hallow this ground. The brave men, living and dead, who struggled here, have consecrated it, far above our poor power to add or detract. The world will little note, nor long remember what we say here, but it can never forget what they did here. It is for us the living, rather, to be dedicated here to the unfinished work which they who fought here have thus far so nobly advanced. It is rather for us to be here dedicated to the great task remaining before us—that from these honored dead we take increased devotion to that cause for which they gave the last full measure of devotion—that we here highly resolve that these dead shall not have died in vain— that this nation, under God, shall have a new birth of freedom—and that government of the people, by the people, for the people, shall not perish from the earth."

As he began reading the speech a third time—not that he believed in Reed's prophecy, but just to see if he could—the boy in the spectacles began to feel his head nodding, his eyes blinking slowly as the coolness of the polished stone combined with fatigue to bring him to the edge of repose. The words of the great speech swam in his mind as he finally drifted off into a deep sleep.

II: Ransford Walks to Town

Ransford walked the rutted road to Corinth. It would take about an hour, he thought, to walk the five miles to the village, enough time to meet the boys at Enos Johnson's barn.

The rounded tops of mountains looming to the west were illuminated by the setting sun, rounded and dark like the backs of old warriors hunched under blankets around a campfire. Soon a hunter's moon lit the way and he puffed like a horse in a steady trot. He'd done his chores, thrown the hay, rounded up the sheep that were ill to keep them from the rest of the flock, and now he was free to go to town and cavort with the boys as he did every Friday night. His father didn't mind, as long as he was back by sunrise. After all, he was 21.

He walked with a steady, strong gait, swinging his arms to keep pace with his legs. Like the struts of a wagon, his legs instinctively absorbed the roots and rocks and potholes along the road, always maintaining a give and a bend, never straightlegged and flatfooted like the men from Saratoga, who lived their lives on planked walkways and paved roads. It was the way mountain folk walked.

In the spectral shadows conjured by the moonlight, Ransford saw pumas crouching by rocks and packs of wolves circling him, and Indians, lots of Indians. He'd suddenly stop and whirl, his imaginary musket leveled and ready to fire at a red man lunging to bury a hatchet in his skull. A month ago, he had read *The Last of the Mohicans*, a great novel of wilderness adventure by James Fenimore Cooper, and it had stirred something in him. He thought about it often, especially on long walks to town, where he could imagine the land around him the way it had once been. Hawkeye and and his Mohican brother, Deerslayer, had fought the rampaging Iroquois just a few miles east of Corinth, hiding in a cave behind the waterfall that was later to be called Glens Falls. Then they had escaped north to Fort William Henry on Lake George, just 15 miles to the north. These places, embroidered in the area's frontier history, were all around him.

The more Ransford pondered it, the sadder he got. And then he got angry. Because now it was all gone—the adventure, the danger, the Indians. Oh there were a few Indians still in town--his grandfather had even married an Indian woman—but they weren't like the ones in *The Last of the Mohicans*. They weren't wild, noble and dangerous anymore. His grandmother had been a sweet, quiet woman who sat mending clothes in an old rocking chair by firelight, and most of the rest were just sad, old, and drunk. They sat on benches in town and mumbled things no one could understand. And the land, so pristine and full of wonder and places to hide just fifty years before, now was crisscrossed by railroad lines and telegraph wires and roadways filled with peddlers in funny suits. It was all mapped and tamed. There wasn't anything left uncivilized in the Adirondacks anymore. The frontier had left him and jumped a thousand miles away to the west.

Ransford could see his life spread out before him, and he didn't like what he saw—an unending series of chores, a thousand Sunday sermons, saying howdie to the same boring people, fixing fences, and tending sheep. Lord, he hated sheep. They were so stupid they'd follow a rabbit over a cliff; they'd stand in the rain until they caught a fever if you didn't shoo them into a barn; and, Lord, they smelled bad. It was a smell he thought he'd never be rid of, it seemed to infect him and his clothes so much that, before he went to town, he would keep a pair of pants and a shirt aside after laundry day just so they wouldn't suffer the stink of those sheep.

His father said that Scots had raised sheep since the dawn of time and it was a fine thing to do. But that didn't square with the other things his pa had told him, about how their clan was a proud people who, back in the old country across the sea, had defended their land from invading English princes in bloody fights, outmatched ten to one. Those Scots had flung rocks down upon the armored invaders on horseback and had ambushed their campsites at night.

"They had fought because they were right and a righteous man fights to the death," he would say, "because a righteous man fights for more than himself."

But the righteous had been overwhelmed and the few that lived or were not enslaved to work for British lords had moved to America, to find a better life for them and theirs, said his father, half lit by a candle and the whisky he often sipped alone.

He loved his father, a hard, gnarly, headstrong man with a knack for woodwork and rambling tales. He had carved out an existence in the Kayaderasseros Mountains southwest of Corinth, building a flock and doing carpentry for businesses and people in town. But it just didn't square with Ransford, that such a proud people would ever find happiness tending to loathesome sheep.

Ransford puffed along towards town, feeling trapped by tradition and the smallness of his world. Coyotes yipped from a hilltop and creatures made strange noises in the darkness, but none of that bothered him. He was comfortable in the woods at night.

Out of the blue, he thought of Sarah, the way her eyes always seemed to be smiling in a warm, happy way and the curve of her lips, like birds' wings in flight, inviting and magnetic. He felt odd around her these days, though, unable to utter anything comprehensible when he saw her at the general store her father ran in town. He had played with Sarah when he was a boy and she was a girl; while filling some order, their fathers would talk of the world and the two children would slip off to the backyard or a storage room. They would challenge each other to feats of knowledge and expertise.

"Ransford, I bet you've never heard of Niagra Falls?"

"Why yes, I have, Miss Sarah, that's the grandest of all waterfalls out there in far west New York . . . and I aim to go there one day and ride over it in a canoe."

"Get out of here, Ransford; you'd be broke in two if you rode over Niagra Falls!"

"'Spect not," he'd say, and then jump up and grab an overhanging beam, hook his legs over the top and dangle with his arms hanging down, as if that proved his point. "Can you do this, Miss?"

"I can . . . but I have no reason to ever want or need to do that."

Back then their talk had flowed as easily as a stream through a glade. But now he felt strange around his childhood friend. The way her slender neck rose regally from her shoulders; the way her hips curved beneath her petticoats; and the breasts that, it seemed, had suddenly appeared one day beneath her blouse . . .. He blushed in the darkness, stopping to ponder the forbidden feelings that had suddenly welled up inside him.

Thwap!

Ransford felt a pain in his shoulder, flinched, and swiveled to his right.

"Are ye sleep walkin', boy?"

There in the darkness were two human silhouettes defined by the moon, one holding a stick above its head. As the stick came down for another blow, Ransford grabbed it in mid-swing. It was Horton Pike, one of the boys.

"Christmas, Ransford, a herd a buffaloes coulda trampled ye!" said Horton, while jabbing his friend in the ribs and laughing hysterically.

Embarassed, Ransford wrested the stick from his friend's hand and smacked him on the ankle with it.

"Ow!"

"That'll teach you to not sneak up on a feller."

"I don't know as we were sneakin' up as much as we were walkin' up, Ransford. You jus' seemed to be in one of those zombie trances."

The reference to the walking dead of the Caribbean seemed to excite Horton's younger brother, Earl, who had kept quiet until this point. "Yes, yes, Ransford you looked like a zombie . . . a zombie!"

"Close yer trap, Earl or I'll make you a zombie," warned Ransford, wanting to be done with the whole thing and not particularly pleased that young Earl had tagged along. "Where's the boys, Hort?"

"You'll be happy to know, we got us a little joy juice tonight, Ransford. That's right, Amos' older brother came back from Saratogee with a jug a fire water. Now he's drunker then a bride's daddy and we got the rest!" Horton declared, while shaking both of Ransford's shoulders with the joyful news.

It'd been a while since Ransford had had a belt and the thought seemed inviting. It would warm him from the inside out and make his worries about the future melt away.

"Well, what are we waitin' for, son? Lead me to it!"

They walked for another mile or so, south and eastward around the outskirts of the village, where townsfolk lived in neat little, whitewashed houses lining Main Street, Center Street, and Palmer Avenue, radiating away and up the hill from the river. Horton led them along a wooded path that emerged on a rocky crag high above the Hudson River. To the north, Antone Mountain crouched in the moonlight like a shrouded sphinx guarding the valley, the river curling lazily beneath its feet.

There, the river straightened and flattened out--like it was taking a breather--for about a mile before it gathered speed and tumbled into the rapids. The water racing through the moonlit palisades glistened like quicksilver, roaring downward through the jagged canyon that squeezed the frothy water into a

27

churning white snake that slammed into the cliff wall one hundred feet below them. There the river grudgingly bent and turned east toward Glens Falls, again picking up speed as it hurtled over another, larger waterfall that the Indians called Palmer Falls. It was spectacular. On the edge of the cliff, Ransford felt drawn into the splendor of the scene, an odd magnetic sense, frightening in a way, that seemed to entice him into space.

"Where the hell ye been? Out dancin'?"

Like a screech owl, the familiar voice cut through the night, coming from another ledge jutting out to the east, thirty feet away. Enos Johnson was a boney boy--all elbows and knees-- with a voice like nails on a chalkboard. He ambushed people with his voice, relishing their scowling faces after he uttered a few syllables. Ransford liked Enos. He was a true country boy, always up for adventure, and a loyal friend who always had his back in a fight. Enos had bad, craggy teeth that pointed out from his gums in odd directions like tombstones jutting out from an ancient burial ground. His friends called him "Chicken," and Enos bore the name as proudly as if it were "Achilles".

His eyes refocused, Ransford could make out the shapes of several lads, sitting and squatting in a semi-circle around a huddled shape who was trying, unsuccessfully, to get a stick match to catch on some kindling. Ransford, Horton and young Earl carefully made their way around the edge of the cliff to the flat, rocky area where their friends had gathered.

"Damn, boy, you tryin' to start thet fire with moss fer kindlin'?"

"Hell, no, you just be my guest if you think you can do better. These twigs are wet from the rain we had this morning," said Zack Eggelston as he held the match's flame under a small pile of sticks.

Zachary had been named after the hero of the Mexican War, the old war horse Zachary Taylor, who had brought the

Mexicans to their knees at the battle of Vera Cruz, later becoming president. Zack's father, William Eggelston, hadn't faired nearly as well in the far-off war to liberate the Texas territory, losing his leg in one of the short war's battles. As a result, Zack's family had suffered hard times. Ransford liked Zack but felt sorry for his 18-year-old friend, who had to work harder than any boy he knew to help support his family. Recognized as a war veteran, Zack's one-legged father was given odd jobs around town and church hand-outs, but, with a carved oak stick strapped beneath his right knee, he could no longer work at the mill or cut down trees or even tend sheep effectively.

Most people in town felt that bad luck, like Bill Eggelston's, had more to do with God's will than just an unfortunate roll of the dice, that it was a visitation of His wrath upon those who had strayed somehow--unbeknownst to all but Him--into the path of darkness. But that didn't keep them from whispering in the square after Bill had hobbled past them. *You know, he stopped coming to services just a short time before he went off to fight,* or, *William was always proud as a young man,* or, *He swore a blue streak when he was angry.* Aware that God moved in mysterious ways, Ransford nonetheless couldn't see that any of these things could be so insulting to God that He would personally direct a Mexican cannon ball to hive off Bill Eggelston's lower leg. It just didn't make sense.

After a while the fire caught and Zack blew into the base of the flame until it lapped around the larger sticks and small logs, growing to illuminate the collection of young men assembled on the rocks. They settled into their positions--some squatting Indian-style near the flame and others lying back on their elbows--and called upon Enos to open up the jug of hard liquor that he had pilfered from his inebriated brother.

"Gimme a pull off'en that jug before I hit ya with a rock!"

Billy O'Rourke's demand was met quickly. He was the mill manager's boy and Ransford didn't like him much. It wasn't because he had things that the other boys didn't--like the spirited pony or the fine boots or the Sears & Roebuck rifle he was so proud of. Ransford told himself he didn't secretly hate Billy because of all that. It had more to do with his princely air; the way he would demand things and expect them without hesitation; and how the world would be turned on its ear if he didn't get his way; and the way he talked about the other boys' lives and their fathers' lives as if his father would decide everything for them--whether they got the job they wanted or whether they would ever amount to anything at the new paper mill they were planning to build at the falls; and the girls, how they fawned over Billy and his pretty lips and his curly black hair.

But, the boys, a good batch of boys all things considered, accepted Billy's haughty air, probably because, by association, it seemed to elevate them somehow. They felt, in many ways, lucky to count the mill manager's son among their group. They were coming into manhood and something deep inside, something they couldn't quite put into words, told them that this would be a good person to call a friend someday. So they bit their tongues at his occasional insults and, in the way of young men, accepted him into their clan. And that, for the time being, was good enough for Ransford.

"Whoooooooeeeeee!" Billy screamed after sucking down a draught of whiskey. He had stood up to hoist the jug over his shoulder and now he mock-staggered around the fire and fell back onto his rump, the group howling its pleasure at his act.

The tone set, the jug moved its way around the fire, each boy taking in a slug of the vile liquid and giving out a grotesque sound that gave evidence of the accomplishment. Howls, grunts, catcalls, and belches accompanied each hit of whisky.

With the jug in his lap, Ransford sucked in a long, enduring pull; he drank deep and purposefully, closing his eyes as the liquor invaded his body, traveling like lava down his throat and into his bloodstream. He felt the warmth flush through his limbs, up into his head, and he leaned back, flat on the ground, staring up at the brilliant stars above. He opened his mouth, but didn't utter a sound.

"I think Ransford's been struck dead!"

"Ransford Densmore, are you dead?" one of the boys asked in a parental way, while poking him in the ribs with a stick.

Laying motionless, Ransford waited a moment, for dramatic effect, before speaking. "If I am dead, this surely must be Heaven."

The gang howled. They spent the next hour passing the jug around the fire, getting drunker and drunker. Before long they were yelping like coyotes and dancing around the fire as they imagined Indians would have on the night before a war party. While one beat a rock against a hollow log, the others twirled and danced and jabbed sticks at the sky, throwing their heads back and yowling at the moon. One by one, the boys fell exhausted into heaps. Occassionally a boy would fall on another and that would start them wrestling until somebody was pinned or someone cried uncle, laughing hysterically. Gradually the commotion ceased and quiet settled over them. They were drunk and tired, rendered stupidly happy. It was exactly the feeling they'd been hoping for, to lose themselves on that ledge where the mill and the sheep and their parents and the girls they were supposed to marry someday were nowhere in sight.

Before long, they turned to talking. The conversations ranged from girls to gunpowder--all the important, volatile things in their lives--before settling on the looming possibility of war. Since they'd been young boys they'd heard the talk in the town square and at the dinner table of the southern states bridling against the north over slavery. There'd been talk of war before, the adults getting worked up over various newspaper articles or the words of passing politicians railing on about the need to stem the evil tide of slavery. But, after years, nothing had ever come of it. Like the threats of the great floods of generations past and the devastation they had wrought, the boys had grown up thinking war talk was something adults did to keep uppity children in line. Mostly, they'd ignored it.

But, Abraham Lincoln had been elected president and the war talk had started again with new fervor. In the spring, news had come of a far off federal fort--a Fort Sumter--being fired upon in South Carolina. The force inside had surrendered to the rebels and suddenly the talk around the supper table had changed from "What if we go to war?" to, "We're at war! What does it mean?" Now the fear in their parents' eyes was real, like the look they got when thunder bolts were striking around the house and a child was still out playing in the fields. Someone had to venture out into the storm to bring the child home, but no one really wanted to.

"My uncle says they're raising up volunteers in Saratoga to go down and fight them rebs," Horton offered.

"You think they'll be askin' us to go soon?"

"Nah, this thing'll be done afore the next snow. My daddy says it's all just a bunch of saber-rattlin' . . .. Just one pack of politicians showing the others who's got the biggest cannon barrel!" Billy O'Rourke chimed in while making an obscene gesture that had some of the boys chuckling.

"Well, I don't know, but from what I heard they're even asking for troops in Saratoga and that means the whole county," Zack said, bringing an earnest tone back to the conversation. "Heck, I don't know if I could go and leave my pappy all alone like that."

"I, for one, would jump at the chance," spurted Peter Johnson, the middle child in a family of nine, who saw himself less outnumbered by a regiment than at a breakfast table surrounded by his siblings. "I hope they come up here recruitin', I surely do. It sounds downright exciting."

"There's nothin' exciting about having yer head blown clear

off, boy!" Chicken said. "I look over at Zack there and I seem to recollect that his pappy had his leg snipped clean in that last little squabble we had, or are you fergettin' that?"

"No, I'm not forgettin' that and that's a terrible thing. But I know of 10 or 20 other men who came back from Mexico without a scratch. Heck, those ain't bad odds. I'll take 'em to get a free ticket out of this stink pit and see some of that world out there!"

There was an uncharacteristic passion in Peter's voice, something that struck a chord with all the boys gathered on the ledge that night. Had they been Baptists, someone would have said "Amen, brother." But they weren't, so they sat there quiet for a moment, soaking up the admission as if it were a universal truth.

"Alright, alright, Petie here's got a point," Billy said. "But, I'm askin' you: why would you want to leave your friends behind, leave your family behind and take all those chances, just for the sake of some know-nothin' blackie pickin' cotton balls down in Alabamie?"

There were quiet nods and uncharacteristic pondering among the group at Billy's point. After all, what was the point of this looming war? Few of them had ever seen a Negro in the flesh, most of their understanding came from the gross characterizations that appeared on rally posters and newspaper illustrations. The competing images of nobly-adorned nubian princes and goofy, big-lipped darkies dancing wildly to a fiddle did battle in their heads. They didn't read the articles that accompanied the pictures; they just glanced at the images.

Ransford's memory was piqued. He began to recall his one encounter with a Negro, not more than a year past. He had been hunting with his friend Charlie Clothier deep in the woods near Mulleyville on a cold October day. The buck they'd been tracking broke from a thicket suddenly, surprising both of them. Ransford had whirled to his right, locked onto a patch of

33

moving fur, and fired, his musket ball ripping into the deer's shoulder. But the shot wasn't clean and the buck bounded off into the forest, leaving a slight trail of blood behind him.

They had followed the wounded deer up over the mountain, scouring the woods for tracks and occasional drops of thick, steaming crimson spattered on fallen leaves. They followed the creature earnestly, hearing their fathers' voices cautioning: "It's a sin to leave a wounded animal in the forest." The boys trudged on into the afternoon, getting farther and farther from home, tracking their quarry through spiny thickets, hemlock swamps, and brush that snapped visciously into their faces. Occasionally the beast would break from cover before them, but always out of reach of their muskets, its white tail bounding up over the next ridge and vanishing out of sight.

After many hours, as the sun dipped onto the western horizon, they slogged dejected over a hill and down into a hollow where a pond stretched out below them, glistening in the twilight. In a little clearing next to the pond sat a cabin oozing smoke from a crude stone chimney. Exhausted and defeated from chasing the wounded deer, the boys walked with relief toward the wood hut, a trappers' cabin, like many scattered throughout the deeper regions of the mountains, not owned by anyone, but there for those who needed it. They slung their muskets over their shoulders, drained and resigned to the fact that the deer had outrun them along with the daylight. They walked onto the rickety wooden planks serving as a porch.

Ransford opened the door to the cabin as if it were his own; indeed, it was as much his as it was anyone's. The boys stepped into the hut, welcoming the warmth and the safety that it offered. They decided to spend the night there and hike back to South Corinth in the morning to face their fathers empty-handed.

But something had felt strange when they entered the darkened, smokey room. A stark wooden table with a clay bowl sat untended. The embers of a small fire glowed feebly in the crude

34

rock hearth against the far wall. They felt edgy and scanned the room.

As they adjusted to the limited light the first thing they could make out were eyes, like two upturned crescent moons that seemed to be floating in the highest, darkest corner of the cabin. Then the rest of the apparition began to come into focu:. a high, furrowed forehead beaded with sweat that dribbled over stark, dramatic cheekbones. A massive neck grew like a tree trunk out of the broadest shoulders they had ever seen, which were strangely pinned back against the cabin's log walls. The man's chest was heaving, almost retching.

Fear filled the room and the boys clutched their muskets tensely at the ready. The eyes in the darkness darted wildly between the weapons and the boys' faces. A dark-skinned man trembled in the corner.

"Who are you? What are ye doing here?" demanded Ransford.

"Don't shoot me. Please don't shoot me!I'll go with you easy, young masters."

Taken aback by the baritone, fearful voice, Charlie Clothier raised his weapon and pointed it at the man. "Don't you move . . .. Don't you move or I'll shoot ya. I swear I'll shoot ya!"

Ransford's memory was jarred; he recalled something he'd heard about escaped slaves using routes through the Adirondacks to make their way to Canada. There were rumors that people--abolitionists, ministers or Quakers from Saratoga--would help them along their secret journey by providing them with shelter and food, hidden from the world in little outposts in the woods, like the very cabin they stood in.

"Put yer gun down, Charlie," Ransford said, gently putting his hand atop the barrel of Charlie's musket. "We mean you no harm sir, and we hope you mean none to us. We been chasing a deer all day and have come up empty. Would you mind if we shared this cabin with you tonight?"

35

The next few minutes were uneasy ones. Charlie and Ransford talked to the strange black man as best they could, deciphering enough through his broken English and southern drawl to relax their fears and settle his nerves. There was an uneasy peace established between the boys, who had no place else to go, and the runaway slave, who'd been told by a kindly man of the cloth to stay there for two nights when he'd be gathered up by an anonymous assistant and brought to his next stop on the Underground Railroad. They spent the night together in the cabin sharing their stories well into the cold autumn night.

The man's master in Mississippi had called him Hercules, changing his name from the one he'd been given at birth by his father, who had been captured in Africa and brought to the South in chains on a slave ship. He was born as Mali, which meant hot wind. His master had changed his name to Hercules because he had grown into such a strong young man, cut like a Greek statue out of black marble, that he could show him off at county fairs and lay bets with rubes who didn't believe Hercules could bend an iron rod across his chest.

The Mississippi master had bought Hercules a wife, a lovely, Nubian girl with big round hips. He'd come to love the woman, Charlise, who'd been raised and trained in a big plantation house outside New Orleans. Like many house slaves, she'd learned to read and to foster the social graces that southern gentility required of their servants. Charlise passed some of her education on to Hercules, particularly an appreciation of the Good Book. When their work was done, they'd read the Bible on steamy southern nights under the stars, stretched out on a matted patch of grass by the Mississippi River.

Soon a a baby boy arrived and Hercules was as proud as any enslaved man could be. The bliss lasted until the master fell upon hard times, losing too many bets on bad nags to maintain his family's lavish lifestyle. He began selling off property, including his slaves, to pay the mounting bills and gambling debts. Charlise and the boy were sold in the spring, taken away in chains to a place far away. Hercules was never told where

36

they'd been brought.

"Don't want y'all to get any ideas, boy. I can't afford to lose a prize bull like you," the master had told the heartbroken Hercules, warning him to work off his pain—to turn his tears to sweat—or face the lash.

Hercules had been rendered unquenchably mad with the loss of his family, his sweet woman, and his helpless baby. At first he thought of breaking free, discovering their whereabouts, and taking them all to safety in the cold land to the north. The railroad; the sketchy, secret route to Canada was whispered about among the slaves who clung to the notion of freedom as if they were afflicted with a disease. Most slaves, however, dismissed such ideas, having seen most of those who had run brought home bloody and in irons, and some beaten to death, for trying.

Hercules' thoughts had turned to revenge then, a seething need to hurt the man who had wrought such pain, to kill the man who had done such an evil thing to him and his. He knew he could do it in a instant, break his neck with one swing of a shovel or a pick axe, hold his head under water and watch his master's face writhe in horror until the water sucked the wretched soul from his body. Cleansed him. Baptized him. These thoughts consumed Mali. But with every sadistic plan he pictured in his mind he heard Charlise's sweet voice reminding him that, "Vengeance is mine, sayeth the Lord, "and that killing another man is a sin, no matter how evil that man might be.

He couldn't find her and the boy. He couldn't kill his master. He couldn't take his own life—as much he desired it—because that, too, would be a sin. But, he realized, he could at least do something that would hurt his master deeply, hurt him in a place that would sting him and keep stinging him like a hundred angry wasps. He could take a prized possession from the man who had taken the world from him: he could steal himself. By running away, Mali would be taking money and pride from his owner at a time when he needed them most. Sure enough, he'd be committing a sin, by stealing himself. But that, Mali reasoned, was a sin he and Charlise, and perhaps, even God could live with.

"So I stole myself from that awful man. For a month I acted like all was good with me. I did as I was asked and kept my tears to myself," Mali explained to the boys, who sat by the fireplace in silent awe. "And then one morning, a long time before the rooster crowed, I took a bag filled with potatoes, bread and other victuals that I'd been savin' and I jumped over the back fence and made my way north."

It had been a harrowing journey, one started without any particular knowledge of where to go or who to see for help, with just the myths he had heard from other slaves during his travels with the master. He knew he should follow the North Star or the Drinking Gourd, as some called it, and stay to the woods, the unsettled places, for throughout the South they were on the lookout for runaways. Bounty hunters and law men would grab up any unaccompanied negro in a heartbeat to fetch rewards and maintain the status quo. As the drumbeat of war built, the South was on full alert.

"I swear a pack of dogs chased me from Mississippi to Tennessee," Mali exclaimed at one point, shaking his head from side to side and smiling broadly at the memory. "Some times I ate and some times I didn't. But after a while, maybe two or three months after I started, I got to the state of Pennsylvania and in a pretty place with big fields and green hills I made contact with the Railroad. I was outside a little town called Gettysburg, hiding in some trees and I called out to a young negro working in a wheat field there and he told me to stay put and that he would fetch a feller to help me. And sure enough, that night a man of the cloth, a nice Methodist minister, gathered me up and brought me to his barn. His wife came out and gave me a good wholesome meal, first one I ate in months!"

Mali had been ferried along the well-established stops along the

38

Underground Railroad. Through Philadelphia and New York City, along the Hudson River to Albany, and then into Saratoga, where another man of the cloth, a Quaker minister, had hosted him in secret just outside the city. Before dawn broke that very same morning, Mali and the minister had ridden horses up the Kayderossas Creek, which wound its way down and out of the valley formed by the mountains of the same name. For the entire day they followed the creek, eventually diverting to the north over a rugged and rarely used logging trail to the isolated mountain pond that had, over the last several years, become a primary way stationon the Railroad . The handful of locals who knew the pond's importance as a secret stop in the Underground Railroad's path to Canada had taken to calling it Black Pond, to distinguish it from the many other ponds and lakes dotting the southern Adirondacks.

After a long but fascinating night in the cabin where all three ended up sleeping curled up and uncovered on the floor's hardwood planks, the boys had been awakened to the sounds of two men talking on the front porch. Ransford swung open the cabin door and was met with a cold burst of autumn air that immediately had him shaking.

"M-m-morning . . .."

"Good morning young man!" A wiry negro man, bestubbled about the face and wearing a distinct black top hat, was standing alongside Mali and holding the reins of two horses. "Now who would you be?"

"Name's Ransford, Ransford Densmore."

"Would you be Elias's boy?"

"Yes, that's my father," said Ransford, feeling suddenly put on the spot by the odd fellow in front of him. "And who are you, if you don't mind me asking?"

"I happen to be Jedediah Smith. Very pleased to meet you. I think quite well of your daddy . . .. A good man. Good with his

39

hands. Does fine work with wood, he does." The man had spoken quickly, his eyes darting around as he talked, as if troubled by something. Although he'd never met Mr. Smith, Ransford had heard of him; he was often described as an eccentric old black man, a free man, who lived alone in a cabin at the top of a small mountain known only as "Nigger Hill," named disparagingly after its only occupant. He was also known to be a man with an uncommon ability to fix broken things, mechanical and otherwise, part blacksmith and part carpenter, and he was called upon begrudgingly by those from the village who sought to keep things—a hitch, harness or bellows—working beyond their expected lives. Apparently, Ransford's father had had some as yet unrevealed dealings with Mr. Smith.

"Now son, I've got something of some delicacy to discuss with you before me and my new friend Mali head off down this trail. Mali has shared his experiences with you two boys as I understand it, yes?" By then Charlie had joined them on the porth, scratching himself and yawning.

"If you'd be talking about the Railroad, then yes, sir, he has."

"Fine. Fine. And that's good, it is. But I'd be asking you two fine young men if we can hope you wouldn't be too free with your talk about this incident? This Railroad, as you call it, has been doing its good work for, hell, half my lifetime. We've saved hundreds of souls; got them out of chains and safe to Canada. And make no mistake boys, that's as close to God's work as you're ever going to find. But it don't work, it *won't* work if we can't keep it secret, even now when so many agree with us. There's still enough hard people out there to stop us if they knew the particulars. Do you understand me, boys?"

"Well, I guess you'd be asking us to lie. Is that what you're sayin'?"

"Not lie,. No, I wouldn't ask you to sin like that, if that's the way you look at it. I'm just asking you not to talk about it. Heck, don't brag about it is all I'm saying. Of course you can tell your daddy, Elias. He already knows. He's a good man." Mr. Smith paused and looked at Charlie. "I don't know your daddy, but I'm hoping he would have some sympathy for us poor colored souls. What do you say, son?"

Charlie thought for a minute before speaking up. "I'll be honest with you, Mr. Smith. I never met a negro before last night. But after talking with Mr. Mali and hearing all he's been through in his life and with him being, well, such a decent man, I don't think I could ever do anything to hurt him or anyone of such similar experience. I guess that's my answer, sir."

"Good! Good then!" Jedediah Smith nodded his head repeatedly up and down, pleased by what he'd heard but anxious to get moving. "Mali, it's time to get going. We've seven hard miles to my home and then more in the morning. We want to get you to Canada before winter sets in."

Mali, who seemed even more physically impressive standing in front of the cabin in the gaining morning light, reached out his massive hand to shake hands with the boys.

"Thank you both. Both you young men give me hope that this here world won't be so crazy some day; that some day good people won't be slaves and bad people won't be masters. I'm hoping, God willin', that I'll be free and that you two fine young men will be long for this world and that you'll be happy all your long life. That's my hope and prayer for you." He said the words with such fervent sincerity that his passionate pronouncement would indeed resonate and remain with them for the rest of their days.

The two men said their farewells, mounted the horses, and made their way north along the barely perceptible trail that led to Mr. Smith's home on the hill that rose above Hunt, Jenny, and Efnor Lakes, three lovely mountain ponds known locally as the Three Sisters. From there, Mali would be ferried on to one of several routes the Railroad took through the Adirondack

41

high peaks, the last great ordeal in his journey before approaching Canada, and freedom.

The boys—still baffled but profoundly affected by their experience—slowly shuffled east from the cabin, pointing themselves toward the rising sun and their homes far away on the other side of the forests around South Corinth. They spoke little as they trudged through thickets and swamps, their muskets heavy in their hands, their stomachs empty, and their heads spinning. They vowed to keep the incident to themselves and their families, suddenly recognizing that the world-changing events that had previously resided only in newpaper articles and sermons, had suddenly visited them in person and stood in front of them, breathing and talking and alive.

Now it was deep in Ransford's thoughts at quiet, reflective times like these. His mind, addled by whisky, had drifted there and he wondered how Mali had fared in his dangerous quest for Canada.

Ransford's ruminations were broken suddenly by Billy ordering Zack to get more wood and stoke the fire. Ransford cringed as Zack jumped up to search out sticks in the dark edge of the woods behind them. Damn, he thought, it's like he's working for the bastard. Maybe someday he'll work for him, but he doesn't work for him now. Ransford propped himself up on his elbows and stared toward the dark shape across the fire that was Billy.

"Why don't you go fetch some wood yourself, Master William . . . or is that too petty a burden for a prince?" The challenge was delivered with a sarcastic bite, different from the way the boys normally picked on each other. It shook the boys out of their delirium.

Billy O'Rourke sat up straight and leered over at Ransford, considering his response and measuring his foe. Ransford was tall, almost six feet, sturdy and strong and, although he rarely fought in earnest, his friends knew him to be a scrapper when he had to be.

His father had told him once, "It's better to get licked in a righteous fight than to win one that had no business being fought."

"So, it's better to lose?" he'd asked his father.

"No! Now listen to what I'm tellin' you, boy," his father had scolded him, giving Ransford a little cuff on the top of his head. "It's that you should only be a fightin' if you have a darn good reason. And that's not just because some fella doesn't look too kindly at ya."

"So, what's a good reason?"

"Well, you'll know the difference when yer older."

Something in Ransford told him this might be one of those times. Maybe it was the whisky. But maybe it was that Billy had no right to treat his friends that way, ordering them about and putting on airs. Still, he wasn't sure and he could almost see his father scowling at him as he braced for Billy's response.

Instead of standing up--widely recognized as a signal for readiness to fight--Billy hunkered down and lobbed an insult of his own Ransford's way.

"You know, Densmore, I've heard that you've some interest in that handsome lass who works in the general store. What's her name again? Sarah, is it?"

Ransford felt a tightening in every muscle, the blood rushing to his neck.

"That might be right, mister," he said, angry and embarassed at having to admit his infatuation in front of his friends. "Why would you be bringing that up?"

"Well I'm just thinkin' that nothing seems to be happenin', boy. I don't see you taking Miss Sarah to the dances or holding hands or even being all that friendly, if you know what I mean . . .. I was just wonderin' if you didn't mind me makin' a play for her? I mean, if you're not going to, I surely think she is a comely lass."

"You can do whatever you want, O'Rourke; you always do," Ransford seethed, a blink away from crossing the thin line that keeps two hateful, but otherwise law abiding men from attacking each other.

"Oh, well, thank you, Densmore, that's charitable of you . . .. You know, boys, it's funny how you can put a mare in a pen with a stallion and pretty soon nature takes its course. That is, most times, mind you. Some times the stallion just doesn't have what it takes, if you know what I mean, and you have to bring in another stallion to get the job done." He said the words knowing the effect they would have. "Now that Sarah, she looks like a fine young filly to me...a good breeder, I'll bet."

As the words left Billy's mouth, Ransford was already scrambling over the dying fire, spraying embers and sparks into the air like a thousand fireflies. In the moment before Ransford fell upon him, Billy saw a black silhouette with an eerie corona of sparks firing off in all directions as if some terrifying spirit had risen up from Hell to exact an awful revenge. He froze at the spectacle. In a whisky-fueled rage, Ransford fell upon Billy O'Rourke with all his momentum, crumpling Billy's defenses. On his back and overwhelmed, the boy covered his head with his hands as Ransford rained punches down upon him. There were sickening thuds and cracks as his fists connected with cheeks, skull, and teeth. Ransford didn't stop, even when Billy cried out in pain and shock.

If ever someone deserved a beating, Billy O'Rourke did; for the fear he put in the hearts of his friends and for his haughty, regal attitude. But this was more than that. Billy's words had unlocked a short lifetime of rage and frustration that he never saw coming. The boy had seen his father cut down men with words, relying upon his status and their fear to deliver unseen blows and get away scot-free. But this was a reaction Billy had never witnessed before. And he was paying the price for it.

The boys watched the violence in silent awe. Fights were common in their world, but they were usually little more than glorified wrestling bouts. Following some slight, the combatants would stand face-to-face and deliver insults until somebody shoved somebody else. Then, only after the proper build up, would they lock in battle. The stronger would pin the weaker, asserting his status for the time being, and then all would be well. Not this time. This time the fight had exploded in front of them in a one-sided, brutal display that shocked them all. They were fascinated by it.

Zack and Chicken finally pulled Ransford, still spitting and swinging, off his vanquished foe. Billy was bloodied and bruised everywhere--his shirt torn, teeth broken, blood streaming out of his nose and mouth. He lay curled up and whimpering on the ground. Others in the group gathered around Billy, as much to inspect the damage as to comfort the beaten boy.

"Damn, Ransford!"

His chest heaving, his eyes wild, Ransford strained against his friends' grips and stared at Billy on the ground, transfixed on the quivering heap that had just insulted him so deeply. If he could have killed him, he would have.

"Calm down, man!" Zack said as he and Chicken pulled Ransford away from the scene, off into a quiet patch of trees. "You coulda killed him, Ransford. And, if you did, his daddy would make sure you hang . . . and then where'd we be? Short two friends . . .."

"Friend! How can you call that sniveling lump of royalty a friend, Zack?" Ransford was shaking, but his senses had returned enough that he could speak and plead his case. "Of everybody, Zack, I'd think you'd back me on this. Didn't he deserve everything he got just now?"

"Shit, sure he did, Ransford!" Chicken piped in, his cockeyed teeth gleaming in the moonlight. "After what he was sayin' to you, I was 'bout ready to jump him myself, but you beat me to it, Ranny boy."

"Well, now, I don't know as anybody deserves a whuppin' like that," Zack responded cautiously. He was thinking about his family and his father and how much they relied upon the help of the community to make ends meet. He sensed that beating the tar out of the son of Corinth's most powerful man might not be a good thing for anyone associated with the event, especially those who just sat around and watched it happen. "Sure you were right, Ransford. I just don't know what's goin to come of it. That's all."

III. The Long Walk Home

Zack and Chicken walked with Ransford to the outskirts of town, at times consoling him and at others wondering aloud about the implications to come. After a while, Ransford cooled down and, while admitting he'd acted rashly, still clung to the notion that "Billy had it coming." He could not accept the idea that others, who had seen what he had seen and had heard what he heard could ever come to another conclusion. And yet, as he would soon learn, they did.

The walk home seemed to take forever. As the whisky wore off, his head began to pound and both his hands—knuckles raw, bloody, and swollen—throbbed. With each step he relived the moments that had transpired around the fire, the words that had hit him like cannon balls, and his violent, instinctive response that had, in the moment, felt so right and now shamed him to his core. At no point in his young life had he ever lost control like that and the thought that it could happen again frightened him.

He trudged along in the darkness, finally arriving at the doorstep of the farm house not long before sunrise. His father was already awake, brewing coffee in the kitchen, when Ransford entered. His younger brother, Sylvanus, sat at the small oak kitchen table, his face illuminated by a candle.

"'Bout time you dragged yerself in here, boy."

"Morning, Daddy. Morning, Sylvanus," he said, exchanging looks with his sibling who was just two years younger and anxious to hear about Ransford's trip to town.

"Well, I hope you can be good for somethin' today, young man . . .. Lord sakes, you smell like a honkey-tonk! What have you been up to, boy?"

Ransford hung his head. "Well, Daddy, we did imbibe a bit last night and you'll find out soon enough that I got myself into a fight."

"Who'd ya fight, Ranny? Did you whip him?" Sylvanus could hardly contain himself.

"Yes, young man, I'd like to know who you fought, but I'm much more interested in the why of it than the outcome." His father's tone became stern, like an earnest prosecutor, and Ransford knew he was expected to tell the whole truth and nothing but the truth.

"Well, we got to drinkin', up on the cliffs above the river, and then we got to talkin' about the war and other things . . .."

"Alright then, go on."

"And then Billy O'Rourke said some things, terrible things, that got my blood to boilin' . . . and so I went over an' fought him."

"Alright. Then you two tussled and that's the end of it, right?" his father asked hopefully.

"Well, not exactly, Daddy. I think I hurt him pretty bad . . .. His face was real bloody and he lost a couple teeth, as far as I could tell, before I left."

Sylvanus, awestruck by what he was hearing, blurted out, "Lord sakes!"

"Why on earth did this thing get so outta hand, son? Can you explain it to me?"

"It's sure hard to explain, Daddy. He said awful things about me and about a gal and I just went outta my head . . ..I just don't know." He stood there shaking his heavy head from side to side and found himself oddly starting to feel frustrated and angry all over again.

"A gal, eh? Well, I don't know if your mama, bless her soul in Heaven, would have ever wanted me to beat a fella bloody over her . . ." he said and then hesitated, thinking of his long dead wife, who had died giving birth to Sylvanus. "But I suppose I might have acted that way just the same, under certain circumstances, mind you. I can't approve of the thing you done, Ransford, even though I understand it."

Ransford was surprised by his father's rare show of empathy. He didn't expect it and was most grateful for it.

"I understand, sir."

"Now you go wash up, son. Have some breakfast and I'll see you and yer brother down at the barn." And he walked out, leaving the boys alone in the kitchen.

"Damn, Ransford! What ya gonna do now?"

"I guess I'm gonna wash up and go down to the barn. What are you gonna do?" he replied, brushing aside his younger brother's desire to probe deeper into the dramatic events of the night before. Ransford didn't want to talk about it anymore; he wanted to put it behind him.

The next day, Ransford, Sylvanus, and their father took the wagon into town for Sunday service at the Methodist Church. Not talking about the previous day's events or caring to revisit them, Elias pulled the wagon into a hitching area next to the recently painted, white steepled church located halfway down Main Street hill in the center of the bustling village. As they passed others dressed for church, the customary tipping of hats and "howdies" were exchanged. Here and there some people they encountered looked away or even scowled slightly, as if the sight of them was repulsive. It had not dawned on Ransford, or any of his family for that matter, that news of Ransford's shellacking of Billy had spread beyond the normal boundaries of young men's social circles and had become something of a village matter.

During his sermon, the Reverend Ringwood extolled the virtues of *turning the other cheek* and *the need to avoid the sin of violence at all costs*. He went on: "Resist the call to raise your hand or your sword against your fellow Christian, no matter how repulsive his transgressions, and then you will walk with angels

. . ..But strike you a righteous blow against your neighbor for slights real or perceived and God will consider you the transgressor. Vengeance is mine, sayeth the Lord!"

On one hand, the bombastic preacher, educated in a southern missionary college, seemed to be railing on with his oft-stated belief that the northern states had no business going to war with the south; that such a war would be viewed as an abomination by the Lord. On the other hand, Ransford felt as if the preacher was directing his sermon squarely at him, and perhaps he was, because throughout much of it, parishioners would turn in their pews to cast sour glances his way.

After the service, as the families shuffled out of their pews and back into the street, a well-dressed man, known to work for Charlie O'Rourke, Billy's dad, asked Elias for a word over by a large oak next to the church. Ransford and Sylvanus watched the conversation from several yards away and could see their father growing increasingly agitated as it progressed. The man, never removing his top hat, remained expressionless while calmly explaining things in a very business-like manner.

"How in God's name does he expect me to be able to come up with $210 by the end of this week? We agreed I'd pay him $5 a week until the note was paid. I've been a payin' him for six months now and I've met my part of the bargain . . .."

"It doesn't matter one way or another to me, Mr. Densmore, but Mr. O'Rourke is calling your note as is permitted under terms of the agreement. You can either provide him with the full amount due—that's $210—or you can turn over the collateral—the wagon—to him by the close of business on Friday. That's all there is to it," the man in the top hat stated matter-of-factly. He then tipped his hat perfunctorily and walked off. "Good day, sir."

The boys' shaken father walked back to them, his mind working on this sudden vexing problem.

"Daddy, I didn't know you owed money to Mr. O'Rourke."

"I didn't know I was obliged to tell you every thing I'm doing in this world, Ransford. But, yes, after we lost the other wagon in that flash flood a year back I had to get me a new one, so I went to the only fella in town that could make me a loan and that'd be Mr. O'Rourke."

"Well, how can he just go and ask for all the money at once like that? Isn't that why you agree to terms?"

"Yessir, we agreed to terms, but terms are writ by them that has the money, son. And in this case, him that has the money just saw his only son come home beaten bloody and senseless by my son!" he said, waving his arms around in exasperation. "I guess I'm not all that surprised by his reaction now that I think about it."

"What you going to do, father?" asked Sylvanus. "We don't have that kind of money, do we?"

"No son, we don't. I'll have to think on it. I need the wagon to do my work on the farm and for the handiwork and carpentry I do for folk in town . . .. I suppose I could sell the sheep but I don't like the feel of that," he said, shaking his head. "It definitely is a quandry. But don't you boys fret now, I'll figure somethin' out."

Ransford was dumbstruck. He couldn't believe how quickly his random act of aggression had rippled through the community and how it was now beginning to negatively impact those around him.

"I figure we best visit the general store and pick up some provisions while we're here in town," Elias said, causing Ransford to feel suddenly even worse. The idea of encountering Sarah at her father's store after all that had happened felt ominous.

When they arrived at the store, Ransford offered to mind the

51

horses and wait at the wagon but his father persisted, telling the boys that he'd need their help to bring feed bags out from the store.

"Good Sunday, Teddy," Elias greeted Mr. McGloughlin, who was poring over a large ledger book while seated behind the counter of the well-stocked general store.

"And to you, sir," the storekeeper responded somewhat flatly. "And what'll it be today, Elias?"

"I'd be looking to purchase four bags of feed and a spool or two of barbed wire if ye have it, Teddy. How are you and the family?"

"I'm sure we can arrange that, Elias. Tell your boys to fetch the items in the storehouse out back. Might I have a word?"

"Of course, Teddy. Now boys, go out back and pull off four bags of feed and two spools of barbed wire onto a wheelbarra and put 'em on the wagon."

The boys did as they were told and the two men, who had known each other for decades, commenced their conversation.

"I didn't want to be talking to you about this in front of your boys, so I best get to it straightaway. I was asked by a certain party, an important party here in town, if you catch my meaning, not to be extending credit for goods and services to Mr. Elias Densmore anymore."

Elias' blood started to boil and just as he was about to mount a loud protest Mr. McGloughlin, perhaps anticipating his reaction, continued speaking.

"Now I heard what transpired among the boys the other night and I even saw the O'Rourke lad myself yesterday. Stopped in here, he did. And, I'll tell you Elias, it was a powerful sight to see. That boy's face looked like it'd been run through a thresher! He ain't so pretty any more . . . .. But after seein' and hearin' all that, I remembered that there's two sides to every story—at least two, sometimes three or four—and that me and Mr. Elias Densmore go back to when we were boys here in this town, and that's a hell of a lot longer than when Mr. High and Mighty O'Rourke first came to our fair town. Right?"

"That's right, my old friend," he said, relieved. "I'd be forever grateful if we could continue our business under current understandings, especially since, as you know, my cash money comes and goes in bunches. But Teddy, I don't want our friendship to be any kind of burden on you or your business."

"Hell Elias, he don't own me or my business, not yet anyways. I think we can keep matters the same between us. Don't you worry about it. I thank you for your business and your friendship."

The sticky matter removed from discussion, the two old friends moved on to other, more mundane matters, while Ransford and Sylvanus brought the wagon around back to the storehouse. There, seated at a little wooden table, similar to the kind found at the Corinth schoolhouse, was the shopkeeper's daughter, Sarah. Her long dark hair tidily braided and wearing a flowery summer dress, she was reading a book, in which she looked thoroughly engaged, when the boys pulled the wagon in front of the enormous red barn that served as a warehouse.

"Good afternoon, Miss Sarah!" Ransford called out to his lifelong friend and the secret object of his affection.

She looked up from the book, startled, straightened her back in the chair and returned her gaze to the pages. Without looking back up, she responded: "Hello, sir. And hello to you, Sylvanus."

The cool and detached response, without averting her eyes from the book no less, was rude even by young peoples' standards. For it to come from Sarah, his childhood friend, was downright alien to his world. Ransford asked Sylvanus to go ahead inside and begin hauling the feed bags off their pallets in the storehouse. He'd be in shortly.

"What on earth has gotten into you, Sarah?"

Feeling ill-treated, he crossed his arms and waited for a response. Then, at the last possible moment before he said something again, she set the book down and looked up at him with a fierce and indignant look in her lovely brown eyes, catching him off guard.

"I was visited by Billy O'Rourke yesterday and he showed me the terrible things you did to him in a drunken rage! He had stitches all over his face, black and blue, swollen, and even missing three teeth! My God, Ransford, how could you have done such things, said such things! He looks scarred for life; I felt such pity for that poor boy! Why Ransford? Why?"

"Said such things? What things did I say?"

"Oh, I can't even bear to repeat them, Ransford. He said you were drunker than everyone else at the party in the woods and that you were muttering things about me, about things you wanted to do to me if you could only get the courage up . . .. Billy said he couldn't stand hearing such vile obscenities any longer so he spoke up and, well, defended my honor. And then he said you just went mad, totally mad, and attacked him!"

"Defended your honor!!!" Ransford yelled, the rage once again rising in him. "Can't you see, he's the one lying? *I* was defending your honor, Sarah!"

"You're starting to frighten me, Ransford. And, if you were defending my honor, why's he the one who's been beaten to a pulp? And why is it other boys say the same thing happened?"

"Like who? Who said that's what happened?"

"Horton Pike and his little brother Earl. They came in with Billy to buy a new shotgun and a pair of boots and they told me what happened to Billy. It's no use lying, Ransford. Please just admit your mistake and ask the good Lord for forgiveness."

"A new shotgun and a pair of boots, eh? Well Sarah, if you don't believe me then I might as well just go home and soak my head in a slop bucket. I may have made a mistake but it's not the one everybody around here thinks I made. I guess I'll be going now, Sarah, and I won't be around to trouble you no more."

"Oh Ransford," she sobbed, but said no more.

And he went off to load the wagon with Sylvanus, exasperated, convinced now that there was no way he could ever get justice in Corinth, not when he was facing a stacked deck and such a powerful, committed, and ruthless adversary. For the first time he was seeing how quickly and effectively the world could be manipulated and how the little worlds that people lived in—his, his father's, and his family's—could go terribly wrong in just moments.

Chapter IV: Ellsworth's Avengers

The boys drove the wagon around front and picked up their father before heading up Main Street hill, past the village square, on their way out of town. At the square, where peddlers and politicians and abolitionists collected to attract the attention of curious townsfolk every Sunday afternoon, Ransford could hear the strains of banjo, fiddle, and voice belting out a popular new tune, one that had been stirring the passions of upstate folk for the past few months. The inspirational lyrics and catchy melody of "Ellsworth's Avengers" carried up and down Main Street, gathering people around the musicians playing it in the square:

> *"Down where the patriot army,*
>
> *Near Patomac's side*
>
> *Guards the glorious cause of freedom,*
>
> *Gallant Ellsworth died.*
>
> *Brave was the noble Chieftan,*
>
> *At his country's call.*
>
> *Hastened to the field of battle,*
>
> *And was the first to fall..."*

The tune went on to regale the tragic end of dashing Colonel Elmer Ellsworth, the first Union casualty in the Civil War and a boy from "just down the road" in Mechanicville, another Saratoga County town 20 miles from Corinth. Everybody knew the story. The people of upstate New York had proudly followed the career of Ellsworth, a native son and a rising star who moved to Chicago, Illinois, in 1860, where he became a law clerk for another rising star, Abraham Lincoln. The two had quickly became friends and Ellsworth had worked on Lincoln's successful presidential campaign, accompanying him to Washington, DC, in 1861. Something of a renaissance man, who excelled in everything from the law and military arts to uniform design, Ellsworth had trained several military cadet units in the Midwest, eventually forming and becoming the commanding officer of the Chicago National Guard Cadets, which became a nationally-renowned drill team outfitted in colorful, if not gaudy, uniforms designed by Ellsworth and similar to those worn by the Colonial French Zoaves' fighting force in Algeria.

Upon the outbreak of hostilities in April, 1861, Colonel Ellsworth went to New York City, where he formed the 11th New York Volunteer Infantry Regiment (the Fire Zoaves), comprised almost entirely of New York City firefighters, whom he considered to be already battle-tested, and brought them back to Washington, DC. A short time later, on May 24th, one day after Virginia voted to secede from the Union, President Lincoln ordered his trusted military aide to take the 11th across the Potomac to take down a highly visible Confederate flag that had been flying above an Alexandria hotel for almost a month, vexing Lincoln and those who considered the flag a symbol of the government's reluctance to act. Colonel Ellsworth complied and, while much of his regiment fanned out across the city to root out resistance, he and seven men climbed to the roof of the Marshall House Inn, where the flag had been flying. After cutting down the flag, Ellsworth was carrying it down the stairs when the hotel's proprietor confronted him and, without warning, killed the Colonel with a single shotgun blast to the chest. After bayonetting the secessionist hotel owner to death, Ellsworth's stunned troops carried their fallen leader's body back across the Potomac, delivering him to Lincoln as if he were Hector being returned to Priam. President Lincoln grieved the sudden loss of his friend and military confidante, ordering an honor guard to place his body in the East Room of the White House for viewing. Noting that Ellsworth stood only 5 feet 6 inches tall, he said famously: "He's the greatest little man I ever met."

Lincoln's personal grief and shock were amplified nationwide.

Just 24-years-old at his death—handsome, gallant and smart—Colonel Ellsworth seemed to represent the bright promise of his generation. His death touched a chord with folks far and wide, from Chicago to New York City, and from Midwest farms to deep into the Adirondacks. When his body was brought to New York City for viewing, thousands flocked to the service and a great call went up to avenge his death. In response to an emotional editorial appeal from Albany's main newspaper, New York State commissioned the formation of the 44th New York Infantry Regiment, which, unlike most county-centric regiments of the day, would be comprised of soldiers drawn from every town and county of the state. "Ellsworth's Avengers," or the "People's Ellsworth Regiment," would be unique in other ways also, as recruits would be limited to proven fighting men, all of whom were required to be under 30-years-old, unmarried (supposedly to ensure their willingness to fight and die if need be), and 5 feet 8 inches or taller (a good two inches taller than Ellsworth himself!).

So when Main Street filled with the notes and lyrics from the familiar ballad extolling the virtues of brave Ellsworth, Ransford took notice, jostling his attention from a focus on his own sorrowful experience to the grander and graver issues being acted out on a great stage far, far from Corinth. Not much older than Ransford, Ellsworth had been places, done things, and accomplished so much before dying gloriously. Hell, Ransford thought, Ellsworth never tended sheep, and Ellsworth would have never been sucked into the kind of useless Shakespearean drama that Ransford found himself in that day. No. Ellsworth was above all that!

"Father, if you don't mind, I'd like to go over to the square and have a listen," Ransford asked his father.

"Why in blue blazes d'ya want to do that? Haven't you heard that song a few times before?"

"Yes, indeed I have, sir, but I'd like to hear it again and maybe go and see if some of my friends are thereabouts. It is Sunday, isn't it, sir?"

"You know it is, boy. Well I suppose I don't mind as long as you don't git yerself in any more mischief."

"Can I go too?" asked Sylvanus, to which both Ransford and his father responded: "No."

"Alright, Daddy. I'll be seeing you later tonight then." He hopped off the wagon and onto the street, jogging back down the hill toward the music and the village square.

The village square was a bustling place on a Sunday afternoon. Tables featuring an assortment of odd products—many of them drinkable and claiming to grow hair, restore lost virility and vitality, or improve intelligence—were manned by gayly dressed hawkers warbling on about the remarkable powers the drinks contained. There were men on overturned wooden soap and fruit boxes addressing pockets of people listening to them pontificate on a wide array of subjects, from Christianity to politics to the evils of slavery. However, Ransford's interested was captured by something new—next to the band, which continued to play Ellsworth's Avengers over and over, a couple of nattily-dressed men had established themselves behind a table underneath a large, brightly festooned banner that proclaimed:

ENLIST HERE!

ELLSWORTH'S AVENGERS

BOUNTY PAID

Ransford had heard that the state was seeking volunteers to join Ellsworth's Avengers, but he'd never seriously considered enlisting. The war had begun not long ago and, in rural places like Corinth, far from the battle lines, it was an exotic thing that only seemed to exist in newspaper articles and Sunday speeches, a subject of debate, but little more. Today was different though; Ransford felt changed. He approached the table and waited his turn behind a couple of men who were asking questions, while others stood back and listened intently to the answers the two gentlemen from out of town were giving.

"So, if I sign up, how long do I have to serve in this here unit?" one fellow asked.

"That would be three years, my good man," responded one of the men, who turned out to be from Saratoga. "We are recruiting men from Saratoga County and once we've raised a company they'll assemble for service down in Albany."

"Ain't there enough boys from Sara-to-gee to form yer company? Why you comin' up here for recruits?" asked another fellow, demonstrating the inherent distrust many in Corinth felt for "city slickers" from Saratoga.

"Indeed, there probably are enough from Saratoga to fulfill our needs sir, but as you know, Ellsworth's Avengers will be an elite fighting unit comprised of men from every town and ward of the state. In keeping with the memory of the unit's courageous namesake, New York State wants its best men—the tallest, the bravest, and the best shots—from every corner of this fine state to contribute to Colonel Ellsworth's fervent desire to put down this wretched rebellion once and for all!"

The short speech had the desired effect upon most of the men gathered there. Appreciative grunts—"Hell yes!" "Here here!" "Yesiree!"—followed and generally eased tensions.

Several men in attendance, clearly intrigued, peppered the Saratoga men with questions.

"So what does a feller get paid for his service?"

"I'm glad you asked that question, my good man. Throughout his term in service to the state and the nation a recruit—a private, mind you—can expect to be paid $13 per month. If he is promoted to a higher rank that amount can be expected to increase."

"What does that sign up above yer head mean when it says 'bounty paid'?"

"The bounty to which the sign refers is paid as a one time bonus to all recruits at the time they commit to serve in the 44th New York Infantry Regiment. Now, mind you, once you sign that paper, you are committed to serve for three years and there's no going back; it's a firm commitment enforceable by military law."

"Oh I git it. If I don't line up with the regiment every mornin' for three years you'll either shoot me or throw me in jail. Now how much is that there bounty? "

The Saratoga fellow chuckled. "You've got a colorful but accurate understanding of how this all works. As for the bounty, we are currently offering a one-time bounty of $300 to any legitimate, signed recruit who musters in at the Saratoga Court House by noon on Wednesday . . .. Now, mind you, that rather generous amount is subject to change and represents a strong desire by Saratoga County's leaders to send an impressive contingent of soldiers to Albany by the time the regiment musters in next month. "

"Cash money?"

"Yes, of course, cash money."

Ransford pondered the information, becoming astonished at its implications. By enlisting he could participate in New York State's noble effort to preserve the Union, perhaps even end slavery. What's more, he could shake free of his own captivity and, in the bargain, be provided with enough money from the bounty to more than pay off his father's debt and right a wrong of his doing. Ransford shook his head slowly from side to side, smiling at the thought of just how perfect the idea seemed. It was long before the casualty lists began to be published daily in the local newspapers and the thought of going off to war still appeared benign, if not downright pleasant, to a young man anxious to see the world. When it came his turn to speak to the men from Saratoga, Ransford stepped up to the table and announced, "I'd like to enlist."

His resolve surprised the two recruiters as they were accustomed to a more spirited give and take between themselves and potential enlistees, who tended to be nervous at both the commitment and the danger that danced equally with the benefits. They questioned his motives and sought to determine with certainty that the young man in front of them was qualified for enlistment.

"That's just fine, young man! First things first, son, please tell me your name, age, and place of residence."

"Ransford Densmore. I'm 21- years-old, and I live with my father, Elias Densmore, and brother, Sylvanus, down in South Corinth."

While one continued the questioning, the other recruiter was digging deep into a great, bound, black tome marked 1850 Census, trying to verify Ransford's age and residency.

"I can see you are tall enough; what are you, about six feet? Now, are you married? You can't be married, and I don't suppose you have any military experience?" The recruiter confessed that the previous military experience requirement had been largely ignored since it was almost impossible to find men under 30 years old who had any organized military experience, the last war—the Mexican War—having ended 13 years earlier. "Are you a good shot?"

"I'm a touch under six feet and, no sir, I'm not married and no current prospects. And, yes sir, I'm a damned good shot if I do say so myself."

"My colleague found you listed in the Census. And you do appear to meet all other qualifications for service. So, Mr. Ransford Densmore , if you are indeed serious about serving in the 44th New York Infantry Regiment, please sign this commitment letter to hold your place when we muster in the company in Saratoga in two days."

Signing the letter that had been drawn up hastily on the spot by the other, quieter fellow, felt more grave than he had anticipated. Other men, less resolved than he, but nonetheless intrigued, had gathered around and there was an air of public formality about it that caught Ransford off guard. A smattering of applause followed his signing the letter and Ransford turned around to see 10 or 15 men and women, most of whom he knew, clapping and nodding their heads in approval.

"Congratulations Mr. Densmore, you are on your way to becoming one of Ellsworth's Avengers! Bring this registration slip to the Saratoga Court House at noon on Wednesday— please be there on time—and you will officially join the company then and, at that time, you'll be given your bounty. Thank you and may God bless you!"

There was another smattering of applause and several well-wishers gathered around Ransford, slapping him on the back, praising his courage and patriotism, and thanking him for being one of the first to represent them in the Great War of the Rebellion. One in particular, Amy Carpenter, a pretty, fresh-faced gal with pig-tails who still attended school with his brother, boldly approached Ransford after his signing, professing how much she admired his commitment to action and his willingness to sacrifice. She breathlessly confessed that she had read and was moved by *Uncle Tom's Cabin*, the ground shaking novel by Harriet Beecher Stowe.

"Honestly, Ransford Densmore, I am most grateful you have summoned the courage to participate in the great battles to come for I feel they are necessary to break the horrible chains of slavery once and for all!"

"Well, I thank you for those kind thoughts, Miss, I surely do," he responded politely to the girl he had hardly noticed until now, who seemed a sudden and beautiful affirmation. In her hazel eyes, he would later recall, he sensed something familiar, as if she already knew him deeply.

"Might I be so bold as to ask if you would mind if I wrote to you while you are away in service to our country? It would truly mean a lot to me, Ransford," she asked.

"Of course, Amy. That would be just fine. I just don't know where I'm going or how a person would go about that, but sure."

"Oh wonderful. Thank you! Don't worry, Ransford, my words will find you."

"Well, I best be going. It's good to see you."

"It's been very good to see you, Ransford. Good luck to you and God bless you!"

He walked off, almost delirious. The warm reaction from his neighbors and the girl surprised him, especially coming so close on the heels of a morning in which he had felt nothing but scorn and derision. Curious, he thought, how things can change so quickly. And yet, he welcomed the change and feeling infinitely better about himself, he began the long walk home with a spring in his step, looking forward to the adventures ahead.

Ransford's father was none too pleased when he learned of his decision later that evening. It took some talking and some hand wringing before Elias Densmore grudgingly acknowledged that the boy, perhaps for the first time in his young life, had made a man's decision, one that took into account every side of a situation and then did what was best for everyone.

"Well son, I can't say there's much about this situation that I like, but I have to admit that you approached this stickiness like a man and that's all a father can ask for. Just the same, I don't know that I like this bounty business, sounds like a bribe to me!"

"Hell, I figure it's more of a reward then a bribe. And I suppose there's no crime in taking Saratoga's money for a good cause, now is there, Daddy?"

"I s'pose it sounds better if you put it that way, Ransford," he said, pausing to look at his boy with a hint of admiration. "You do this thing son, but you serve your time smart and come back to me and yer brother safe. You understand me, boy?"

"I do, sir."

Come Wednesday morning, Elias, Sylvanus, and Ransford were back in the wagon, heading south out of the mountains toward Saratoga. They plodded past many miles of bustling mature forest, the oaks, beech, and maples already shifting from green to hues of yellow, purple, and crimson. It was Ransford's favorite time of year in the mountains, a crisp colorful time that blew away the oppressive heat of summer and seemed to re-energize folks. They traveled steadily downward for several miles until they reached the flatter lands outside Saratoga. Here they rode past large farms, many with sprawling fence-lined paddocks dotted with pretty horses grazing happily.

"Damn! I don't think I ever saw horses treated so nice!" exclaimed Sylvanus, who hadn't been to Saratoga in some time.

"They breed race horses down here, boy. It's big business." Elias hadn't spoken through much of the trip as he pondered the momentus change. Not only was his son going off to war, taking risks that he didn't want to mention aloud, but he was losing Ransford's daily contribution to the family's work. There'd be more for he and his younger son to do. They were healthy and capable enough and many got by with less, he thought, but they'd just have to work a little harder.

Soon they were rolling through the outskirts of Saratoga, past the great pillared homes and assorted commercial establishments that provided for every need (or desire) imaginable. There were haberdasheries, flower shops, book stores, and purveyors of saddles, along with places that sold only canes and baskets. As they pulled the wagon onto Broadway, bustling with fancy black carriages and gentlemen on horseback, the towering hotels and elaborately adorned casinos dominating the streetscape came into view. They churned with activity as men, most in bowlers or top hats, and women dressed in all sorts of finery, poofy chiffon dresses and frilly hats, breezed in and out of the hotels and gambling houses. The boys were fascinated.

"This is where rich folk come to play, boys! This here's a different world from ours; you just remember that."

"True it is, sir! But it surely is a spectacle!" Ransford said as he exchanged glances with a particularly fetching young woman, dressed like doll in a store display, walking arm in arm with a prim older gentleman that he assumed was her father. The man shot Ransford a derisive look.

"Rube!" he said and walked off down the stone sidewalk.

"Mind yerself, boy," Elias warned his son, sensing his reaction. "We're almost there and don't need any distractions."

Further south on Broadway, just past a glorious park sporting tidy footpaths and a large central pond with fountains and swans, they pulled in front of the Saratoga Court House, yet another impressive building fronted by marble steps and grand ionic columns heralding its importance in civic affairs. They ventured inside and encountered a uniformed man, a lieutenant by rank, who directed them to a small courtroom being utilized for registering the new recruits. Another man in uniform with sergeant's stripes ushered them inside the richly-panelled room adorned with several larger-than-life paintings of great jurists who had presided in the court over the last century. Feeling uncomfortable in the hushed setting and its austere trappings, they were directed to sit in pews that faced an ornately-carved bench, that was currently vacant. Several dozen young men, some with family or friends accompanying them, anxiously but silently awaited the arrival of an official to tell them what would happen next. After an interminable wait an aged judge in black robes took his seat at the bench and the sergeant ordered those assembled to rise and remove their caps for the Honorable Judge Rosewater.

"Good day, gentlemen. Let me tell you that I am most pleased to meet you and that I am quite honored to oversee your enlistment into the 44th New York Infantry Regiment. You bring with you onto the field of battle Saratoga County's profound appreciation for your commitment and sacrifice. I also wish to offer my thanks to your families, your fathers and mothers, brothers and sisters, for giving you up to this noble cause. For this is their sacrifice as well. When I read your name please come forward and take the oath of allegiance."

Upon hearing his name called Ransford shuffled out of the pew and went forward.

"Do you, Ransford Densmore, vow to serve Saratoga County, New York State, and these United States of America willingly and honorably for the full duration of your service to the 44th New York Infantry Regiment?"

"I do, sir."

"Thank you son and God bless you. Now sign the oath you just took with the clerk in the back of the room there and he'll give you a receipt for your bounty."

As he signed the oath, Ransford could overhear the Lieutenant and the Sergeant speaking to each other nearby.

"Don't look like much of a company to me, if you don't mind me sayin', Lieutenant . . .."

"They don't look like a bad lot, Sergeant. Just not a lot of 'em."

"Exactly my point sir. I thought Saratoga would raise at least 75 to 80 men, if not a full company. We got us less than 30 here, by my count."

"True enough. It is surprising; I'll give you that, especially given this was Ellsworth's county. Well, let us hope that Albany delivers a good showing."

"Maybe a higher bounty would have done the trick," said the Sergeant derisively. Ransford could tell these two were familiar and had possibly served together for some time.

"Heh, you may have a point Sergeant. Now let's gather these babies up and get them saying their good byes. We've got a long trip to Albany."

"Yes sir." The Sergeant then straightened noticeably and announced to all assembled: "Attention, all recruits gather your belongings and follow me to the back of the courthouse where you can redeem your bounties and say your farewells."

Behind the court house the men lined up in front of another uniformed man, a quartermaster, seated at a little folding table under a broad ancient oak casting shade over a pleasant clipped grass yard. The men shuffled along in line, each holding a little slip of paper redeemable for his bounty, while a gathering of relatives, loved ones, and others, perhaps less emotional than the rest, watched with interest.

Ransford's turn came and he presented his slip, which the quartermaster matched with a name in a lined book in front of him.

"Are you Ransford Dinsmore?"

"Why no sir, I am Ransford Densmore," he said surprised at this odd complication. "Maybe somebody wrote down my name wrong?"

"I'm sorry son, the army doesn't make mistakes. Maybe there's another fellow named Ransford Dinsmore out there somewhere?"

"With all respect sir, I signed the paper up in Corinth just this Sunday."

"We cannot spend any more time on this. The book states the name Ransford Dinsmore, and Ransford Dinsmore must be the one I release the funds to."

It was Ransford's first encounter with miliary logic and far from the last. Flumoxed, he conceded that he was, indeed, Ransford Dinsmore, and signed the form accordingly.

"Very good, private. Here's your bounty," said the Quartermaster, immensely satisfied, and handed a small stack of money to Ransford, which he carried over to his father and brother.

"Sakes alive! That's a lot of money Ransford!" Sylvanus couldn't contain himself but his father's countenance was far from joyful. He cast his eyes downward at first and then raised them to look purposefully into his son's face, tears welling in his eyes. It was the first time he'd ever seen his father cry. Elias took hold of his son's shoulders.

"I can't say I ever pictured this day coming for you, son. I figured you, me, and your brother would be living in Corinth all together until you planted me in the ground. I never saw this coming—a father doesn't like to admit a thing like that—and it grieves me, son, it grieves me!"

"I know, Daddy. It came as a surprise to me too. You know it did, but I do think it's a good thing." He didn't know quite how to respond to this sudden outpouring of emotion from his father, something he'd never experienced. "So here's the $300 I just got in bounty and that should more then make things right."

"I don't want it, boy! You keep it. It's a noble and good thing yer doin'. You hold onto that money!"

"Well, if neither of you two fine gentemen have need of that money, I can certainly put it to good use!" The interruption came from a tall mustachioed man in a bowler hat, a fellow recruit, who smiled and tipped his cap. Then he turned and ceremoniously handed his full bounty to another, tough looking character who had been watching his every movement. "Now, my good man, I certainly hope this settles my account with you and your employer."

"It does, it does. You're a lucky one, Jack. Woulda enjoyed takin' it out of your hide. I'll tell Mr. Brady you're square now," the burly fellow said, smiling devilishly. "Come back and see us again in three years!"

"I'll be looking forward to it!" said the mustachioed man, turning to his new acquaintances and introducing himself. "The name's Jack, Jack Finnegan. Very pleased to meet a fellow recruit. It will be a grand adventure, don't you think?"

Ransford liked Jack immediately, but the same couldn't be said for his father, who already sensed that his son was in danger.

"Thank you kindly Mr. Finnegan, but my son and I are saying our good byes, so if you don't mind?"

"Not at all, sir. I'll take my leave of you and—Ransford is it? I'll see you shortly." Again he tipped his cap and made his way toward several wagons that had been brought around to transport the new recruits to Albany.

"You best watch out for that one," Elias warned his son, resuming his discussion with far less emotional intensity, which relieved Ransford. "Now me and the boy aren't the best writers in the world but we'll do our best to send you letters and we're hoping you'll do the same, time permitting. You be careful out there, son, and there ain't no shame in coming back from a fight alive. Keep yer head down, is what I mean."

"I will do my level best to come home to you, Daddy. Now here's that bounty; I don't want any more arguing about it. And, I'll save up as much of my pay as I can and send it back to make up for my not being there to work the farm. Alright, Daddy?"

"Well then alright son, how about I'll take about enough to cover the wagon and a little extra and you keep the rest? You'll be needing it and you won't be getting paid for another month . . .. I guess I never told you that you mean a lot to me and your brother and, hell, I'm real proud of you." Elias gave his son a lasting hug and sent him on his way, the tears returning to the proud man who was quite unaccustomed to such displays.

Ransford turned to Sylvanus and shook his hand fervently. "You can't be slacking around the house no more. Time for you to earn your keep. You hear me, boy?"

"You bet, Ransford. Heck, you'll be back afore you know it!"

"Sure hope yer right . . .. Off I go!" Ransford pulled his rucksack, which he'd stuffed with extra clothing, a jacket and sundries, over his shoulder and loped over to one of the covered wagons there to transport them to Albany. He climbed up into the back of the wagon and found a seat inside with ten other recruits sitting on benches facing each other. He scanned the faces of the men inside; some nodded to acknowledge him; others just stared ahead, lost in thought.

It was a long, bumpy ride to Albany, one with very little conversation as the men tended to keep to themselves. Most had never ventured more than ten miles from their homes and none, it seemed, had ever been to Albany, the state capital, nearly 50 miles, as the crow flies, from Corinth. The wagons stopped along the way a few times to let the men out to stretch their legs and relieve themselves. Ransford could hear Jack Finnegan chatting up recruits further ahead.

It was dark by the time the wagons pulled into a large mowed field on a hill overlooking the city of Albany. As they climbed out of the wagons the men could make out a rather large assemblage of tall, white tents with peaked roofs and in front of

71

every fourth or fifth tent, a large bonfire stood, illuminating the vicinity. The Lieutenant and the Sergeant jumped down from their perch on one of the wagons and started barking orders to the men, telling them to form a line in front of the wagons. Naturally achy and lethargic from the long ride, the men complied slowly with the order, listlessly forming a ragged, uninspiring line in front of the wagons and facing the camp, where other recruits milled around cook pots and came and went, some stopping to watch the newbies' arrival.

"Did you not hear me, babies? Get your sorry arses in line!" Bellowed the Sergeant. "This morning you may have belonged to your mamas and your daddies, but now you belong to me! I swear, if you do not form a neat and soldierly line in 30 seconds each one of you poor excuses for a soldier will roll a rock three times around this entire camp!"

The men jumped at his words which exploded out of his throat like shotgun blasts. The Sergeant noticeably held a pocket watch connected to a fob he had pulled from his vest and was scanning intently as the men fell into line.

"Glory be to God, I think they made it!" he announced as he surveyed the line in front of him. He smartly snapped to attention and pivoted around to face the Lieutenant who had been standing to his left. "Lieutenant Knox, I present the Saratoga company -er- squad for your inspection, sir!"

"Thank you Sergeant Tinkham . . .. Men, welcome to the 44th's temporary camp. We will bivouac and train here for the next few weeks as the regiment completes its muster. Now you are a ragged group of recruits much in need of training. It is my job to transform you into a commendable fighting force, one that Colonel Ellsworth would be proud to lead into battle. I intend to do just that. That is all, men. Sergeant Tinkham will show you to your quarters."

Talk among the recruits revealed that Lieutenant Knox had served with Ellsworth back in his early days with the Chicago

National Guard Cadets Drill Team and had followed the Colonel to New York City, helping him form the 11th New York Infantry, the Fire Zoaves. He had seen his Colonel fall that fateful day in Alexandria and, with barely time to grieve, had taken the field with the 11th New York in the first major battle of the war at Manassas Junction. There, near a little creek called Bull Run, he witnessed firsthand how poorly-trained Union troops had lost their cool in the thick of battle. In places, green recruits under the command of Brigadier General Irvin McDowell failed to follow rudimentary battle commands while under fire, losing the army's advantage due to superiority of numbers. Toward the end of the long bloody battle, many simply broke and ran, surrendering the field to the enemy. The shameful day's events (that some pinned as much on a lack of leadership as poor soldiering) easily could have resulted in the fall of Washington, DC, and perhaps the loss of the war, had it not been for waning sunlight and the brave work of the 11th, which lost many men in guarding the main force's haphazard retreat to the capital.

Ransford and his compatriots would learn the history of the 11th from several men who had served in that unit but transferred to the newly constituted 44th after the ill fated battle. After Bull Run and the shock waves it sent through Washington's political and social elite, President Lincoln sacked General McDowell and replaced him with the diminutive but fiery General George McCellan, who immediately set about building a massive, well-trained army—the Army of the Potomac—that would never be bested again. For his part, Lieutenant Knox left the 11th New York, which he considered to be one of the best trained fighting forces on the field, and worked to recruit and train the 44th – Ellsworth's Avengers—into a force that would have made his dead colonel proud.

The men followed Sergeant Tinkham to a line of empty tents on the far edge of the encampment, counting off ten men at a time and telling them they'd be bunking there for the foreseeable future. Ransford and his bunkmates, Jack Finnegan included, entered the large peaked tent, each man picking a cot upon which a rolled up wool blanket had been placed. Minor squabbles about select locations were resolved without incident and the men, exhausted from the long day's events, settled into their cots by the light of a few oil lamps. Just then, the familiar face of another Corinth boy, Solomon Hickok, appeared in the half light and greeted Ransford.

"Well howdie, Ransford! I guess I didn't get a chance to say hello up in Saratoga."

"Hello to you too, Solomon! So you're in this unit too? Anybody else from Corinth that you know of?"

"Well yes, as I understand it, Elijah Earls, Dwight Earls' son, signed up too, but he's comin' down separate tomorrow or the next day. He had to finish up some business with his family . . . .. It's sure good to see another fella from back home!"

That's when Jack Finnegan felt compelled to interrupt.

"Far be it for me, a no account miscreant from Saratoga, to break up this touching reunion of two long lost country boys, but the scary sergeant—who does seem to mean what he says—mentioned something about not wanting to hear a peep out of us until morning, did he not?"

"I heard him, Jack. He's got a point, Solomon. I'll talk to you in the mornin'," he said in a hushed tone.

"Night boys!" whispered Solomon, a likeable young man, about 20, who sometimes worked with his uncles and cousins cutting timber in the mountains around Corinth. Solomon Hickok belonged to the Towers' clan, a group of wild lumbermen who lived and worked deep in the forest, occasionally venturing into town for supplies and special occasions. They tended to make village folk nervous with their volatile and intemperate ways, but Ransford had always admired their courage—lumbering was a dangerous way to make a living and many a young man lost a limb or even their lives engaged in it—along with their

74

bluntness, which he took for honesty. Ransford went to sleep relieved that a couple of Corinth boys would be along with him on the adventure.

V. The Sacrifice of Private Whitney

The night sky was still hanging over the camp when the strains of a harsh and unrelenting bugle roused them from sleep. At first, Ransford incorporated the melodic entreaty of reveille into his dreams until finally he was jarred awake by a torrent of orders and admonitions. Sergeant Tinkham barked from outside the tents, exhorting his new recruits to dress double quick and face the morning for the first time as soldiers. They pulled on trousers, shirts, and boots while hopping up and down on the cold packed dirt that served as a floor, then assembling in lines facing their commanders. For the first time, in the gathering light of the morning, they could see the makings of their regiment, a ragged line of men, indiscriminately dressed and evidencing assorted postures and poses, stretching off into the foggy distance to the west.

Appearing out of the fog, a uniformed man on a tall bay horse rode slowly toward them. He cut an impressive figure—as most uniformed officers on horseback did—with a double breasted navy blue coat sporting bright bronze buttons, his clean shaven face and head topped with a dramatic plumed hat, and a saber dangling from his side. As his horse strode along the line, the Colonel—Colonel Stryker—addressed the troops within earshot in a deliberate, developing fashion, apparently not worred if the soldiers heard the entirety of his speech. It was enough, he felt, that everyone see him and hear a portion of it and, perhaps, he reasoned, they would collectively re-assemble his thoughts later on in camp like some verbal jigsaw puzzle. For his part, Ransford heard the tail end of the address:

" . . . You men can take pride in knowing that the 44th New York Infantry Regiment is perhaps the only regiment from New York to truly represent the totality of this great Empire State. You come from Erie County out west to Herkimer County in the lofty Adirondack Mountains and many of you come from Albany, our capital city, and many more from the great metropolis of New York City. And we have come together thusly to defend this grand state and our nation as well as our sacred constitution against forces that would strive to destroy our Union. I know you will, to a man, comport yourself with honor on the field of battle and so I am honored to have been chosen to command you in this coming struggle!"

At that, he drew his saber and twirled it several times around his plumed cap, his horse spurred into rearing up, to conjure up quite a dramatic scene, one that Ransford would remember vividly in years to come. Similarly impressed, the men along much of the line—even those who hadn't heard or seen the dramatic flourish at the end of the speech—spontaneously erupted in sincere and throaty "hurrays" and "huzzahs." As the Colonel trotted triumphantly from the scene, he was replaced by several lieutenants on foot who led a squad of some 20 sergeants to the center of the field in front of the line, where two large wagons had been parked. They pulled back the burlap tarps that covered the cargo, revealing prodigious stacks of freshly milled pine two-by-fours, cut five-feet-long. Each sergeant fanned out to areas along the line that roughly approximated their companies and selected a handful of privates to go and collect several of the raw yellow sticks, instructing them to distribute one to each man in his vicinity. When every enlisted man in the regiment had been given a two-by-four, sergeants began addressing the men in their respective companies.

"Right shoulder arms!!!" Sergeant Tinkham bellowed. Some of the men placed their sticks over their right shoulders hesitantly, but many men looked around nervously, holding their pieces of wood haphazardly, leaning on them, holding them perpendicular to their bodies and the like. They shuffled their feet and listlessly mumbled to one another in a display of confusion and disharmony that elicited a colorful response from the sergeant.

"Confused are you? Confusion in battle will get you killed, babies! I don't think I've ever seen a group of men more ignorant, more slow on the uptake than you upstaters! Do I need to talk more slowly for you babies?" He paused, waiting for a response which never came. "I'll only say this once—if I ask a question, I want to hear an answer and it had better be either 'Sir, yes sir' or 'Sir, no sir'. Do you understand me?"

"Sir, yes sir!" most responded, starting to capture for the first time how this game was played.

"If I have to drill you pathetic morons every day for a year you will become soldiers! You will learn how to march in formation, the manual of arms, how to load and fire as a unit, bugle commands, and all the basic commands for an infantry man; and you will learn them so you do them while sleeping. You will learn them so you do not get me or the men in your platoon killed. Do you babies understand me?"

"Sir, yes sir!"

"Because you are still babies, we are not giving you real rifles, we are giving you pretend rifles to drill with. These two-by-fours will be your rifles until I think you are worthy of real rifles. Do you understand me?"

"Sir, yes sir!"

And so it went. From that day forward, from dawn until dusk, they drilled every day—except Sunday—for the next several months. Drilling consumed them, haunted them, and ultimately broke them. Long before they could be brought to battle and asked to function as a modern military unit they were required to learn a mind-numbing litany of infantry commands—over 90 in all—designed to move men quickly and decisively in the chaos and smoke and carnage of battle. Painfully deliberate and degrading, boot camp had proven itself over a hundred generations as the best way to break down undisciplined young men and rebuild them as members of an army. Ransford thrived in this simple new environment, as did many of the young men, who were inclined to embrace the structure and the clarity of command. Others, however, did not flourish in this strange new universe; they instinctively bridled against the constrictions and mindless obedience required of military order. And they did not fare well.

One fellow, a Saratoga boy from a well-off family named Horace Whitney, who had enlisted but refused the bounty, seemed incapable of following the simplest of commands without some complication or complaint. Sometimes he would raise his hand, as if in grade school, to ask a question while an officer was explaining a certain drill or maneuver.

"Pardon me, sir, but wouldn't it make more sense if one were to parade left instead of parading right under these particular circustances?"

Such questioning, perfectly reasonable in civilian life, would prompt an immediate, visceral response from officers, particularly among sergeants, who had earned their stripes precisely because of their blind obediance to military cannons. So it was with Sergeant Tinkham who was not a man to be trifled with and took his task of preparing men for battle with fearsome sincerity.

One day, after a particularly long and grueling stretch of drilling that focused on a somewhat complicated battlefield maneuver, Private Whitney, after an order had been given to wheel right, inscrutably wheeled to his left, causing the ranks of the entire company to spasm. Such mistakes were not uncommon; they tended to elicit stern and public rebuke from the sergeant in charge followed by repetition and more repetition, the army's cure for most mistakes. But, in this instance and almost certainly due to the person causing this particular misstep, Sergeant Tinkham called Private Whitney out of the line and proceeded to dress him down mercilously in front of the entire company.

"Private Whitney's foolish blunder in the ranks has just killed off his company! Because he wheeled left instead of right the column could not form a firing line and because the company could not form a firing line in time a good many of his comrades were shot and killed by Johnny Reb! Now boys, this here isn't about Private Whitney, who appears to be floating just a little bit above the rest o' us. No, it's about his squad mates as much as it's about his royal fuckin' hi-ness, if you catch my meaning. There's no royalty in the ranks! There's only rank, and rank is earned. There's only royalty in the ranks if it's allowed. So I do believe this punishment needs to be divvied out, not only to Prince Whitney, but also to those that allows this condition to occur . . .. So, Prince Whitney, I would like you to select six of your platoon to share in this little punishment I'm cooking up for you."

"Sir, yes sir." A shaken and embarassed Private Whitney dutifully selected six men, including Ransford, for this dubious but as yet undefined punishment.

"You six privates have been chosen by Prince Whitney. Now, I'd like you six to lift his highness above your heads and carry him once around this camp. Mind you, the whole camp, around the mowed edges. Now get to it! And do it on the double quick."

"Sir, yes sir!"

The men formed two lines of three and clumsily hoisted Private Whitney, a good-sized man of nearly 180 pounds, above their heads, arms stretched up to the sky as if forming the death pyre for a fallen Greek warrior about to be set ablaze. They shuffled along, at the double quick, just as embarrassed as Whitney to be parading around the camp in front of their peers. Different companies drilling in other parts of the great mown field halted their maneuvers and watched as the odd assemblage lumbered outside their perimeter like some strange six-footed beast. Catcalls, hoots, and huzzahs erupted as they passed—tacitly condoned by the commanders—forever burnishing Private Whitney's shame into the mind of the regiment. Some officers would eventually credit the "sacrifice of Private Whitney," as it would later be called, as doing more to build 44th's unit cohesiveness than a hundred drills.

"I'll tell you, boy, you'd best be learning your steps or we'll be carrying you to a cliff to throw you off!" Embarrassed at being visibly associated with Whitney's shaming, Private Wiggins, one of the six chosen pallbearers, threatened Whitney about halfway around the camp.

"Now we don't need to threaten ol' Whitney, do we boys? He's gonna snap to attention and learn his steps right away now; aren't you Private Whitney?" Ransford grunted under duress. Perhaps because he sensed that Whitney was being unfairly singled out for a mistake any one of them could have committed or possibly because this sort of public shaming felt all too familiar to him, Ransford stood up for the young man. "By God boys, if we can make Whitney a soldier we can make Company E the best dang company in the regiment! I aim to make that happen!"

Stiffly accepting his ride atop the men of his choosing, Private Whitney declared his contrition and vowed, under the sight of an all-knowing God, to change for the better. "Gentlemen, I truly apologize for putting you through this embarassment. I am ashamed and will work night and day to be a better soldier and a better comrade to you all. Lord willing, I will make you all proud some day!"

"Amen to that, brother!"

True to his word, in the ensuing weeks, Private Whitney drilled with a new found intensity, following each order and executing each step as if a life—his or someone else's—depended upon it. He would practice outside his tent after mess, often with the help of members of his squad, many of the same men who had carried him around the camp that day. He did, indeed, become a serviceable soldier, and, after nearly a month, so did the others in Company E and the rest of the 44th Infantry Regiment.

The drilling and the monotony of camp life were momentarily reprieved on Sundays, when soldiers of the 44th were granted an opportunity to engage in personal matters. Many pious recruits, particularly the country boys, attended Sunday services delivered by chaplains of assorted faiths—Catholic, Methodist, Baptist (but exclusively Christian)—in large Chataqua-type tents that served as both mess halls and churches. Those less attentive to religious matters might be found lazing with their brethren around campfires in front of their tents, mending torn clothing, writing letters to loved ones back home, whittling sticks, or just sipping coffee and listening to the birds. In places, the strains of fiddle and mandolin music would call together appreciative audiences, often inspiring spontaneous dancing and knee-slapping jigs by soldiers ready to release a slew of pent-up emotions.

After attending services at the Methodist tent, Ransford increasingly looked forward to Sunday afternoons in the camp and the kind of free wheeling comaraderie that they engendered among his fellow soldiers. Only then could he meet and talk with men from exotic places he'd never heard of, places like Buffalo and Syracuse and Plattsburgh and, of course, New York City, which produced men, many of them of Irish or Italian descent, who talked strangely and quickly and, much like Jack Finnegan, always seemed to be selling something.

On one particular Sunday, only a few weeks after arriving in camp, a group of the New York City boys made their way to a flat patch of the expansive mowed field that served as the regiment's parade ground and, like field surveyors, began pacing and marking out the boundaries of a large diamond in the field. This attracted the attention of many of the men in the camp, who gathered around, intrigued at the odd goings on.

"What are them boys doing?" asked Ransford.

"Looks to me like they're laying out a baseball field," replied Jack Finnegan. "And, lad, that's the most marvelous thing I've seen in many a month!"

"Why is that, Jack?"

"Because yours truly happens to have an affinity for this game, Ransford, my boy. Now you just watch; don't let on, and maybe we can have a little fun."

Jack approached one of the men involved in carving a baseball diamond out of the mowed field, asking him what on earth he was doing. The man, a swarthy fellow with a pencil thin mustache, responded derisively as he carved out a chunk of sod that would serve as home base.

"I'm not building a pyramid here, buddy. My friends and I are getting tired of watching the grass grow in this upstate, backwoods paradise of yours, so we thought we'd play a little baseball. That's called base-ball, rube. You ever hear of the game?"

"Why yes, I have, in fact, heard of the game, my good man," responded Jack, not acknowleding the insult in the least. "In fact, my friends in E Company and I have played the game on occasion. Would you and your fellows consider playing against us, as feeble as we no doubt would be to you?"

"Come on rube, we play this game hard and fast. We wouldn't want to hurt nobody."

At this, Jack proposed that they make things "more interesting" for the New York City boys. "To make this worth your while and to reward your obvious generosity of spirit, how about we make a friendly wager on the outcome?"

"Hmmmm, what did ya have in mind, rube?"

"I don't know. It's only money. How about a dollar a man?"

At that, the swarthy Irish fellow looked Jack up and down, figuring him for a dandy, and brought the idea to several of this mates who were wrapping up their work in the field. They looked over at Jack and Ransford and a collection of the squad that had gathered around them, and nodded their heads in consent.

"What are you doing, Jack? I've never played baseball in my life and I don't want to lose a dollar to those no account snake oil salesmen. We'll never hear the end of it!" Ransford said. He liked Jack but, of course didn't trust him, not completely anyway.

Jack leaned in to Ransford's ear and earnestly said: "Trust me on this, lad. I may be a gambler, but when it comes to this game, I'm not gambling . . .. If we lose I'll cover your and everyone else's; just go along."

As nearly half the regiment collected along the first and third base lines, the experienced team from C Company of New York City faced off against nine hastily selected men from the Saratoga squad out of E Company, a few of whom had played before, the rest hopelessly new to the game. Jack placed each man in a position either in the outfield or infield and very broadly instructed them in their roles on the defense. Then Jack took to the mound that had been created from a pile of dirt and horse manure pounded with a sledge hammer.

He preceded pitching by engaging in an elaborate stretching routine, touching his fingertips to his toes, twirling each arm in a dramatic circular motion, and pulling his long, wiry arms over his head. Jack's lanky frame combined with the deliberateness of his routine to create a comic air that elicited laughter and catcalls among the troops, prompting several side bets favoring the New York City boys, and at long odds.

The same swarthy private that had rudely challenged Jack happened to be the first batter and stood at the plate grinning from ear to ear in anticipation of teaching the rube a lesson and taking his money. Jack smiled back and then motioned to his catcher that he had best move back several steps, prompting more laughter from the men. One of the lieutenants, who hailed from a neutral company and agreed to serve as umpire, stood behind the squatting catcher.

Jack took the roughly-stitched, horsehide ball and bent over, the ball cradled in his right hand, his arm hidden and cocked like a musket hammer behind his back. The regiment let out a sustained roar as he progressed into his wind up, stepping back with one leg and then tucking it high up onto his chest, his knee almost touching his chin. Jack's contorted body remained suspended above his left leg and then uncoiled suddenly like a cobra striking, his right arm following high over his head like an unleashed catapult, exploding forward with incredible force and sending the ball zipping above the block of sod representing home plate. The private meekly swung his carved oak bat a full second, it seemed, after the ball had split the air over the plate. He stood there stunned, staring dumbfounded at Jack, who simply caught the ball retrieved by his catcher, meandered cooly around the mound, and prepared, workmanlike, for the next pitch. The soldiers roared and clapped as Jack wound up again and delivered another cannon shot by the helpless batter.

To the delight of most of the regiment, except for those who had wagered against the upstate boys, Jack proceeded to strike out every batter he faced. Some even stood back away from the plate out of fear of being hit by the hurtling horsehide ball. As the innings went on, however, the only path to victory for the boys from E Company depended upon them eking out at least one run. And, despite their inadequacy in dealing with Jack's fastball, Company C had a pitcher of their own who had limited Jack's squad to a handful of hits, two of them by Jack, that didn't amount to anything. That was until the bottom of the ninth inning, when Jack strode to the plate.

By then, Company C's team had had their fill of Jack Finnegan and were feeling embarrassed and angry, even duped by this ringer from the north, enough so that their pitcher (perhaps, it was later rumored, under orders from his lieutenant), wound up and plunked Jack square between the shoulder blades with his first pitch. Members of E Company rushed the field. Had it not been for the timely intervention of a few officers, things might have dissolved into a bloody fist fight between companies. Once order was restored, with both sides warned against any further beanings, Jack was awarded first base and E Company's next batter, Private Whitney, stepped to the plate. Whitney, it turned out, had played some of baseball while attending a Boston preparatory school in his youth. In previous at-bats Whitney had made good contact on the ball, but without a favorable result.

He stood at the plate, facing his foe, the bat gripped firmly but comfortably in his hands, a determined look on his young face. After a strike and hitting a ball that sailed far but clearly foul, Private Whitney shifted his weight onto his back foot and waited for the pitch, which hurtled fast but straight over the center of the plate. He swung and heard the clear unmistakable sound of the bat hitting the ball cleanly and fully, sending it high into the autumn sky. The ball's trajectory took it deep into the outfield between the two fielders who scrambled to retrieve it, splitting their outstretched arms and continuing unabated into the high grass at the outer reaches of the parade ground. Jack had taken off from first at the crack of the bat and easily rounded the bases, leaping onto home base with his arms thrust triumphantly in the air.

Private Whitney followed, rounding the bases as the two outfielders from C Company futilely searched the tall grass and brambles for the lost horsehide ball. The private was met at home by a rabble of happy comrades, most from E Company, but many from other companies who either shared in the sudden euphoria or had just come into considerable winnings. In the happy chaos that followed, six members of Private Whitney's squad, the ones who had once labored beneath him in public shame, collectively and spontaneously agreed it was time to carry him once again. To Whitney's great surprise, Ransford, Jack, and the others hoisted him above their heads and began carrying him triumphantly around the patchwork baseball field, much of the regiment recognizing the irony and expressing their approval with howls and huzzahs. It was a joyous moment for E Company, and indeed for much of the regiment, one soon branded in their memory.

When the commotion died down and the victors from E Company returned to their tents on the far eastern side of camp, a steady stream of soldiers, including some officers, from other units stopped by to congratulate them and chat with Jack, Private Whitney, and the boys, who were holding court around their camp fire. One in particular, a private from C Company, shook Jack's hand intensely and thanked him for bringing him a considerable windfall.

"I figured it was you when I heard you challenge the boys to a game and, boy, you proved me right!" the Private blurted out, still shaking Jack's hand. "That's when I pressed the bet. You were going off at 10-1 odds, buddy!"

"Well, I'm not sure what you're referring to, my good man, but thank you nonetheless," Jack stated innocently.

"What is he referring to, Jack?" Ransford inquired.

"Why this is Jack Finnegan!"

"I know his name is Jack Finnegan, fella, what of it?"

"This Jack Finnegan is the same Jack Finnegan that was the star pitcher for the New York Knickerbockers, only the best professional baseball team in the whole mother-loving country!" said the starstruck private. "His picture was on the front page of the *New York Herald* and any other paper that mattered at one time or another. Everybody wondered what happened to you, Jack. You just up and vanished a couple years ago!"

"Well, truth be told, I found it necessary to leave the confines of New York somewhat suddenly one day and realized it wouldn't be wise to leave a forwarding address, if you catch my meaning."

"And why on earth would that be, Jack?"

"Let us just say the matter involved the daughter of a

remarkably powerful man, an industrialist of some repute, who had friends high up in the New York Police Department. I found it quite necessary to—what's the term you country folk use—oh yes, I found it necessary to skeddadle," Jack admitted nervously. "I packed a steamer trunk and took a clipper up the Hudson, then a train to Saratoga, where I settled in quite nicely. That is, until that unfortunate incident with Mr. James Brady."

"You are a character, Jack! Well, your secret's safe with E Company!" the private announced.

The squad erupted into more huzzahs and hoo-rays and proceeded into many hours of happy revelry. Someone broke out distilled spirits, a jug of joy juice smuggled into camp by a teamster. That night the men of E Company laughed and danced to fiddle music under the stars. The next morning came all too soon, beginning yet another week of drilling and training.

Weeks past and then on one bright and crisp autumn morning, after being summoned awake to the now familiar bugle call of reveille, the men assembled in a line, two deep and stretching nearly a quarter mile facing north. Unlike the ragged, undisciplined line of a month earlier, the men stood straight and true; spaced impeccably and holding their two-by-four "rifles" on their shoulders smartly, facing front and at the ready.

Once again Colonel Stryker, astride his big bay horse, rode along the line from west to east and addressed the men. They had not seen him since the first day and there was an air of anticipation among them.

"Men, you have acquitted yourselves well in your training these last few weeks and have demonstrated a commitment to drilling that is exemplary. You have come far in our communal quest to appropriately represent the exalted memory of Colonel Ellsworth! (There was a smattering of "huzzahs" from the ranks.) We are now ready to show the world the 44th Infantry Regiment, the Ellsworth Regiment, and bring it to the fight!"

Again, the Colonel reared up on his horse and flourished his saber above his head, prompting yet another round of hoorays and huzzahs. Some cynics in the company would later theorize that drumming up morale with dramatic displays of horsemanship and "speechifying" was about all the Colonel was good for, but they did, nonetheless, admire the tactic and its effectiveness upon the men.

Upon striding off the field, as the colonel had done before, teamsters drove several heavily laden wagons upon the field. They pulled back flaps of the covered wagons to reveal a colorful cargo piled neatly inside. Some wagons were loaded to the brim with pine wood boxes containing hundreds of brand new Enfield rifles. The other wagons were stacked with piles of uniforms.

Members of the quartermaster's staff each sat behind several small tables, one representing each company, in front of the wagons. Cartons containing rifles and stacks of uniforms, each bundled and tied up with twine, were piled up behind the tables.

Lieutenant Knox stood in front of the men of E Company and instructed them to proceed to the table one at a time to collect their uniforms and rifles. The proceedings felt strangely official, like a graduation of sorts, attended by all the pride and underlying fears that came with ascending from one status to another. It was, after all, an acknowledgement of achievement, but also a heart-stirring reminder that soon they would be going off to war—the real war they had only read about in newspapers.

At his turn, Ransford went forward and gave his name to the quartermaster's representative.

"Private Ransford Densmore."

The sergeant peered up over his spectacles at Ransford and looked back down at his list of names. "No Densmore here private. I have a Dinsmore. Is that you?"

"Sir, yes sir." Ransford thought better than to make issue of the mistake. "Military intelligence," he thought to himself. He collected his rifle—a clean, impressive weapon standing nearly as tall as himself—and his uniform, which was given to him without consideration of size or fit, and carried them proudly back to his unit.

"Men," said Sergeant Tinkham (referring to them as men for the first time). "Return to your tents, change into your uniforms, and report back in thirty minutes time to form up. Dismissed."

Several of the men in Ransford's squad burst into their tent. Brimming with excitement, they pulled apart the packages containing their uniforms and inspected the contents. Each included a pair of bright red pantaloons, an indigo woolen jacket with ornate bronze buttons, white leggings that strapped over black boots, and a simple red cap with a brim that was designed to approximate a fez. Some of the men stared at the exotic clothing assembled on their cots before them, not quite knowing what to make of them.

"Well, ain't that something!" said Solomon Hickok with a puzzled look on his face.

"I won't say a thing in public, boys, but it kind of reminds me of something an organ grinder's monkey would wear," admitted Whitney.

"And so it does, my good man," chimed in Jack Finnegan. "It will make us the prettiest soldiers on the battlefield!"

Ransford was busy pulling on the red pantaloons, which hung down uncomfortably from his waist in a loose, baggy fashion. After pulling his white undershirt over his head and tucking it into his trousers, he covered it with his blue jacket, marveling that it fit snugly and comfortably. Then came the new black boots which were stiff and a bit large. He strapped the white leggings over the boots and reluctantly pulled the red fez-like cap onto his head.

"My, my! Aren't we a sight!" a bemused Jack announced after looking around the room at his fellow soldiers.

The others simply nodded in agreement.

"We best get back out there." Ransford picked up his rifle and headed back with his squad to the field. As the line formed in the bright autumn sunlight it became clear to the men that they had, indeed, become part of an army. Gone was the motley collection of individuals hailing from a hundred disparate towns and cities throughout New York, men born of different classes and education. They had become a homogeneous and structured regiment that, at least from all outward appearances, could move and react as one body, like a machine; and, despite the men's initial misgivings, appeared downright dashing.

VI. A Long Strange Journey to the Front

After more days of drilling—many devoted to loading and firing their new Enfield rifles in an array of formations that might someday be dictated by battlefield realities—the regiment received word that it would, at long last, break camp and move south. The men awoke the morning of October 24th before dawn to corporals and sergeants barking orders, each squad responsible for breaking down its tent and packing it on wagons brought in by the teamsters. After a quick breakfast of hot coffee and hard tack—the ubiquitous rock-solid biscuit that they would eventually both despise and long for—the regiment formed in marching order, beginning with Company A (the Albany boys), followed by Company B, and so on through Company I. Colonel Stryker and his top officers, several captains and lieutenants among them, led the column of more than 1,000 men down the hill they had occupied for the last several weeks into the City of Albany, many of its 60,000 inhabitants lining the parade route and anxiously awaiting their arrival.

Flag bearers carried *Old Glory*, New York's Empire State flag, and the regimental colors along with a line of drummer boys, who rattled out a constant stream of rat-a-tat-tats representing battlefield commands. They marched in good order from the outskirts of the capital, eventually reaching State Street and the heart of the bustling city that lay where the Hudson and Mohawk Rivers met. The Dutch-settled city once known as Fort Orange had grown substantially over the past several decades and Albany had become one of the nation's largest and richest cities, due to its strategic location along the Erie Canal and its key railroad hub. Steamboats, barges, wagons, and trains laden with goods and people flowed through the city from throughout the Northeast and the city's entrepreneurial captains—many of Dutch, English, and German descent—had built small empires in publishing, lumber, transportation, banking, and manufacturing in the great city. Despite being 150 miles north of New York City—already one of the world's greatest commercial epicenters—Albany commanded its share of respect and treasure, due in no small part to its political importance as the state's capital. As commerce boomed in the humming metropolis to the south, the political might that meted out laws dictating winners and losers in the world of commerce flowed through Albany.

On that glorious fall day the city was festooned with gaudy red-white-and-blue bunting and thousands of its best-dressed citizens lined State Street for the spectacle of the People's Ellsworth Regiment, as it was called by the press. The people of Albany were bursting with pride in their regiment; after all, it had been promoted and largely paid for by Albany banks, businesses, and politicians, who viewed the regiment as their Spartans, the best of the best, being sent off to vanquish the barbarians who had snuffed out the bright light that was Ellsworth, one of their most promising native sons.

Ransford and the soldiers of the 44th marched in step down State Street, eyes fixed forward, looking polished and precise— a smartly dressed regiment making its way through Albany to the delight of its inhabitants.

"Have you ever seen anything like it, Ransford?" Solomon Hickok whispered out the side of his mouth.

"Indeed, no, I haven't," Ransford replied, never averting his gaze.

Halfway down the street, the unit stopped, standing sharply at attention in front of a fine three-story red brick home. An elegantly dressed matron stood at the balcony overlooking the head of the column. Ransford learned she was the wife of the late Erastus Corning, the longtime mayor of Albany, under whom the city had flourished both economically and politically.

"Brave men of the Ellsworth's People's Regiment, noble members of the 44th New York Infantry Regiment, this city salutes you!" A great cheer rose up from the ranks at Mrs. Corning's words. "You carry with you today our profound gratitude for the sacrifices you have made and will make for our grand state. Were he here today, my husband, Mayor Corning, would tell you how proud we are to have such exemplary young men representing us in this terrible conflict and that, because of you, we cannot imagine losing. Go forth, young warriors. Go forth to victory!"

She presented the regiment with a new battle flag, consecrated by an Irish priest at her side and lowered to a captain waiting below. An aide fixed the flag to a standard and the regiment resumed its march through a loving Albany, crowds growing more raucous as they approached the docks along the Hudson River, where the city's commerce came and went, day and night, via trains, ships, and wagons, from all directions. Within sight of the river—which Ransford noticed had swollen much larger and more substantial than its modest proportions back in Corinth—the column passed what appeared to be the largest lumberyard in the world. Sprawling for acres in every direction, save the eastern boundary of the river, the yard looked like an enormous chess board with giant blocks of piled lumber of all types—hemlock, spruce, beech, maple, and oak—laid out in grids with many, many men and wagons moving to-and-fro, filling the holds of waiting ships and train cars.

The men were herded unceremoniously like cattle, bound for New York City onto waiting barges strung together by massive cables and trailing a large steamer boat. By company, the men clambered over the sides of the cumbersome, flat-bottomed barges, only the tallest among them able to see over the sides of the thick creasote-soaked walls of the vessels, which emitted a powerful stench.

"Who-eeeee! What the hell is that smell?" one of the soldiers exclaimed upon boarding.

"I truly do not know. But it ain't a thing I look forward to for more than a minute . . .. Kind of like hot tar and chicken shit, all mixed together!" replied another.

"Quiet in the ranks! Now this will be your chariot for the next day. So let's settle in and make the most of it, men." Sgt. Tinkham didn't much care for the mode of transport either, but he couldn't abide complaining. He'd never seen any good come of it in life or in battle.

Most of the men of E Company took seats atop their packs and bed rolls at the bottom of the foul craft and felt a great lurch followed by a deep unmistakable groan as the steamer began straining to pull the barges downriver. They plowed ahead through the morning, making slow but steady progress down the Hudson, lumbering through numerous craft that dotted the river. The river was alive with commerce. There were sloops with grand white sails, hauling all manner of cargo and manned by toiling roughnecks, and steamer ships, their decks lined with well-dressed travelers peering across and pointing at the formidable string of barges. Along the east and west shores of the gray-blue waters of the Hudson, trains belching white clouds of steam curled along the shoreline and could be heard chugging in the distance. Although the boys from the Adirondacks and the far western part of the state had seen many of these things before, they were awakened for the first time to a new magnitude of things and a sense that the world was much bigger, faster-moving and more dramatic than they had ever realized. As they progressed down the river, the impression only grew.

After several hours of slow progress downriver the steamer and its trailing caravan of barges began to lose momentum, gaining less distance despite the steamer's best efforts. The steamer altered its course and made for a small city built on a hill in a hodgepodge fashion from the river's eastern shore. The boat angled to its port where a bustling series of docks and warehouses awaited with a team of longshoremen who grabbed ropes tossed to them from the craft and, straining mightily, pulled them close, securing the line to the dock.

"Men, welcome to Poughkeepsie! We'll be waiting out the tide here for the next four hours before we head back down the river. Each company will be given some time on the docks to stretch legs, eat, and do their business. Let us proceed in orderly fashion to our business," announced one of the captains as he walked down the dock addressing each company directly.

Ransford didn't pay much attention to what was being said. Like most young soldiers he wasn't as inclined to listen to the why of a thing as much as the what or the when of a thing. All he knew was that soon, hopefully, would come food, a chance to relieve himself, and possibly a breath of fresh air.

"What did he say was the name of this here town?" Solomon Hickok asked.

"Po-Kip-See is what I heard. What the hell kinda name is that?" replied another soldier.

"I'm guessing it's an Indian name," said Ransford.

"Well why in blue blazes can't they call it by an American name? Damn Indians are nothin' but no account fools and drunkards, talking gibberish all the time," said one of the recruits from Saratoga, riling Ransford.

"First off, my grandma was an Indian woman and she wasn't a drunkard and she didn't talk gibberish. And second off, where in hell do you think the name Saratoga came from?" Ransford again experienced that odd feeling, the one he had succumbed to when he confronted Billy, rising up in him as he stood to face the Saratoga boy, who also rose to face him.

Private Whitney stepped between the two young men and turned to admonish his fellow Saratogian. "Alright now Johnny, be a good lad and apologize to Ransford here. We know you didn't mean those ignorant things you just said, now don't we? You're just tired and hungry like the rest of us, aren't you?"

Johnny Corcoron's father worked for Private Whitney's father back in Saratoga at one of the elder Whitney's factories and the boy knew his place; at least, he knew his station back in the proper, well-ordered world they had left behind. As others stood to back their man in what might be a looming fight, Private Corcoron, sizing up the situation, offered a somewhat concilliatory response.

"I don't know nothing about your family or your views concerning this subject and so I didn't mean any offense . . .. It's a sad day when a fellow can't just speak his mind among his friends, but if I made you angry, boy, then I guess I apologize."

"My but isn't that about the sweetest of apologies?" Jack Finnegan's unmistakable voice suddenly chimed in. "Well, Ransford, in the face of such abject sincerity from my fellow Saratogian, how would you have us proceed? Do you accept this noble fellow's offering or should we hoist him over the side and toss him into the river?"

"I don't suppose the sergeant would like that solution very much," said Ransford, chuckling. "Yes, of course, that will be just fine, Corcoron, and that's the end of it."

Ransford felt embarassed by the commotion and unwanted attention, but another side of him appreciated how cooler heads, young men he counted as friends, had divined the situation before it escalated and had defused it with humor and diplomacy. Our country, he thought, might have avoided this war if they'd been in charge.

A short time later, E Company was summoned onto the deck for a much needed break from the bitterly cramped hold of the barge. The men scrambled over the side and leaped onto the gray weathered planks of the deck. They gathered to receive rations and were led into a small vacant alley behind one of the many large buildings collected along the busy waterfront, where they were told they could relieve themselves. Emerging, Ransford could see the waterfront buzzing with activity, ships being loaded with cargo, along more than a mile of docks fronting massive warehouses and factories that seemed built one atop the other. There were taverns and inns tucked between the commercial buildings, places where the longshoremen, sailors, deckhands, peddlers, and travelers were gathering for drinks and food. This Poughkeepsie, he thought, is very much alive.

E Company made its way, far too soon, back into the hold of the foul barge and were told that the regiment would be moving in an hour or so. Ransford, looking out over the river toward the high bluffs across from Poughkeepsie, wondered aloud why they were waiting if all the companies had concluded their business.

"Because the river flows against us." An older, dark-skinned soldier in civilian clothes with raven black, close-cropped hair, that Ransford had never noticed before, was standing next to him, leaning against the barge wall, also looking west over the river.

"What are you talking about?" Ransford asked.

"Look there at the river. What direction is it flowing?"

Incredibly, the river was clearly flowing due north, the opposite direction that it had been flowing a few hours before. Ransford was dumbfounded.

"How can that be?" Ransford stared at the phenomenon, trying to make sense of it.

"The Indian would say one thing and the white man would say another. To the Indians who lived north of here—the Mahican tribe—this river is called *Mahicanituck* or *the River that Flows Both Ways*. It is a very sacred place to them, a place of great magic."

"But how can it flow both ways?" Ransford asked incredulously.

"The white man's answer is that this river, most of it, all the way from New York City to Albany, is a tidal estuary and that whenever the tides change, the direction of the river's flow changes with it. It flows north with the high tide and south with the low tide."

"But aren't we a hundred miles from the ocean?" Ransford looked more closely at the man's face and observed his high cheekbones and slightly ruddy complexion, which were less obvious due to his mustache and cap.

"That's how powerful the ocean's tides are. It reaches this far because there aren't any barriers or waterfalls from Albany to New York." The man noticed Ransford's quizzical look. " My name is Ely Samuel Parker," he stated. "Very good to meet you, Private."

"Pleased to meet you, Mr. Parker. I guess I didn't notice you before, when we were camped in Albany, I mean."

"That may be because I didn't join you until the day the 44th departed Albany."

"If I may be so bold, why aren't you in uniform Mr. Parker?" asked Ransford, still staring with disbelief at the water flowing north, slowly carrying ducks and sticks and other flotsam back north toward Albany. "And how did you know all that, about the Indians and the tides?"

"Among my tribe, the Seneca, I am considered a chief. I've been asked by General Ulysses Grant to join him on the western front but there are some people in Washington, some officers in the war department, who'd like to meet with me first," he explained with a sort of resigned exasperation. "They find it hard to believe that General Grant would want a native American—an Indian, as you say—to join his staff. I think they find it even harder to believe that I'm an engineer, trained at Rennselaer Polytechical Institute back in Troy."

Now Ransford was looking at Ely Parker much the same way he had stared at the river that had suddenly changed directions. He couldn't help himself.

"Surprised, son? You certainly look it." Mr. Parker said, chuckling quietly.

"I am sorry sir. It's just that . . .."

"You've never met a smart Indian? One who wasn't a fool or a drunkard who always talked gibberish?" He looked at Ransford knowingly and gave him a nod. "Yes, I overheard your little conversation with the delightful Private Corcoron. I thought you acted quite nobly. First you stood up for your grandmother and then you resisted the urge to throttle the buffoon. There's a saying that I've gone by my entire life, Ransford, and that's that great men only fight great battles. Are you familiar with that concept?"

"Not entirely, sir, but it sounds a lot like something my daddy tried to teach me, something about righteous fights being the only kind worth fighting."

"Yes, I think you're father had it right. Now this is a battle worth fighting, don't you think?"

"I do, sir. I just don't know what to expect when I'm in the thick of it," Ransford said, confiding in this stranger, this Indian, hinting at his fears.

"I think you will do well in battle, Ransford. I feel that your *orenda* is strong. Quiet, but strong," Mr. Parker said matter-of-factly, as if a doctor delivering a prognosis. The pronouncement, rendered by such a wise and affable fellow, both comforted and confused Ransford.

"What is o-ren-da, Mr. Parker?"

"The closest thing I can say to you so you'd understand is maybe the word 'spirit'. The Iroquois and many tribes have a word that explains how all things are bound together, unseen, and how they all—people, animals, trees, wind, rocks—have their own share of this energy. Some more, some less. Private Cocoron has very little in my opinion. For the Iroquois it's

100

called *orenda*. I sense you have a lot of *orenda*. But of course, I could be wrong. Who really knows these things?"

"Thank you, Mr. Parker. I truly hope you're right about me having a good share of o-renda. From what I'm hearing I'll be needing it!"

"You're most welcome, son."

They were quiet for a while, each looking out over the grand river, the sun slowly creeping toward the mountainous western horizon. Soon the river had stopped flowing northward and had slackened, creating a glassy, flat veneer, looking more like a lake than a river. Just then the steamboat throttled its engines; the longshoremen cast the ropes back to the barges, and they were off again, the caravan of barges and its blue-clad cargo lurching southward toward the war.

They chugged along through the night, passing through a particularly dramatic valley where the river narrowed and the mountains, illuminated in the moonlight, appeared to loom menacingly over them on either side. On the western bluffs overlooking the river, West Point Military Academy stood like a sentinel tracking their movements.

"Look up, boys; take a good look to your right at West Point. We wouldn't have a nation if it hadn't been for that fort right there!" Lt. Knox proclaimed from the front of the barge, waking some of the soldiers who had nodded off to sleep. "The British couldn't take her, though they tried, over and over again. Even bribing that bastard Arnold (and he spat for emphasis) was to no avail. Because that fort stood tall, the Brits couldn't take this river and because they couldn't take this river they couldn't take New York State and because they couldn't take New York State, they couldn't win the war!"

Some of the men responded to the Lieutenant's fiery oration with half-hearted hoorays, but many were lost in slumber, curled in the bottom of the fetid barge or leaning on each other's shoulders for support while they dozed.

Ransford gazed at the collection of black granite buildings and prodigious fortifications dotted with gun turrets that appeared cut into every nook and cranny of the rocky mountain above them. The country's most prestigious military academy—from which most of the war's generals on both sides of the conflict had graduated—stood like an emblem of a nation's resolve. If that fort held the young nation together, could its students, who learned the art of war there, go forth and now tear it apart?

Onward they progressed through the night, passing an unrelenting stream of vessels, both under sail and steam-driven, heading north. Faster moving boats overtook them in the well-defined shipping channels of the Hudson. Eventually the river widened substantially and they began to pass larger cities on both the eastern and western shores. Increasingly, immense red brick factories appeared, sprawled for acres along the shoreline, dark clouds of smoke rising from incredibly tall stacks, dotting the industrial landscape like barren trees, stripped of their limbs. As they drew closer to New York City, there was more of the same, more of everything, as the city expanded outward and upward in all directions, unbroken except by the river.

Ransford and many other soldiers hadn't slept at all during the night. As the sun began to peak above the eastern horizon, they approached Manhattan, a city of incomprehensible dimensions. Buildings were piled, it seemed, one atop the other and divided neatly by a gridwork of streets, each bustling with more people than Ransford had ever seen in one place, walking, riding bicycles, horses, carriages, and wagons. Ringing the densely-packed island were piers, hundreds of them, each jutting out into the waters of the Hudson like the spokes of a wagon wheel, accepting ships, boats, and ferries of all size and purpose.

With some dexterity, the captain of the steamship maneuvered the line of barges along a massive pier and the men disembarked for the first time since Poughkeepsie. Achey and sleep-deprived, they were ordered to form up by company and make ready for a hastily prepared parade down Broadway. Word of the arrival of Ellsworth's Avengers had spread throughout the city whose citizens had adopted the young colonel as one of their own. Just five months earlier, Colonel Ellsworth had marched his gaudily dressed 11th New York Infantry Regiment, the Fighting Zouaves, down Broadway, on a sacred mission to quell the rebellion. Recruited almost entirely from the roughneck firefighters that protected the city day and night from the scourge of fire, the Fighting Zoauves and their dashing colonel were adored like no other fighting unit arising out of the enormous city of nearly a million souls. And, just as passionately, the city mourned the death of Ellsworth, just a month later, when his body was displayed at one of the city's great meeting halls to lie in state before throngs of grieving citizens. The arrival, therefore, of Ellsworth's Avengers in the autumn of 1861 was proclaimed by the press—the *New York Tribune*, the *New York Times*, the *Herald* and others—as the city's own "terrible swift sword," a vehicle for retribution and vindication for the awful, almost personal, hurt its people had suffered.

Colonel Stryker, astride his fine bay stallion, shiny saber unsheathed, led the procession with an assemblage of pipers, drummers, and flag-bearers. They marched four abreast at a deliberate pace down one of the mid-city side streets and then turned south onto Broadway in the heart of the city. Quite suddenly the regiment found itself immersed in a roaring sea of admirers, who lined the streets and hung out of windows at every level. Hundreds of New York City police officers, clad in indigo uniforms with brass buttons and bowler hats, took positions along the streets and intersections as the regiment passed, in places locking hands to hold back the impassioned crowd. Ransford couldn't resist glancing out the corners of his eyes at the surprising make-up of the crowd, how different people—whites, Latins, blacks, and Asians—from different stations, seemed to be altogether mixed and unreserved. Unlike other places, such as Saratoga and Albany, where poor and rough and tumble types would never rub elbows with nattily-dressed gentlefolk, here they all seemed to share the same sidewalk quite comfortably. Throughout the ranks, the men's spirits rose, a far cry from their lowly experience on the barge the night before. They were buoyed by the adulation and excitement and their pride showed smartly in the manner of their march. Ransford felt it keenly; he was proud to be a member of the 44th. Curious, he thought, this must be how Caesar and his legions felt as they marched through Rome.

The unit advanced down Broadway, past grand hotels, banks, trading houses, newspaper offices, and government buildings, until they had returned once again to the edge of the river. There, at the southern tip of Manhattan, they were marched onto a waiting steamer. This one, the *Baltic*, was much larger than the boat that had towed them to New York and could carry the entire regiment on her ample decks. The men, heads still spinning from their exciting romp through Manahattan, were only able to relax aboard the *Baltic* a short while, however, as it was commissioned to shuttle them across New York Harbor to Jersey City. There they would board a train for Philadelphia.

That afternoon, the regiment packed itself into the longest train that Ransford had ever seen. It was one of many lined up in a massive and sprawling train yard, awaiting troops that had converged there from throughout the Northeast, all bound for Washington, DC. Some men sat while others stood in the aisles as the locomotive engine idled. Ransford and his squad had just settled into their seats at the front of the train when Sergeant Tinkham entered the car looking for "volunteers."

"I'll be needing four men for a detail. Who will it be, then?" he asked without expecting an answer as he looked over the men before him. "Densmore. Hickok. Whitney. And you. What's your name again, Private?"

"Jones, sir."

"Alright then, men. Follow this fellow, Mr. Meisner; he's the engineer, to the front of the train and do what he tells you, just like it's coming from me. You mind me, boys?"

"Sir, yes sir!"

Special details were the bane of a lowly private's life. They came in all shapes and types, but were generally unpleasant jobs, like digging latrines or hauling a wagon out of mud or catching a snake that had invaded the mess tent. Rarely were privates asked to escort the general's daughter into town. For some ungodly reason Ransford and his friends seemed to be called upon to man details with some regularity; perhaps, they thought, because they performed these unpleasant tasks so well or perhaps because Sergeant Tinkham just didn't like them very much. No one could be certain which it was. So it was with some trepidation that the men followed Mr. Meisner, a soot-faced, wiry fellow in a tattered gray smock and striped hat.

They went along the side of the train and climbed a steep metal ladder into the sleeping locomotive's engine house. Mr. Meisner herded them into a surprisingly small space that served as his command post.

"You und you!" he spoke in a strong German accent, tapping each man, all much larger than himself, as if to get their attention, and proceeded to explain the procedure he wanted them to follow. "Take deeze shovels und get de coal from de coal car. Den you bring it dere and shovel it into der fire hole dare. Den you und you (tapping Ransford and Solomon similarly). You two do da same."

He explained, as best they could make out, that he did not have the full crew he would normally have for such a heavy run and that he would need them to be stoking the flames of the engine with plenty of coal to get up a good head of steam.

"You work hard, boys. You work hard an I give you strudel!" he laughed hysterically, and began spasmodically coughing, out of control. Shuffling about the car like Quasimodo, he took a curved metal rod and used it to open a thick iron door to the firebox, where faintly glowing embers could be discerned deep inside. "In dare, in dare you throw it boys."

As Mr. Meisner took to the tall stick handles that controlled the train's speed and brakes signals, he beckoned the men to start hauling coal. He reached up, pulling the handle on a dangling chord, causing a drawn-out, high-pitched scream to explode out of the locomotive, warning all within a mile or more that the train was about to leave the yard.

"Now boys! Now!"

The men complied, each digging his shovel into the small mountain of coal piled in the trailing coal car, carrying it 15 or so feet, and shoveling it into the mouth of the firebox. Like a water brigade, they timed their trips and kept their human chain moving in sync. The work was hard and, after several trips, particularly draining to their shoulders and lower backs. Mr. Meisner, sensing a loss of speed, began a series of verbal harangues designed to motivate them, if not drive them mad.

"What is dis? What is dis? Is you strong men or weak little daisies? Come on now, boys! I need steam to get you soldiers to da war! Steam!"

Their backs and shoulders screaming in agony, Ransford and the other men hardened their resolve to pick up their pace and bring the coal faster and faster to suit their diminutive German master. As Ransford tossed load after load of hard black fuel into the firebox, the fire began to come alive, soon roaring and straining to get outside its container. Almost delerious, Ransford faced the flame that, in a matter of minutes, had grown from a few benign embers to a raging inferno, leaping and licking manically at the opening, while emitting a searing heat like nothing he had ever experienced. Both fascinating and frightening, Ransford found himself staring far too long into mouth of the bedevilling firebox when he was unceremoniously brought back to attention by a whack on the shoulders from Mr. Meisner.

"Wake up, boy! Wake up and get da hell out of da way!"

Ransford pulled himself away from the glaring face of the inferno just as the locomotive began to move, chugging and spitting steam as it lurched toward Philadelphia. The men had only worked twenty minutes but they were likely the hardest minutes they would ever experience. Mr. Meisner informed them that their services were no longer needed and had a brakeman (who had been sitting atop the mound of coal, watching them work the entire time) take them back to their car along a dangerous catwalk that led around the coal car. Before they left, the little German man handed each a package wrapped in newspaper.

"Strudel! Like I promised, here it is!"

Sweating and coated with coal dust, they climbed into their designated places in the car with the rest of E Company. Private Hickok was the first to open the package. Driven by hunger that overcame caution, he bit into the odd-looking pastry and pronounced it good, very good. The rest of the detail followed suit, sharing bites of the German delicacy with their mates. For the rest of his life, Ransford would remember the supremely delightful taste of Mr. Meisner's strudel.

The men settled into their seats or places on the floor for the oft-interrupted ride to Baltimore, as the train halted every 30 miles or so to take on water or stop at crossings to allow other trains to pass. At Philadelphia, they disembarked briefly to be served a meager meal of bread and coffee before packing back onto the overburdened cars for the run to Baltimore, where they left the train behind—Mr. Meisner waving and cackling almost incomprehensibly from his perch in the fire house: "Fight good, boys! Fight good!"

Upon setting off, the 44th's commanders alerted the troops that the city was not to be considered a welcoming place, reminding them that Baltimore was a hotbed of anti-Union and secessionist sentiment. While the city was under martial law and patrolled by federal troops, they were nonetheless told to keep their weapons at the ready, and ordered to fire only if fired upon.

As they marched through the historic American city past Fort McHenry—the noble defense of which had inspired Francis Scott Key to pen the Star Spangled Banner—the tension in the ranks was unnerving. For the most part, the city's streets were curiously quiet for an autumn afternoon; small groups gathered on corners to watch the regiment as it passed, the fifers and drummers that had greated them in New York noticeably missing. The citizens of Baltimore were subdued and strange. Even those who favored the Union's cause did not express themselves loudly—in stark contrast to the raucous, adoring crowds of New York—only waving small versions of Old Glory, blowing a silent kiss or simply smiling. It was a place divided, an unhappy place wrestling with itself.

Ransford and the rest of the soldiers were greatly relieved when they had cleared the city's southern boundary and boarded the last train to Washington, a ride that ended deep into the night. They marched through the darkened capital, a city swarming with military encampments and sentries at practically every street corner. Looking past the bustle of soldiers and fortifications, Ransford noted how unimpressive the city—the nation's capital—seemed. Unlike the other cities he had marched through, this one was built broad and low to the ground, with very few tall impressive buildings, except for the Capitol Building, a glorious structure, as yet incomplete, that the men passed in their march through the city.

Bedraggled and hungry from their lengthy journey, the regiment was led to an enormous warehouse on the outskirts of the city where they piled their muskets and spent the rest of the night sleeping on the floor.

The 44th spent the next three days camped temporarily a couple miles south of Washington before pitching their tents and forming up for inspection by none other than General George McClellan, supreme commander of the Army of the Potomac. The sergeants were especially brutal, Ransford recalled, in getting the men prepared for the review at dawn, waking them a half hour before sunrise, barking orders with special ferocity, and warning them all to look especially sharp and orderly for their "special guest." The men complied and looked downright impressive when they stood at attention at the foot of a small ridge called Kaloram Heights.

Ransford got a good look at Little Mac, as some called him, when the diminutive general strode by E Company atop a jet black horse and accompanied by Colonel Stryker. Neatly groomed and impeccably attired in a double-breasted overcoat with a bright red sash around his waist, General McLellan viewed the ranks in with much more sincerity, it seemed, than other generals or officers, who usually attended reviews with a kind of perfunctory detachment. No, McLellan looked long and hard at the men in front of him, asking Col. Stryker about the unit's origin and history.

"So these are the boys chosen to avenge Ellsworth?" he asked the Colonel.

"Yes sir, General. They've got the makings of a fine regiment, I think, sir."

"I'm certain they do, Colonel. A fine line of men you have here, but I'm sure you understand this army is raw and as we learned to our distaste back in May in Manassas, raw troops can be worse than no troops at all. They cut and ran, sir! And by God, no troops of mine shall cut and run. We shall prepare them, Colonel, and we shall prepare them well. We owe these brave men that much!"

"Yes, indeed, General McLellan . . . .. What are your orders, sir?"

"I would have you and this fine regiment winter—and drill mind you!—across the Potomac with our forward elements in Camp Butterfield. Get them ready, Colonel. We shall fight in earnest next spring when the Army of the Potomac will be the greatest fighting force on earth! That is when we shall invade and bring these rebels to their knees!"

"Yes, of course, sir! Thank you, sir!" One could tell that Colonel Stryker, a man of some words himself, was duly impressed and rendered somewhat speechless at the General's impassioned oratory.

To a man, Ransford and the others who had heard the exchange agreed that Little Mac was a soldier's general and that they would be in good hands with him leading their army.

VII: A Wonderful Reception

Knapsacks packed and rifles at their sides, the men of the regiment began their long trek south for the inhospitable lands of northern Virginia about midday. After boarding ferry boats that took them across the Potomac River, the march began in earnest as the regimental commanders aimed to reach their destination—Camp Butterfield—by day's end. After a hard eighteen-mile march with few stops along the way, the 44th trudged into Camp Butterfield at Hall's Hill, Virginia, at 8 p.m., tired, dusty, and famished. The sight that greeted them when they dragged themselves into the encampment was, under the circumstances, about as warm, welcoming, and unexpected as any soldier could imagine.

The 83rd Pennsylvania Infantry Regiment, part of Butterfield's Brigade, had, in anticipation of their arrival, prepared a grand feast—or at least the military equivalent of it—for the men of 44th Regiment. A lengthy line of makeshift tables comprised of planks on sawhorses had been erected at the center corridor of the camp, lit by a line of bonfires, that revealed mounds of good fresh food, the likes of which the men hadn't seen in weeks: jugs of cider; pots of fresh, steaming coffee; piles of bacon; cauldrons of bubbling stew with beef, potatoes and carrots; platters heaped with cornbread and biscuits; and a surprising variety of freshly killed game—duck, venison, geese, and squirrel—roasted and appealing.

The sight and smell of it brought some of the boys near tears. They had been traveling nonstop since Albany for more than a week in trains, boats, barges, and on foot, never staying one place longer than a night or two. They had slept on floors and open ground and had been fed the barest, skimpiest, and least appealing meals—bread and coffee in New York and salted horse in Washington—the entire way. And though they had weathered these privations without complaint, the trip had worn their collective spirit down considerably. This, Ransford would recall, was dreamlike, an oasis after crawling across the desert.

"Can this be real, Ransford?" asked Elijah Earle, one of the other Corinth boys in the regiment.

"If it isn't, don't wake me up," replied Ransford, speaking out despite still being in formation. The commanding officers didn't seem to mind; they were just as dumbfounded at the incredible act of generosity afforded them by their colleagues from Pennsylvania.

"Let's hear it for the 83rd men!" one of the lieutenants called out to the regiment. "Now, by God, let's break ranks and eat!"

A chorus, approaching a roar, of "Hoorays," "Huzzahs," and "Here-Heres!" went up from the haggard and hungry men of the 44th, before they stacked their rifles and dropped their packs, practically where they stood.

Meanwhile, the men of the 83rd stood at loose attention lining the banquet tables, each a few paces away with beaming smiles fixed to the their faces like proud maitre d's at a fancy French restaurant.

"Well boys, don't wait to be asked twice. Dig in!" one affable Pennsylvania private yelled in the direction of Ransford's squad.

The next hour was spent consuming the feast; the men spread throughout the camp, some eating where they stood, others finding seats around various campsites the 83rd had established during their weeks already spent at Hall's Hill. Consumption eventually gave way to conversation as the men of the 44th, sated and rejuvenated, engaged with their new colleagues.

"I can't thank you boys enough. I don't know if you knew it, but we were about ready to start eating each other if you get my meaning!" Solomon Hickok broke the ice at a campfire where some of the men from Company E had collected.

"You are welcome, son," replied one of the Pennsylvania privates. "It was our commanding officer's—Colonel Strong

112

Vincent—idea and a darn good one, we thought. We been here quite some time now and, to be honest, there ain't much for us to do except drill and hunt. This campsite turns out to be a fine place to forage. Lots of game and trees around here."

"You boys have our gratitude," said Ransford. "We haven't had a decent meal in what seems like forever and this was one for the ages!"

"So you say you splendid fellows haven't been doing anything but drilling and foraging for the last few weeks?" asked Jack Finnegan. "There's still the little matter of a war going on down here, isn't there? I mean, I couldn't imagine 1,000 well-armed men traveling so far just to hunt wild beasts, fell great trees, and dine together on sumptuous meals . . .as nice as that sounds."

"Heh, heh! This one does have a pretty way of expressing himself, doesn't he? No you all came to the right place. Johnny Reb isn't more than five miles that way," said the Pennsylvania private, gesturing south. "But nobody's done much of anything for quite some time now. A pop goin' off here or there and rumors of cavalry sightings, but nothing that ever amounts to much."

"Yep, we call this here Camp Wait 'n' See!" chimed in another private. "Might as well make the most of it, I guess."

Indeed they did appear to be making the most of their stay in northern Virginia. The encampment had evolved into a tidy makeshift village, with company streets clearly marked and rows of small log cabins where ten to twenty soldiers could be comfortably housed. There were larger canvas tent structures with wooden floors that served as messes, kitchens, churches, and provision storehouses, along with enclosures that bustled with livestock. The camp spread across the foot of Hall's Hill, itself covered with a pleasant grove of hardwoods that provided plenty of game, firewood, and logs for building. It would have been the pleasantest of places for a homestead, some remarked, if it weren't for that damn war over yonder.

With the 44th's arrival, Camp Butterfield had reached its full complement of four regiments, including the 44th, 83rd Pennsylvania, the Michigan 16th Infantry Regiment, and the 20th Maine Infantry Regiment. With more than 4,000 soldiers, they would serve as the Third Brigade, attached to the First Division of V Corps, Army of the Potomac. None of them could know that their brigade would fight side-by-side throughout the entirety of the war and in some of its bloodiest, most decisive battles of the Civil War, and manywould end up wounded, captured or killed along the way.

But not tonight. Tonight the boys were as yet unbloodied by battle and unsullied by their actions in combat, the taking of human life, or the gruesome sights and sounds that awaited them. As happy and as innocent as 2,200 men could ever be in each other's company, they danced jigs around the campfires to rousing fiddle tunes, shared jugs of moonshine (as was occasionally allowed by their commanders), and swapped stories. The steam from their breath mingled in the cold autumn air and there, under the stars, they formed bonds that would never be broken.

When the officers gathered up the men to turn in for the night, yet another surprise greeted them.

"Where we camping tonight, Sergeant?" an exhausted member of E Company asked Sergeant Tinkham.

"Don't trouble yourself, lad. You see that tidy row of tents off to the north? They've been erected for us, courtesy of the 83rd!"

Yet another gift from their new brothers in arms, the men stumbled into the high-tipped white tents, laid out their bed rolls and slept deeply, resolutely. It had been quite a welcome; one no member of the 44th would ever forget. Ransford drifted off to the assortment of odd sounds that collections of sleeping men make, a strange chorus of grunts, teeth grinding, jabbering, and gaseous expulsions, knitted together into a strange symphony that had once kept him awake but now served as a strangely comforting lullabye.

The next morning arrived too quickly, reveille jarring the men from a deep sleep at the break of dawn. The last days of October brought with it the first hints of winter, especially in the morning, as the recruits pulled on their clothes in the dark. The coffee brewed in great pots over a hundred camp fires demanded their attention first and foremost, beckoning to them to force open the tent flaps and answer what had already become a profound addiction.

"Gimme some of that tar, boy!" Private Hickok called to a dark silhouette huddled over the pot hanging over the campfire outside the company's collection of tents.

"Me too. Load me up!"

The men gathered around the fires every thirty feet or so along the many "company roads" that crisscossed and defined Camp Butterfield. They huddled in small circles, clutching their steaming cups closely with both hands and loving the warmth and smell and power it had to awaken and stimulate them once again.

After several minutes of obligatory silence, whether out of reverence for the coffee or a need to collect thoughts, conversations, at first perfunctory and simple, would begin to spark.

"That was some feast those Pennsylvania boys threw us last night, eh boys?"

"About as neighborly a thing as I've ever encountered!"

"Don't think I've ever eaten as much in one sitting!"

"Yes, indeed."

After a moment of silence and appreciation, Private Whitney changed the subject. "I was talking to a private in the 83rd and he said they've been on alert for the last week or so after that unpleasant business at Balls Bluff, which isn't too far from here."

"What happened at Balls Bluff?" asked Ransford.

"Nasty business, Ransford. It was in the paper, back in Washington," explained Jack. "Apparently, Colonel Edward Baker, a close friend of our esteemed President, by the way, took a sizeable force across the Potomac and got himself ambushed and soundly whipped, as they say in your neck of the woods."

"I heard they lost some 1,000 men, killed and wounded," said another private.

"Land sakes! That's our whole regiment!" Ransford was impressed at the scale of the defeat. It was inconceivable that such a large force of men could fall in one day, one battle. It had come too close on the heels of Bull Run and that, combined with a painful dearth of victories on the Union side, contributed to a sense of foreboding among the troops encamped at Hall's Hill. So early in this young war, the new recruits were no longer buoyed by grand promises and arrogant proclaimations of a short war. They were both green and doubtful.

"I heard a couple of the Pennsylvania sergeants talkin' about it during the feast last night," said Elijah Earls, one of the Corinth boys. "An' they were sayin' that Colonel messed it up somethin' fierce. That he shouldn't have split up his forces and didn't do near enough re-con—whatever in hell that is—and that the problem so far ain't been the men; it's been the dang generals. Now that Little Mac is in charge, they said, things is gonna be different."

"From your mouth to God's ear, my good private," Jack chimed in. "As I understand it, Little Mac, as you call him, is being most deliberate in his resolve to encircle Washington with an impenetrable ring of fortifications while simultaneously transforming this huge rabble of untrained men—that would be us, by the way—into an indomitable fighting force: the Grand

Army of the Potomac! He refuses to move on the enemy until he is convinced we are good and ready to soundly whip these shameless rebels."

Jack's oration was followed by silence, as often happened when Jack spoke at any length.

"I'm not all the way certain, Ransford, but isn't that sorta what I just said?" Private Earls asked mockingly. A round of knowing chuckles resounded among members of the squad, who had come to appreciate each others foibles as much as their strengths.

"Yes, Elijah, I think you got us to the neighborhood, but Jack took us inside the house and showed us around the living room and the parlor and the kitchen!" responded Ransford.

"Har-dee-har-har!" Jack spurted with feigned indignation. "I should have one or two of you rubes at my side at all times so as to translate to the barbarian hordes we will no doubt encounter down here in Dixie." He waved his arms around with a Shakespearian flourish, which brought on more laughter. "All I can tell you, my fine brethren, is when I look into my crystal ball I see a vast sea of men, many thousands of men in blue, doing nothing but drilling, drilling, and more drilling!"

Jack's vision that chilly autumn morning proved prophetic. That day and practically every other for the next several months the regiments at Camp Butterfield drilled, and drilled and drilled, following a neat prescription that proved out daily:

6:30 A.M.	Reveille
7:00	Breakfast
7:30-9:00	Squad drill and company drill
10:-11:30	Batallalion drill
12 P.M.	Dinner

2:00-5:00	Brigade drill
5:00	Retreat and dress parade
6:00	Supper

VIII: The Battle for Camp Butterfield

The undifferentiated days crawled on as autumn gave way to winter. Unlike the relentless snows of the Adirondacks, which built one upon the other until impeneratable piles formed several feet deep, the season in northern Virginia was markedly milder, the winter less committal. It came and went as it pleased, at times leaving the camp blanketed in snow followed by a warm snap that quickly melted it all away. As the men went about their business, with thousands tramping to and from the great fields adjacent to the camp that served as their parade grounds, what followed was mud. The camp was, in places, awash in mud so profuse that is had the consistency of a sticky pudding; one that afixed itself to everything below the knee and made moving to-and-fro a challenge. Makeshift walkways made of wooden planks laid end-to-end provided the only passage on these days and soldiers would walk upon them in plodding, unhappy, soundless lines like cows to a barn.

At drills the sergeants, lieutenants, and captains, watching from horseback, barked incessantly at the men, chastising them for any breach of step or any sign of confusion. The mind-numbing array of formations, steps, and marches that occupied their time in autumn soon gave way to firing lines and battle formations, where the men drilled in loading and firing their Enfield rifles, their commanders fixated on meeting lofty performance standards while glaring at stop watches.

"You boys will load, aim, and fire your weapons three times a minute or I swear to the blessed Lord above you will be out here all night long every night until you do!" bellowed Sergeant Tinkham on the field one day in December.

The companies practiced firing in different order, sometimes all firing simultaneously so as to deliver a maximum blow in one awesome fusillade, and sometimes alternating fire by rank or position in the line, so that they could maintain a constant volley. Ransford and his cohorts had to learn to prime, load, aim, and fire their bulky weapons under duress through the thunderous cacophony of a battlefield shrouded in billowing blue smoke. Generally they practiced firing while standing in line, but their commanders also gave them turns at loading and firing while prostrate.

"There ain't no easier target to hit than a man in blue standing straight up tall as a flag pole!" Sergeant Tinkham declared one brisk sun-splashed day at Camp Butterfield. "Today you boys are gonna drill and load from yer backs. Follow all the firing steps, just do it on your backs. When it's time to fire, roll over— make sure there ain't no friendly in front of you--and then fire."

"Hell, Ransford, I don't mind shootin' from my belly, but I don't particularly like comin' back to camp lookin' like I just a-wallowed in mud like a happy hog." Solomon Hickok confided after such a drill.

"I don't disagree Solomon," said Ransford. "But I do like the idea of not standing up there like a six-foot target for them rebs to take aim at."

The musket and cannon fire went on relentlessly, Camp Butterfield's regiments joining scores of other camps stretched out around Washington in a daily barrage that shook the countryside in all directions, like a great line of thunderstorms revisiting the region daily. Only the North could afford to waste so much ammunition on trees and targets, some thought, while others recognized General McLellan's all too deliberate intent to build an army that would never lose the field again.

The papers out of Washington kept up a steady drumbeat of criticism of the generals and their lack of progress against a brash enemy scarcely a day's march away. The Army of the Potomac's reluctance to engage the rebel army soon began to vex the nervous politicians and elected officials safely seated behind McLellan's impeneratable ring of forts and encampments encircling Washington. In response to the travesties at Balls Bluff and Manassas, they formed the Congressional Joint Committee on the Conduct of the War and used it to call into question virtually every military decision that didn't have a happy outcome. At that period of the war, the Committee had much to question.

"Damnable politicians wouldn't know their ass from their elbows!" proclaimed a private who sat on a log near the campfire one late January night while holding a copy of a newspaper, slapping it against his leg disdainfully. A protracted discussion followed—similar to many those days—concerning the merits of biding time and training versus taking action against the rebs who had taken up residence, comfortably it seemed, just a few miles to the south.

"Well I hears ya, Private," responded another. "But I'm just about all trained out. Hell, I'd like to be shootin' some rebs right about now. I figure I've done killed all the trees a fellow should in this life! It's time to put my lead to some good use."

"Here, here!" resounded from a gaggle of privates and corporals that had assembled around the lively debate.

A snowstorm, sizeable by Virginia standards, had blown through camp the night before, leaving a foot or more of wet heavy snow in its wake, forcing the men to stomp out places to stand and sit around the fire.

"That same newspaper you're presently holding, my good man, also tells of some notable exploits of our troops down south and out in the western territories," Jack joined in, expressing his own growing skepticism about the wisdom of waiting. Union forces were winning battles in far off places, like New Orleans and Missouri, but one of the grandest armies ever assembled—the Army of the Potomac—sat on its haunches, waiting.

A smallish but decisive victory at Dranesville, Virginia, on December 20th, where Union General Edward Ord drove rebel General Jeb Stuart from the field at a key crossroad several miles from Camp Butterfied, had given the troops a measure of optimism and anticipation. The army would be on the move now, they theorized, readying themselves for battle. But the orders never came. The unyielding cold of January followed, accompanied by the pitiless tedium of training and camp life that kept men edgy and itching for a fight.

"For some mysterious reason, *these* Union soldiers, our bretheren in arms, have been able to gather enough gumption with just enough leadership to defeat Confederate forces elsewhere," Jack continued, relishing in his growing audience. "Why, pray tell, can't we, the brave and impeccably-trained forces of Camp Butterfield, achieve similar results? Let me answer my own question gentlemen: Because nobody's asked us to!"

"Now just settle down, Jack," Ransford responded. "Who are we, lowly privates from upstate New York, to speak for the Army of the Potomac? But there is a fellow of some stature—a very tall fellow I'm told--who tends to agree with you."

"And who would that be, Ransford old boy?"

"I believe his name is Lincoln, President Abraham Lincoln. Why just the other day he sent a telegram to Little Mac—and I read this in the paper too—asking him if he wasn't going to use his army would he mind if the President borrowed it for a little while!"

That brought on a chorus of guffaws and laughter from those who sided with the notion that the Army had trained enough and should set about its business. This was by no means a unanimous sentiment in the camp, especially among different companies and regiments who tended to adopt consistent positions on such matters. In fact, there were those who felt statements critical of the army's leadership were sacrilegious, an outright insult to General McLellan, about whom many felt a certain reverence.

As the laughter died down a squad of privates from the 83rd Pennsylvania happened by the group, passing on their way from a detail in the woods to their regiment's portion of the camp, several acres that were separated by a hundred yards from the 44th 's neighborhood by a slight gully, formed by a little stream that drained the hill. As they passed they were drawn in by Jack's diatribe around the campfire and, as it turned out, these boys held the strongest of opinions regarding what they felt were meddling, know-nothing politicians. To them, an attack upon their commander was tantamount to treason.

"Now that's downright humorous, isn't it boys?" said one Pennsylvania private, who, along with the rest of his squad, had elbowed their way into the circle around the fire. "That's so funny I don't know if I'm listening to a loyal soldier of the Union army or a rebel spy tryin' to make us fight amongst ourselves." Several of his compatriots leaned into the light illuminating the men around the fire, creating a semi-circle backing the private and a demonstrable show of support for him and his derisive statement.

"Since when is it that men can't speak their minds without being called traitors? Aren't you supposed to be Pennsylvania boys?" Private Whitney asked incredulously. "Have any of you ever heard of a thing called the Liberty Bell or maybe the Declaration of Independence? Maybe you skipped that class in school but the Liberty Bell is in Philadelphia—Philadelphia, Pennsylvania, that is—and that's where they signed the Declaration of Independence."

"I don't know what yer talkin about, son," responded another member of the squad. "All I know is, we're at war and it ain't right to tear down our leader like you just done."

"Well, I don't know how democracy is done in your part of Pennsylvania, but where we're from in New York, we say it's okay to say what's on your mind without worrying about some knucklehead attacking you for it," Whitney went on, obviously moved.

"Oh, well, it's one thing to speak poorly of General Mac, it's a whole other thing to call us knuckleheads!"

The men on both sides of the argument, which despite mixed feelings among both regiments, appeared poised and ready for a good old fashioned brawl between the men of the 44th and those of the 83rd, a brawl that normally would have devolved into a messy mix of fisticuffs and wrestling. But at that critical moment someone from the 44th—an anonymous soldier who has never confessed to his transgression—tossed a well-aimed snowball square into the face of one of the Pennsylvania boys, sparking a chain reaction among the men, who eschewed traditional methods of dispute resolution in favor of what would soon become an epic snowball fight.

The Pennsylvania squad, badly outnumbered, fled under an unrelenting fire as the men of the 44th, barely 20 or 30 of them at first, chased them down the gully, across the stream, and into the safe confines of their part of the camp. Within seconds, men of the 83rd rallied to the call of their stricken comrades and, disorganized but with superior numbers, met the advanced corps of the 44th at their border, driving them back with an impressive volley of snowballs that forced a measured retreat.

It did not take long before calls, shouts, and even buglers brought the majority of both regiments to the the contiguous boundary of their camps, facing each other across the snow-covered divide and the little stream that ran through the center. Soon, the scene adopted a degree of primitive hilarity as men from each side tossed hundreds of snowballs at great distances, arching high into the night sky, mostly missing, as the men laughed and sang like drunken fools at a wedding party. Soon sergeants and officers arrived at the scene and began to exert influence upon their respective mobs. Firebrands and torches were staked into the ground behind and flanking the forces so troop movements could be seen and assessed.

For his part, Sergeant Tinkham, at the urging of Lieutenant Knox, gathered as many of the men of Company E at the center of the evolving battle directly across from the 83rd 's main firing line. "I want two lines of men with alternating fire. You know the drill, men. Fire by rank and concentrate your fire on their center. We will advance to the edge of that stream and hold our ground!"

Instinctively, the men complied, packing snowballs as if they were loading Enfield rifles. As one squad packed the other would unload an impressive barrage upon the "enemy's" center, advance ten steps and then halt while the other unit fired. Soon they were at the stream's side and making good progress when, without warning, the 83rd unleashed a sudden and shocking charge, as two entire companies swept down the hill and peppered E Company's neat and orderly line with direct and vicious fire. Hard and icy projectiles struck the boys at nearly point blank range, in some cases breaking noses and shattering spectacles. Badly beaten, Company E fell back, while reserve units of the 44th came down the hill and, with a good deal of concerted fire, kept the 83rd from crossing the stream.

Sergeant Tinkham and Lieutenant Knox gathered the bruised and, in some cases, bloodied members of E Company behind the lines as other companies of the 44th advanced towards the 83rd's right and left flanks under orders delivered from a collection of captains observing the activities from above. The "battle" had evolved into a spontaneous training exercise, an opportunity for commanding officers to test their men under battlefield conditions without much risk of losses. Most of them appeared to take the opportunity seriously.

"Sergeant Tinkham!" Lt. Knox barked, getting Company E's attention.

"Yes, Lieutenant!"

"Do you see that little hill off our right flank?"

"I do, sir!" snapped the sergeant.

"The captain has ordered artillery be placed on that

commanding hill immediately."

"Artillery, sir?"

"Yes, Lieutenant, artillery," Lieutenant Knox explained. "In this case, I'd like you and a squad of your men to accompany Private Finnegan to the top of that little hill and I require that your speed balling pitcher, with the squad's full complement and support, deliver an unrelenting fire down upon the enemy's center."

Jack Finnegan and the rest of E Company immediately understood the Lieutenant's meaning, broad grins appearing on their faces.

"You heard the Lieutenant. Private Finnegan and his squad will follow me, double quick to the top of that hill where we will establish an artillery position."

"Sir, yes sir!"

The squad ran as a unit through the lines and clambered up the little hill, backed by the tree line, that looked down upon the two battling regiments. The squad quickly established itself with Jack at the center and Sergeant Tinkham, Ransford, Hickok, Solomon, Whitney, Jones, and the others packing snowballs and making "ammunition" stacks in preparation for the attack.

"I want you to pack 'em hard boys. We want those Pennsylvania boys to know it when we hit 'em!" yelled the Sergeant. "Now, Private Finnegan, you see that big fellow in the center of their line, about 20 yards up from the stream? I want you to take him out first and then fire at will into their center. You boys keep feeding ammo to Finnegan here, one from the right, then one from the left, and so on, so he can fire without stopping. You got me, men?"

"Sir, yes sir!"

Earnest but smiling, Jack took the first snowball—an icy orb about the size of a baseball—and powered into a throw that whistled through the night in a tight arc that found its mark, square against the temple of the enormous Pennsylvania corporal who stood like Ajax at the center of the 83rd's line. The blow knocked him clean off his feet and surprised several men around him. Fed a steady stream of hard-packed snowballs by his comrades, Jack continued to fire at their center, eventually driving a large hole in their ranks as they scattered from the concerted barrage raining down upon them. A prodigious roar went up from the men of the 44th as they witnessed the effects of the artillery barrage upon the opposing regiment.

Companies A and B were ordered ahead towards the stream and the breech in their opponent's line. A detachment of men from the 83rd, sent to extinguish the artillery unit, crossed the upper stream and began an assault upon the the little hill. Jack continued firing into the melee at the center of the Pennsylvanians' line, but his cohorts, under direction of Sergeant Tinkham, began peppering those attempting to win the hill with snowballs. Unable to maintain their footing and under contstant fire, the attackers fell back, eliciting yet another round of huzzahs from the regiment.

Just then, Companies A and B forded the little stream, still in formation, and began pushing their way into the hole in the 83rd's line. More men from the 44th started to mass behind them and, in the instant when it appeared Ellsworth's Avengers were on the brink of taking the field, an officer—a colonel—rode a dashing black stallion into the center of the fray between the two lines. It was Colonel Strong Vincent, the 83rd's commander, and he was waving his cap around and hollering as he came.

"Hold on, boys! Hold on now!" he said, laughing heartily from atop his rearing horse. "A fine and noble display, men. Great courage and resolve under fire from both regiments. Pennsylvania and New York should be proud! Now let us save our hostilities for the real enemy and retire for the evening."

Exhausted, in some cases bloodied, but relieved, the men stood down and, under the encouragement of their officers, slowly made their way through the trampled field of snow back to their quarters.

As they trudged back to their tents, the men laughed and shared stories of what would later be called the Battle of Camp Butterfield, an episode that would further bound the two regiments throughout the many real battles they would later face together. Like brothers close in age and vying for attention, the 83rd and 44th would, from that point forward, dream up many creative ways to test each other. On any given Sunday, the men would concoct inter-regimental challenges that broke the boredom of camp life. There were bare knuckle boxing matches, wrestling bouts, foot races, horce races, louse races, and fiddling contests; each resulting in someone being proclaimed the official Champion of Camp Butterfield. While the men of Michigan and Maine occasionally participated in these epic contests, they rarely matched the brotherly zeal aroused in the 83rd and the 44th. But nothing would ever surplant the spectacle that was The Battle of Camp Butterfield and so it occupied a special place in camp lore from that night forward.

Ransford and the others from his squad returned to their tents and settled in for the night, each man removing his boots and coat near the door, tip-toe-ing quickly across the frigid plank floor to gain the sactuary of his cot and his welcome wool blanket. As lumpy and hard as an army cot could be, on such nights it felt like a Victorian featherbed, receiving their aching bodies with a warm embrace so foreign to their recent experience that it had the effect of laudanum. Many would drop off into slumber soon after their heads hit the pillow, while others, like Ransford that night, would linger by candlelight, reading a book or a letter.

Earlier in the day, Ransford had pocketed a letter from home that he had received during mail call, a weekly ritual that held for soldiers the solemnity of communion for Catholics. To be called forward to receive correspondence brought an anxious joy to a soldier's face at the anticipation of hearing news from home or a sweetheart. The fact that the news contained in the letter often ended up being bad—informing the long departed lad of a recent death, financial difficulty, or an undesired break up—didn't diminish the willingness with which it was received. Letters were, in many ways, a form of magic, welcomed, beloved, and feared all at once.

In the dim flickerings of the candle Ransford opened the letter, penned in an opulent hand but smudged in places where melting snow had intruded upon the paper:

My Dear and Noble Friend, Ransford,

I pray, dear Ransford, that this correspondence finds you well. It has been too long since my pen last scribbled words to you and, as such, I was beginning to feel derelict in my duties as a friend and supporter of our troops and their righteous mission. As I have said previously, I shall write to you as if I were writing to all the soldiers in the Union Army, who truly represent God's will on this earth. I shall also write to you because I feel, if you do not mind my sounding too bold, a kinship to you that, strangely enough, arose in me when you volunteered for service that day in Corinth. It seems so long ago, Ransford, but still I cannot forget your spontaneity and bravery when you stepped forward before all the other men and signed your name to avenge brave Ellsworth. I think you became a symbol for others in our little town, and now many of the boys are considering enlistment. I see your father and brother, every Sunday in church and I make it a point to ask about you. I can tell from their faces that they miss you, Ransford, and that they are proud you represent them and all of us in this great struggle. I will leave you with an impetuous thought—a secret hope, if you will—that soon you will return home to Corinth victorious and healthy, having vanquished an evil foe and set the world to right, and that when you return, you and I will have a sumptuous picnic in a grassy place I know by banks of the Kayderossas Creek where you will tell me tales of your grand adventure. Please consider this heartfelt expression of my affection and appreciation of you, Ransford, my brave knight. You are in my prayers nightly.

Most sincerely yours,

Ransford re-read the letter several times, pondering its many meanings. He smiled at the thought of a pretty girl back home in Corinth thinking so highly of him and her apparent interest in him. Did she want to be his friend because she admired his patriotism, adventurousness, or was it something more? He shook his head as the candle dwindled down to a nub and he drifted off to sleep.

IX: A Good Death

Sleep. It was always too short in this place. He awoke to another dreary cold day, pulled on his scratchy wool trousers, shirt, socks, boots, and overcoat, and pulled back the flaps of the tent. The familiar scene of black silhouetted men stomping around campfires, clutching coffee cups, greeted him again.

"That you, Ransford?" asked one of the silhouettes.

"Ayep. Howdie Earle."

"Did you all hear bout that feller from B Company?"

"Can't say as I did."

"He up and died yesterday. Just up and died."

"Died? From what?" asked Ransford.

"The shits." Earle replied, to the acknowledgement of a few others gathered around the fire.

"Hell, Earle, haven't we all had the shits at one time or another whilst we was here?" asked Ransford incredulously. "I had 'em last week myself. Nobody's died from 'em."

"Well they have now," added another soldier. "And I heard there were a couple other ones from the 83rd too."

"Died?"

"Yep. Died."

That brought on a period of sustained silence as the group of men sipped their coffee and pondered this information. They had expected death in the battles to come. Quietly, every soldier explored the same question—over and over—in his mind: will I die in battle and, if so, what will happen to me and my loved ones back home? Deep inside, most had steeled themselves to that bitter reality, accepting it as God's will, should it come to that. But they had never prepared themselves for dying prior to battle, certainly not in camp. Almost all, to a man, were strong, healthy, and young; hell, they were the cream of the crop from their communities. Only the old and infirm died of illness, for the most part. So this news was particularly unsettling to the men.

"Why in sam hell did this happen? What do the officers say about it?" asked one private.

"Not much from what I hear'd. As a matter of fact, I hear'd one tell his men they ought to get over to the chapel more often on Sundays."

"Well, I don't like the sound of that very much," confided Ransford. "That's the best answer they got? Pray?"

"Praying can be a powerful ally, my friend," a new voice came into the circle. "Very pleased to meet you boys. My name is Reverend Pease and I'm your chaplain. Couldn't help but hear you all discussing the current state of affairs here at Camp Butterfield."

"Why, it's good to make your acquaintance, Reverend!" said one of the boys. "I must say I hear'd you speak a couple Sundays ago and found it right exhilarating, especially when you said: 'I want to stand as an electric telegraph line between the 44th and Heaven.' That was somethin'!"

"Heh, heh, well my lad, yes, I did say that in one of my more passionate sermons," the Reverend acknowledged modestly. "Now what troubles you lads on this brisk winter morning?"

"We were just discussing this unfortunate business of some of our men in our unit dying all of a sudden from something as silly as the shits—er, sorry pastor—I mean from a pretty common kind of sickness. We heard there was others about in the other camp who died from that too. To be honest Reverend, it was downright disturbing," Ransford was trying to capture what he sensed to be the men's mood on the subject, as well as his own.

"Indeed, it is disturbing, Private. What is your name, son?"

"Ranford, sir."

"Well Ransford, I could tell you that the Lord moves mysteriously and it is not for us to question His actions; that He has called these young men home for His own reasons. But I don't think that answer would be all that satisfying when you consider the circumstances," he opined, catching the men off guard with his willingness to explore more than just the pat answer most of them expected from a man of the cloth. "You are young, strong men, readying yourselves for battle and a righteous battle, at that. You expect to be treated better by your God than to die ignominiously in some forsaken place far from home. If you are going to die in battle, so be it. You are ready for that. But deep down inside you yearn for a good death. It is my fervent hope that you, brave soldiers of the 44th, will indeed, if it is God's will to take you in this glorious struggle, earn yourselves a good death!"

"Yes, yes Reverend!" exclaimed one private, moved by the accuracy of the preacher's description. "Yer right on the money with that, Preacher. I'm at peace with dying in this here war. But I want me a good death, somethin' me and my family can be proud of. Please don't tell me I'm gonna die of the shits in Camp Butterfield, Virginny!"

There were many spontaneous and enthusiastic amens surrounding the fire. The Reverend had touched a nerve, or exposed it, and the men would employ the phrase "a good death" many times afterward as a way of differentiating between positive and negative mystical outcomes in the war.

Whether it was due to his upbringing or a sense that he'd be riling most of his platoon unnecessarily, Ransford did not challenge the Reverend's assertion. He couldn't help questioning how a man of the cloth could ascribe such fickle motives to the Lord Almighty. Is God really more pleased with a man who dies from a bullet to the heart than He is with a poor fellow who dies from the shits? Or should a family be less proud of a son who dies in camp from illness than one who dies gloriously in battle? Is there ever a *good death*?

The days continued to bleed together in a mundane succession punctuated by occasional news of fights elsewhere. Meanwhile, in Camp Butterfield, word of death cropping up in various corners of the camp visited the morning fires with increasing regularity, giving rise to feelings of helplessness and doubt among the men. One day it was a likable boy from Herkimer County and another it was Corporal Johnson, a Saratoga lad, who had a knack with the fiddle. They all died in a prolonged and horrid way that taxed the young men around them, who vainly sought to make sense of the unseen enemy taking their lives. It was as if they had been marked by malevolent spirits, who came into their tents unseen while they slept, annointing some for death and passing by others without rhyme or reason.

Camp life went on, even as the regiment's ranks thinned slightly, and the soldiers became oddly accustomed to the news of death among them. It was, Ransford thought, like the beasts of some African herd of grazers--zebras or gnus maybe—that quietly go about their business, grazing and frolicking under the savannah sun, until a lion attack throws the entire massive herd into a panic. Hooves pounding, calves bleating, the big cats snarling and roaring, until they make their kill. And, then, with strange regularity, the entire herd goes back to its business, grazing and frolicking, as if nothing had happened. At Camp Butterfield the men would stop talking about Corporal Johnson; a new fiddler would step into the light of the campfire on Saturday night, and life in the camp would go on.

One March morning, however, the bugler called early and the sergeants barked wildly at the men, bringing half-dressed soldiers from their tents in the still frigid night.

"Break camp! Break camp, men!"

This was it. Finally. The 44th was on the march at last! The whole camp was in motion as the entire brigade began dismantling its home of the previous five months. Men feverishly stuffed their belongings into knapsacks and worked in squads to take down tents, kitchens, and command posts. Teamsters drove their teams of oxen and horses through camp, loading up everything the army would need in the field. There was a buzz whirring through the men.

The regiment formed for review as the first light crept over the hills of northern Virginia. The fog and the steamy breath of thousands of men and horses combined to create an eerie cloud moving slowly about the assembled line of soldiers. Officers called to sergeants and sergeants called to the men to prepare to march. They would be marching east to Centreville, where they expected to face the Army of Northern Virginia. Finally.

"This is it, Ransford!" Private Solomon said in an excited whisper.

"It appears so," Ransford replied out the corner of his mouth.

"Quiet in the ranks!" Sergeant Tinkham would have no jabbering in the lines. He was excited too, but for a whole different reason. He had seen the green and jittery men falter on the field at Mannassas; he had seen them run and die in droves, ingloriously. This, at long last, would be his chance to right that wrong. These men, he believed, were ready and able to fight. He had trained them to do so. And, if used rightly by their commanders, they would bring honor, once again, to Ellsworth's name.

"Fall in behind D Company, men. Step lively!"

The march was on. Nearly 4,000 men from New York, Pennsylvania, Michigan, and Maine said farewell to Camp

Butterfield and made for war. Before long an impressive line of marching soldiers formed in the valley beneath Hall's Hill, the 44th led by Col. Stryker and his staff of majors and captains, all on horseback, their bright brass buttons and sabers glistening in the morning sun. They were followed by a coterie of pipers and more than twenty drummers, all young men who carried no weapons, only drumsticks and flutes, and accompanied the force with pomp on all its marches. The players struck up a tune, familiar to most in the regiment, *Always Stand on the Union Side*, that enlivened the start of the march and had many in the ranks singing along.

"…Always stand on the Union side,

And battle for the right.

With conscience clear, we'll laugh at fear

In the midst of the boldest fight.

Always stand on the Union side,

And 'keep your powder dry.'

We'll soon rejoice both far and wide

To see secession die.

'Tis better in defense of truth,

To be both brave and bold,

Than side with traitors and at last

Be left out in the cold…."

They tramped west along a well-traveled road, still hard from the evening frost, bound for Centreville, the strategic lair of the Army of Northern Virginia, which had held it ever since the rebels' infamous rout of Union forces in the first major battle of the war at Manassas Junction. A key railroad junction located not far from Manassas, Centreville's train station had allowed the Confederates to quickly bring up a fresh division to support its faltering army late in the afternoon of the battle, turning the tide and bringing them an overwhelming victory. They had held the town and the heights around it ever since, fortifying it for the expected assault. As the brigade advanced away from the safe confines of Hall's Hill, they were soon joined by other elements of the Fifth Corp's First Division, growing considerably in size.

"An awesome sight, ain't it Ransford?" Solomon Hickok said as E Company marched four abreast along a pike through Fairfax County, Virginia.

"It surely is, Solomon. Must be 10,000 men in this line!"

"Can't see the end of it, nor the beginning," added Private Whitney.

"I do admit that I too am quite impressed, my good bretheren," Jack Finnegan chimed in. "But I would be remiss if I didn't remind you that the rebel army up yonder did whip a force as large as this several months ago and did so not far from where we're headed."

"Well aren't you a breath o' fresh air today, Jack?" Ransford chided him, but knew he was correct. "That army wasn't this army."

"You make a point with some merit, my country cousin . . .. Perhaps I should just start singing *Always Stand on the Union Side* again?"

"Please don't, Jack!"

The men chuckled. They marched throughout the morning and well into the afternoon, part of a great blue snake crawling slowly but inexorably through the pretty countryside of northern Virginia. Ahead and along the sides of their column small contingents of cavalry galloped forward and outward to the north and south, probing and scouting for the enemy, who could be anywhere. After several hours their knapsacks—jammed with nearly 40 pounds of gear—began to dig deeply into the men's shoulders, the rifles getting ever weightier in their arms. With increasing regularity the column would simply halt, forcing the men to stand in place, unsure of what the delay meant.

"What's happening up ahead? Are we about to fight?" they thought. And then, without explanation, the company would be ordered to march once again.

Eventually the column made its way to Centreville, the village and train station visible nearly a mile to the west. No discernible sign of the enemy could be detected, but nonetheless the men were unsettled as they stood in place, scouring the horizon for any sign of Johnny Reb. He was an unpredictable foe, after all. Off to the south of town they could make out the black barrels of cannons poking from a series of redoubts and earthworks that had been constructed on the heights overlooking the valley. It was a formidible and, quite possibly, unassailable position. But no men appeared attached to them.

Small bands of men on horseback, some sporting uniforms and some in civilian garb, galloped furiously toward the the officers at the head of the column, now visible several hundred yards away from E Company. Ransford saw them gather around the head of the great snake; all apparently conferring and reaching some conclusion that would, he could only hope, be shared soon with the men, who stood in a state of agitated ignorance. Riders were dispatched to follow the line and convey orders to each regiment and their companies, eventually bringing word that there would be no fight that day.

Word circulated that General Joseph Johnston and his army had evacuated Centreville a day earlier, preferring to fall back toward Richmond, rather than face the full brunt of the Army of the Potomac. They had abandoned the ground won at great cost at Manassas, perhaps recognizing that this new federal army was indeed formidable, while theirs might be vulnerable so close to Washington and the troops massed around it.

On one hand, the news came as a reprieve to every man that had, earlier that morning, quietly feared today could well be his last. On the other, the troops couldn't deny their profound disappointment at not being given the opportunity to do what they had come to do: fight rebels.

Orders came to deploy on the ridge overlooking the town and the men of E Company occupied the formidable redoubt they had spied earlier. However, the cannons guarding the valley from numerous gun placements turned out to be nothing more than wooden poles and posts, painted black and positioned to look like cannons from afar. Yet another ruse from a crafty enemy.

"Look boys, Quaker cannons!"

"Why do they call 'em Quaker cannons?"

"Cause they wouldn't harm a flea!"

"I wonder if this is the type of tomfoolery that kept our generals from attacking these many months?" pondered Jack as the company pitched tents and made camp for the night in the earthworks above Centreville. "These shifty rebs appear to have our leaders bamboozled."

"I don't know who's bamboozling who, but I do know I'm about ready to burst if I don't get a chance to do somethin' other than march, drill, and shoot targets," admitted one soldier shortly after a sparse dinner of hardtack and coffee.

"I'm with him."

"Me too!"

Next morning, after just one night in their bivouac at Centreville, the men were called back into line and ordered to return to Camp Butterfield. The long, uneventful march back to their erstwhile home was a somber one—one of quiet resignation and pessimism that oozed through every man like a sudden sickness. The men, now well-trained and soldierly, re-established the regiment at Butterfield and resumed, for the time being, with the routines of camp life, as if the sad march to Centreville had never happened.

When not drilling, Ransford busied himself with re-reading the precious few books he had been willing to bear on his back along with all the other necessities in his knapsack. Aside from the Bible his father had given him, the rest were lofty tomes—Moby Dick, the Count of Monte Cristo, and Walden—that had once abetted his escapes from a bleak and repetitious existence in upstate New York. Now, they helped him escape from what had ostensibly become a repetitious (and at times terrifying) existence encamped in a strange and hostile world. When not reading, Ransford would write, mostly letters to his brother, father, and, occasionally, to Miss Amy Carpenter, who began to occupy his thoughts more frequently.

In letters to his father or brother he would insert an occasional inquiry about Miss Carpenter in the third or fourth paragraph, hoping to avoid any detection of his interest in the gal. But such subtleties were lost on Sylvanus, who quickly exposed Ransford's sentiments in his most recent letter.

Dear Brother Ransford:

I hope this letter finds you well. I am certain you must be doing better than me, since it is I, and not you, who must now feed and tend the entire herd of sheep at our homestead, given your long and unrelenting adventure! (Please know I say this in jest and hold you in the highest esteem.) In fac,t I may, at some point in the near future, be joining you in the glorious ranks. Although this concept has not been fully discussed with our father, it is quite commonly accepted in the community that more and more of our young men, of which I now consider myself one, are enlisting. Calls for new regiments go out with regularity and my ardor to contribute to the noble cause that drew you in late last year has taken hold of my sensibilities. I will inform you of any further developments as soon as I have something to report, dear brother. In the meantime, I must also report that a certain young lady, Miss Amy Carpenter, has been asking about your activities with increasing regularity. This interest on her part, combined with your inquiries regarding this same fair person of our community, cannot lead me to any other conclusion than to wonder if you have become sweet on this lass? If this is indeed the case, rest assured that I and others of your acquaintance believe your mutual interest to be a good match for both parties concerned. I will end my communication on that note, dear brother, and it is my profound hope you will be victorious and will stay safe in your journeys.

Most affectionately,

Your brother,

Sylvanus

Ps. Father is well and sends his affection. He asked me to admonish you again, as he did in Saratoga that day: Do not forget to duck!

Ransford read his brother's letter several times over, repeating various clauses under his breath as he studied the note by candlelight. It both troubled and pleased him, evoking concern for his younger brother's plans to enlist while feeling reassured that his instinct about Amy Carpenter was not a figment of his imagination. "A good match, eh!" The thought inspired him, making the idea of returning to Corinth some day not nearly so unappealing as he'd once imagined. Ransford resolved to write his brother:

My Dear Brother Sylvanus,

I am most grateful for your recent letter and the thoughtful package that came along with it. I do not know which warms me more, your kind news from home or the socks and good coffee that accompanied it. Your generosity is much appreciated, Sylvanus and, quite frankly, demonstrates most clearly that you have indeed grown into a fine young man. You should know that down here, in Camp Butterfield, the smallest of comforts are cherished above all else and I will leave it at that.

I must admit, however, to being somewhat vexed to learn of your interest in enlisting. While I understand your desire to join the growing list of young men volunteering for service at this critical time, my thoughts travel to selfish places when I ponder your enlistment. I worry that father may have neither of us at home to help him with the considerable work that comes with our family farm and his carpentry business. I worry that, should you follow through with your plans, he will have not one, but both of his sons, to fear after. Although we in the 44th have not, as yet, "seen the elephant" as they say, the time is coming soon and, when we do engage, the likelihood of casualties is high. You, of course, must make your own decisions as you now enter the challenging club of manhood. I only ask that you weigh honestly all sides before proceeding with a decision that will impact others.

As to your thoughts regarding Miss Carpenter, I am, perhaps for the first time, willing to admit to being sweet on the lass, as you put it. She and I have corresponded extensively since I departed and I have found her to be a young woman of sincerity, spirit, and wit. Please, do me this favor Sylvanus, now that my secret is out, would you keep a watchful eye out for her on my behalf? I would be grateful, brother.

Thank you again, young man. Please know that I truly look forward to your letters and observations. They mean the world to this poor soldier.

With love and warm affection,

Your brother,

Ransford

With the last few strokes of his pen Ransford felt sleep overtake him. He dreamed of home: the blue-green mountains, the great river flowing through them, the refreshing clarity of the seasons, like the people, who were, for the most part, warm and honest, Amy Carpenter.

It wasn't long after the debacle of Centreville that word spread of another impending move. Such news was met with derision around the campfires, but it was attested to with fervor and corroborated by enough others that the rumor appeared to have merit.

"I'm tellin' ya, it's true, boys. We'll be moving afore the week's out," Private Wilcox announced breathlessly, barely a week after the march to Centreville.

"I heard that too," confirmed Private Whitney.

"Well, I heard that General Joseph Johnston had surrendered to some boys on picket duty in B Company last week and was having coffee down the road with Colonel Stryker and that didn't quite pan out, now did it?" remarked Jack, taking a drawn out sip from from his coffee mug, as if for emphasis.

"My source of this information, Jack, appears reputable enough. Lieutenant Knox was telling some fellas we'd be heading out in the next day or two," Whitney responded.

"Fair enough. But where did the good lieutenant say we we're heading?"

"To the ocean! Said we'd be boarding steamers for the coast," Whitney answered. "Not sure exactly where we're going though."

"So we're going on a cruise!" Jack mocked excitement at the idea. "I haven't been on a nice sea jaunt in quite some time. Time to pack my steamer trunk."

"I haven't ever been on a sea jaunt," said Ransford, nervously. "Why in heck would we need to go out to sea? I can point to Richmond. Hell, it's right over there about a hundred miles away. Why on earth don't we just march over that way for crying out loud?" After reading Moby Dick, several times, he was convinced that the ocean was a mysterious and utterly unsafe place for humans; the idea of traveling in small wooden boats out into the vast, dark void of the sea—a place teeming with monsters and malevolent weather—unsettled him more than facing the entire Army of Northern Virginia.

"That would probably be bacause there are six rivers to cross between us and Richmond, Private. And all the bridges have been destroyed." The unmistakable baritone of Sergeant Tinkham broke into their circle.

"Sir, yes sir!" They all perked up, surprised, and stood at attention.

"At ease, men . . .. The private has a point, but larger military minds than ours are convinced that we should avoid fording all those nasty rivers and do an end run on Johnston's flank. Little Mac is moving the whole dang army down the coast to Yorktown . . .. Then we're gonna march straight up the penninsula and take Richmond. You heard it hear first, boys."

Ransford and his squad were taken aback by both the content of the conversation and the fact that Sergeant Tinkam was conversing with them at all. Such full explanations of army thinking were extremely rare, leaving lowly privates and corporals to constant conjecture about where the army would move and why.

"Well, thank you most kindly, Sergeant," Ransford said sincerely. "We had been hearing some things and weren't all that sure what was true and what wasn't. You've cleared that up for us and for that we're grateful . . .. Is it true we're gonna be riding in boats out in the ocean?"

"Yes, that's the plan, son, but it's not like we're sailing off to China or anything all that dramatic. The trip won't take much more than a day and we'll be hugging the coast the whole way, in sight of land."

Ransford was relieved at the thought of "hugging the coast."

"When will we be departing, Sergeant?" asked Jack.

"Tomorrow. First light," the burly sergeant responded before moving to the next campfire, continuing to inform his squads personally of the plan to break camp in the morning.

"Yorktown. Why does that ring a bell?" asked one of the men.

"Does Lord Cornwallis ring a bell? The little matter of the British surrender at Yorktown and the end of the Revolutionary War? That was at Yorktown." Jack's abbreviated history lesson jarred most of the men's recollections of lessons learned long ago in primary school.

"Well, that sounds just fine," Ransford responded. "As long as we're playing the role of Continental Army and the rebs are the British!" Several men laughed uncomfortably.

"Well said, Ransford. Let's be on the right side of this fight."

Few men slept well that night as the exotic notion of migrating south with the entire Army of the Potomac, boarding ships, and heading to sea occupied their mind Many took the opportunity to pack their knapsacks or write a last letter home before the campaign began in earnest.

Again the brigade was gathered at dawn and again they broke Camp Butterfield, this time for good. The troops marched east, back over roads they had taken out of Alexandria several months earlier. Once in the city that stared across the Potomac at Washington, they were funneled into enormous queues with other regiments, what seemed like hundreds of them, each waiting to board one of the steamers, scows, and sailing vessels lined up at the city's docks. The excitement that at first permeated the lines waned as the day dragged on and the men waited in place, hour after hour, for their ride to Yorktown. While they waited in the streets of Alexandria, more than one soldier pointed out to his compatriots that it was here, in Alexandria, that Colonel Ellsworth had met his untimely end. A bustling conversation moved through the lines as the men realized that this place, to them, was truly hallowed ground. One private in the ranks spied the Marshall House just a few blocks away from where they were standing and, upon being so informed, representatives from several companies of the 44th requested permission to briefly visit the famous hotel.

Lt. Knox offered to take members of his company—E Company—to the site with the understanding that as soon as the regiment began to move they would quick step back to the lines. Ransford's squad and several others elected to join the lieutenant and soon they were standing before the Marshall House, staring at it with a mixture of curiosity and reverence.

"Ain't all that much to look at, to be honest," said one soldier. "I mean, it's not all that big, is it?"

The four-story, red brick colonial inn at the corner of King and South Pitt streets was indeed indistinct from the other red brick buildings lining the streets of Alexandria, except for the prodigious flag pole poking high out of its gabled roof. It was this pole that had displayed the offending rebel flag that irked President Lincoln so much on that fateful day—one day after the Virginia legislature had voted to secede from the union— that he ordered his most trusted adjutant, Colonel Ellmer Ellsworth, to take his 11th NY infantry regiment across the Potomac and take it down.

"We were only too happy to comply," said Lt. Knox, who stood staring at the pole along with the men of his unit. "We'd been seeing that damnable flag for weeks across the river; it vexed the hell out of us. But the Colonel told us to be patient, our time would come."

"You were there, Lieutenant?"

"I was there. First lieutenant, A Company, 11th New York. We'd been handpicked and trained by the Colonel, raised up out of the hellish life of a New York City firefighter," he said wistfully, almost unaware that his entire company had gathered around him and were hanging on his every word. "We went about our work quickly and cleanly, quelling resistence and pacifying any seccessionist sympathizers we encountered throughout the city. Doing our jobs as ordered by Colonel Ellsworth . . .. But he wanted to personally remove that damn flag. He'd promised President Lincoln he would do it himself.

So when we got here he took a small squad, me out here in the street, guarding the entrance, and he went on up those stairs with four of our men."

"What happened, Lieutenant? Did the rebs have a squad o' soldiers up in there? Did they fight it out?"

"That would have been an honorable way for the Colonel to go, Private. No, after the Colonel took down the flag and was carrying it down a flight of stairs, a grimy innkeeper, who had appeared drunk and disorderly when the men first arrived— Jackson his name was—stepped out a doorway and, unprovoked, let go on him with a shotgun. The blast went straight through the Colonel's heart. Corporal Brownell killed the coward straightaway with his bayonet."

"Damn!"

The lieutenant paused, emotional at the recollection, and looked around at the young, mostly unproven soldiers gathered around him.

"Men, Colonel Ellsworth was the best soldier, the best leader, and, hell, the best man I've ever had the privilege to meet. As it turned out, he was the first of us to die in this bloody struggle, murdered without good cause by a man, a civilian, who was protecting nothing more than a flag, a flag that represented an ugly institution called slavery. If a flag doesn't stand for something honorable then it's not worth dying or killing for. Don't be fooled by anything they tell you about this war being about state's rights or sovereignty or some such nonsense. This war is about slavery, the domination of privileged white men over subjugated black men, and the south's willingness to kill anyone in sight to protect their evil industry. Colonel Ellsworth was the first among us to die in this fight and he won't be the last. You fine young men will carry his name and memory into battle soon. I look forward to leading you in the fights to come."

The men, some moved to tears, others to raucous applause and hoots, were genuinely surprised at the Lieutenant's passion and eloquence, especially as it was displayed in front of them. They would, henceforth, always view him as a trusted leader and friend. Their reflection was rudely interrupted as a runner came upon the company, alerting them that the 44th would be boarding shortly and that they should make their way back double quick.

X: The Peninsula

The 44th lined up by companies and boarded a massive paddleboat that had been parked in a sleeve in the Alexandria docks. Two great black stacks, each belching plumes of gray smoke, jutted up from an elaborately adorned three-tiered upper deck and bridge. The men were herded onto the main deck by navy seamen, who roughly ordered them into the deeper recesses of the ship until each section distributed with men and the ship was filled, stem to stern. With the regiment aboard she cast off and began steaming down the Potomac. Ransford sat atop his knapsack on the forward deck surrounded by the soldiers of E Company.

"Settle in, boys. We'll be on this lovely vessel for a day or so!" bellowed Sgt. Tinkham over the screams of the ship's horns.

"So this is what a cow feels like," said Private Earles.

"Not the most comfortable of accommodations. But it surely beats marching to Yorktown," added Jack.

"That it does," said Ransford, peering out over the oak railing at the broad river bringing them toward the war. It was the last day in March and a gentle breeze blew. The day was surprisingly warm and pleasant. "I suppose this isn't too bad a way to travel, is it Jack?"

"No lad, it isn't. Under the right circumstances, it can be a lovely way to see the world."

"I suppose you've spent time on steamships?"

"Oh, indeed I have," Jack offered. "A few times down the coast and once to Europe. Now that little jaunt was something special!"

"Tell us all about it, Jack. It appears we've got plenty of time."

"Well I'd rather not delve too deeply into my, at times, privileged past Ransford, so as to not foment any sort of class warfare among us. But I will share that cruises are one of the reasons the rich like to remain rich, if you know what I mean," he went on, wistfully recalling his pampered days and nights on a cruise ship bound for Ireland, home of his forbears. "After a fine repast of quail and caviar in the gilded trappings of the dining room, we gentlemen would take our brandy on the upper deck, high above regular folk on the decks below. There we would perambulate and smoke fine cigars, discussing the day, dreams, beautiful women, whatever. You could gaze a hundred miles out into a perfectly mysterious ocean, under a sky sparkling with a million stars . . .. Life was good then."

"Well that surely does sound lovely, Jack . . .. So how in the world did you end up here with us, sitting on your rucksack and heading to the front?"

"That's a tale for another day, if you wouldn't mind."

"Certainly not, Jack," replied Ransford, sensing his friend's discomfort. "You've got the right to keep your story to yourself, but I'll be a willing party to it when you're ready."

Throughout the day and well into the night, the ship steamed ahead, making good time at ten knots per hour, soon becoming part of a great procession of vessels of all sorts—sail and steam, large and small—making their way from docks in Washington, Georgetown, Alexandria, and other cities along the Potomac. The prodigious migration of ships, each fully laden with men and materiel, was designed to shift the main body of the Army of Potomac from its defensive ring around Washington to a landing point at the tip of the peninsula formed by the outlets of the James and the York rivers.

After a long, uneventful, but somewhat relaxing voyage, which afforded many men the opportunity to catch up on their sleep, the paddleboat plied into the great harbor at the mouth of the Chesapeake Bay as the sun rose over the ocean to the east. Viewing the Atlantic Ocean for the first time, Ransford was struck by its immutable beauty, the relentless rolling waves crashing onto rocky promontories packed with yacking sea birds and barking seals. A pod of dolphins frolicked in the wake made by the ship's bow, causing the men to jam against the railing and gaze down at the scene in wonder. It was an incredible, mystic experience that quickly gave way to another spectacle as the ship turned away from the sea and headed toward the sprawling harbor at Newport News, Virginia.

The paddleboat churned its way through a formidable line of warships, cannon poking out of gun portals lining their sides, that girded the opening of great waterway against attack. The boys had been informed that just weeks earlier the harbor had been the scene of a great battle the likes of which the world had not yet seen, as two ironclads—the Confederate *Merrimack* and the Union's *Monitor*—slugged it out for an entire day, their cannon balls bouncing off each other's metal plated sides, while crews of the Union's wooden warships watched and prayed the *Monitor* would emerge victorious. One day before the *Monitor's* arrival, the *Merrimack* had torn through the Union blockade, sinking one Union frigate and disabling another before retiring for the night. It returned the next day; its crew fully expecting to finish its rout of the outmatched Union navy. But by morning the *Monitor*, an odd creature with a flat deck almost flush with the water line and adorned only with a round rotating turret— similar in shape to a cheese box that hosted two massive guns— arrived on the scene. Although the two battled to a draw that day, the *Merrimack*, vastly outnumbered and wounded from too many blows, withdrew to safer harbors along the southern coast (eventually scuttling to keep her out the hands of the enemy) and never again threatened northern ships.

Once through the defensive ring, the men on deck could see a great armada spread out before them as ships of every discernible type dotted the harbor, some under sail and others moored. Ransford was struck with awe at the incredible number of craft bustling before him like bees in a hive and wondered if this was how Priam must have felt as he looked out over the walls of Troy at the terrifying sight of King Agamemnon's fleet bearing down upon his beloved city.

Soon they were steaming under the watchful gaze of Union defenders manning Fort Monroe, a colossal fortress situated at the tip of the Virginian peninsula. A sprawling island unto itself, separated from the mainland by a protective moat, with its own docks, farm, and hundreds of buildings, Fort Monroe featured seven stout walls, each bristling with cannon. It commanded every natural passageway into Virginia and Union generals were very pleased that they controlled it.

The 44th's paddleboat approached its docking assignment, waiting for more than hour before it could tie up and allow the regiment to disembark. As the men clambered across planks onto the dock below, they were struck by the sheer magnitude of the military operation unfolding around them: soldiers and seamen bustled by the thousands on the docks, cranes unloaded every manner of materiel from the ships' holds—cannon, barrels, ammunition, and livestock, still bleating and squirming—were all sharing the docks with whole divisions formed on the fort's parade ground. Captains and quartermasters barked orders, straining to be heard over the commotion that naturally followed such endeavors. The 44th's officers worked feverishly to assemble the men as they themselves had been admonished to get their "asses off the docks in 30 minutes" or face disciplinary action.

"I think they mean business, boys," said Private Whitney as he and the squad lined up in front of the ship amidst the chaos and cacophony.

"Ayep, if the officers get in trouble you know who else will suffer, don't ya?"

"That would be us, Private."

Soon they were marching through the mad hive on the docks and toward the busy but open ground near the western walls of the fort. The 44th and other regiments from their brigade—the 83rd Pennsylvania, 16th Michigan, and 20th Maine—rejoined each other on the expansive parade grounds, receiving orders from on high to form up and march to a new bivouac further up the peninsula. As they gathered, the men noticed clouds forming to the west and soon a steady rain, not driving but prolific, began to fall. The entire brigade formed up and started marching over one of the bridges spanning the moat separating Fort Monroe from the tip of the peninsula. Rumbling, dull but distinct, was discernible to the west and the men debated whether the sounds were thunder or cannon fire.

The brigade marched to a non-descript patch of ground slightly higher than sea level and began carving out a campsite, felling trees, digging latrines, staking their canvas tents, and foraging for firewood. The fact that nearly 100 other regiments—more than 100,000 men—were busying themselves with the same activities in a surprisingly compact area made for some tense moments as the units competed for resources and space. One detail returning to the 44th from foraging recounted a run-in with some boys from another regiment. As they came into camp, each soldier carrying a small bundle of fire wood, they were asked about their experiences scouting the territory.

"All's I can tell you, boy, is: be watchful out there," said one recruit, pointing to his right eye to reveal a nasty purple contusion.

"Who-eee lad! How in hell did ya git that shiner?"

"Well, I fancied a nice piece of ash laying on the ground up in that stand of timber over there and went to claim it when another fella—looked like he was from some Ohio unit—took a fancy to it too. I got into a discussion about it with him and he just up and walloped me! Hit me right in the face, musta been an Irish boy because he hit me solid; knew how to use his hands, he did!"

Ransford's squad began to debate the news.

"Did you get wind of that, boys?"

"Not at all neighborly over there in Ohio are they?" replied Jack.

"I don't know if it's Ohio as much as it's any unit that doesn't have a history with the others," theorized Ransford. "Heck, some of those fellas from the other units that we talked with back in Alexandria were downright rude when we talked to them. It was like we were dogs and they were cats."

"Or we were Capulets and they were Montagues," added Jack.

"Well, I don't know who's Romeo or who's Juliet, if that's what you're saying, Jack, but I do know we're all in the same darn army and we should treat each other with respect," Ransford said.

"I don't disagree with you, son, but until that happens it sounds like we better forage together, in groups, until we find kinder company around us," Whitney proposed. The rest nodded in agreement.

They made camp in the rain and waited anxiously—the mud getting deeper and more prevalent--over the next several days for orders as to when they and the massive force would move up the peninsula toward Richmond. The army, it appeared, had stalled before it started, stymied by Confederate Brigadier General John Magruder's stubborn line of defenses stretching nearly eight miles across the narrow isthmus along the Warwick River and around the City of Yorktown. The men heard occasional reports of attacks by forward units, but, for the most part, the great Army of the Potomac waited as General McLellan, convinced that a force of 100,000 rebels awaited him on the other side of the Warwick, dug in for a long siege.

For the next 30 days the 44th was brought forward to assist in the digging of fortifications and trenches to support the coming siege. The men gave up rifles for shovels and pick axes, constructing an impressive system of trenches and parapets to support the nearly 200 siege guns General McLellan wanted installed along his front. As they worked, rebel snipers and artillery fired constantly at their positions, occasionally inflicting casualties and causing mayhem when a projectile found its mark. One day in late April, Private Guernsey from H Company was struck by shrapnel from an exploding shell and killed instantly, becoming the regiment's first casualty from battle. It was a telling moment for everyone in camp as they attended a military funeral for the Herkimer County boy.

There were also moments of odd wonder when the recently formed "Balloon Corps" was called into service. An enormous clattering and shaking box attached to a steam engine worked for hours, it seemed, forcing helium gas into a sprawling rubberized skin spread over the ground, slowly inflating it until the balloon's expanded girth could carry a large wicker-type basket and a man aloft. Wearing a comical white trench coat and thick riding glasses, the good Professor Lowe, sometimes accompanied by an officer, would ascend, tethered by strong ropes held by stout soldiers, above the tree line to make observations of the rebel lines. Knowing his time was limited by both scientific realities and the tendency of the enemy to aim its guns at the massive balloon as soon as it came into view, the Professor would sketch and scribble furiously for several minutes before giving the signal to the men, who looked for all the world like they had roped the moon, to haul him back to earth. The "Balloon Corps" always merited a huge cheer by the hundreds of Union soldiers who had gathered around to gaze at the strange contraption.

Despite the occasional moments of entertainment or tragedy, life was predominantly mundane for the men camped in the muggy and marshy patch of the peninsula and it eroded their resolve. They were anxious for something, anything, to happen.

"I don't know about you boys, but this here camp is starting to feel a whole lot like Camp Butterfield, just muddier and with worse provisions," chided Private Hickok.

"That it is, Solomon," agreed Ransford, expressing a sentiment that had darkened everyone's mood since the day they had disembarked from the paddleboat.

"Well, they're bringing up some guns the likes of which this world has never seen," said Private Whitney. "These mortars they call 'em can toss a 200-pound round almost a mile. They've been building and digging and setting up hundreds of cannons for the siege of Yorktown!"

"The devil you say!"

"It's gonna be something!"

The troops had been alerted that on May 5th the greatest concentrated bombardment the world had ever known would commence. It was universally believed that Little Mac's fastidious preparations of the prior month would lead to the devastation of the Confederate defenders around Yorktown and deliver a smashing blow to the Army of Northern Virginia. The invasion would truly begin and they would finally get off the accursed patch of ground where the army had been languishing for so long.

The 44th joined with several divisions at the ready in anticipation of the coming barrage, the men excited for the spectacle. But the long-awaited bombardment never came; men stood for nearly an hour before being informed that General Magruder and his men had slipped away from their defenses the night before, retreating toward Richmond rather than face the cannonade they knew was coming.

Many elements of the army, including the 44th, were ordered forward into the vacated works and entrenchments of the enemy. Ransford's squad inspected one of the redoubts near the City of Yorktown and discovered another "battery" of Quaker cannon, much like the ones they had encountered in their visit to Centreville two months earlier. As they poked leisurely through the leavings of their foes—firepits, coffee cans, a chicken bone or two—they were jarred by an explosion that erupted from just below the western wall of the redoubt and they scrambled to investigate. Below them, they could see a soldier—his leg clearly shattered and hideously mangled below the knee—writhing on the ground next to a path that connected two redoubts, a considerable crater still smoldering beside him.

As men from his unit—a company from the 16th Michigan—rushed to his side, others hunched and took defensive positions, anticipating an artillery attack. But this made no sense to Sgt. Tinkham, who announced that there weren't any Confederate artillery positions within miles of the location; they had all retreated toward Richmond. He ordered the men to stand in place and conferred with Lt. Knox, who had come forward to inspect the site of the explosion. As the mortally wounded man was carried from the field, Lt. Knox dispatched a runner to the commanders, alerting them of the hazard.

"I've read about this, but never seen it, men," he announced to many assembled troops from the top of the parapet. "It's called a land mine and it's a bomb or cannon ball that's rigged with a compression fuse. Basically, it blows up when you step on it."

Audible gasps went up from the men.

"I want you all to back away from this place, try to step on ground you already covered and pull back to the river. We're going to bring up some engineers to clear this ground."

What kind of evil trickery was this? And how could they know where they'd already stepped?

"Alright soldiers, you heard the lieutenant. We're going to carefully depart this place and do it in an orderly way," said Sgt. Tinkham. "Let's look for our tracks in the dirt and work our way back down the walls of this redoubt and back to the river. It'll be safe there."

"Sir, yes sir!"

The exercise was less of a chore for Ransford and many of the upstate boys who had plenty of experience tracking creatures in the woods. They could differentiate a recent footprint from older ones; but many in the company were petrified at the prospect of stepping somewhere that might suddenly explode beneath their feet.

"Just follow me Jack, you too, Whitney. Do what we do," Ransford said, nodding to the other boys from Corinth, who could lead them to safety. Jack and several others complied without argument, gingerly following the country boys down the parapets and across the fields, mimicking their every step along the way, until they reached the banks of the Warwick River. As they progressed slowly, deliberately across the fields, they heard another explosion and then another several hundred yards to the south as other units encountered this new and entirely unexpected form of warfare.

The scattered and infrequent land mines were eventually cleared by army engineers and small squads of Confederate prisoners captured in previous engagements, who were commanded to search out and dismantle the hidden bombs. General McLellan, who personally gave the order, thought it only fitting that rebel soldiers take the greatest risk in removing the nefarious armaments from the field. Nonetheless, the land mines would have a much greater psychological effect than practical, thanks to the trepidation they caused among the ranks from that day forward.

Later that day, Brigadier General Stoneman led his cavalry, followed by divisions under the command of Generals Hooker and Hancock, in hot pursuit of the fleeing rebels, who turned to face their pursuers around Williamsburg and a series of earthen redoubts called Fort Magruder. It was here that the first true battle of the campaign occurred. The battle raged for much of the day as four divisions of McLellan's army slammed into the hastily established lines of General Magruder and General Longstreet's forces, numbering about 30,000 men. The roar of the fight could be heard far from the front, where the 44th waited in reserve, the men nervously anticipating their first call to action.

"You hear that, boys?" Private Hickok remarked, as the men stood at ease with the rest of the brigade in a large swampy field a few miles from the front. "It's like the biggest thunder storm you ever hear'd, times ten!"

"Couldn't have said it better myself," agreed Jack, who was intently gazing forward at nothing but noise, as if the booming sounds themselves might suddenly materialize in front of him. "It does sound rather . . . big."

"It's big alright," noted Sgt. Tinkham. "I'd venture it's almost as big as Manassas, and this is only the first punch."

"Reckon those boys up thar have seen that there elephant, haven't they, Sergeant?" Private Earles asked.

"They're seeing him right about now, son. And I guarantee you they won't ever be the same."

Every member of the squad took in what the Sergeant was saying and quietly mused about this fabled creature: what on earth must this particularly horrid elephant look like to inspire such dread?

As the shadows lengthened and the evening drew near, the distant sounds of battle began to subside, transitioning from an unrelenting roar to a few scattered reports, like the last few kernels of popcorn exploding in a pan until finally, it was over. The sound of riders on horseback soon followed, doubtless bringing news back to generals in the rear. A few called out as they galloped past the anxious ranks of men who'd waited in ignorance throughout the entire battle: "We got 'em on the run!"

Cheers of "hoo-ray!" and "huzzah!" followed the victorious news and relief flooded the men who were relieved that they would not witness anything approaching the disorderly retreat the army had experienced at Manassas. A repeat of that shameful disaster had been the unspoken worry of many men in the lines that day. But the happy mood of the troops who stood in reserve was short-lived as their compatriots began to slowly return from the battle.

A column of Hancock's division appeared above a small ridge, the sun setting behind them as they marched deliberately, but not smartly, down the road. They carried themselves erect and maintained good order, but there was a weariness to them that was unmistakable to anyone who knew what to look for. And their colors—the regimental flag and Old Glory carried aloft at the head of the column—told as much as the men's demeanor: they were ripped and ragged and spotted with holes. Some of the men limped, others had their heads or arms wrapped in bloody bandages as they approached with a hard stare to the front, oblivious to the men lining the road, gazing at them with great curiosity. It was the same with each passing regiment: either blank emotionless stares or pained, almost shocked expressions that were maintained as they walked by, immutable, as if painted on their faces. They had seen the elephant.

Stretcher-bearers and the wagons followed the columns—hundreds of them—filled with wounded soldiers collected from the field. The open wagons were heaped with a strange cargo that writhed and bled, elbows and legs cocked in odd positions, sometimes dangling over the sides or off the back of the wagon so it looked as if their bodies might tumble out. Medics standing in the jumbled piles, jiggling uncomfortably as they bounced over rough roads, tried to tend to the gravely wounded but did so futilely without the benefit of medical supplies or support.

Some of the wounded men screamed incessantly of their pain, their shock or their anger, launching into inscrutable, obscenity-laced grievances with God Almighty; others simply whimpered, sad and soulful cries, for mothers or girlfriends or even dogs back home; others slowly died, saying nothing. The men watched the procession silently. Gone were the huzzahs

160

and banter that were so common among men standing together in the ranks. This was something quite awful.

The men of the 44th returned to their soggy bivouac that night in silence, their reticence smothering the normally festive mood around the campfires. Sporadic fiddle music and occasional harmonica tunes could be heard intermittently, mournful songs and dirges that took the men to a somber place before retiring for the night.

The next morning the men rose to more rain and word that the brigade would be on the move. While most of the brigade was ordered to transport ships that would take them up the James River, the 44th would occupy the City of Yorktown for the foreseeable future. It was odd for the men of the regiment to see their compatriots march off without them, especially the 83rd, with whom they'd established a lasting bond. As they followed Colonel Stryker into the conquered city, the men wondered why they'd been kept behind, apparently away from the action around Richmond.

While most of the regiment occupied positions throughout the historic city of Yorktown, Captain Conner took companies D and H across the York River to garrison Gloucester Point, where there had been rumors of Confederate cavalry still skulking about. The Captain took a detail of some 100 men several miles into the countryside to investigate, eventually returning without having any encounters.

Meanwhile, with the conquest of the Confederate army (temporarily) complete in the lower portion of the peninsula, the countryside around Yorktown began to fill with slaves seeking the protection of the Union army. They streamed into the city—men, women, and children—singing and waving their arms as they approached the men in blue, who had established defensive positions at various check points, guard posts, gates, and fortifications in and around the city.

Ransford recalled it being a series of joyous encounters, each one memorable and passionate. One family of slaves—a man, his wife, and three small children, ragged and barefoot—walked directly up to his squad, unafraid and convinced that they had at last been delivered to their freedom. As they approached the soldiers they sang a song of freedom that lilted high into the muggy southern sky, defiant and happy:

"Free at last, free at last
I thank God I'm free at last
Free at last, free at last
I thank God I'm free at last

Way down yonder in the graveyard walk
I thank God I'm free at last
Me and my Jesus going to meet and talk
I thank God I'm free at last

On my knees when the light pass'd by
I thank God I'm free at last
Tho't my soul would rise and fly
I thank God I'm free at last

Some of these mornings, bright and fair
I thank God I'm free at last
Goin' meet King Jesus in the air
I thank God I'm free at last."

Ransford's squad welcomed the family, their guarded nature dissolving as they marveled at the sweet harmonies emanating from the squalid family of slaves. Recognizing they probably hadn't eaten in days, the squad offered their rations to them, which they gobbled down eagerly.

"Thanks to you, thanks to you, Yankee boys!" the father, a wiry, short fellow with a stubbled face, cried. "We been waitin' a long time for you all; long time!"

"Mhmmm, yes we have. A blessed long time," confirmed his wife, who was taller than her husband with a passel of long black hair pulled in a bun atop her head. "Now children, you thank these nice soldiers for all they be giving you."

"Thank you most kindly!" all three of the children—little ones about 3-5 years old—pronounced in harmony, with delightful wide eyes and solemn looks on their faces.

"Why, you're most welcome little ones," said Private Whitney, who was perhaps the most smitten of the entire squad. "We have come to help you folks achieve your rightful freedom and we won't leave until we accomplish that goal. M'am, Sir, you have a lovely family!" He shook their hands, all around, leading to similar pleasantries by the rest of the men. The father, overcome with emotion, took up yet another song:

"I love to shout, I love to sing
Let God's saints come in
I love to pray my heav'nly King
Let God's saints come in;

Come down, angels, trouble the waters
Come down, angels, trouble the waters
Come down, angels, trouble the waters
Let God's saints come in;

I think I hear the sinner say
Let God's saints come in
My Saviour taught me how to pray
Let God's saints come in;

I hope to meet my brother there
Let God's saints come in
That used to join with me in pray'r
Let God's saints come in;

Didn't Jesus tell you once before
Let God's saints come in

To go in peace and sin no more
Let God's saints come in."

The heartfelt scene was interrupted by Sgt. Tinkham, who felt obliged to return the squad to a more soldierly demeanor and to remind them to focus on their mission. Before they could mount another chorus, he stepped in to inform the family, hospitably but firmly, that they needed to continue to the center of the city, where hundreds of Africans seeking asylum had been brought.

"Now please, folks, I need you to walk on into Yorktown and there'll be people there to help you. Alright now, you folks head on in there," he stated, waving his arms and pointing toward the city.

"Yassir, we be goin', but God bless you all. May God truly bless you!"

As the family moved along down the road into the city, Sgt. Tinkham admonished the men, pointing out that there still weren't any guarantees that these or any slaves in the rebel states would ever be legally freed.

"It doesn't much matter what you think or what I think, lads. President Abe Lincoln and his friends in Congress haven't freed anybody, so we best not be filling these sorry folks up with wrongful ideas," he said. "You hear me, Private Whitney?"

"Yes, sir."

The 44th continued to garrison in Yorktown, acting more like police than soldiers. Many of the men grumbled that they shouldn't have come so far to have such an inconsequential role in the invasion. It was rumored by some with ears in high places that Colonel Stryker himself had requested the duty, preferring to keep his unit well away from the front. Meanwhile, other officers bitterly disagreed with his approach and, it was also rumored, made their dissatisfaction known to the regiment's primary benefactors back in Albany.

As a result, when Colonel Stryker and his quartermaster were away visiting Washington to retrieve the unit's traditional Zouave uniforms—which had been stored away in favor of a more battle-friendly version of Union garb—the regiment was ordered to proceed up the York River to join the rest of the division, which was encamped now along the banks of Pawmunkey River. Livid at the back-channel communications, but unable to suss out the culprits, Col. Stryker complied and reluctantly moved the 44th upriver via steamboat to the famed plantation known as White House, home of Robert E. Lee's in-laws, the Custis family. Ransford and the rest of Ellsworth's Avengers arrived at White House and the large federal encampment there on May 19th in a driving rain storm. The division marched, again in the rain, northwest of White House several miles to a new bivouac well north of the Chickahominy River. They were within several miles of Richmond and battles were brewing all around them.

XI: Aura Lea

The men awoke early on the 20th. Edgy and alert, they went about the many duties that accompanied life in a camp deep in hostile territory. It had rained for most of the month, resulting in the soldiers' clothes being perpetually dank and the men's morning began in the dark, pulling on wet woolen socks, pants, and jackets over soggy undergarments that emitted a powerful stench of mildew and sweat. This least appealing moment of the morning was followed closely by a most desirable one as the men engaged in the comforting routine and addictive relief brought on by a hot cup of coffee. A couple of pickets returning from all-night guard duty stepped into the firelight with an anxious look in their eyes.

"Morning boys," said one of the pickets, a man from G Company, who had guarded the western edge of the camp. "Mind if I grab a cup o' Joe? My unit's still a good ways from here and I jus' can't abide waitin'."

"No trouble, friend," said Private Hickok, handing him a steaming mug of the black and bitter liquid. "It's good fer what ails ya."

"Thank you kindly. You boys hear that commotion up ahead last night?"

"Can't say as we did, fella."

"I s'pose I woulda slept through a tornado too if I had the chance . . . .. Lots of big guns firing a few miles to the west; hell, it looked like a lightnin' storm. Musta been our boys shootin' at Richmond."

"It does appear we have found the war, gentlemen," Jack imparted as the picket expressed his gratitude and moved on toward his company's encampment.

"And, we've been ordered to go out there and look for the enemy, men," Sgt. Tinkham's familiar voice preceded him into the circle. "Look sharp, men. We've got 15 minutes to form up. Half our company and half of Company C will conduct a reconnaissance patrol at dawn. Leave your packs here."

"Sir, yes sir!"

They formed up with five squads selected from each company under a dreary gray dawn. It was announced that they would be commanded in the field by Captain Ephram Underhill, a recent West Point graduate who was in charge of C Company. Meanwhile, E Company's Captain Walsh would remain in camp.

The column, approaching 100 men, marched out of camp in the rain, tramping along a muddy road with a small detachment of cavalry watching their edges. The march was slow and sullen but marked by a profound awareness that they were now probing the enemy, looking for him in his own country.

The men had marched much of the day into the teeth of a hot afternoon along the road that led to their latest objective. It was a farm; eight miles from camp where scouts had sighted Confederate activity the night before. The column was parched now, marching uninspired along the dusty track in the midday sun, when the captain reared his horse and raised his white-gloved hand. A sergeant on horseback met him and they each pointed off to the west toward a line of trees a half-mile away.

Ordered to stand at ease, the men drank from their canteens and listlessly shuffled their feet, surveying the ground around them. Two hundred yards ahead stood a quaint cream-yellow farmhouse next to a large, weathered maroon barn, its doors open, chickens poking about the grounds. To the west stretched a field of wheat, hip high, glistening and golden like the fur on a tiger cat's back. Between them and the woods, squarely in the middle of the wheat field, stood a little hilltop that rose up oddly like a breaching whale's back in the middle of an otherwise flat sea.

Near the front of the column, Ransford could hear the captain and the sergeant talking. The sergeant had spotted a rebel infantry column double-timing into the woods. He estimated their numbers at half their strength—maybe 40 men—and without cavalry or artillery support.

"I'm telling you, sir, we could march over there and clean 'em out. They wouldn't know what hit 'em." The gnarly, black-haired sergeant spat for emphasis.

"I don't have the luxury of guessing at troop strength, Sergeant. I'm not going to commit this column without the benefit of reserves to a risky venture based upon your suppositions. I've been told Jeb Stuart's cavalry might be patrolling this region . . .. So we'd best proceed cautiously."

"Yes, sir!"

Captain Underhill, a slight man who'd graduated from West Point only months before hostilities erupted, wore a large brimmed hat that seemed too big for his head, at least to Ransford. Members of the column began pointing in the direction of the trees where a troop of 40 to 50 Confederates had broken from cover and were running, full out for the little hill.

"They're tryin' for the high ground captain! We'd best beat 'em too it . . .. Don't you think, sir?"

"Who is running this unit, Sergeant? By the time we get skirmishers organized and commence up that hill, the enemy will already have it and we will be assaulting an unassailable position. No. No. We must proceed with caution."

"Yes sir, with caution, sir. What are your orders, sir?"

The captain fidgeted slightly in his saddle, feeling the anxious eyes of the men upon him. He adjusted his ponderous hat and gazed at the rebels, bounding and yelling as they loped through the wheat, now nearly halfway to the little hill.

"We'll make for that farmhouse ahead. Use it for cover and, from there, maneuver around their left flank. That's it."

"Yes, sir!" The Sergeant barked urgent orders to the company—the commands rippled down the line through the platoon leaders—for all soldiers to turn and quickstep in formation down the path to the farmhouse.

As the men gathered themselves and turned to face their appointed direction, little puffs of dirt popped around them and strange zipping and whirring sounds filled the air. The delayed cracks of musket fire followed, telling the men the rebels had made it to the top of the hill and were now shooting down upon their column. It was the first time most of the men had found themselves under fire and, despite many months of training in moving quickly together as a column, the maneuver soon began to spasm and break down as fear took hold and minié balls found their marks.

While clumsily holding his musket high on his left shoulder, Ransford ran only half as fast he as could to avoid stepping on the heels of the man in front of him. His heart boomed like a kettledrum and the heat dragged upon him as if he were trying to flee some dark force in a nightmare. Somehow, in the midst of this horrid scene imposing itself around him, he became focused upon the yellow farmhouse now less than a hundred yards ahead. It was salvation, a shimmering haven in the sea of golden wheat. He saw it through the commotion with a clarity that occurs when all else is blocked—by fear or pain or love of purpose—from one's mind, like an oasis, or a mirage.

As he ran toward it he saw the door to the farmhouse open. Odd, Ransford thought, amid this deadly commotion to see a door open, almost welcoming. And then a young woman, clutching a bundle of some sort close to her bosom, stepped fully out upon the front porch. She stood there, a vision in white flowing petticoats and flaxen hair like the wheat around her, striking a dramatic pose as she gazed across the field toward the men and the din coming from the hill. Then she turned and glared at the advancing Union soldiers with an unmistakable look of reproach, as if scolding them for bringing such awful business to such a wholesome place. Perhaps she was a school-marm, Ransford thought as he ran, remarking how such a handsome teacher would have rendered a young man's attention to studies difficult. But what, he wondered, was in the bundle, held tight to her breast?

By now, the front of the scrambling column was getting perilously close to the farmhouse and bringing with it, like a following cloud, a steady rain of lead. Near the head of the column, a few rows in front of Ransford, a bullet had found the knee of a Saratoga boy, crumpling him in a heap on the spot. Wits dulled and without time to adjust, the men behind the stricken soldier toppled over him. Others fell upon the growing heap and so on until nearly 15 men had tumbled onto each other, creating a churning pile of navy blue elbows, knees, caps, and muskets. It would've been comical if it didn't make for such easy shooting for the Confederates, who trained their rifles upon them and released an unrelenting fire. Soon it was a writhing pile of anguish as screaming, wounded men and shocked soldiers looking to flee mingled in an awful mass not 15 yards from the farmhouse.

Ransford scrambled to free himself from the bloody pile. A man to his right with a shattered shoulder tried to grab Ransford with his one good hand, blood pulsing from the wound, his damaged arm dangling like the wing of a crippled bird. He pulled Ransford close, face-to-face and with mouth agape, he tried to speak words that couldn't escape. Just an other-worldly groan, that seemed to come from deep inside his throat. Another soldier, shot through the abdomen, hoisted his musket to his shoulder, took a knee, as if in training, and fired into the crowd around him—striking one of his own in the back of the head. The lunacy of it drove Ransford to twist violently, shaking his arms and head wildly like a man who awakens to discover he's covered in ants.

"God free me from this!" he implored, begging the God he rarely spoke to for deliverance.

He finally broke free from the awful gravity of the pile and resumed running, this time as fast as he could without soldierly reservation or concern for anyone but himself. The farmhouse came back into focus. The woman holding the bundle on the front porch was still there. It seemed she was just realizing the horror that would soon be visited upon her. As the frantic Union soldiers clambered toward her so did the fire from Confederate muskets.

Ransford thought he heard himself yell to her, "Go back in the house!" or perhaps he just willed her to do so. He could clearly see the young woman's face now and her outrage had melted into unbridled fear. She turned and stretched her graceful arm for the farmhouse door when some invisible force seemed to grasp her by the shoulders, stopping her in her tracks. Her back arched, her one free arm thrust upward like a ballerina on a music box, she pivoted slightly and fell a step from the door, still cradling her bundle, shielding it from the fall and the bullets that now spattered like a hard, steady rain upon her home.

Ransford stopped running, frozen at the sight of an angel shot dead in front of his eyes. Had he come so far for this? Was he freeing Negroes from bondage or bringing wanton death to innocents? A bullet ripped the front of his pant leg, searing a crimson line in his thigh, when he saw the bundle begin to move. A tiny hand and then a face emerged from under the swaddle. The baby opened its big blue eyes wide and stared, it seemed, straight at Ransford.

What a lovely child, he thought. Lord, she must've been proud of that child. Ransford stood mesmerized at the spectacle for what seemed an eternity, watching the baby rooting for its dead mother's breast. And then the child turned again to face the soldiers, propping itself up with its little, stubby arms. The babe's white, moon-pie face held its strange, passionless expression for a moment before exploding in a full out wail. Its mouth opened, it seemed, wider than its face, bigger than its head, and unleashed a frightful cry. Primal outrage, anger, shock, all took part. Of the untold number of sounds he would hear in his life, Ransford would remember that one. It would always make him shudder.

The gnarly, black-haired sergeant, now off his horse, grasped Ransford by the shoulder and towed him the remaining few steps to safety behind the farmhouse. Ransford never felt his feet move; he just arrived there, where some sixty of the men had found a haven in the farmhouse's shadow. Some collapsed. Some wept. Some just stood staring into each other's eyes, as if verifying their common experience. How could such a sunny, average day turn so brutal, so quickly? In seconds, the smartly-trained column had disintegrated into an exhausted, frightened mob—all confidence gone. Looking back upon the grisly scene they had escaped only made matters worse: a small writhing pile of dead and wounded soldiers, moaning and screaming.

"It's hell out there, I tell you!" one shocked soldier, remarked, staring deadpan at the sight.

"Can't we do a thing? Can't we do a thing for those poor devils?"

"The best we can do for them devils is to stay alive, boys. It's a shootin' gallery out there. Let's start shootin' back at those rebs. The only way to save your brothers is to drive them off that hill! Now let's get to it!"

Sgt. Tinkham's voice suddenly became clear above the madness. Tinkham and some of the other sergeants were exhorting the men to form up and re-take the field, where several dead and wounded men still lay, including Captain Underhill, whose fractured leg was pinned beneath the body of his dead horse.

Ransford and members of his squad took up positions around the edges of the farmhouse, primed their rifles and started firing at the Confederate men standing atop the little hill. It was the first time Ransford ever fired at another man and the strangeness of it gave him pause. Looking through the sighting bead at the end of his Enfield rifle, he lined up on a rebel soldier 300 yards away. He was a young lad, clean shaven, with a red and tattered button-down shirt and baggy gray trousers. Ransford saw him fire and then re-load his musket and fire again workmanlike in the direction of his unit, towards his friends and compatriots. It was hard, he thought, to pull the trigger. But when he noticed out the corner of his eye a Union soldier not far from him on the line recoil from a fresh wound, Ransford refocused, took aim at the red-shirted rebel and fired. It seemed like forever before he squinted and saw the young Confederate lurch forward and fall, mortally wounded from the minié ball that had just passed through his abdomen.

"My God, I've just killed a man," Ransford thought, while re-loading. He continued to fire from the corner of the farmhouse porch, where, above the raging reports of gun fire, all could hear the orphaned infant wailing incessantly.

The sergeants and a first lieutenant from C Company worked to form a line of battle to the right of the farmhouse and ordered a burst of fire upon the enemy position that clearly shook their ranks. They then marched over the road and up the hill, stopping at intervals to fire as they made clear progress, closing the gap between themselves and the rebels to a few hundred paces. At this point, what was left of the rebel contingent turned and ran, galloping back across the field toward the cover of the tree line. Although the men of C and E Companies fired after them, they did not pursue the fleeing enemy. It was late in the day and Lieutenant McRoberts, now the highest-ranking officer on the field, decided they should bury the three men who had been killed and transport their wounded—including Captain Underhill, who was suffering greatly and in shock—back to camp as quickly as possible.

"What's to become of the child, Lieutenant?" asked Ransford as the men worked to bury their fallen comrades and build stretchers for the wounded who couldn't walk.

"I'm thinking we should leave the child to its people, who must be about here somewhere . . .." Lt. McRoberts was ill-prepared for such a question and was concerned, nervous even, about the readiness of his new command to safely return to the division. "Listen, gentlemen, I recognize your concern for the child and I most surely do appreciate it, but I've got to get a badly bruised company back to camp safely. There's no telling what might be coming for us."

The men in Ransford's squad exchanged nervous glances, sharing the same sentiment without speaking.

"With all due respect, we can't leave this baby out here alone for a night much less an hour Lieutenant. Heck sir, we feel responsible, that's all," said Ransford, his emotions welling up as he struggled to explain their point of view.

"Permission to speak, sir?" asked Sgt. Tinkham. "I think the private has a point, sir. There's a baby over there a-wailing who needs tending. Through no fault of her own, the momma's lying dead on her front porch and there ain't no kin in sight. Now we could go looking for folks to take this poor child in but I imagine a bunch of Yanks knockin' on doors in this vicinity wouldn't be the wisest move, especially with the sun going down . . ., with all due respect, sir."

The Lieutenant took off his cap, scratched his head and thought for a moment.

"Of course, of course, you men are right. But I'm telling you, this squad right here, are taking responsibility for this child from now until you find it a safe and satisfactory place to be. You hear me, Sergeant?"

"Yes sir. Thank you, sir!"

"Now gather your gear, I want to be away from this accursed spot in ten minutes!"

The three fallen soldiers and the young mother were buried in shallow graves beneath a peach tree near the farmhouse. The chaplain not being present, one of the men, a preacher's son, spoke a few words over the graves, exhorting the Lord Almighty to take their souls into heaven and, in the case of the young woman, to ask for His special consideration for her baby in the coming years.

"We ask you Lord to be especially mindful of this innocent child and ask our forgiveness for unknowingly bringing such an insult to its life. Please bless this baby, Lord, and know that the 44th will do all in its power to find it a safe home," the Private said, eliciting "amens" from those soldiers gathered around the graves.

Solemnly, the column moved back down the pike toward the brigade, nervously alert for any sign of the enemy as stretcher bearers bore the wounded at the rear of the line. Despite his protestations, Ransford had been elected by the squad to carry the baby, who wriggled and squealed constantly in the crook of his arm. The tiny child's inconsolable crying, which varied between whimpers and full on howls, made the men uncomfortable. With any pretense of normal order in their ranks lost, Private Hickok made comical faces in front of the babe in a vain attempt to get it to stop crying. Others made odd whooping noises or attempted other distractions, to no avail. Finally, as Private Whitney began singing a lullaby, the baby stopped fussing and stared up into the Private's grubby face, not smiling but content, at least momentarily. It was a popular tune for the time, *Aura Lea*, and the Private sang it with a surprising sweetness that seemed out of place for the circumstances:

> "…*When the blackbird in the Spring,*
> *'On the willow tree,*
> *Sat and rocked, I heard him sing,*
> *Singing Aura Lea.*

Aura Lea, Aura Lea,
Maid with golden hair;
Sunshine came along with thee,
And swallows in the air.

Aura Lea, Aura Lea,
Maid with golden hair;
Sunshine came along with thee,
And swallows in the air.
In thy blush the rose was born,
Music, when you spake,
Through thine azure eye the morn,
Sparkling seemed to break.
Aura Lea, Aura Lea,
Birds of crimson wing,
Never song have sung to me,
As in that sweet spring.

Aura Lea! the bird may flee,
The willow's golden hair
Swing through winter fitfully,
On the stormy air.
Yet if thy blue eyes I see,
Gloom will soon depart;
For to me, sweet Aura Lea
Is sunshine through the heart…"

"She's a right pretty little thing, isn't she?" said Private Earles, staring down at the baby. "What should we call her? Shouldn't we call her somethin'?"

"I don't know as we have the right to call her a name since we ain't kin and all," offered Private Hickok.

"Looks like we're all the kin she's got at the moment," Ransford said.

"Aura Lea. I vote we call her Aura Lea until we learn anything to the contrary," Jack said, to which everyone agreed. "Aura Lea it is!"

"Far be it for me to interrupt, gentlemen, but I'm guessing Miss Aura Lea is going to be getting hungry soon. Any ideas on how we're going to accommodate her?" asked Private Whitney.

"There's a couple o' milk cows I seen back at brigade headquarters a few days back. Maybe we can get 'er some milk there?"

"That's a good idea, Solomon," Ransford agreed. "When we get back to camp we'll go get Aura Lea some milk and maybe clean her up a bit."

Sgt. Tinkham concurred but warned them they'd need an officer's pass before they went off on a humanitarian errand. "I'll accompany whoever you choose, but we're going to need approval from someone with bars bigger than mine," he said.

The rest of the march passed without incident as the column cleared the Union sentries and filed past many curious onlookers in camp, who were drawn to the procession by the sounds of the baby crying, quite unusual for an army in the field. Well past sundown the bedraggled men made it back to the 44th's encampment, crying baby and the wounded in tow. Before long the wounded, some severely, were brought under the care of Hospital Steward Howard Frothingham, who had established a makeshift field hospital on the outer edges of the camp.

Ransford, Sgt. Tinkham, and several members of the squad sought the counsel of Lt. Knox, who had recently been elevated to the position of adjutant. While sympathetic, he was nonetheless circumspect about their plan to sustain the child with the brigade's milk cows.

"This thing you're trying to do is laudable, men. And I support it within the limits of my office, of course. However, I must say that your plan is somewhat short sighted," he explained while gazing with wonder at the baby. "Think this through with me: were you to get permission to feed the child with milk from the brigade's cows, what will happen tomorrow or the next day when we're ordered to the front to fight the Army of Northern Virginia? Will the child accompany us into battle? Will I have to leave a valued squad behind to tend to a baby while the rest of E Company is engaged on the field? No, gentlemen, I think we must search for a more permanent solution, one that is satisfactory for both the child and for the 44th. Ideas?"

The men had thought the brigade cow idea was brilliant, but now realized that it was limited in both its scope and its lack of permanence. Some, those who had already become smitten with the child, had even harbored the fantasy that they could both fight and care for the baby collectively, perhaps throughout the course of the war. The Lieutenant had brought them all back to reality, but no clear solution presented itself. With some reluctance, Jack stepped forward, offering an option.

"Perhaps . . ." Jack spoke haltingly. "Perhaps, I know of a possible answer to this conundrum, but I must say it is an odd and possibly unsuitable option."

"I'm listening, Private," said Lt. Knox sternly.

"Well, Lieutenant, please understand that I present this with a degree of hesitancy . . . but I am familiar with a certain group of ladies who are, for want of a better term, attached to General Hooker's division. Are you by any chance familiar with them, sir?"

"I am not familiar with them, Private, but I am aware of their presence."

"Well, there happens to be one of my acquaintance, who has in recent weeks given birth to a child and who might—might, mind you—be open to an arrangement involving caring for this child, at least on a temporary basis." Jack spoke these words as if suffering from a recent tooth extraction. Some in the squad smirked while others stared at him as if he were speaking a foreign tongue. But the Lieutenant apprehended his meaning and pondered it long and hard.

"I am both repulsed and intrigued by the solution you are offering, Private Finnegan, and I also recognize the discomfort with which you rendered it. You were loath to admit these things, yet were willing to do so for the sake of your unit and this child. Commendable."

"Thank you, sir, I'm glad you see the merit in it. I, on the other hand, am not sure I do. Perhaps, it's the fever?"

"No fever, Private Finnegan; it's called concern for your fellow man," said Lt. Knox, who then launched into a hastily conceived strategy that had all the hallmarks of a battle plan. "Alright then, here's how we're going to handle this 'conundrum' as you put it: First a few of you will go with haste to get a goodly supply of cow's milk from the brigade cows to feed the baby short term. I will give you a pass for this mission. Second, and this is the more difficult part, I will endeavor to secure a pass from our commanding officer, Colonel Stryker, that will allow Private Finnegan and another soldier—I'm not sparing all of you—to accompany him to the rear where they might seek the 'camp angel' that Private Finnegan referred to earlier. Here he will attempt to strike a bargain with said angel regarding our needful baby here . . .. Does this sound suitable to this child's 'uncles' assembled here?"

The men, who felt pride at being called Aura Lea's "uncles", glanced among themselves and gave their assent by nods and grunts and the plan was laid. All (except Ransford) agreed that Ransford should accompany Jack on his mission to secure a wet nurse for Aura Lea. And Private Whitney and Private Hickok were asked to secure milk for the baby from brigade headquarters. Armed with a pass from Lieutenant Knox they made their way through the quilt of interconnected campsites that provided a home for the brigade and were, after quite a bit of tale telling and cajoling, able to procure sustaining cow's milk for the baby. While they were gone, Lt. Knox ventured past two sentries into an adjacent tent to meet with Colonel Stryker in hopes of securing a pass that would allow for safe passage through the lines.

The men overheard a heated discussion ensue as the Lieutenant described the unique circumstances and the novel approach to solving the problem.

"It's bad enough, Lieutenant, that I have been humiliated by my subordinates and their 'connections' in Albany into moving our regiment from a perfectly comfortable situation back in Yorktown to a much more intemperate circumstance here, but now you tell me I need to worry about some rebel baby and make special accommodations as if it were my own. Is that what you are telling me, Lieutenant?"

"In a manner of speaking, yes, Colonel. But I am also presenting this as an opportunity to demonstrate to your men, who view this child with great affection, that you are a beneficent leader, someone who cares for them and their interests," Lt. Knox explained with great deference to his commander's ego.

"I see you are a man of some eloquence, Lt. Knox, and that is partly why I made you my adjutant. I will accede to your plan and grant a pass for these soldiers, but only with your assurances that this will be handled with efficiency and discretion. Can you assure me of that, Lieutenant?"

"Indeed I can, sir. I can vouch for these men."

Lt. Knox emerged from the tent with two passes, one for Private Finnegan and the other for Private Densmore, allowing them free passage and all accommodations necessary to travel to the headquarters of General Hooker accompanied by an infant child "in the interest of army business."

"I can spare you for no more than 48 hours. I don't expect the army to move until then, but after that you will be considered absent without leave. Do you understand me?" he said, looking directly at Jack and Ransford. "First thing tomorrow morning be on the first boat you can catch down the Pawmunky River. Hooker is supposed to be camped around Yorktown, licking his wounds. God speed, gentlemen!"

"Yes sir . . . and thank you sir!"

After a long and sleepless night tending to Aura Lee, Jack and Ransford bundled the baby and set out on their mission with the regiment's blessings. As they made their way out of camp, soldiers, many of whom they didn't know, wished them well and blessings to the child.

"There goes Miss Aura Lea. She's the 44th's baby now. You boys take good care o' her."

A few miles down the pike, with help from Col. Stryker's pass, they were able to board a steamer filled with men, many of them wounded, that brought them to White House and the great military encampment that had been established there. Another vessel took them to the docks at Yorktown, which was bustling with activity, wagons loaded with supplies and stagecoaches brimming with travelers of all sorts. Jack inquired of a sergeant guarding a check point at a busy intersection as to the location of Hooker's division and he directed them to an encampment near the southern outskirts of the city, not far from the 44th's original bivouac a few weeks earlier.

"And might you know the whereabouts of the ladies of the camp, Sergeant?"

The Sergeant looked him over and then Ransford, holding the baby, who was fussing considerably.

"Don't you two boys have enough to worry about, Private?" he said, motioning to the baby.

"That we do, Sergeant," Jack said, showing him the pass. "And as you can see this happens to be army business, so I'd be most grateful if you'd convey any contributory information you might possess."

"Well, yes indeed, Private . . . .. Said establishment was moved recently to a pretty little red brick house with white trim over on Bacon Street, not far from General Hooker's headquarters. Over that way," said the Sergeant, pointing to the southeast.

"Much obliged, Sergeant," said Ransford, as they both began navigating through the quaint colonial city until they came upon the house, nestled on a cobblestone street and guarded by two sentries at a gate in a white picket fence ringing it. After presenting Colonel Stryker's pass to the guards, Jack and Ransford knocked on a large mahogany door, which was opened by a negro servant, elaborately dressed in colonial garb.

"Yes sirs, may I help you?"

"Indeed, you may, my good man. Would Madame Sophie be available?"

"Who may I say is asking for her, sir?" the servant, who was quite formal, asked while looking the two shabbily-attired soldiers up and down.

"Jack, Jack Finnegan."

"Indeed. Please make yourselves comfortable in the sitting room," he said, gesturing to an elaborately furnished parlor where a trio of officers were being entertained by three elaborately adorned young women flitting fans and fawning over the captains. They all paused, however, when Jack, Ransford, and Aura Lea entered the room, regarding them with great curiosity. Just then a woman who figured to be Madame Sophie entered the room.

"Jack! Jack! Jack! Is it really you?" A jubilant woman, tall but curvaceous, with a dramatic main of curled, yellow hair piled upon her head, appeared before them. Fluttering dramatic eyelashes and smiling broadly, she engaged Jack with her sharp dark eyes, glancing quickly at Ransford and Aura Lea. "What on earth have you brought me, Jack?"

"Dearest Sophie!" Jack's flowery tone matched hers, theatrical and lacking sincerity. "It has been some time my love, but you look as ravishing as ever."

"Oh, thank you Jack; you always were a flatterer! Now tell me, sir, what brings you to my establishment and who are your friends?"

"Always to the point, Sophie. This is my friend, Ransford, and this lovely child is, well, we call her Aura Lea . . . .. If we could remove to a more private setting, I'd like to discuss a matter, a proposition, with you."

"Very pleased to meet you," Madame Sophie nodded to them politely. "I am a simple woman of business, Jack, and as you can see, the house does have regular clientele at the moment. But, for an old friend, I can certainly spare what appears to be some unproductive time, if you catch my meaning?"

With a turn of her skirts, Madame Sophie led them to the kitchen toward the back of the house and, upon closing the door behind them, proceeded to light into Jack quite differently from her earlier demeanor.

"Jack Finnegan, you foolish scallywag! Why would you come into my establishment, looking like you've been dragged through the mud and smelling like a wet dog with a similarly ripe friend—no offense, sir—and toting a baby? A baby, Jack?"

"Let me explain, Sophie . . . .."

"Oh, please do, and I'd be grateful if you made it quick. I love you, Jack, but right now you're not good for business!"

Jack went on to explain, with some embellishment, the elaborate circumstances of the previous two days. He described the great quandary that faced the men and their special bond with Aura Lea, how they felt an obligation to the child and her dead mother. They needed to know the child would be safe and away from the front while the battles raged, and their future was uncertain. From a previous visit to her establishment, when Madame Sophie's charges were encamped outside Fort Monroe along with the soldiers, Jack had been told that one of her charges, a young woman named Sally, had recently given birth. Might it be possible, he asked, that this woman would consider accommodating two children, at least for the duration of the campaign. Afterward, Jack postulated, the regiment could seek a more suitable, permanent arrangement.

Madame Sophie sat quietly through the entire fascinating tale before speaking. "I am sincerely moved, Jack, truly I am. But there are a few matters that must be discussed before any arrangement could possibly be made," she said.

"I thought there might be, Sophie . . .."

"Firstly, any commitment of this kind would be entirely up to the young lady. Sally is already quite in demand, if you know what I mean. Second, would be the matter of compensation. Not only does the lady deserve special consideration for this great service she would be performing for the brave lads of the 44th, but I would venture that her patron—that would be yours truly—deserves some level of recompense as well. Wouldn't you gentlemen agree?"

"Why yes Sophie, we anticipated this very issue. The men of the 44th are prepared to offer the young lady the sum of $10 each week for as long as she is providing this service."

"That's most generous Jack, and that would help Sally reduce her work load to accommodate the increased parental attention necessary to account for the needs of two infants," she conceded, sounding much more conciliatory than before. "And, what, pray tell, would be my compensation?"

Before Jack could answer, Ransford, who had remained quite silent through the entire negotiation, cleared his throat. "Jack, might I have a word?"

"Certainly, Ransford. Sophie, could you spare us for but a moment while I consult with my partner?"

She nodded, but looked irked at the interruption while Ransford and Jack stepped out onto the back porch.

"Alright, out with it, lad. We're close to reaching an accommodation here," Jack said with some urgency.

"Well, here it is," Ransford replied uncomfortably. "It just doesn't feel right, Jack!"

"Of course it doesn't feel right, Ransford. There's nothing about any of this that is, as you put it, right. The war's not right. The battle wasn't right. The fact that Aura Lea's momma died certainly isn't right . . .. But here we are, needing to make this as right as possible under the circumstances so we can get back to the war."

"All true. But do we really want this beautiful child's life to start off this way? Is that how we settle our vow to Aura Lea's mother, by leaving her daughter with these camp ladies? I'm not passing judgement on these women. But heck, Jack, they'd only be doing this service for us for the money, not because they love this child."

"I'm not saying you're wrong, lad, but who on earth are we going to find—in the next 24 hours mind you—who would possibly love a stranger's baby?"

They stared at each other for what seemed like a minute.

"A church?"

"I suppose you might be right, Ransford. But which church and do we have time to find a Christian ministry in Yorktown willing to accept a rebel baby from Union soldiers?" asked Jack, exasperated. "I'm willing to give it a go, if you are. But we've got to agree that we come back here if we are running out of time. Agreed?"

"Agreed."

Jack explained their thinking to Sophie who was losing patience with the entire situation. She nonetheless accepted that all alternatives should be explored before the child was left in her care.

"I may be a business woman, Jack, but I'm not a heartless business woman. If we need to leave this place in a hurry I'd greatly prefer knowing the child was in good hands," Sophie admitted. "Now I happen know there are some thriving congregations a few blocks over."

"Thank you kindly, Miss Sophie," Ransford said, tipping his cap to the madam, before leaving the pretty red brick house on Bacon Street with Jack and Aura Lea.

They walked two blocks north to the aptly named Church Street and soon came across a simple stone building that had suffered some damage, it seemed, from a recent artillery round. Workmen were busy trying to repair a gaping hole in Grace Episcopal Church's eastern wall while parishioners came and went through its two heavy oak doors.

The two soldiers entered the church, which was illuminated internally by numerous candles and the sunlight that streamed through the hole in its wall. As their eyes adjusted they could make out the silhouettes of parishioners huddled in pews praying and a minister standing at the center of a resplendent altar embellished in fine wood, brass, and flowers. The preacher was not sermonizing from the pulpit that commanded a high right corner of the altar; rather, he was speaking informally to those assembled before him, a mix of parishioners, travelers, and even Union soldiers who had sought the comfort of scripture during the discomforting time.

Jack and Ransford made their way into the chapel, moving toward the altar, but keeping to the outer aisle. As they drew near, the rector and members of the flock were soon distracted by the fussing of Aura Lea, who was whimpering noticeably despite Ransford's best efforts to distract her.

"Come forward, gentlemen, and please bring the little one to me," Father McKeon said in a warm and welcoming way.

"Thank you, Father," said Jack, aware of the others watching them. "We come to you on a matter of a sensitive nature, er, involving this child here."

"Certainly, certainly," he said, recognizing immediately the need for privacy. "Pardon me for a moment please, friends, while I meet with these soldiers in my vestry." Father McKeon, a tall, stately fellow, perhaps 50, with close-cropped raven black hair and wearing a simple white robe with a leafy green stole draped over his shoulders, ushered them into a room to the right of the altar and offered them a seat. "Now tell me boys, are you fresh from the front?"

"That we are, Father," said Ransford as he adjusted Aura Lea's blanket. "And, I'll get right to it, sir, we've been sent by our commanding officers to seek out a fitting home for Aura Lea here. Well, we call her Aura Lea, but, truthfully, we don't know her real name. You see her mama's passed away."

"I see," the preacher said gravely. "So, you boys have left the war on a humanitarian errand, condoned by your superior officers. But why, may I ask, have you brought this lovely child to me?"

"Father, my name is Jack and this is Ransford, and we were delegated by pretty much the entire 44th New York Infantry Regiment to find a suitable home for Aura Lea. You see,

187

Father, it pains me to say it, but we feel responsible for her mother's demise." Jack proceeded to explain the sad circumstances behind their predicament, adding that it had been Ransford's idea to seek out a church to render assistance. "My initial approach was quite pragmatic, Father, but I realize now that it was unsuitable for the lass, who we've all grown quite fond of . . .. In fact, we've taken to calling ourselves her uncles. Aura Lea has a whole regiment of uncles."

"Indeed, that does sound like a formidable group of uncles," said the minister, smiling and shaking his head from side to side as he pondered the situation. "As I'm sure you gentlemen will appreciate, we find ourselves in a most untenable circumstance, complicated greatly by your very presence here. Normal life in Yorktown has ceased to exist and my parish has swollen with needful families, many suffering great losses. Many have died and many are missing. And it is only through a profound faith in God's mysterious purpose that we are finding our way through this darkness.

"I shall be frank, boys: we do not like that you are here, regardless of the purpose or even if we may share some of your beliefs. But none of the pain or resentment or disdain we may hold for you and your invading army should be visited upon the lovely innocent you have brought to us. As a man I am conflicted, but as a servant of God my duty is clear: I must do all that I can to save her."

Relieved almost to a point of tears, Ransford reached out with his free arm and hugged the minister, surprising him and imparting a grimy residue upon the rector's pristine white vestments. "I'm sorry, Father, but thank you, thank you so very much!"

"That will do, son. That will do. Please make no mistake, I'm not absolving you men or your unit for this or any other injustice you may have committed while invading our land. Terrible things have happened here and it may well take generations for these many wounds to heal, if they ever can. But today you present me with an opportunity to help heal at least one; we may be able to make one thing better."

"Yes, Father, we share that hope."

"Good. Good." And then, without further discussion, Father McKeon left the vestry briefly and returned with a young woman. She was pretty, perhaps in her early twenties, with dark brown hair pulled into a neat ball behind her head. She wore a tidy white blouse tucked into a long, gray, patterned skirt that gave her the appearance of a school marm. As Father McKeon introduced the woman to the men, her face, which had been tilted downward toward the floor when she entered, rose up to reveal a melancholy expression, a sadness that appeared to weigh down and beleaguer her otherwise handsome features.

"Men, I'd like to introduce Mrs. Talmadge. This fine lady has been indispensable to my work in comforting my flock."

"Very pleased to meet you, ma'am," said Ransford, removing his cap.

"Indeed, it is good to meet you, Mrs. Talmadge," parroted Jack.

"Thank you, gentlemen," she spoke politely and softly, glancing at each of them quickly and then back at the Father, as if questioning why she had been summoned. At this point, Aura Lea began to whimper demonstrably in Jack's arms, catching the young woman by surprise. "And what is it you have there?"

"This happens to be Miss Aura Lea. And these young soldiers have brought her to us, Mrs. Talmadge."

"Why on earth is this child with these soldiers, Father? And where, pray tell, is her mama?"

Father McKeon explained Aura Lea's unique predicament to Mrs. Talmadge and how Jack and Ransford had come from the front looking for a safe and loving Christian home for the child.

He explained that he had committed the church to finding a suitable home, even if only temporarily, for the orphaned child.

"Why yes, of course, Father," she said, her voice beginning to tremble.

"I wonder, my dear—and I know this is asking much of you and you are entirely free to decline without any negative judgement whatsoever—if you wouldn't mind taking care of young Aura Lea here, at least until we can find her a home among our congregation?"

"Yes, Father, I would be most honored to look after this lovely child." She reached out enthusiastically for the baby, tears beginning to well in her deep brown eyes. Ransford handed Aura Lea to Mrs. Talmadge without hesitation. The baby seemed immediately at home in the arms of the young woman, whose face, once somber and cast in shadow, appeared suddenly revived and fascinated.

"That is music to our ears, Mrs. Talmadge. Now would you mind finding this poor child some milk and possibly a warm bath? Meanwhile, I believe these Union soldiers are obligated to return to the front, yes?"

"Yes, sir, we are, but first I would like to make my good byes to Aura Lea, if that's alright?"

"Of course, son."

Ransford and Jack gathered around Aura Lea, who had found a comfortable place nestled in Mrs. Talmadge's arms.

"Miss Aura Lea," said Ransford, looking down into the child's big azure eyes. "Me, Jack here, and all of your uncles at the 44th want you to know we are truly sorry for the trouble we brought upon you. But we're not sorry we got to know you, even for a short time. It has been an honor, young lady. Now we feel much better knowing that you are here, in this church, with these good Christian people. And I'm sure Mrs. Talmadge here will take wonderful care of you. I can tell she's a fine woman."

"I couldn't have said it any better, Ransford," said Jack. "Miss Aura Lea, it is our fervent hope that you will thrive with these good people. And perhaps we—myself and her hundreds or so other uncles—might be permitted to write to her occasionally, Father?"

"Yes, of course lad."

Mrs. Talmadge left the vestry with Aura Lea held tightly to her bosom, all the while gazing into the baby's eyes and smiling.

"That young woman lost her own baby to sickness just two months ago. I do believe this is the first I've seen her smile since that terrible day," Father McKeon confided. "I will see how things progress between them, but my sense is what we've done here today will help heal more than one wound." It was welcome news to Jack and Ransford, who found it comforting to know that they had left the child with someone who valued, even needed, her.

After exchanging addresses and other pertinent information along with a donation to the church to help provide for Aura Lea's care, Jack and Ransford made their way back into the streets of Yorktown. Silently they walked several blocks to the docks where they boarded a paddleboat bound for the federal camp at White House. Throughout the journey up the York River the boat chugged past some of the loveliest scenery Ransford could have imagined: great sweeping plantations comprised of columned mansions and tidy collections of outbuildings, herds of livestock grazing in rolling green pastures, and grand trees—oaks, magnolias, and maples—punctuating the landscape. It was like a living painting everywhere he looked; except occasionally, the painting was marred by pockets of devastation—places where a mansion had been reduced to a smoldering ruin, odd black craters pockmarking the meadows, and the bodies of dead horses and livestock littering the fields. These places marked where the advancing Army of the Potomac had encountered a desperate enemy and pushed them back toward Richmond.

A gentle breeze brought forth a sweet unfamiliar fragrance, possibly from blooming azaleas, to the air and both men felt a calm wash over them as the boat plied its way through the bucolic countryside. They sat back on their packs and, perhaps for the first time in weeks, relaxed.

"Well Jack, I think we've accomplished our mission!"

"My dear boy, I believe you are correct. Well done!" Jack proclaimed, leaning his head back and gazing up toward the heavens. "All we have to worry about now, Ransford, is the war."

They both laughed.

"Speaking of the war, Jack. You still haven't told me how on earth you—a child of privilege you called it, right?—ended up in this predicament."

"I suppose now is a good time for a good story, eh Ransford?"

Jack described how he was born into the lap of luxury in the bustling heart of New York's elite. As a child he was tended to by governesses and private tutors, who pampered and trained him for a princely life among the wealthy denizens of New York's upper crust.

"The only catch, as they say, was that my lovely mother and my dear father were not married, not in a conventional way, if you get my meaning."

"No Jack, I'm sorry but I don't get your meaning," replied Ransford, who was truly in the dark.

Jack explained that his mother had been his father's longstanding mistress. Often, he said, powerful, wealthy men like his father, the owner of several fabulously successful companies, maintained their mistresses in separate households that were just as opulent as those inhabited by his legal wife and children. In this case, Jack said, his mother wanted for nothing, being treated to all the wealth and privilege that his father could provide. What's more, the man, who Jack declined to name, treated Jack with great affection and showered him with gifts, providing the boy with opportunities to travel and experience the finer things in life.

"I went to the finest schools, learned French, played tennis and dined at the best restaurants. That, for me, was normal," said Jack in a resigned, whimsical way. "That was until my good father—the great industrialist, the great provider—died suddenly one cold February night. I heard he'd eaten a bad oyster or something. He fell incredibly ill and then, within a few days, he was gone."

"I'm so sorry, Jack!"

"Thank you, lad. But that wasn't nearly the worst of it. You see, his legal wife, the harpy, in no short order turned viciously on my mother. She'd resented mother for years, secretly seething at her place in her husband's life, yet unable to do anything about the arrangement, something that was, and still is, a common custom among powerful men in high society . . .. Not much different from kings and princes and sultans throughout time."

"You lived in a strange world, Jack! Never would have happened back in Corinth. But go on." Ranford was fascinated.

"Within weeks of my father's death we were completely cut off. Couldn't pay for the apartments, the servants, the cooks, maids—they all left us, of course—and by April we were out on the streets looking for a new home." He paused and took a heavy sigh before continuing. "My mother secured a temporary apartment from a friend, but that was an exception as most of her "friends" turned a cold shoulder to us as soon as word got out that we were *personae non gratae* and basically penniless."

Jack explained how he was forced to drop out of Harvard and returned home to support his mother, a sweet, lovely and cultured woman, but someone without the intestinal fortitude for survival. Jack sold off some of her jewelry to stake him with enough money to buy his way into the more lucrative card games popular among *nouveau* rich young men at the time.

"I found I was quite good at separating these arrogant twits from their parents' money and, with that, I was able to put my mother up in fairly adequate accommodations. It would never be the same, of course."

"Damnation Jack, that's quite some story," Ransford said sincerely. "I'm truly sorry you and your momma fell so far so fast. It must've been hard on her especially."

"It was, Ransford. She never quite recovered. There was a sadness about her that reminds me of that young mother back in Yorktown," Jack halted. "She could never quite shake that sadness, whether it was the sudden loss of my father, who I'm convinced she loved dearly, or the fact that someone could be so cruel to her . . .. Well, one beautiful spring morning she went and took her life . . .. Just drank a full bottle of laudanum, went to sleep, and never woke."

Ransford was struck silent by this rare personal admission from Jack, who spoke a great deal but rarely revealed anything about his true feelings. He looked over at his friend, head down, staring at the deck of the boat. Ransford put his arm around Jack's shoulders and looked out at the northern Virginia countryside passing by as the sun was setting in the west.

Before long Jack took a deep breath, thanked Ransford for listening to his "maudlin tale" and, feeling obligated to continue his story, explained that he had quickly sunk into a state of debauchery. While his abilities as a star pitcher for the New York Knickerbockers baseball team brought him some level of fame it hardly did much for his fortune. Before long the combination of gambling, womanizing, drinking, and other excesses caught up with him, leading to the unfortunate turn of events that forced him to flee to Saratoga. It was there that he'd hit rock bottom, wagering more than he could possibly cover in a poker game at one of the town's swanky casinos.

"Another thing about wealthy, powerful men Ransford: they always travel with a particular breed of well-dressed troglodyte who are only too happy to bash your skull with a pistol handle if you should offend their master," Jack pointed out, reminding Ransford of the day they'd met. "Enlisting in the 44th was my best, and frankly only, option at not only saving my skull but starting fresh."

"That's an incredible story, Jack! Sounds like a book you should write some day."

"I don't have the patience to write a book, Ransford. Maybe you can write it for me," he said, patting his friend on the shoulder.

"I'd be honored, Jack . . .. So, how is this part of your story working out so far?"

"Honestly, Ransford, I'm finding this whole adventure strangely enjoyable. Meeting new and interesting people, wearing strange clothes, traveling to exotic locales. It's kind of growing on me!" Jack said, sounding much more like himself.

Ransford felt relieved.

"But seriously, lad, I've learned something this last year. I've been with some of the prettiest and wealthiest people in the world, but when all is said and done I much prefer the company of rubes like you. You say what you mean and mean what you say. And at the end of the day, you have more sense than a room full of professors."

"Thanks for the compliment, Jack, or at least I think I should thank you."

They were jostled by the high-pitched scream of a steam whistle announcing their arrival at White House Plantation. It looked like the entire Army of the Potomac was spread out before them: high-peaked white tents dotted every acre of the sprawling fields, various regiments marched to and fro, and cavalry detachments galloped off in all directions. It had the look and feel of a camp readying for engagement.

As men grabbed their packs and scuffled off the boat, Ransford and Jack approached a naval officer on the deck, asking him if the boat would now be traveling up river.

"Not until morning, boys. Too many reb snipers to chance a night trip. You can camp here the night." He pointed to a sergeant on the docks below and suggested they ask him about accommodations. For his part, the sergeant, who was busy ordering troops and teamsters about on the dock, briskly suggested they visit the hospital tent located along the river bank a few hundred yards to the west. There, some tents were set aside for soldiers in transit.

In the waning light, Ransford and Jack approached what turned out to be a series of tents devoted to the care of wounded men who were arriving sporadically in wagons and via stretcher bearers. Other men, sporting white bandages over bloody appendages, walked and hobbled up the field hospital, some supported by comrades. Most tents were open on the sides, letting air flow freely in the hot and humid conditions, and revealing a series of illuminated tables laid out in a grid roughly ten across and ten deep.

As they drew closer, it was clear that a desperate scene was unfolding at each table where a surgeon or nurse tended to a man mangled by some ungodly wound. Horrid screams filled the night as surgeons sawed shattered limbs from all-too conscious men who were being pinned down, writhing and kicking, by teams of soldiers. Other men, some appearing to be negroes, perhaps emancipated slaves, fetched buckets of water from the river and ran back into the tents, sloshing the water onto blood soaked operating tables to prepare them for the next wounded man. On another side of the tent, stretcher bearers carried the bodies of those who had ultimately succumbed to their wounds, laying each in a lengthy row in the matted, gloomy field. It looked for all the world like some sort of ghoulish factory, laid out with a kind of logic that was designed to efficiently process the dead and dying.

Appalled by the sight, Ransford and Jack instinctively detoured around the entire complex, looking for someone who wasn't engaged in a life or death activity or something resembling the transit tents that had been described to them. When they reached the far western side of the complex they could see farther up river. Along the bank a small collection of tents with a smattering of soldiers gathered around fires. As they passed, they felt compelled to look back once more upon the gory but fascinating scene. Off to their right, they could perceive the outlines of two shirtless men, hard at work, plying a pitchfork and a spade into a pile of some sort and depositing objects onto a wheelbarrow. As the scene came into focus, Ransford could clearly see that the pile was composed of limbs, nothing but dismembered arms and legs, pale and bleeding from the ragged edges of their respective stumps. The men, either soldiers or black men, it wasn't clear in the evening light, were heaping the gory pieces into the barrow methodically as if they were piling wood or completing a mindless chore. With the wheelbarrow now brimming with a perverse pile of disembodied limbs, one of the men hoisted the load, rolled it a few hundred feet to a recently dug hole, and tipped it upwards, allowing the bloody remains to tumble into the pit.

Ransford and Jack proceeded to the campsite silently. They joined several men gathered about a campfire and nodded acknowledgements all around. After a skimpy meal of hard tack and coffee, the two men, weary from their long eventful journey, laid their bed rolls out in one of the tents and fell off to sleep. Ransford slept fitfully, however, unable to get images from the hospital tents out of his mind, particularly the one of the wheel barrow.

The next morning Jack and Ransford drank their mugs of coffee and headed to the docks, once again circling the hospital tent, which appeared just as busy with its grisly work as it had been the night before. Unconsciously, the men turned their heads away, looking toward the south at the vast military encampment occupying the area. The camp was buzzing, like a hive, with activity.

They boarded a smaller boat that promised to bring them and a small contingent of reinforcements up the Pawmunkey River within a few miles of the 44th's encampment. Ransford felt anxious to return to his regiment, especially now that talk of imminent battle was on everyone's lips. Soon, the army would be on the move; the only questions were where and when.

Jack and Ransford found their way into camp by late afternoon and were greeted like conquering heroes by much of the regiment. Upon learning of the successful resolution of their mission, rank and file soldiers, even those they didn't know, called out their praises as they passed through the camp.

"Huzzah!!! Aura Lea has been saved!"

"The prodigal sons have returned!"

"Long live the 44th!"

"Thank you, brave souls! Hoo-ray!"

Embarrassed by the attention, the two men retreated to the section of the camp occupied by Company E, whose members happily engulfed them. After much back-slapping and hubbub, Ransford and Jack sat down near a campfire and recounted their tale, much to the fascination of their brothers-in-arms. They were peppered with questions, all dutifully answered, some with occasional embellishment from Jack.

"All right men, looks like you've had your fun," Sergeant Tinkham chimed in suddenly, as was his way. "Welcome back, wayward lads. Glad I didn't have to send a squad out looking for you. Now it's time we all got back to the business of soldiering."

"Good evening, Sergeant Tinkham, so good to be home!" said Jack wryly.

"And it's marvelous to have you back, Private Finnegan. Are the accommodations suitable?" asked the Sergeant sarcastically.

"Lovely, sir, just lovely."

"Well, that's dandy, Private. But let's not get too cozy, gentlemen. We're moving out in the morning. Got a bit of marching to do before breakfast!"

The Sergeant went on the explain that the entire division would be moving forward along the south bank of the Pawmunkey River well before dawn. Each man was ordered to take provisions for three days and to procure 60 cartridges.

"That's a lot of rounds, ain't it, Sergeant?" asked Private Earles.

"I'm just passing down what I've been told, Private, but if we get into a scrape tomorrow, you'll be glad you've got 'em," Sgt. Tinkham replied. "I'm not going to put flowers and bows on it, boys, the rebel army is up that road and Brigadier General Fitz John Porter wants us to go up there with the whole Fifth Corps and take 'em on. That's what we came here to do. Best we do it, do it well, and go home."

That was about as inspirational a speech as the Sergeant had ever uttered and the men were duly impressed.

"Here, here, Sergeant!"

"Let's get 'er done!"

Meanwhile, the camp had swung into action in all quarters—riders on horseback coming and going, wagons laden with provisions and ammunition being positioned, and lines of men requisitioning their allocations of cartridges and supplies from their quartermaster. After getting their share of provisions, the men fell out of line and returned to their squads for what many felt would be their last full dinner for a while. The lack of specificity in their orders—fall into line at 3:30 a.m., march north, and bring provisions for three days—left many anxious about what might lay ahead. Considerable speculation was ladled up along with the beef stew consumed at dinner.

"What do you boys think the generals are up to? This another Centerville? All march and no action?" Private Hickok offered up, almost hopefully, as they ate around their campfire.

"Well, you never know with generals," said Whitney. "But it's a little different story down here. I mean we're in Johnny Reb's backyard now."

"Private Whitney's got a point, at least judging from what Ransford and I witnessed during our travels," added Jack. "We saw signs of serious fighting, considerable destruction, and, well, many wounded men all the way here. I hate to be the bearer of objectionable news, fellows, but the 44th is about as close to Richmond as anyone. We are at the mouth of the proverbial lion's den."

"And that lion hasn't got any place to go," added Ransford. "She's got to turn and fight to protect her den and her cubs. And she's spittin' mad!"

The men sat back silently, assessing the gravity of their circumstances; some puffed on pipes, some poked the fire with sticks, others just stared into the flames intently, each man suddenly alone with his thoughts and his doubts.

"So, it's on then," said Private Hickok.

"It's on, Solomon," replied Ransford gravely.

"If it's on then, boys, I think we're ready as we're ever gonna be," added Private Earles. "And I guess it's gonna be God's will whatever happens to us, right boys?"

"It might just be God's will, son, but I'd still suggest you hit what you're aiming at and keep to your training," said Ransford.

"Amen to that," replied Private Whitney. "I believe the Lord looks kindly on those that are well prepared and work hard."

"And ain't nobody work harder than the men of the 44th, right boys?" said Hickok, suddenly energized.

"That's right, son. We're not cocky but we're damn good in a fight!"

The men's spirits were buoyed up by the confidence and sincerity pouring out around the fire. Even Jack, usually an insufferable cynic, joined into the pre-battle banter playing out throughout the camp that night. Harmonicas and banjos were played in places; groups of men gathered around the chaplain, who made a point of visiting each campfire and leading every squad in prayer; but many of the men preferred solitude. Each man privately harbored his doubts, you could see it in their eyes, but the squad was confident, and that would help many through the interminably long night. Most went back to their tents and wrote letters home before turning in and trying to sleep.

XII: The Battle of Peake's Turnout

The bugle sounded harsh and unwelcome as morning approached, calling the men to the line hours earlier than normal. Adding to their discomfort, a steady rain greeted them as they emerged from their tents, pelting them and soaking their jackets before they could slurp down their first cup of coffee. Relentless sergeants barked orders with urgent ferocity throughout the camp, driving the men into line without any opportunity for the customary pleasantries associated with waking. Within half an hour the men, practically sleep walking, were in line and ready to form up with the rest of the regiment. They left the campsite intact, tents still standing and cookpots still simmering over firepits, and marched out silently into the darkness like a long zombie army. Several other regiments attached to the Fifth Corps preceded them on the march along an unknown pike that shadowed the Pawmunkey River and the tramping of ten thousand boots combined with wagons, cannon, horses and oxen, made the road a muddy trench. The men slogged along in the driving rain, making slow uncomfortable progress toward an unseen enemy that was "out there somewhere."

The march continued for several hours at a painstakingly slow pace as the men slogged through knee-deep mud, the consistency of pudding. At times, whole companies would abandon the road in favor of the woods and brush along either side; other times they would gather to haul a hopelessly stuck wagon or cannon out of the mud. And, still, the army progressed up the road—New Bridge Road, they later learned—getting ever closer to their objective: a strategically-important railroad crossing at Hanover Court House. This railroad line brought nourishment, supplies, and reinforcements to and from Richmond, an important lifeline that, if cut, would hasten the rebel capital's surrender. As is often the case with foot soldiers, the men would learn more as their mission unfolded, picking up bits and pieces about their plans from other soldiers and officers along the march. A private, after all, was the first to fight, but the last to know.

Mercifully, the rain stopped around mid-morning, replaced by a stifling combination of sun and humidity that made the men's soggy garments clingy and uncomfortable. The 44th was ordered to stop in place and await orders from their commanders, who were now some distance ahead with the main body of the force. Sleep deprived and exhausted, the men took the opportunity to drink lustily from their canteens and take a bite or two from the rock-hard biscuits they kept in their pockets. Before long, they could hear sporadic popping of musket fire off to the north followed by more consistent reports, occasionally punctuated by the unmistakable roar of cannon. The men, many of whom had been laying in the tall grass by the road, jumped up and craned their necks to listen as if to better ascertain what the gunfire meant. Riders came from the front, bringing news of an engagement ahead at a place called Peake's Turnout, near the intersection of New Bridge Road and Ashcake Road some ways south of Hanover Court House. A nasty fight between the 25th New York and a North Carolina regiment was underway and Brigadier General Butterfield's brigade, including boys from the 83rd Pennsylvania and 16th Michigan, were moving up to reinforce the New Yorkers. Still, no orders came telling the 44th to advance, frustrating the men who were itching to come to the aid of their friends.

"What in sam hell we doin' standing here while our friends are up there getting shot at?" Private Hickok said, under his breath, so no nearby officer might hear.

"I'm not disagreeing with you, Private Earles," said Private Whitney. "If it's time to fight, let's get on with it."

"Here, here."

"I'm with you."

For nearly an hour the 44th stood anxiously in place, seeing riders come and go from the front, each time bringing conflicting descriptions of enemy size and position. Some accounts had the North Carolinians routed and on the run through Hanover Court House and others had a strong force of North Carolinians threatening General Butterfield's flank from the south. Meanwhile, the gunfire went on unabated, some of it from farther north and then some, disturbingly, from fairly close, making the men uneasy.

Finally, a rider approached Colonel Stryker at the front of the column and, after an earnest discussion, the commander gave the order to move forward with haste. The men were both relieved and excited to be moving toward the action and their comrades who were obviously engaged in a pitched battle. After a hard, fast march up the road, their rifles at the ready, a volley of fire burst out a grove of trees to the regiment's left, causing the men to pivot left and fire into the woods at an unseen enemy that quickly evaporated. The captains deployed two companies of skirmishers to comb the woods on either side of the regiment so as to avoid any further ambush.

As they came within sight of Peake's Turnout, it was clear that two other regiments—the 2nd Maine and the 25th New York—were clinging to the east side of New Bridge Road and facing a large Confederate force massing for attack across a broad open field. A battery of cannon placed strategically in the center between the two units was blasting away at the rebel center doing significant damage, but still they approached, unflinching across the field. The 44th's leaders called for the men to move smartly and, despite a withering fire from across the field, within minutes the regiment was stretched out along a ditch anchoring the left flank of the fighting line.

By now the sergeants were dressing the line, closing gaps and preparing the men for the advancing columns of several hundred rebel soldiers who were still some 500 yards from their line, but looming and determined. Meanwhile, Col. Stryker and Lieutenant Col. Rice sat on horseback to the rear, surveying the scene and sending out orders via captains and sergeants who shouted encouragement to the boys, most of whom were facing their first real fight.

"Hold the line, men. Whatever you do, hold the line!"

"Load your weapons, lads!"

"Hold your fire until you hear my command!"

Following a rote procedure he'd done a thousand times before at Camp Butterfield, Ransford took a cartridge out of his ammunition satchel. Ripping the paper covering at the top of the cartridge with his teeth, he poured the gun powder down into the muzzle of his Springfield rifle and then used a lengthy steel ramrod to push the 50-caliber lead minié ball deep into the barrel. He then placed a percussion cap on a small nipple attached to the flash pan and cocked the hammer. He was ready to fire.

The North Carolinian unit, which had been ripped apart in places by several well aimed artillery rounds, had advanced stubbornly against the Union forces lining New Bridge Road and was preparing to fire, when an order was given along the Union line to drop to prone position. Hundreds of blue clad soldiers dropped to their bellies on cue, just as the rebel line erupted in gunfire, most of the shots sailing high over the men's heads. After the volley had passed, the men were ordered back to their feet and to fire at will. The fusillade that followed appeared to knock the rebel soldiers back on their heels, felling and staggering many of the men dressed in various shades of gray and butternut. Their commander ordered a retreat into the woods facing the field to the south, which brought up a great cheer from the Union soldiers along the road.

Their relief was short-lived as the Confederate regiments—both the one that had just fled the field and another unit positioned in a clump of woods to the north—began firing upon the entire Union line from the safety of the trees. The 2nd Maine was soon engaged in a desperate struggle with the other rebel regiment that had swept through the forest unseen from the north. A steady fire rained down upon the men of 44th, which found itself trapped and exposed to fire from both rebel regiments, whose soldiers could not be easily ascertained from their hidden positions in the woods.

Ransford saw men falling from wounds to his left and right as puffs of thick gray smoke consistently belched from the foliage to either side. Private Haskell, not ten steps from Ransford, was struck in the belly, doubled over, and fell to the ground. He saw another Company E boy, Private Lawless, writhing in the ditch behind them, his leg spurting blood from a gaping wound to his thigh. Now minié balls were whirring through the air so close to his head that he could feel a hot wind as they passed.

"Go to prone firing positions men!"

"Load and fire prone!"

Sergeant Tinkham or some other sergeant was bellowing orders above the commotion and Ransford and the rest of his squad instinctively reacted, falling to the ground and loading and firing their weapons from the prone position. Although it afforded more protection from enemy bullets, it was an ungainly procedure that slowed their ability to return fire. At this point, Lt. Col. Rice was riding his horse along the back of the line exhorting the men to steel against the sudden onslaught. Perhaps sensing fear in his well-trained but green troops, he galloped back and forth, his sword raised high, encouraging his men to hold the line, keep firing, and do their duty.

"Be careful, men. Be careful, men. You are making history!" Colonel Rice yelled while brandishing his sword.

But there atop his stallion, the Colonel presented a large target to the enemy and, with many rebel rifles trained upon the dashing Colonel, a fusillade of concentrated fire first knocked his saber high into the air and then felled his steed, the noble horse falling back into the brush and the officer tumbling off unhurt. Colonel Rice rose, fetched his saber and continued shouting encouragement to the men, who were greatly impressed by their commander that day.

Ransford picked a recent cloud of smoke rising out a patch of green across the pike and fire at it, hoping to hit the hidden rebel who'd made it. He rolled onto his back and commenced loading his rifle, flat on his back and without the benefit of gravity.

The firing went on unabated for more than an hour. The harried men of the 44th, still taking fire from two angles, loaded and fired their rifles furiously, matching their attackers' shot for shot. At one point Private Hickok yelled that his barrel was getting too hot to handle and he feared it would melt.

"Pour your canteen water over the barrel!" bellowed Jack.

Soon prodigious clouds of acrid gray smoke hung like a dense fog over the battlefield, making it impossible to see more than thirty paces. The men on each side were firing from one dirty cloud into another, watching anxiously for any sign of a massed assault. They were firing at ghosts.

Between firing Ransford would look to his right and left to check on those in his squad who had been firing without relief. All of them had become strangely energized by the experience, almost manic, and it showed in their eyes and their faces, which had become coated with a grimy black residue as they accumulated black powder from relentless and hurried ripping of the cartridge paper to load their weapons. As each soldier rubbed his irritated eyes, the powder mixed with the sweat building on his face to create a ghoulish appearance. Through the smoke, he could see his friends' faces turned dark and foreboding as deep black smudges emanated from their wild eyes and drizzled down the corners of their mouths making them appear like demons or Pacific island cannibals painted for war.

He shuddered and turned back to his grim business. Ransford fired his weapon over and over and over again, aiming at nothing except the idea of the enemy lurking in the trees he knew lay behind a veil of smoke. He accepted that he had become one of the black-faced ghouls just as he accepted that his entire life had boiled down to this protracted, horrific moment. Nothing else mattered except keeping his enemies at bay and protecting the lives of his friends. He wasn't fighting to avenge Col. Ellsworth anymore and he wasn't fighting for his father or his girl back in Corinth or to free the slaves anymore, he was fighting for his squad. They were in mortal danger and he couldn't bear the thought of any harm coming to them.

Soon he sensed that the line was failing, that the 2nd Maine had finally faltered on the far right, that the 25th New York had collapsed, surrendering the cannon in the middle of the line, and some companies of the 44th were just now starting to buckle. Through the roar of battle—the melded cacophony created by thousands of muskets blasting, bugles sounding, drums banging out notes, and men screaming—he could suddenly hear something discernible and familiar. It was Lieutenant Knox triumphantly standing just a few paces behind the men, his saber raised gloriously above his head. He looked strangely clean, almost glowing, and fearlessly shouting that this battle could still be won if only they would "...press on, press on, press on and hold the line!" At that moment, Ransford saw Lt. Knox's outstretched arm, the one holding the gleaming saber, explode. It just burst, it seemed, at the wrist, sending shards of bone and blood in all directions, the sword falling meekly to the ground. Ransford gasped and returned to firing with a kind of vengeance and hatred that he'd only experienced once before.

By now the rebels, sensing victory, emerged from their haunts in the forest and began a slow assault against the last companies holding out along the 44th's line. As they drew closer in the tall grass, Ransford could finally see the outlines of the enemy, darkened silhouettes that would stop, fire, and then move forward toward their position, drawing ever closer. He smiled like a maniac, happy that he could finally see the bastards. He took down one, then another, watching them recoil from his shots and crumple into the grass. And, as he was taking aim at another, a reb in an oddly familiar red button-down shirt, Ransford was distracted by an entirely new set of sounds, bugles and drums announcing the arrival of new troops to the field.

"Are they ours, or theirs?" he thought, just as a huge and soulful cheer arose from the lines to his right. Ransford squinted and rubbed the black sooty mixture from his eyes to see, rising above the smoky field, the familiar banner of the 83rd Pennsylvania and other fresh regiments driving down the New Bridge Road from the north. "Friends," he thought. He turned back to the reb he had targeted just a moment before and saw that the man had taken a knee and was now clearly aiming his rifle at Ransford. The moment was chilling, odd and incredibly distinctive; it became frozen in his mind, like a painting, for what seemed an eternity.

"Keep your head down!" He heard his father say, as if he was lying next to him on the blood-soaked ground. "Keep your head down!"

Ransford ducked his head onto his hands just as a 50-caliber minié ball slammed into the top of his skull. And the world went black.

XIII: Nurse French

There was no sense of time, only a profound darkness and silence that felt very peaceful to Ransford. But then, as if being wakened from a fine dream, a flood of undifferentiated noises bombarded him; at first distant and cacophonous like an orchestra without a maestro, each instrument practicing without regard to the others. Soon, though, he could make out distinct sounds: a bugle, a sergeant barking orders, horses clomping by, and flies, yes flies, buzzing around him. He tried to open his eyes, but his eyelids seemed glued together and were vexingly immoveable. He tried to move his arms and they, too, felt frozen. Then there were voices, some of them familiar.

"Ransford! Ransford's over here, boys!"

It was Private Whitney's voice sounding very urgent. I wonder why.

"Oh, good Whitney. Check 'im, check to see if he's . . ."

A Corinth boy. Elmer Earles. See if he's what?

"His head doesn't look good. But he's breathing, boys, he's breathing!"

Well, of course, I'm breathing.

"Alright lads, we need to get our friend to the hospital. Let's all gather him up and get him to the field hospital. There's still time."

That was Jack. Oh, it's good to hear Jack's voice.

"Everyone take hold and lift! I'll support his head . . .. My, that is a prodigious wound!" said Jack, marveling at the wound that had transformed the upper left side of his friend's head into an undifferentiated bloody mess.

Is it me he's talking about? I don't feel a thing! He tried to speak, to shout out to his friends, but no sound came out his lips.

Ransford felt himself rise off the ground, as if floating, as his friends carried him several hundred yards to the field hospital that had been established at Dr. Kinney's farm, a well-appointed house belonging to a local physician. The regiment's assistant surgeon, Elias Bissell, a young man draped in a smock smeared with blood, was outside the house assessing each wounded man's condition. Based upon his decisions, orderlies would either carry seriously wounded soldiers into the house for immediate attention or, in some cases, if he found the wounds too severe to be addressed with any hope of a favorable outcome, the mortally wounded men, many suffering from inoperable belly wounds, were carried to a tent erected in the shade some distance from the house, where they would be comforted until they inevitably succumbed.

Ransford's friends placed him on a stretcher and Jack entreated the assistant surgeon to look at his wound.

"Please sir, take a look at our friend here. He's suffered a most severe blow to his head."

The harried surgeon, not pleased at being distracted from his work on another patient, whirled about to look at Ransford.

"We can't do much with head wounds. Nothing to cut off . . .. Nurse, please get me some water and a rag. Too much blood to see a thing here."

He drenched the rag in crimson stained water, squeezed out the excess, and carefully rubbed the dried blood from around the wound, revealing an odd gap in a portion of Ransford's skull. The bullet had clipped the upper left portion of his cranium and it was slowly, but clearly oozing blood.

"I'm sorry, boys. He's not conscious and a part of his cranium is gone. Likely he'll never wake up. Best to just ease his pain and let him go men. I'm sorry."

The doctor's harsh clinical assessment dashed their hopes for their friend.

"My good doctor, do you know who this is?" asked Jack urgently.

"No, Private, I don't."

"This is Private Ransford Densmore. He's not a fancy colonel or a prince. He's just a good man. He's a good man, sir. And we're his friends . . ." said Jack urgently. "Now I know a bit about chance and I can tell you here and now I wouldn't wager a nickel on our friend's chances if he gets deposited over yonder in that death tent. But if he gets into that house and gets in front of your superior, he might just have a chance."

The assistant surgeon adjusted his spectacles, coughed, but then retreated to his "policies" and how he'd been ordered not to send those soldiers "highly likely to die" into the hospital where they might absorb valuable time and resources.

"I care not for policy, sir. If ever this regiment had a heart it resides with this man. And I personally attest to the fact that if he is given even the slightest chance to live, our friend Ransford will survive. For God sakes, man, he is the regiment!"

"Here here!" Several men chimed in with support after Jack's impassioned speech. They had seen many comrades killed and crippled the day before and as such had no tolerance for what appeared to be a bureaucratic response to a life or death matter.

"Fair enough, men. If the surgeon can possibly suture those bleeding veins and patch the wound this man might—might, mind you—stand a chance at survival." He directed two orderlies to carry Ransford into Dr. Kinney's home. A cheer went up among the men and Jack wiped his eyes.

Ransford heard the entire dramatic discourse but was unable to respond in any way. He was touched deeply by what Jack had said and wanted to leap off the stretcher and thank him for those words. But, of course, he couldn't; he was trapped inside a body that would no longer do his bidding.

Orderlies carried him into the country doctor's substantial house and into an ornate, book-lined study that had been transformed into an operating room. Ransford was laid upon an oaken door straddling two saw horses; blood-soaked straw covered an Oriental rug. Surgeon William Frothingham, a tall, bearded austere fellow, inspected Ransford's wound and wasted no time prescribing a course of action, almost relishing the challenge before him.

He had been sawing limbs off writhing and retching men all day and was beginning to feel akin to a carpenter. Lead minié balls traveling at slow velocities shattered bones and expanded inside the body making wounds to the torso virtually impossible to cure. His clinical responses to most battlefield injuries were, therefore, quite predictable; except in a few cases like this one. Amputation certainly was not an option and, here, the only vital organ affected was the patient's brain and there was no way of knowing the extent of the injury.

"Interesting," Frothingham pronounced to his nurse. "I'm surprised Mr. Bissell sent me this patient given our protocols, but there is a glimmer of hope here. This man still has a good pulse . . .. If we can just stanch the bleeding and safely cover the wound."

He asked for more water and carefully cleaned the area around the wound. Then he shaved much of Ransford's light brown hair away from the borders of a rather large gouge in his cranium while the nurse dabbed the spot with sponges to absorb the blood. In places where he could clearly identify them, the doctor used tweezers to carefully remove bits of bone, hair and detritus from the wound, which exposed part of the brain.

"The finest silk you can find, please, nurse," he said before ascertaining the location of at least three blood vessels that were slowly leaking blood into the cavity. He moistened the ends of the silk between his lips before threading it into the tiny eye of a sewing needle and then deftly sutured the three bleeding vessels.

"I'll tell you, Nurse Johnson, this man may have benefited from having a bit of his skull exposed. It may actually help reduce the threat from sub-cranial swelling."

"Indeed, Doctor," said the young nurse, who had been by his side, assisting in his brutal tasks without sleeping since the battle began 24 hours earlier.

"Now please give the wound a thorough cleaning, Nurse, and let's prepare to close it off. I'd prefer to use a natural bandage, one of his own skin, rather than exposing his brain to further damage."

He identified an area of Ransford's scalp that had been ripped back by the passing bullet, a flap of sorts, that he could use to cover the wound, and proceeded to carefully suture the flap over the cavity.

"There you have it!" pronounced Dr. Frothingham proudly. "Let's hope we have saved this man . . .. Next patient!"

Ransford was carried outside the house, placed in a large open-sided tent to the north of the hospital, and added to the rows of other wounded soldiers, awaiting transport away from the front. There the men of the squad, who had been waiting anxiously outside, gathered around his makeshift cot to pay their respects and wish him well.

"You look a whole lot better, Ransford. Looks like that doctor fixed you up good."

It was the voice of Solomon Hickok, another Corinth boy. Ransford contemplated his strange situation. Piecing together that he had been shot in the head, seriously wounded, but for some reason he was unable to move or respond physically in any way. It was vexing. But, at the same time, oddly intriguing; never had he been such the center of attention and never had he heard such nice things said about him. The fact that he felt no pain, made it even better.

"He does look better, doesn't he lads?" Jack said with uncharacteristic affection. "He is a tough one, a resilient rube . . .. If you can hear me, Ransford, I'm here with Whitney, Earles, and Hickok and we want you to know that we're quite jealous. You'll be going home now, you lucky dog. Back to your backwoods paradise and that pretty young lady you've been fancying, while your old bunk mates will be eating bad food and following Sergeant Tinkham's orders for another year or two."

"That's right, Ransford," Private Whitney said. "God's speed back to Corinth. We're praying for you. And once you heal up, please go visit my father in Saratoga. He'd love to hear how I'm doing."

"Hell, boy, I wish I was a going back with you. I do miss Antone Mountain and the Sacandaga River and all my crazy uncles. Tell 'em howdy for me, would you, Ransford?" said Private Earles.

Before long, two corpsmen came and picked up Ransford, installing his stretcher in a waiting ambulance that was bound for better medical accommodations behind the lines. Ransford's long trip home had begun.

From the sounds he could tell the wagon was bouncing along a long difficult pike, probably the same one that the 44th had slogged up two days earlier, the drivers cursing its mud and debris that jostled the bodies of the severely wounded men aboard. He could hear expressions of the wounded men's discomfort and pain as they moaned and screamed consistently throughout the long uncomfortable journey. At last they arrived at some flatter, more appropriate destination, a camp of some kind, where they were removed and brought to another hospital, and he could hear another doctor reading his chart aloud and commenting to a nurse about his care.

"Let's see if we can get some water and nourishment into this one. He's been unconscious for nearly two days. We need to keep him hydrated."

He heard a woman's gentle voice suggesting that they prop his head up to see if he could ingest some water. Ransford recalled a tingling sensation when the nurse propped him up and inserted a spoonful of water between his lips, the cold liquid surprising him as it flowed into his mouth and drizzled down his chin.

A feeling! It was incredible to experience a feeling! Ransford gulped to keep the water from going down the wrong pipe.

That feels good! he thought, as he swallowed the rejuvenating water.

"He swallowed, sir!"

"That's a good sign, Emily! Let's be careful about it but let him drink as much as he can handle . . .. Good sign!"

More sensations came when she spooned warm broth into his mouth. *Warm*, he thought. And then more when she covered him with a blanket. *Warm.* But with the arrival of a limited set of sensations a degree of pain crept into his consciousness, a throbbing in his head that slowly advanced from annoyance to a sharper discomfort that eventually became unbearable. *Pain.* Unable to communicate his plight to the medical staff that he knew were hovering in his vicinity, Ransford tried to distract himself by concentrating on all the things he missed from home, imagining himself tramping through the autumn woods around Corinth, picnicking with pretty Amy Carpenter on a grassy bank of the Kayderossas Creek, or singing hymns with his father and brother in the Methodist Church on Main Street. Laughing with his friends around the campfire. Fishing for brook trout in a mountain stream. Eating fried chicken . . .. But the pain barged into his dreams and became consuming as if a wolf was gnawing slowly and deliberately on his head.

"Doctor, please come here and take a look," said the nurse.

"Yes, Emily," said the doctor, coming over to Ransford's cot.

"He's sweating quite a bit and his eyelids are twitching . . .. Do you think he could be in some pain?"

"I believe so, Emily. He suddenly has an uncomfortable aspect about him. The senses may be slowly awakening and bringing the pain with it. Let's give him a dose of morphine and see if that helps."

Thank the Lord, thought Ransford. *Thank you, Nurse Emily!*

Nurse Emily administered the morphine via a liquid dosage spooned into his mouth and it took some time for the drug to do its work. Ransford clung to the hope that this medicine could stop the pain that had become all-consuming, maddening. After what seemed like an eternity, he could feel an odd warmth invade his body, similar to whisky, but much more pervasive. It was remarkably effective and calming.

Dearest Emily . . . he thought, as he drifted into another deep sleep, this one wholesome and fulfilling that lasted several hours. He woke to the sound of a steam whistle and men yelling orders. A breeze was blowing across his face and, once again, he could hear sounds of medical personnel in his proximity. They were different voices, however, from the previous hospital, different nurses and doctors. He would miss Nurse Emily, he thought, wishing he could've seen her face.

He discerned that he was on a boat, a hospital boat, probably headed back down the Pawmunkey River to the James. From there, who knew where he was bound? Would they ask him to recuperate at Fort Monroe and then send him back to the front? All kinds of thoughts flooded his brain, which was now considerably more active. Meanwhile his body, while still not under his complete control, would occasionally twitch violently as if it were waking from a nightmare. That would bring a member of the medical staff scurrying over to investigate.

"This boy appears to be waking up, Doctor," another nurse said, addressing a nearby doctor.

"It's a small miracle, Nurse Shelby. He's been in the dark for days. Had a goodly portion of his skull removed by a musket ball. Let's just continue the care plan established by the doctors up river. Gradual introduction of liquid nourishment, wound treatment, and morphine for pain . . .. Hopefully we can get this boy home."

"Yes, Doctor, he has been through quite a bit." She wiped Ransford's brow with a cool, moist cloth and adjusted his sheets. He was pleasantly surprised that he could feel it all; he could even smell the woman's fresh scent with a hint of lilac, perhaps coming from her or wafting in through the boat's portal.

Many of Ransford's senses eventually returned, but both sight and motor control over his limbs eluded him. He settled into a comfortable rhythm nonetheless as the medical treatment made him stronger and the morphine kept the pain at bay. A matter of days passed, though Ransford's conception of time was discombobulated by the drugs, as he remained on board a vessel that had apparently stopped and started several times.

There were times during his passage that Ransford could hear anguished cries from other wounded men who shared the floor. Mixed with the soulful moans and weeping of soldiers in pain were smells of feces and vomit that penetrated his nostrils and reminded him where he was. Sometimes it was difficult to separate what was real from nightmares as the screams would at times transport Ransford's mind back to the raging battle at Peake's Turnout and the ghoulish gray figures advancing toward him through the smoke. In an instant, he could be back there on his belly firing from the ditch, re-loading his musket and firing again and again and again while men were torn apart all around him. He would shudder at the images that haunted him with regularity until his dose of morphine would arrive like a visiting angel, bringing relief and a deep, dreamless sleep that vanquished the demons, at least for a little while.

After several days Ransford's transport had made its way to a distant port where the sounds were amplified dramatically, booming horns, whistles, and bells marked the presence of many ships and the seamen on deck could be heard swearing lustily at the sight before them.

"Thar she is, boys! New York City!"

"Liberty tonight!"

New York City! They've brought me back to New York!

Ransford was excited and totally unaware he had come so far. He wished he could jump up and see the great metropolis again. After the boat had docked, orderlies and soldiers hoisted Ransford up and carried him down a long incline to the docks. There was a lot of commotion as ambulances were loaded to take the men to various hospitals within the great city. A doctor looked over Ransford's file and directed that he be brought to a waiting train bound for Albany. His smooth, comfortable marine voyage had come to an end, replaced by an uncomfortable wagon ride through the mayhem of Manhattan with all its shrieks, honks, voices, and horses clomping on cobblestone. Soon he was being inserted into a specially outfitted car attached to a locomotive idling in a trainyard, hissing steam.

Before long, the hospital train was chugging out of the yard and on its way north with hundreds of wounded boys from upstate New York, on its way to Albany. Ransford could hear the train whistle and the loud puffing of the smokestack, but the noises seemed amplified and more shrill than before. He felt uncharacteristically uncomfortable, even after receiving his daily dose of morphine, which dulled the pain but did nothing to bring him either comfort or sleep.

This discomfort continued unabated for some time and began to be punctuated by intense shivering and dizziness. *Why am I so cold?* he thought.

"Doctor! This man is burning up!"

"Indeed, he is, Nurse. Cover him in blankets and try to get some water into him," said the doctor assigned to the car, who then inspected Ransford's wound. "The wound is red and emitting puss. Please rinse it out and apply a new bandage."

The blankets and water did little to quell the raging fever that had suddenly consumed Ransford's body. Like a lit match dropped into a barn, the fire inside him spread quickly, engulfing his body in sweat. The nurse applied bundles of ice wrapped in bandages to his forehead and chest and opened the windows of the train car, flooding the room with fresh air. Little else could be done.

Ransford felt the train car lurching along the tracks, belching smoke from its prodigious black stack, as the wind sucked acrid air into the cabin. His senses were flooded with insults: foul smells, cold spasms, hot spikes, strange discordant sounds, and competing voices that melded into a chorus of whispers. They all conspired to induce in him a poignant apprehension that something or someone was conspiring against him, yet he knew not what or whom. The cacophony expanded inside his head as he perceived the train car dissolving around him and, suddenly, he was alone and exposed on some type of flat railcar hurtling down an attenuated track, taking him from daylight into a foreboding darkness.

Fascinated and no longer feeling pain or discomfort of any kind, Ransford observed his surroundings with keen interest. There was a profound clarity everywhere he looked, much more so than life normally afforded. At first, the tracks stretched to a distant horizon on an undifferentiated plain as flat as a table top with no features on either side. But suddenly the landscape transformed as the train car—pushed forward at great speed by no foreseeable source of power—sped into a pronounced valley, bordered on each side by a series of rounded mountains running parallel to the tracks.

In the distance, at the point where the tracks intersected the horizon, he could make out a faint light, a glimmer, like hope, beating back the darkness. He gazed at it with much anticipation even while the mountains on either side loomed ever closer and closer. The car accelerated, the wind rushing past Ransford's face and his hair streaming back, as it plied its way through the odd canyon toward the light in the distance.

What is this place? he asked. No answer came.

Soon the car began to shake, at first only slightly, but growing more violent as the car sped through the dark valley, growing ever closer to him. And then the mountains began to move, rising as apparitions that were silhouetted by the approaching light. In a moment, the mountains transformed into living beings, revealing their true nature after casting off enormous black shrouds. Before him, on either side of the tracks stood a row of giants, terrifying in their splendor. Some were Nubian and some Native, each chiseled and gloriously festooned with the garb of warriors. They stood facing the tracks and his oncoming car, staring down at him. He shivered at their ferocious painted expressions.

The light on the horizon was growing brighter now, revealing a distant platform, and upon it there appeared to be a central figure generating the mysterious light. The tracks were bringing him to the light and, despite the ominous creatures rising around him, Ransford felt the light would bring him to something positive and good, something that might give him answers to questions he had never uttered. Frightened, horrified, he awaited the light anxiously and hopefully.

Take me there. I want to know. He heard himself say.

"Oh, we will take you there. You shall know." The voice, powerful and omnipotent, came from some undiscernible source.

Like living sculptures, the Native and Nubian behemoths standing along the tracks gathered themselves near the place where the tracks arrived at the light that now glowed with impeccable brilliance. And there they set to work. Ransford squinted to see what task the great warrior giants were performing, hunched over and toiling with tools or implements, tossing heaps into a growing flame.

Ransford's fascination grew as he approached the mysterious light, which revealed itself to be emanating from a tiny child, an infant, sitting naked and cross-legged at the center of the entire commotion.

One immaculate child, glowing, at the center of the universe, Ransford thought, smiling at the realization. *It makes sense.*

As he pondered the child, he glanced down at his rolling transport and realized that it had again transformed. Now he was sitting back, his hands supporting himself with his knees poking upward, on a rubberized belt, like the kind used to bring coal or wood to a factory furnace, that was advancing inexorably toward the child at the center of the glowing stage.

Flanked by the terrible warriors, the baby soon became clear and, to Ranford's great delight, it had all the appearance of the same child he and boys of the 44th had saved on that terrible day in Virginia. It was Aura Lea!

Aura Lea, it's me . . . !

As he drew closer, Aura Lea's eyes made contact with his, fixing on him. Her benign, soulful expression had dissolved and, after one contemplative moment, the tiny babe began to expand. At first slowly and then exponentially, as if she were a carnival balloon expanding with new gas, Aura Lea grew and grew until she was as large and as terrible as the native warriors. Her mouth opened wider and wider until it overwhelmed her features and out of it came a horrid, blood-curdling scream, even more harsh than a train whistle, that penetrated Ransford's skull. An embodiment of outrage; it was a call to action that appeared to energize her giant servants. They began shoveling something into her gaping mouth, something that the conveyer belt was bringing to her in great numbers.

Terrified, Ransford looked down at the belt that was bringing him to a massive pit in front of the baby's gaping mouth. The pit was brimming with all manner of carnage; the bodies of soldiers, Union and Confederate, were intermingled with piles upon piles of limbs, torn from their hosts, all moving and alive, but heading toward the pit at the end of the conveyer belt.

Horrified, Ransford tried to scramble back up the belt and away from the pit. But he was frozen in position and compelled to watch all that was transpiring as if ordained to do so. The belt was emptying prodigious piles of wounded and dying men, along with thousands of squirming bloody limbs, into the deep and writhing pit that seemed to know no bounds. The Nubian and Native princes were using spades and pitchforks to toss the carnage into the mouth of the infant and the formidable fire that burned deep in her throat. They worked incessantly to ply their way through the pit but never seemed to complete their work as the pit was constantly refreshed with new bodies.

He was being carried closer and closer to the pit. Unable to move, much less flee, Ransford awaited his fate: to be cast upon an infinite churning heap of carnage and fed to the insatiable beast that devoured all in its sight without judgement or circumspection.

Is this to be my fate?

Just then, a powerful other-worldly voice that came from no source discernible to Ransford shook the scene, bellowing:

"Until every drop of blood drawn with the lash shall be paid with another drawn with the sword, as was said three thousand years ago, so still it must be said: The judgements of the Lord are true and righteous altogether!"

Ransford shivered in awe. He wrapped his hands around his knees, peering ahead in terror at the pit that awaited him while asking God to forgive his offenses.

Ransford lay flat on his back, folded his hands over his chest and prepared for his fall into the pit, closing his eyes in anticipation. He realized he wasn't being punished for what he had done in his life, but for the transgressions others had committed against God's children for generations. He could feel the incredible heat emanating from the furnace inside the babe's gaping mouth and he could hear the anguished cries of men languishing in the pit. Terror had been replaced by resignation and a profound sadness.

Just then, he felt himself clenched by a great force and abruptly lifted high into the air. It jarred Ransford's eyes open and he found himself staring into the painted face of one of the giants that had been feeding bodies into the fire. It had stopped its labors to pluck Ransford away from the conveyer belt moments prior to his dropping into the pit and now, it was inspecting him. His fierce black eyes, adorned with an array of brightly colored ceremonial paints, seemed to be penetrating Ransford's soul, looking deep inside for something from the puny creature he held, limp and quivering, in the palm of his massive hand. He squinted and uttered something in a language incomprehensible to Ransford, and yet he understood what the Native giant was saying:

Orenda is strong with this one.

Instead of eating Ransford—which is what he expected—the giant brought his other hand over to rub, with surprising gentleness, the top of Ransford's tiny head with the tip of his pointer finger, which was as big as a tree trunk. The giant stared for another moment into Ransford's eyes and then, with the flick of his wrist, tossed him high over his shoulder. Ransford found himself flying, for miles it seemed, propelled far over the mountains and the dark plain, over the train tracks, arcing downward with great velocity and then landing suddenly, with a thud, in a hospital bed.

He shook violently from side to side, wrestling with the soaked sheets that now covered him, using his hands to reach up and feel his face.

My God, I can use my hands! I can feel my face . . .. I'm alive!

Alerted by the commotion, a nurse rushed to Ransford's side and tried to calm him.

"Let's try to calm down, Mr. Densmore. All is well with you." The reassuring, sweet voice was new to him.

"Am-m-mm . . . a-ah-ah-live?" he heard himself stammer.

"You most certainly are, dear. Although for a while we had our doubts you were going to make it . . .. You had quite a raging fever when they brought you in here a few days ago."

"F-f-few d-d-days! N-n-n-not on t-t-train?"

"No, lad," she chuckled slightly. "You were on the train a while ago. You're in Albany now."

"C-c-c-an you hear m-m-me m-m-miss?"

"Why, yes I can! Sounds like some things are coming back to you. That's good, very good . . .. And it's Mrs. French, Mrs. Jacqueline French."

"P-p-pleased to muh-muh-eet you, M-m-mrs. F-f-f-french."

"You can call me Jacqueline. Now let's not try to speak so much, dear boy. You rest now."

"Yessss, ma'am."

"I have had the privilege of caring for you these last few days. I have a special affection for your regiment, Ransford . . .. I once knew Colonel Ellsworth, you see. He was, well, a special man

225

and I remember him quite fondly . . .. Now that your fever has broken, I think we should get you into some fresh linens. These are soaked!"

Nurse French set about removing the sheets that had become drenched with sweat and peeling his bed clothes away from his body. She moved efficiently over and around him without any hint of embarrassment or reservation at seeing the young man unclothed. For his part, Ransford had lost any humility as a patient and surrendered himself to the requirements of his caregivers. Soon he felt clean and refreshed but famished. She brought him a substantial bowl of chicken soup that he consumed voraciously, asking for seconds and even eating a crust or two of bread with the broth. It was his first hard food in nearly two weeks.

"*Tres bien*, my dear! *Tres bien*! It's so good to see you eat, Ransford."

"S-s-s-sorry ma'am . . .. T-t-t-tray wh-what?"

"Oh, sorry, *chou chou*! That is the French language. I am Mrs. French and I grew up speaking French. It is a coincidence, no?"

"Ha ha!" Ransford laughed, the first time in a quite a while. It felt good. "S-s-s-sounds p-p-pretty."

"*Merci*! Maybe I will teach you."

"I'd l-l-like th-th-that."

The doctor visited Ransford and pronounced that he had made a significant recovery, especially after arriving in Albany delirious and burning with fever. He was pleased with the return of many of Ransford's physical abilities, particularly speech.

"This indicates the brain is returning to normal function. Nurse French, maybe we see if he can stand tomorrow, eh?"

"Absolutely, Doctor."

The next day Nurse French helped Ransford take his first steps since the minié ball had clipped his brain. She swung his legs over the edge of the bed and placed his arm over her shoulder, encouraging him to raise up onto his legs. He felt strange, dizzy, but, thanks to Nurse French's support, persevered in standing on his wobbly legs.

"I have you, *mon cher*. Try to give me a step, one step *s'il vous plait*."

He concentrated on telling his right leg to move forward and it slowly responded, awkwardly, to his command. He steadied himself and then did the same with his left leg, pleasing Nurse French.

"*Tres bien*! Very nice, Ransford! You are doing so well!"

After a few more halting steps, she pronounced that their work was done for the day and helped him back into the hospital bed, tucking him in and fluffing his pillow. Although he couldn't see Nurse French, his senses soon became attuned to her many attributes: her sweet, melodious voice that he looked forward to every morning; her optimistic, doting way—a maternal luxury he'd never experienced—encouraging him day after day to achieve certain goals during his long convalescence; and her singular smell—a curious blend of freshly-baked vanilla cookies and spring flowers—that told him she was in the room well before she spoke.

But, one morning, Ransford experienced another side of his caregiver, one that remained with him long into his life. By now, his speaking, as well as his ability to walk, had greatly improved and his vision was returning enough that he could see the blurred outlines of people and things around him. Mrs. French was bustling about the room that housed Ransford and several other wounded men in the sunny room in the mansion that had been converted to a convalescent home for veterans along State Street in Albany. As was his habit, he'd anxiously anticipated Mrs. French's arrival and then, after a few pleasantries,

Ransford would request his "medicine"—the bitter red elixir, laudanum—that would ease his pain and put him in a pleasant stupor for several hours.

"Hmmm . . .. I think not today, *mon cher.*"

"Why not, Jacqueline?"

"I think you are liking the laudanum more than you are needing it now. Your wound is healing, Ransford, and your pain should be much less now."

"Oh, w-w-well, I think I'm still in quite a bit of pain, Nurse."

"Perhaps it is more lust—lust for the drug—than pain you are experiencing, my dear. I am sorry, but I have spoken with the doctor and he agrees."

He felt an uncharacteristic anger spark within him. How could she deprive him of what he needed? Especially when she had never been stern or disapproving in any way, always supportive and willing to accommodate his every need. He felt betrayed.

"I think you are being foolish and not very helpful at all, Mrs. French! I'm the one who was shot in the head in service to his country, not you!" He was surprised at the harsh words jumping from his mouth as the anger rose in him, already feeling pangs of desire in his belly for the drug he had become accustomed to having whenever he wanted for weeks.

"I am sorry you feel this way, young man," she said sternly. "What I do, I do for you . . .. You have not seen the men, and even women, who love this drug too much. It destroys them."

He curled up in a ball in his bed, refusing to walk the halls with her as he normally did. The sulking continued for the next few days as Ransford suffered long uncomfortable nights that made sleeping impossible and had him pacing through the halls of the mansion in the darkness past the shrouded figures of men recovering from every imaginable kind of wound, some sleeping and some calling out for deliverance from their ever-present pain. One of the shrouded figures, silhouetted by a street lamp, its light streaming through a tall, arched window, raised up a hand and beckoned for Ransford to come to him. It turned out to be a captain from the 25th who had lost both his legs to an artillery round at Peake's Turnout. They spoke in whispers, hoping to avoid the attention of any nurses patrolling the hallways.

"So, you're with the 44th, eh, son? We were sure glad to see you boys coming down the road when you did."

"Glad we got there in time, Captain."

"Had myself a bad piece of luck back there," he said glancing down at the two stumps outlined by the sheets. Ransford noticed there was a nervous energy about the man, who occasionally twitched and scratched himself.

"Sure am sorry about that, sir."

"Want to do a favor for a brother, soldier?"

"If I could, sir."

"As you might rightly guess, I'm in a pickle, lad. Can't exactly jump up and walk down these halls," he said, laughing uncomfortably. "Now they—those damnable nurses—promised me a dose of morphine hours ago and they haven't gotten it for me. And, well, I have a powerful need for it right now, you understand?"

"Would you like me to go fetch a nurse for you, sir?"

"No, no, that's not necessary, son. I believe there's a cabinet over there, in that closet over there," he gestured to a large wooden wardrobe in the corner. "You just go over and get out a flask or two of laudanum and bring it to me. No need to bother anyone."

Ransford could see his eyes now and it was clear that he was agitated, wild even, like a trapped animal, making Ransford uncomfortable with the task requested of him. Was this what Nurse French had been warning him of or was the Captain looking to laudanum for something more permanent, much like Jack's mother? Ransford grasped both feelings now with a clarity that rarely reveals itself to a young man.

"No sir, respectfully, I cannot do that for you. I must be going now, Captain, but I wish you peace."

The Captain protested bitterly, snarling at Ransford and questioning his devotion to the army for disobeying an order from a superior. "I'm a captain, damn it!"

But Ransford saw through his anger, turned, and walked slowly away down the dark hallway to his bed. The next morning he awoke to the sound of Nurse French humming a familiar folk tune and fussing around his bed.

"*Bonjours!*"

"Good morning, Jacqueline," said Ransford, hesitating before speaking again as he chose his words carefully. "I, um, wanted to apologize for how I spoke to you recently. You did not deserve the way I spoke to you."

"My dear boy. You have no reason to apologize. I have seen the strongest men laid low by these drugs. The drugs, not you, were talking to me, *chou chou*," Jacqueline said, looking into his eyes and smiling warmly. "It is good to have you back!"

Ransford spent that summer re-learning everything. With Nurse French by his side, seemingly day and night, the young man painstakingly re-acquired the skills he'd long taken for granted. Walking, talking, tying shoes, eating with utensils, and dressing were all chores that felt strange and incomprehensible to him, requiring the kind of repetition and practice generally reserved for toddlers and young children. Although she shared her time with many of the men recuperating in the ward, Mrs. French tended to Ransford with unparalleled devotion.

"You can do this, *Cherie!*" she'd say as he fumbled with his shoelaces or the buttons on his shirt. "Focus. Focus."

They would practice these things, over and over, until eventually Ransford's muscle memory returned and he could perform each step as he had once done. It all took time, months even, and Mrs. French's patience combined with Ransford's perseverance to slowly regain his faculties and his self-esteem.

Perhaps the greatest challenge Ransford faced was re-learning how to read and write. An avid reader before being wounded, Ransford awoke from his injury to discover that pages of text now appeared like some uncracked code, a cuneiform of symbols strung end to end that meant nothing to him. Various doctors visited and tried to assess Ransford's unique condition, marveling at his sudden loss of higher brain function and puzzling as to how to fix it. One opined, without regard for Ransford's presence, that the bullet had so damaged a part of his brain that controlled language that he should accept that his limitation would likely remain permanent.

This diagnosis did not sit well with Nurse French, however, especially since she had seen innumerable skills return to Ransford through repetition and obstinance. With this in mind, Mrs. French instituted a program designed to rediscover Ransford's ability to read and write, to find wherever it was hiding in his brain and unleash it once again. While the sweltering days of summer in Albany were punctuated by sweaty and monotonous rehearsals for the requirements of daily life, Ransford's evenings became wonderous affairs as Mrs. French sought to immerse the young man in literature and language. For one hour each evening, before she left for home, Nurse French would read something to him.

"We will start, Ransford, with me reading to you. Perhaps we will start with a novel and then eventually, we will move on to articles from the newspaper or letters, whatever you like, *nes pas?"*

"Yes, *merci*, Nurse Jacqueline!" At times he punctuated his conversation with French phrases, not so much to impress her as a wish to communicate with her freely and on her own terms. Although unable to put it into words, the young man had become smitten with his nurse. And whatever pain or frustration he experienced throughout those long, mundane days, Ransford gladly suffered them in return for their time together, reading for an hour or two every evening.

After sharing a simple, but satisfying meal of beef stew or mutton, Nurse French would assist Ransford in getting established in his bed, seated upright, and commence reading from an oak chair parked next to his side. She would read various chapters from popular novels—*The Scarlet Letter* or *Ivanhoe* or *Oliver Twist*—and ask Ransford to imagine what was being described as if it were a picture in his mind.

"Do you see the lovely lady all dressed in blue watching the knights battle, Ransford? Can you see brave Ivanhoe tilt his lance and charge?"

Her words were melodic and captivating in the lilting way that French folk speak, and he would often drift away to sleep, as if drugged, after several pages. In that case, Nurse French would tidy the sheets around him and leave for the night. But, upon returning in the morning, she would make a point of inquiring about the passage they had read the night before, asking him to recall specific events and imagery described in the novel. And, sometimes they would discuss the novel, explore what the author implied or what was being taught.

"Do you like this Henry James, Ransford?"

"I'll be honest, Jacqueline, I like the story, but I find his writing a l-l-little hard to f-f-f-follow."

"*Oui, moi aussie . . ..* But I like how he makes you wonder about the governess . . .. Is she crazy or are there really ghosts haunting her?"

"Yes, m-m-mademoiselle, I do see your point," he said, smiling.

Within a few weeks, Ransford's ability to retain and recall information showed marked improvement. It was as if someone—Nurse French actually—had applied oil to a rusty hinge, working it back and forth until it finally, begrudgingly, started working smoothly again. One evening, after dinner, she produced a letter from her handbag and asked Ransford if he would like her to read it to him.

"It is from your brother, Sylvanus."

"Yes, ma'am, p-p-please do."

> *Dear Brother,*
>
> *Greetings from your family back in Corinth. We recently received a letter telling us of your present circumstances. We understand that your nurse, Mrs. French, was kind enough to write to us explaining that you were quite severely wounded but reassuring us that you were making a remarkable recovery. Father and I were quite relieved to hear that you had survived the battle. Many apparently did not and so we are most grateful for your good fortune. I will add that Miss Amy Carpenter, who remains an ardent admirer of yours, is also quite relieved and happy to hear that you are expected to make a full recovery. She joins us in wondering when you might be allowed to return to your home and people here who miss you very much.*
>
> *I must also add the news that I have chosen—after much sincere thought, big brother—to enlist in the service of my country. Along with several other lads from Corinth, I will be joining a new regiment, the 115th Volunteers, in Fonda later this month. As you might expect, father is not pleased but I believe he understands that the Union needs every available young man if it is to win this war and restore the Union. As you know more than anyone, Ransford,*

this is the noblest of fights before us. I hope I have your blessing and, if God wills it, I look forward to the day I see you again.

Most sincerely,

Your loving brother,

Sylvanus

Ransford sat silent, taking in what Nurse French had just read to him. The thought of his little brother experiencing battle, or any of the horrors that he'd been through, made him shudder. Unashamed, Ransford put his face in his hands and wept.

"Oh, *mon Cherie* . . . I am sorry you feel so bad. Your brother is doing what so many young men are doing now. These are sad times." She placed her hand on his shoulder and caressed his back.

After news of his brother's enlistment, Ransford began to request that Nurse French bring him any newspapers she could find so he could follow the movements of Sylvanus' regiment and his other brothers in the 44th. The dreamy evenings filled with the exploits of Ivanhoe and Oliver Twist were supplanted by articles describing news from the front—much of it bad. Ransford was pained to learn that the 115th NY Infantry Regiment, along with his brother Sylvanus, were shipped almost immediately to Harpers Ferry, West Virginia. His brother's regiment had not been given the benefit of the many months of training Ransford experienced after he first enlisted. And, now, following the Army of the Potomac's disastrous retreat from northern Virginia, an emboldened Confederate Army was attacking the North, threatening Maryland and Washington, DC, in a bold counter punch designed to terrify Union leaders. After his defeat at the Second Battle of Bull Run, Union General Pope retreated to the outskirts of Washington to defend the capital against attack. Completely turning the tables on the Union army and sensing an opportunity for victory, Confederate General Robert E. Lee consolidated his forces and invaded Maryland.

The compendium of news about his comrades and kin increasingly agitated Ransford, who longed be useful again. His strength and mental agility had largely returned, surprising many in the medical staff which featured him in rounds with visiting doctors, congratulating themselves for their innovative treatment of this soldier and his unlikely outcome. Few, other than Ransford, credited Nurse French for his remarkable recovery.

As his ability to read and write demonstrably returned, so did Ransford's fervent desire to do something, anything, productive. He even flirted with the notion of returning to active service in the 44th. But this idea was promptly shot down by the doctors and Nurse French who pointed out that, despite his incredible strides, Ransford's health had been compromised far too much to endure the rigors of military life.

"You have given enough, *mon amie,*" Nurse French said firmly one bright September morning. "Actually, Doctor McDermott is recommending that you be discharged next week. I must agree with this assessment, Ransford."

Ransford thought about the word: discharged. "What does that even mean?"

"It means you go home, *cherie,*" she said cheerfully. "You go home to your father, who needs you now more than ever. And you go home to that nice girl who has been writing to you almost every day. You go home!"

"And no longer be a soldier?" The words echoed deep in his mind and seemed impossible to imagine. Something he had never known or experienced just a year earlier was now an inexorable part of his identity. "I am a soldier and I'll always be a soldier."

"*C'est vrais,* Ransford. But you have also become a man and you have responsibilities to the people you love. So many of these poor boys I treat will never go home again. You are one of the lucky ones."

He looked at Nurse Jacqueline, drank in her beautiful face and figure, and tried to imagine not seeing her, speaking with her, and smelling her every day. This, too, was hard to comprehend. Painful even. For a moment he entertained the idea of proposing to her, right then and there. But he didn't. It wasn't fear of rejection that held him back so much as it was the idea that he wouldn't be anything but a burden to her in his later life. He wanted better for her.

"I find it hard to imagine not seeing you anymore, Jacqueline," he said.

"I know, my dear . . .. I'll be honest, Ransford, I have favored you. Perhaps too much. *Oui?* You remind me very much of someone now gone. That is all I can say. But you have been a bright light in my darkest days and I will truly miss you." Tears welling in her gentle eyes, Nurse French said this in a whisper, leaning into his ear so others would not hear. "Now you go home to Miss Amy Carpenter and you love her. I guarantee you, my young Ivanhoe, she will love you back and give you a wonderful life."

XIV: Return to Corinth

One day late in September, Ransford received papers from a military adjutant honorably discharging him from service in the army. The next day he prepared to board a train bound for Saratoga. His ragged and bloodied uniform had been cut away and discarded shortly after arriving at the hospital in Albany, so he wore ill-fitting gray trousers, a button down white shirt and tight black shoes that had been donated to him by the ladies of the Albany Sanitary Commission. Toting a cloth bag that contained all that remained of his personal items, Ransford bid farewell to Nurse French—who bestowed a lingering kiss on his cheek and a hug that he would long remember—along with members of the staff (who had become quite proud of Ransford and his recovery). Walking gingerly, aided by an onyx cane and Nurse French supporting his elbow, Ransford made his way down the mansion's polished granite steps and into the street. After bidding her farewell again and promising to write, Ransford climbed into a carriage that had been called to take him to the train station. As the vehicle wound its way toward the station, the hubbub and noise of the bustling city made his head spin and, suddenly exposed to the real world, Ransford realized just how physically compromised he had become.

The train sped its way along the west bank of the Hudson River, which was brimming with steamships and sloops laden with people and trade goods. The cities and villages hummed with peaceful activity that appeared to belie the great battles raging to the south. All they knew of the war, Ransford thought, was from newspaper reports and tales of returning veterans like himself.

The seats in the lurching train car were occupied by a mix of well-dressed men, couples bound for Saratoga, and a few small families with children, who whispered and giggled, their excitement at the boats, mountains, and life in general, were hard to ignore. This world, the one so familiar before his journey to the war, seemed foreign now, almost mocking him and his uniquely horrid experience. Throughout the nearly three-hour ride, he found himself growing increasingly agitated and couldn't quite understand why.

As the train pulled alongside the platform at the Saratoga Train Station, travelers rose from their seats, gathering bags and small trunks that they had stowed in compartments overhead. Ransford instinctively remained seated, waiting for them to finish their activities and disembark before he rose and slowly made his way down the aisle and the steep iron steps to the platform. Everything he did now, he did slowly, deliberately. When he finally stepped down to the worn wooden platform and looked up, only two people remained waiting.

"Hello, Son!" Surprisingly, there was his father not a few steps in front of him and, next to him, Amy Carpenter stood smiling broadly, beaming.

"Hello, Father . . .. It truly is good to see you, sir!" His father reached out to embrace Ransford, but with some hesitancy out of concern for his condition. Ransford drew him in and hugged his father deeply for a long time, tears welling in his eyes as he looked across his father's shoulders to Miss Carpenter, who stood patiently, still smiling. So very pretty, he thought.

"It is good to see you, Miss Carpenter. I thank you for making the trip."

She reached out her hand and clasped his in both hers, pulling up to Ransford's face and giving him a soulful kiss on his cheek.

"I am most happy to see you, sir!" She spoke breathlessly, sincerely, while continuing to hold Ransford's hand. "Your dear father was most kind to extend the invitation, Ransford. We have been looking forward to your return for many days now. If you are by any chance hungry, I packed us a basket with lunch."

"Why, yes, Miss Carpenter. I welcome anything you have cooked . . . and I am anxious to return to Corinth."

"Your bed is waitin' for you, Ransford . . .. Lord, it's good to see you, boy!"

With his father's help, Ransford climbed onto the front seat of the wagon for the trip to South Corinth. The three of them slowly made their way north, back to the mountains and the life Ransford had left behind but one year earlier. It could have been a hundred years, he thought, struck by the bright autumnal display surrounding them, the oak, maple, elm and walnut leaves exploding with color on the crisp fall day.

Their conversations centered on tales of his home town and the people in it as Ransford sought to catch up on Corinth, what he'd missed, and how his friends were faring. He learned that most of his friends and young acquaintances had, over the course of the previous year, enlisted in the many new regiments that had sprung up since he departed. In all, some 70 young men from the town and surrounding hamlets had enlisted; aside from the handful who had joined the 44th in '61, most locals had mustered in with the 30th NY Infantry, the 77th NY, and of course, the 115th NY Infantry Regiment, which Sylvanus had joined a short time before Ransford's return.

"When the call went up for the 115th that just about took any young men left hereabouts, including your brother, Ransford," his father said sadly. "About 30 marched off to Fonda back in August. I won't lie to ya, I'm all for the cause, but this war has put a whole lot of families under the yoke."

"It surely has, Daddy. Any word from Sylvanus yet?"

"All's we know is that the regiment was rushed down to Harper's Ferry, West Virginia, with less than a month of training and already they're in the thick of it . . .. The papers say there's been action down that way but nothing clear. Nothing clear, son. I admit I'm powerful worried."

"Now Daddy, you never really know something until you know it. Lots of times we heard things in the newspaper that didn't turn out to be true. Let's just wait and see."

Ransford tried to reassure his father but kept to himself that, just a day before, he had read in an Albany newspaper about the fighting around Harpers Ferry as well as a major battle brewing in a tiny Maryland town called Antietam.

After bringing his father to their home in South Corinth, Ransford saw Amy Carpenter to her family's house in the village, and so began their courtship. As was the way of the time (and owing somewhat to Ransford's deliberate nature) their wooing evolved slowly over the ensuing year. As promised in her letter, they would have their picnic on the banks of the Kayderosseras Creek—a delightful and revealing time for the couple, where Ransford shared as much of his memories and fears as he dared, keeping some of the most terrifying details to himself, while she told of her concern for his safety and growing admiration. There, along the banks of the lovely stream that meandered out of the mountains, through forest and meadows, between Corinth and Saratoga, their love grew beyond the letters they had shared and became a three-dimensional thing. Every Sunday, they would meet for services at the Methodist Church, where folks in the congregation soon marked them for marriage. In the eyes of the community, it was a good match.

While, in more normal times, their story might have been a serene, even mundane tale of love in the Adirondacks, it was destined to suffer many foul intrusions that wafted with bitter regularity into the brisk, clean air of the mountains from the war in the south. Like an unrelenting storm lasting for years, each tortured family waited for news of their young men who lived in perpetual danger in strange and distant places. Manassas. Antietam. Cold Harbor. Gettysburg. Petersburg.

Sometimes the news arrived like a swarm of hornets, stinging several families at once as the casualty lists from a major battle were hung on the whitewashed wall of the post office or read aloud on the front porch of town hall. Sometimes the terrible news struck a mother or brother alone by firelight in the form of a letter, written in the flowing hand of a commanding officer, informing them that their son, like so many others, had perished in camp from one of the countless diseases plaguing the army.

Already, Ransford was to learn, at least two young men of his acquaintance who'd enlisted in the 30th New York, had died of disease. Joe McCouchie and Justin Combs, both privates, had succumbed to what appeared to be all too common sicknesses. Their families and others were vexed to think that these robust young men in the prime of their lives could have been felled by something as common and unimpressive as diarrhea. What's more, their passing was often quietly eschewed by those who equated such deaths as lacking in nobility or courage, almost deeming them a divine judgement of some sort. The idea that a "good death"—one suffered in combat in a noble cause—was to be prized above all else pervaded the thinking of many in Ransford's town, as it did in most towns. But it was something that didn't square with Ranford's thinking or his experience. He'd seen many good and vital boys, born leaders of impeccable character, fall ill and die. "A death is a death," he would say to anyone who cared to listen. "The pain and the loss are the same to his family."

Just a few days after his return, Ransford, his father, and Amy Carpenter were attending Sunday services at the Methodist Church on Main Street when the preacher began his sermon solemnly, using the opportunity to share painful news with his flock and call upon them to pray for and support aggrieved families in the congregation.

"Brothers and sisters, it pains me to report that, in the recent struggle between our noble forces and the rebels in a town called Antietam, one of our own, Alexander Walker, a good and loving son of Corinth and a member of this congregation, fell on the battlefield," the minister paused, allowing the muffled sounds of weeping from the Walker family to be heard, as the young man's father comforted his wife and his youthful children

241

sobbed in their pew. "Hiram Walker has asked me to share a few lines from a letter sent to him by Colonel Searing which I will do now with your indulgence."

> *"My Dear Sir,*
>
> *I write to you today to inform you of the death of your son, Sergeant Alexander Walker, who served most honorably under my command in the 30th New York Infantry Regiment. I can in no way diminish the pain and shock which must consume you and his loving family at a time such as this; however, I hope it gives you comfort to know that your son had been recently promoted to rank of Color Guard for his company, and that, in that capacity, during the recent bloody engagement at Antietam, Maryland, Sergeant Walker nobly comported himself, holding the Stars and Stripes high throughout an awful battle that claimed his life. I am told by the Captain of his company that your son heroically withstood several rounds and led his unit forward before succumbing from his wounds. I and the Nation are grateful for his service and sacrifice on behalf of us all. You can be most proud.*
>
> *Your most humble servant,*
>
> *Col. Searing"*

By now, the scattered sounds of weeping could be heard throughout the congregation. Ranford saw that Amy too was sobbing quietly next to him. The preacher asked his flock to rise and sing a rousing hymn that punctuated the glorious sadness that permeated the chapel.

Following the service, as the congregants mingled under the rustling trees in front of the church, Hiram Walker approached Ransford. Holding his cap in his trembling hands, the grieving father asked for a private moment with him, catching him by surprise.

"It's good to see you back from the war, son. I am most pleased you survived your wound."

"Thank you, sir. I am so sorry that Alex was taken . . .. He was a fine man and a good friend. It truly grieves me, Mr. Walker," Ransford told him, speaking sincerely but without any sense of what was the right or wrong thing to say in such circumstances. He felt extremely awkward.

"Thank you, Ransford. You are most kind . . .. I wonder if I might ask you a favor on behalf of my son?"

"Of course, sir, anything."

"Through some wonder of modern science—em-balm-ing they say—they're sending my boy's remains home to us in the next few days. He'll be coming home on the train to Saratoga. I, I honestly don't know how I could fetch him and bring him here, son. And I have no one else to call upon for this difficult task. Would it be in your power, would you consider doing this service for me? I am happy to pay you for your time, Ransford."

"I would be honored to do this for you and your family Mr. Walker . . .. And for Alexander."

Mr. Walker's stoic demeanor dissolved. He hugged Ransford and thanked for absolving him of this worry.

A few days later, Ransford was alerted that Alex Walker's body would be arriving in Saratoga the next day on the 10 a.m. train. He drove the wagon to the station, armed with a letter from Mr. Walker releasing his son's body to Ransford's care. The transaction went surprisingly smoothly as there were several bodies of departed soldiers kept in a refrigerated railroad car cooled by walls of ice and under the care of a Union sergeant, whose job it was to deliver the remains to responsible parties at the Saratoga station.

Armed with a fluttering candle, the Sergeant sorted through the dark, frigid railcar, divided by shelves containing several primitive caskets stacked to the roof, until he came to a rough-hewn pine box with "Sgt. A. Walker-30th NY" scrawled in black paint on its side.

"This be the one, son," said the Sergeant. "Now please give me a hand and we'll haul him out onto the platform."

Once out in the light, the Sergeant took a small black crowbar and, quite surprising Ransford, pried open the lid of the box, revealing the remains of Ransford's boyhood friend in the stark daylight. "Need you to identify 'im, son. If it's Sergeant Walker make yer mark on this sheet."

"Stop calling me 'son', Sergeant. I saw action in Virginia with McLellan . . .. Now let's have a look at him."

"My apologies, brother . . .."

The Sergeant removed the lid and there was Alex Walker, or a version of him, tucked oddly into the pale yellow walls of the pine box, his broad shoulders hunched against the sides. Although the embalmers had done their level best to prepare Sgt. Walker for his journey, the ragged reminders of his violent end were quickly apparent. His uniform was marked by several holes and tears where Minié balls had torn through his torso and thighs, small red halos surrounding each where his blood had stained his jacket and trousers. His face had not been struck but it bore a sunken and sallow appearance, as if the 20-year-old man had aged dramatically since his enlistment. And yet, despite these insults, Ransford could see the young man before him had once been his friend.

"It's him, Sergeant. It's Sergeant Walker."

Ransford completed his business with the Sergeant, who had drawn this unappealing duty back in New York City, where hundreds of corpses arrived steadily into the great port daily and were then transported outward by trains, boats, and wagons throughout the Northeast to the many small cities and towns awaiting return of their fallen heroes.

The Sergeant explained to Ransford that as long as the body was kept cool—"I put some blocks of ice in there with 'im for the trip," he said—the powerful chemicals that had replaced the blood throughout Sgt. Walker's circulatory system would stave off decomposition for quite some time. He admitted that, "this whole embalming business being so new and all," there were times when it didn't work so well.

After they hoisted Sgt. Walker's coffin onto the wagon, Ransford started north along the familiar road to Corinth, his horse trudging forward slowly under the new burden. An easy breeze blew across Ransford's face and the surprising pleasantness of the bright autumn day helped him forget his strange chore, at least momentarily. Soon, though, he began thinking about his friend, Alex Walker, not the sullen body crammed into a pine box behind him.

"Well doesn't this beat all, Alex . . .. Who would have ever thought you'd be back there and I'd be up here under these circumstances?" He paused, as if anticipating a response. "I recall you were a wild, fun loving fella. You did have a wit about you, always made us laugh."

He pondered his interactions with Alex Walker while growing up and sharing experiences in their small mountain town. They'd fished for brook trout in Sturdevant Creek together and, on sweltering summer days, they'd swung from a rope into the Hudson River, falling wildly into the cooling water.

"I must say, Sergeant Walker, you did make a name for yourself on that battlefield. Your family is truly proud of you, my friend, and, well hell, I'm proud of you . . .. Not many would have had the courage you showed that awful day."

"You must have loved your brothers, Alex. Your brothers in arms. I know how that feels." Ransford continued his one-sided conversation with his friend for a good part of the trip. It was oddly fulfilling to him, even knowing that it might appear strange, to someone who had they been listening in.

After the nearly three-hour journey, Ransford delivered Alex Walker to his home at the outskirts of Corinth, where his father, mother, brothers and sisters had been waiting on a sprawling front porch that overlooked the Saratoga Road and a deep green pasture where sheep dotted the landscape. They all rose and stepped cautiously down from the porch, the children gathering close around their mother, who bowed her head and wept. Mr. Walker opened the gate in the picket fence encircling the yard and stepped out to great Ransford, shaking his hand sincerely.

"So that's my boy back there, eh Ransford?"

"It's Alex, sir."

Hiram Walker, who looked too young to have a son as old as Alex, held back his tears, his voice quivering.

"I am most grateful, Ransford. You are a good friend to me and mine. Could I ask you another favor, young man? Would you help me bring him into the house? We'll be setting him up in the parlor."

As they carried the coffin into the home and laid it on a large oak table in the parlor, Mr. Walker explained that the family would be hosting relatives at the house the next day and that the minister would be holding a service for Alex at the church on Sunday, prior to his burial. "It would do us an honor if you would join us at the funeral, Ransford. Could you?"

"Of course, Mr. Walker . . . .. Sir, if it's no offense, I'd feel better about Alex's circumstances if he were in a better, well, a better box. I'd like to send him off in better accommodations if you know what I mean."

"I surely do, son. Is that even possible with Sunday just a few days off?"

"I think, with your permission, my daddy and I can make something more suitable in that amount of time, sir."

"By all means, do, Ransford. We would greatly appreciate anything you can do to send our son off to Heaven in a proper way. Thank you!"

Ransford returned to his home in South Corinth worried he'd taken on too much by promising to fashion a new casket for Alex Walker's funeral in three days. But Elias Densmore was known locally as a proficient carpenter and joiner, who could layer strips of wood using hot glue and small nails to create ornamental moldings and trim that many in the community valued greatly. He and Ransford set about their work immediately and within a few days had constructed an impressive casket out of several fine pieces of cherry he'd purchased from a local lumber yard.

The next day, Ransford delivered the varnished red casket to Mr. Walker. He helped the grieving parents clothe Alex Walker's cold, stiff body in a freshly-laundered white button-down shirt and black Sunday-service pants, and they transferred the young man's body into the coffin, which had been lined tastefully with white cotton cloth. Hiram Walker and his wife expressed their gratitude.

"My boy looks so much better now, Mr. Densmore. And his coffin is quite beautiful . . .. We can't thank you and your father enough," said Alex's mother, who offered Ransford a freshly baked apple pie as a token of her appreciation.

For his part, Hiram Walker gave Ransford yet another sincere hug and handed him an envelope that contained $50, quite surprising Ransford, who tried in vain to give the money back.

"You take this small token of our appreciation, Ransford. You and Elias have a gift, a gift, I tell you. We are most grateful."

"Thank you, Mr. Walker. I'm honored to help send Alex on his journey in a proper way," Ransford replied. "I'll see you at the service tomorrow and please don't hesitate to ask if I can be of any help."

So began Ransford's gradual and unexpected journey into what would become his lifelong profession, a profession that was largely unheard of in rural places, where funerals had traditionally been simple (and unhygienic) affairs carried out by family members in living rooms, kitchens, and parlors. As time passed and the war dragged on, more young men were sent home to Corinth in pine boxes, each of them needing special handling and attention that was foreign to the culture of the day.

Several times Ransford was asked to help grieving families in some way, either by fetching the body in Saratoga and transporting it home or by preparing a proper casket or improving the appearance of the body. Increasingly, families sought to dress their loved one in a favorite outfit or "enliven" their face with cosmetics. Soon an array of specialists—from embalmers and beauticians to carpenters and stone masons—were required to achieve what was regarded as a "proper burial."

Much as families yearned for a "good death" should their young men be killed in battle, in the late 19th Century, the desire for a proper burial would take root among grieving families nationwide—from rural areas to great cities—as something to be prized and encouraged. Ransford evolved into this role quite naturally, almost unintended, as his special talents and his unique disposition drew him to those who needed them.

Many of the 20 young men from Corinth who ended up dying during the war, never had their bodies returned home, as most soldiers were buried where they fell in distant corn fields, along rivers and next to barns throughout the South where most of the fighting took place. But the families of those who were sent home, by virtue of the relatively new art of embalming, invariably summoned Ransford. He was viewed as someone particularly sensitive to their needs and it helped that, in most cases, he had known the lads personally.

Several boys from Sylvanus's unit—the 115th NY Infantry—were sent home over the next few years. Nathan Ide was killed at Darbytown Road, Virginia; Archie Brooks died of disease in Camp Douglas; Hiram Woodcock (one of three brothers from the Woodcock family) died from wounds suffered in a disastrous battle fought in the swamps in Olustee, Florida.

But the harshest news came when Ransford learned that during the madness of Olustee, his brother, Sylvanus, had been taken prisoner. Ransford was devastated. Just a few weeks before the Olustee battle, he and Amy had been married in the Methodist Church. As often happened for joyous events that helped townsfolk forget the war's perverse realities, the celebration that followed at the Grange Hall brought out much of the community. The joy from these events rarely lasted long and Ransford and Amy's wedding was no exception. There would be many more funerals than weddings.

Word of the battle at Olustee, the only major battle fought in Florida, and its toll on several Corinth boys, soon took hold. Some had been wounded and some—Hiram Woodcock and Lloyd Wesson among them—had been killed. And, as the defeated Union brigade retreated through the swamps and pine thickets of north central Florida, many were taken prisoner. According to reports, soldiers from the so-called "colored regiments" that fought alongside the 115th who had been captured during the battle were executed by the rebels, who had promised no quarter would be given to Negro soldiers who sided with the Union.

As dire as the circumstances were, the poor lads' fate was preferable to that of men taken prisoner by the Confederate Army late in the war. As the war turned decidedly against the rebels in 1864, Confederate prisoner of war camps became treacherous hell holes, renowned for severe overcrowding and lacking in basic needs, such as food, housing, and medical supplies. By far, the worst among them was Andersonville Prison Camp in Georgia. A short time after the battle, Ransford learned that Sylvanus had been shipped to Andersonville.

For more than a year Ransford's family suffered in silence. There were no letters, telegrams, or articles to reveal Sylvanus's condition, just a gnawing doubt. The war was raging unabated throughout the South and General Ulysses S. Grant was using his well-equipped army as a cudgel against General Robert E. Lee and the Army of Northern Virginia, battering them almost daily in a series of bloody battles that drained the rebels of men and materiel. Late in 1864, General Sherman's armies marched through Georgia from the conquered city of Atlanta to Savannah and the sea, gashing the very heart of the South. A detachment to liberate Andersonville (not far from his route) was never sent and the nearly 30,000 Union prisoners confined there in squalor, ravaged by malnutrition and disease, continued to die at a savage rate.

With news that General Lee had accepted General Grant's terms for surrender at Appomattox Court House in Northern Virginia, Corinth erupted in spontaneous celebration. Steam whistles screamed from the mills along the river and rifles shot into the air as beleaguered townsfolk ran into the streets of the little town, hugging and dancing jigs on Main Street. They had suffered together for five years, weathering a long horrid ordeal that touched every family in profound ways. Soon their boys—many of them anyway—would be coming home.

But not Sylvanus.

Not long after Lee's surrender, a recently returned veteran knocked on the front door of Ransford and Amy's cottage in South Corinth, a place of their own they had built not far from Elias Densmore's home. The man was bearing a telegram, a piece of paper folded upon itself.

"Good day, Ransford. Ma'am," he said, nodding respectfully to Amy, who stood next to Ransford at the door.

"Good day, Thomas. How have you been getting on since returning?" Ransford inquired of Thomas Austin, an acquaintance who had seen plenty of action with the 30th and was suffering the ill effects of a wound to his shoulder. Like many of the lads who'd returned to Corinth after mustering out from their units, Tom Austin suffered from more than the flesh wound that pained him constantly and hampered his movements.

Bouts of melancholy mingled with occasional outbursts made the young man difficult for others to be around, particularly those who hadn't fought in the war. Fifty young men eventually returned to Corinth from the war and all were wounded in one way or another. Increasingly, these veterans would find solace in morphine or whiskey, which would, in turn, make them less reliable workers, partners and friends.

"I'm doing as well as can be expected, Ransford. Thank you for asking . . .. I have a telegram for you concerning your brother. It came in early this morning and I told the shopkeeper—I've been doing some odd work for him, you know—I told him you'd want to be knowing this as soon as possible."

"I imagine I would, Thomas," said Ransford, taking the paper from the young man's trembling hands. "I am grateful you brought it out straightaway."

The news contained in the telegraph was not unexpected. But its finality and its certitude shocked him nonetheless and he wanted to be alone with Amy now, unexposed.

"Here's a dollar for your trouble, Thomas. I do appreciate your effort and my best to your family."

"Why thank you, Ransford. I thank you kindly . . .. I hope you and the Missus find peace."

"Thank you, kind sir," Amy added sincerely, before escorting Thomas out the front door and closing it behind him.

"Oh, my love!" She held Ransford for what seemed like hours, stroking his sandy hair and shoulders, which would occasionally shudder spasmodically. Still clutching the telegram, Ransford eventually felt weak and retreated with Amy to the parlor sofa. They sat there together without speaking for quite some time before Ransford cleared his throat and read the terrible telegram aloud.

"RANSFORD DENSMORE,

I REGRET TO INFORM YOU THAT PRIVATE SYLVANUS DENSMORE OF THE 115TH NEW YORK INFANTRY REGIMENT HAS BEEN CONFIRMED AS HAVING DIED DURING HIS CAPTIVITY IN CONFEDERATE ARMY PRISONER OF WAR CAMP AT ANDERSONVILLE, GEORGIA STOP

THE US ARMY'S RECENT INVESTIGATION INTO THE RECORDS THE ANDERSONVILLE CAMP DIVULGED THAT PRIVATE DENSMORE DIED OF STARVATION AT THE CAMP ON OR ABOUT JUNE 22, 1864 STOP

PLEASE KNOW THAT THE NATION IS GRATEFUL FOR HIS SERVICE AND HIS SACRIFICE STOP

SINCERELY,

COL. JAMES HOUGHTON"

He shook his head from side to side as he reread the telegram several times.

"They should have never been in that infernal part of the country. What in hell were the generals thinking, sending 115th into some swamp in the south? Damn Confederates should all be hanged for this!"

Amy just listened.

"Why Sylvanus? There never was a sweeter boy. And I'm not just saying that because he's my brother . . .. I wished I'd done more to talk him out of going. I should have done more, convinced him that Daddy needed him at the farm."

"This is not your fault, Ransford Densmore," Amy said sternly. "Your brother wanted to serve like so many other boys. He was proud to join in the cause . . . .. It's just God's will that some died and some came home."

"Why on earth should I come home and not him? Why me and not Charlie Washburn or Alex Walker? I'm no better than them; not by a long shot. God's not making any damn sense, Amy!"

The words took Amy aback. She wasn't accustomed to such frank and blasphemous talk, certainly not from her husband. But she also chalked it up to anger speaking more than anything.

"I don't doubt that you're angry and hurting, Husband. I'm hurting right here with you. But please don't let your anger cast your faith aside. We are God-fearing folk, Ransford, and we don't presume to know why He does what He does. But I will say that I've had some notion of His plan for you."

"And what might that be, Wife?"

"I've seen you with grieving families, mothers, fathers, widows, and such. I've seen how you help them through times like this, how you ease their burden just enough so they can go on and face another day. You've got a gift for that, Ransford, and if that doesn't come from God I don't what does . . . .. I've also seen you handle the bodies of the departed with the respect and care that they deserve. You send them on their way in the afterlife with love and reverence. There aren't many among us that have the temperament for such things."

He sat silently, absorbing what Amy was saying as if realizing for the first time that these tendencies came naturally to him. He had found strange comfort from performing the services associated with caring for the dead as well as the living that they left behind.

"You have become Charon, Ransford, and it's your duty to ferry the souls of the dead to the afterlife. Without a proper burial, you know that their unsatisfied spirits will wander aimlessly along the shores of the river Styx . . .. You provide them with honor in death, Ransford. You are the ferryman."

That was the first time Amy had invoked the Greek myth of Charon, the ferryman, and it resonated with Ransford, who had stumbled across references to the mysterious god while reading a translation of Dante's *Divine Comedy* recently. He paused and gave his wife an appreciative gaze.

"Yes, I suppose that about covers it. But, isn't Charon an ugly, smelly, old man?"

Amy erupted in spontaneous laughter.

"Why yes he is, Ransford. But you happen to be a young, handsome, and sweet-smelling version."

They laughed together, gratefully, after being so drained of emotion, before conversation returned to the dire matter at hand.

"Amy, I'm going to have to fetch him."

"I figured as much, Ransford. My goodness I can't even begin to fathom how long a trip that might be. Would you like me to come with you?"

"No, my dear. The baby will be coming soon. I'd sleep much easier if you could stay with your parents until I return with Sylvanus . . .. I don't know how it's going to be traveling these days. Maybe a week or two. What do you think?"

"I think you need to bring your brother home."

XV: Andersonville

The next day Ransford boarded a train in Saratoga Springs, beginning an odyssey that took him several days and traversed through many of the recently warring states. With no direct means of traveling from the northeast states that comprised the Union into the deep southern states of the Confederacy, Ransford found himself navigating along a patchwork itinerary that included numerous railroads crisscrossing the eastern half of the nation and stops in several cities.

As he ventured deeper into the cradle of the rebellion, the scale of misery visited upon the people of the South revealed itself to Ransford. The trains chugged past mile after mile of devastated countryside, pockmarked by scorched forests and demolished villages. In places, lonely red brick chimneys and smokestacks poked up from piles of rubble that had once been grand homes or factories. Dead and bloated farm creatures that had been caught in the crossfire of recent battle littered the roadsides and pastures.

Small groups of black men, women and children in ragged clothes, burdened by packs and bundles atop their heads, trudged along the railroad tracks, seemingly headed north to some unknown future. Others toiled in the table flat fields under a sweltering sun, picking cotton or tending vegetables, ceaselessly laboring as if the great war and their hard-won freedom had never happened. Detachments of victorious federal soldiers were stationed in city squares and crossroads, keeping the peace in a place that abhorred but feared them. Contingents of Union cavalry galloped here and there, patrolling or chasing rebel bands that still refused to concede defeat. In the cities, packs of poor, displaced families wandered through the streets, desperately searching for food, shelter, or protection from marauding thugs who preyed upon the weak and helpless. Wounded rebel veterans seemed to be everywhere, many missing limbs with primitive bandages covering bloody stumps. They lined benches inside the train stations in Savannah; they were propped against trees in parks in Charleston, holding tin cups and begging for Union silver from the thousands of northerners that had descended upon their cities after hostilities ended. The scale of it revolted Ransford; he clearly saw how thoroughly his reviled foe had been destroyed—not just physically and economically, but psychologically as well. The vaunted and terrifying rebel yell had been replaced with a plaintive cry for help.

Before long, Ransford found his way to a village not far from Andersonville, where he hired a local lad with a wagon to drive him to the former prison camp. Having no idea what to expect, he labored under the hope that someone at the facility, possibly a Union commander, would help direct him to the whereabouts of his brother's body. Nothing had prepared him for the ungodly reality of the wretched place.

The first sign that he was nearing the infamous prison camp wafted past his nose and caused the old brown mare pulling the wagon to start. The pervasively foul stench, like nothing he'd ever experienced, built steadily and became almost unbearable by the time they were at the gates of the sprawling wooden fort.

The nearly 20-foot tall stockade, an impenetrable wall fashioned of perfectly hewn pine poles with sentry towers every 50 feet, ringed the entire massive encampment, making it impossible to see what activities were occurring inside. Outside the fortress teams of workers, some shirtless soldiers and some black laborers, were digging what appeared to be trenches in the flat mowed area to the west of the gates. A small military encampment commanded a hill just to the south, not far from a large wooden warehouse-type structure where wagons came and went.

"I'll be dropping you here if y'all don't mind, sir," stated the young man who had driven Ransford out from Oglethorpe, Georgia. He had kept mostly to himself, rendered silent by Ransford's Union roots, but willing to carry out distasteful tasks like this one in order to procure much-needed funds.

"That'll be fine, young man. I thank you." Ransford handed the lad a silver dollar and walked up the path to a sentry, a Michigan private, guarding the entranceway to the former prison.

"Good day, sir. What's your business?" asked the Private, maintaining a resolute gaze forward.

"Good day to you, Private. I'm not sure how to say it other than: I've come to see if I can find my brother."

The Private's eyes softened. He looked more closely at Ransford and made note of his brass service badge, his cane, and the odd shape of his head, which, though healed, lacked a goodly portion of his skull.

"44th NY, eh?"

"Yes, I served in the 44th in the Grand Army, until I was wounded outside of Richmond. That was some time ago, I'm afraid."

"Wish you boys would have won it back then, sir. Woulda saved us a whole lot of trouble."

"You and me both, Private."

"I'm, happy to try to help, sir, but I can't promise anything. I am sure sorry for your loss but it's the damnedest thing I ever seen in there," the young private confided, shaking his head from side to side.

He reached out his hand, at first to shake, and then took a small brown bottle out of his trousers. "This here is Eucalyptus oil. Slather some of this under your nose, sir, it'll help."

"Thank you kindly, Private. Now, if I was looking for my brother, if there's any chance of finding him, what's my best bet?"

"I'd recommend you going right up to the Quartermaster himself. He's been put in charge of this operation . . .. Up there to the right, in the big tent."

"Thank you, brother," Ransford said sincerely, once again shaking the soldier's hand.

He walked nearly a quarter mile along the perimeter of Camp Sumter, known to most of the world as Andersonville, before he encountered another sentry outside the encampment. After once again demonstrating his noble intentions, Ransford was escorted to a tent in the middle of the camp where a high-ranking officer was speaking to three aides while pointing to an enormous map splayed on a prodigious table.

"Here. Have the men dig here!"

At that point, an orderly who had listened to Ransford's story, politely interrupted.

"Pardon the interruption, General, but this fellow—he's a veteran—has come some distance to inquire about the whereabouts of his brother."

Quartermaster General Montgomery Meigs, a handsome, middle-aged man with a meticulously tended beard, asked his three aides to return in five minutes while he addressed Ransford, who was quite impressed to be standing before a general.

"Sir!" Ransford straightened his back and snapped a spontaneous salute.

"At ease, son . . .. What can I do for you?"

"General, I know you're a powerfully busy man, but I've come a long way to see if I can locate my brother. I know it's a long shot but it's hard for me and my family back in New York to know Sylvanus is buried somewhere down here. I told my wife and father I'd do anything in my power to try to bring him back."

"It's a noble crusade you're on . . .. What's your name?"

"Ransford, sir."

"Ransford, I'm not in charge of this operation but I personally accompanied the leaders because I couldn't abide the thought of our boys, who suffered so much languishing in this infernal place— 13,000 of them dying here—that I vowed to President Lincoln a short time before he was murdered that I wanted to do a complete accounting of who died here, locate their bodies, and, if humanly possible, re-bury them with dignity.

"This travesty should have never happened. You take a man prisoner, you're responsible for him, plain and simple. I come from the South, born and raised in Augusta. The southern honor we hear so much about was nowhere to be found in Andersonville. We have a solemn obligation to these brave souls, including your brother, to make this right."

He described how the specialized unit, included handpicked staff who had distinguished themselves in graves registration and logistics throughout the war, were painstakingly reviewing documents maintained by prison staff (including its infamous commandant, who had been recently hanged for war crimes) and verbal and written reports from Andersonville's survivors.

In fact, he said, one long suffering captured soldier, Dorence Atwater, one of the first to be taken prisoner, maintained a secret list of every Union soldier who had died and been buried there. This list, General Meigs said, had been extremely helpful in locating and identifying thousands who were buried unceremoniously in trenches outside Andersonville's walls.

"Private Atwater is here, helping us identify graves and match them with his list. But when all is said and done, neither Private Atwater nor I are in charge of this mission. Our real commanding officer can be found in the next tent over. Her name is Clara Barton.

"Miss Barton ranks all of us. I'd like you to take your noble search to her. If anyone here can help, she can."

"Thank you, sir. Thank you!"

Accompanied by one of the general's aides, Ransford was introduced to Clara Barton, who was poring over a document of some sort at a desk in tent. She rose and shook Ransford's hand while looking into his eyes. She was a handsome woman, he thought, with fastidiously kept black hair, braided and pinned back to the sides of her head. Despite the humidity, she wore a dark, long sleeved dress that buttoned to the top of her neck. And yet she seemed cool and comfortable, gazing deeply at him with dark, clear eyes.

"Very pleased to meet you, sir."

"Miss Barton. Pleased to make your acquaintance," said Ransford awkwardly. He wasn't prepared to have met a general, much less a woman, on his grim errand. But something about her felt familiar and non-threatening. *Nurse Jacqueline*, he thought, *she reminds me of Nurse Jacqueline.*

"I am told you seek the whereabouts of your brother. Honestly, we are unraveling a great and terrible mystery here. So many men suffered and died here—including your brother, apparently, for which I am quite sorry—and they were unceremoniously interred under extremely disorganized circumstances, I'm afraid. But we have devoted ourselves to the task, Ransford. I will do my utmost to help you because I know how this must grieve you and your family . . .. If you would kindly give me his name and unit, and about when he might have been sent to Andersonville, I'll see what I can do."

"His name was Sylvanus Densmore, Private, 115th New York Infantry Regiment. He was captured after the battle of Olustee, in March of '64."

"Hmm.. .. That would put him here pretty early in the cycle," she said, opening a large ledger, each page featuring hundreds of handwritten entries, each one offering the name and unit of a deceased union prisoner. Using a ruler to mark her place on each page, like a teacher might, she scanned the lists that had been entered chronologically from the first death to the last. After several minutes, she halted, staring down at the page as if to be certain.

Then she read the line aloud: "Number two-thousand three-hundred and twenty. Densmore, S. F. 115th NY Infantry. June 22. Diarrhea . . .. I think we found him, Ransford. I'm so sorry."

Surprised at the impact of hearing the cold accounting of his brother's death read aloud, Ransford leaned over Miss Barton's shoulder to see the entry for himself. He felt suddenly shaken, even slightly dizzy, and Clara Barton stood and gave him a sincere hug. Then, upon pulling slightly away, her hand went to the side of Ransford's head, pulling aside the shock of hair that he tended to comb over the scar at the top of his head. She was looking at him clinically now.

"May I . . . have a look?"

"I suppose so," he said, taken aback, but accepting her sudden but sincere curiosity about his wound. He leaned downward slightly.

"This work is really quite remarkable, Ransford. I would like to know the surgeon's name. From my experience on the battlefield, I would have never expected you to have survived with a wound like this, under field conditions. Quite remarkable."

"To be honest, miss, I wasn't awake for any of it and not for a week or so after. But he was the surgeon attached to the 44th New York Infantry Regiment . . .. It took me a long time to get my bearings again."

"I'm sure it did, soldier," she said, marveling at his recovery. "I think I'll look into your doctor if you wouldn't mind."

"Not at all, Miss Barton."

"Well, Ransford, we know your brother is here somewhere. Now we have to find him. The one thing in our favor is that, I'm sorry to say, he was one of the earliest to die. Back then, they buried the men with a little more care and with better marking . . .. I'll ask Dorence if he can locate your brother's remains and, if so, I will grant permission for him to be exhumed and released to you. Does that sound suitable?"

"It surely does, ma'am. I would be profoundly grateful, Miss Barton."

"Very good to meet you, Ransford. Blessings to you and your family."

The rest of the day was spent searching for Sylvanus' body among the thousands of poorly marked graves, more like trenches, that had been dug in various locations outside the stockade. Using clues such as the date of death and the fact that Sylvanus had been the 2320th prisoner to die, Dorence Atwater, the young soldier who had survived nearly two years of excruciating captivity, was able to pinpoint the spot.

Two Union privates dug into the black soil near the edge of the pine forest that bordered the prison grounds, revealing the skeleton of Ransford's brother, a familiar silver cross still dangling from around the vertebrae of his neck. The men fashioned a small pine box, about a quarter the length and width of a normal coffin, with two hemp rope handles attached to either end, that Ransford could use to transport his brother's bones on the long trip homeward. As the evening sun neared the western horizon, Ransford bade farewell to Andersonville and its many horrors. As the years passed, however, the things Ransford would most remember of his trip to Andersonville were the incredibly dedicated people—Clara Barton, Dorence

Atwater, and others—who had volunteered to bring order and dignity to a place most would've fled from, a place that God had, for a time, abandoned.

The long, disjointed trip home was uneventful but exhausting as Ransford hauled the heavy unmarked wooden box through many stations and onto many trains. Some two weeks after starting his journey, he returned home to Corinth with his brother's remains in a box.

Ransford, Amy, and Elias Densmore hosted a small memorial service at the Methodist Church which attracted many townsfolk who came to offer their condolences and share memories. Along with relatives and friends, the pews were lined with veterans, young men with assorted wounds, many with odd, blank stares on their faces, still trying to adjust to life after war. After the service, Ransford thanked each person for coming and, taking a special interest in the veterans, many being his friends, he inquired about their activities and offered help when warranted.

They later buried Sylvanus' remains in a pretty spot beneath an ancient crabapple tree along the banks of the upper Kayderossas Creek, near a grassy embankment overlooking a small pond that had grown behind a beaver dam. When they were boys, Sylvanus and Ransford had liked to fish there for native trout on spring mornings and swim there in the sweltering days of summer.

With the war over and the Sylvanus' tragic death behind him, Ransford began to follow a happier, more traditional path. Despite his obvious wound, which continued to weep throughout his life, Ransford appeared to be better suited to his post-war life than many local veterans. Some attributed it to his open embrace of Christianity, some said the war had somehow changed him for the better, others placed the credit squarely on Amy's shoulders. Of course, few, other than Amy, were there when he woke in the middle of the night shuddering at the ghosts and demons that still visited his dreams. Few saw him wince at the pain that often shot through his head without warning. Nonetheless, in the eyes of the community, his experience and bearing brought him a certain status that few achieved at such a young age.

Ransford grew into his role as the town's only undertaker, providing a range services in support of grieving families from embalming and burial to grave digging and head stones. He and Amy worked together, sharing the burdens of business along with the growing domestic demands that came from a rapidly expanding family. Their children arrived early in the marriage and the four—two boys and two girls—were born in close succession, each barely a year apart. Soon, their pleasant cottage in South Corinth felt cramped. Over the next several years, they expanded the building in various ways to accommodate their growing brood as well as the funeral and furniture business that had begun to flourish in myriad ways.

When his eldest son, Isaac, achieved manhood, he chose to join Ransford in the funeral business, beginning an apprenticeship that would form the basis of a family succession plan for several generations to come. The family thrived and so did Corinth as an unparalleled post-war economic boom found its way to every corner of the northern states. A short time after the war, outside investors led by a German man named Pagenstecher coalesced around a plan to construct one of the nation's first modern paper mills on the rocky promontory above Palmer Falls. After being built in 1870, the Hudson River Pulp & Paper Company continued to grow and expand, becoming something of an industrial behemoth built into the Gibraltar-like rocks above the rapids, which provided boundless power for the factory. Before long, many of Corinth's men worked in the factory, which produced a superior brand of paper in high demand at the time.

Two decades after the end of hostilities, life had normalized, or so it seemed on the surface. Veterans, who hadn't succumbed to the ravages of their wounds or their addictions, had mostly assimilated back into the day-to-day life of the community, finding constructive strategies for dealing with their demons. Civilians, who had weathered the war at home, had turned their attentions to positive pursuits such as growing new crops, flocks, businesses, and families. Efforts to remember and memorialize the great sacrifices offered up by 70 young men and their families—such as the commissioning of a great granite statue that would stand in perpetuity at the key intersection of Main and Maple streets—were completed and celebrated with significant fanfare. But when all was said and done, many in the community preferred to look away from the war and its toll. It had been a bad dream, one best pushed back into the recesses of the memories of aging men and women.

The war's purpose and the messy truce with the South that followed was soon to be muddied by talk glorifying the nobility of southern generals and their *Lost Cause*. Their leaders' steadfast resistance to give up the barbarous practice of slavery and their treasonous attack upon federal forces had been recast, replaced with a narrative about a people's reasonable resistance to "outside invaders" and the preservation of states' rights. Although they wouldn't admit it in polite company, regular folk up north just wanted things to get back to normal. Of course, veterans and their families couldn't go a day without revisiting the war in their minds. It shaped them and gave their lives meaning.

One particularly hot July day in 1885, Ransford was summoned by a resolute knock on the door of his South Corinth office. There stood a young uniformed man, a captain, who cut a dashing figure in a black cavalry hat festooned with crossed sabers, shiny brass buttons lining his indigo shirt, and a sword attached to his hip.

"Good day, sir. Would you be Ransford Densmore? Formerly of the 44th New York?"

"That would be me, Captain. What can I do for the Army?"

"Sir, I've been asked to escort you to Mount McGregor. Former President Grant has passed and your services are needed."

Everyone knew that former President Grant had, in recent months, taken up residence at a cottage on the shoulder of Mount McGregor not far from Corinth in order to finish his memoirs. He had taken ill with cancer and was racing against time to complete the manuscript in hopes of raising enough money to restore his family's lost fortune. In the years after leaving office, the great commander had fallen into bankruptcy, thanks in no small part to a series of bad investments promoted by his son. At the urging of his friend Mark Twain, Grant dedicated his last breaths to an effort to resurrect not only his solvency but also his good name.

"I am truly grieved to hear the news, Captain. I regarded him highly as both a general and my president."

"Yes, thank you, sir. Are you able to ride or would you prefer to take a carriage?" replied the Captain, who maintained his soldierly discipline.

"I'll fetch a horse." Ransford informed Amy that he had been summoned to Mount McGregor and to prepare for dinner without him. Funeral directors and their wives were accustomed to such interruptions.

Ransford followed the captain along a series of back roads that led to the foot of Mount McGregor, a steep promontory that rose up suddenly from the relatively flat flood plain formed by the Upper Hudson after it broke free from the Adirondacks and headed south toward Albany. From there they followed a switch-backed road steadily upward until, near the top, they reached a substantial house with a large front porch that commanded an incredible view of the valley below. It was here that General Grant had furiously dictated his memoirs to a team of aides assigned to the task, having completed the first and final draft just a few days earlier.

They rode up and dismounted in front of the porch. Several men had gathered and were standing and conversing near the front door, where two federal sentries stood at attention. One of them, a stocky middle-aged man with a ruddy complexion, stepped forward to meet them.

"Is this him, Captain?"

"Yes, he's your man."

"Thank you, Captain. That will be all." The Captain re-mounted his horse and rode up to a stable at the back of the cottage. Then the ruddy faced man turned to Ransford and reached out his hand.

"Good afternoon, Mr. Densmore. My name is Ely Parker. I served as General Grant's adjutant during the war and I have remained an aide and associate for quite some time . . .. Under these trying circumstances and quite aware of his imminent demise, the general was quite specific in his directions as to how he would like things handled," said Mr. Parker, all the while scanning Ransford up and down. "Have we met, Mr. Densmore?"

"I do recognize you, Mr. Parker, but I can't quite place it. I was with the 44th New York. Served under McLellan . . ."

Parker suddenly took a step back and slapped his slacks.

"Poughkeepsie. We shared a boat ride down the Hudson. As I recall you had a few choice words for another private and were close to blows . . .. Correct?"

"That's it! You have a quite a memory, sir."

"It's good to see you again, Ransford Densmore. I am glad you survived."

"I almost didn't. But thank you, sir. And you as well."

Mr. Parker explained that, while the former president's family had insisted on retaining an undertaker and embalmer from Saratoga Springs, the general had asked if an appropriately trained veteran could be present for any preparations that might be necessary. The staff had made inquiries, he said, and had learned of Ransford's service and occupation.

"He always trusted his soldiers more than civilians in life and he told me that wouldn't change after his death either."

"I am here for you and the general, Mr. Parker. Who are the local directors?"

"Ebenezer Holmes of Holmes and Company and his associate, a Mr. William Burke. They seem like reputable men. Do you know of them?"

"I only know of Mr. Holmes through his reputation as a skilled embalmer. I have worked with Billy Burke in the past though and I've found him to be an enthusiastic young man and one hell of a carpenter."

"Good. Good. The family will be relieved, Ransford. Would you do me a favor and have a look at President Grant? Maybe size things up until the others get here?"

"I'd be honored to help in any way needed, Mr. Parker."

He escorted Ransford into the house, through a large well-appointed sitting room, and into a darkened parlor where Ulysses S. Grant's body lay on a large oak table. The General was still in a light blue cotton robe and bed clothes, a pair of black leather slippers on his feet. The ill-fitting clothes appeared to puddle around his body, producing almost skeletal insinuations in the fabric. His vaunted black beard had become gray and unkempt; his face barely recognizable from that of the man who had doggedly led the nation to victory in 1865.

"My lord, he was far gone wasn't he?"

"Indeed, he was," Mr. Parker replied. "Weighed less than 100 pounds at the end. It's good he's found peace finally. No one gave more."

"I hate to say it, Mr. Parker, but there's not much to work with here in terms of embalming," Ransford said. "Forgive my indelicacy, sir, in this heat decomposition will be an issue."

"I appreciate your honest assessment. Were he a Seneca warrior, he would have been buried already, in the ground with his feet facing west after a brief gathering. But General Grant is an American hero, Ransford, and, as we learned with President Lincoln, this nation loves you much more when you're dead than alive," Ely Parker explained. "There are already plans for his body to travel considerably over the next few weeks and for it to be viewed by many thousands of people. We are hoping you and your colleagues can do your best. That is all we ask."

"Yes sir." Ransford responded with military sincerity as if still in the service.

Mr. Parker left Ransford and General Grant's body alone in the dark parlor where the heat and lack of air movement combined to create a stifling atmosphere. Ransford pulled back some of the dark curtains and opened a few windows, helping him to both see and breathe better as he inspected the body. Soon he was removing the general's clothing in preparation for the arrival of the funeral directors from Saratoga, who were expected shortly.

As was now his custom, particularly when he dealt with a person with whom he had some acquaintance, Ransford addressed the body in familiar terms, speaking softly, deliberately as he worked.

"Pleased to meet you, General. Honestly sir, I couldn't have imagined this in a thousand years.

"I was long gone from the service by the time you took over. But I know from some of the boys in the 44th, who wrote me over the years, that they didn't like you much when you commanded them. You drove them hard. One bloody battle after another. Wilderness. Spotsylvania. Cold Harbor. Petersburg. Day after day the dead piled up and you just kept hitting Lee again and again, like a man beating a snake . . ."

Ransford paused, looking down at the emaciated remains of the once formidable leader. The confident, glowering look, an omnipresent cigar jutting out from above his hard-set jaw was a distant memory, a photograph for a book that sat somewhere in this house, waiting to be published. At death he had become a pathetic remnant of a man, oddly similar to the men in the photographs he'd seen of the survivors at Andersonville. He thought about Sylvanus and how he must have looked near the end of his life in the hellish muddy pit that was his prison.

"I suppose you could've saved my brother if you had ordered Sherman to turn south for a week or two. But that didn't happen did it, General?

"Damn. These thoughts could drive a man mad, couldn't they, General? Half a million mothers and fathers, were they standing here where I am today, might be saying the same things about their loved ones to you. Blaming you.

"But you did end the war. Didn't you? You were probably the only general that could have. All those other fancy pants, perfumed, chess-playing, over-educated military minds couldn't beat Lee. But you did. And for that, I am grateful, sir . . .. I just wish you would have done it sooner.

"And I have to give you credit for staying alive long enough to finish your book. Hell, General, it looks like you were dead a month ago. Those horrible beasts were trying to pull you down into that bloody pit, but you beat them off. You beat them off for a while. I'm sure you're facing your judgement now . . .. I wish you well on your journey, General."

At that moment, Ely Parker re-entered the parlor along with two other men.

"Ransford Densmore, I'd like to introduce you to Ebenezer Holmes and his associate William Burke. Mr. Densmore is a veteran and a fellow undertaker from over in Corinth. He is here to provide you two gentlemen with any assistance in your endeavors," Mr. Parker said.

"Very good. From what I hear we can use all the help we can get. Good to make your acquaintance, Mr. Densmore," said Ebenezer Holmes. "Could you and Bill Burke be so kind as to fetch our equipment from the wagon? And we'll be needing the box as well."

"I'll be happy to go with Ransford to get the equipment Mr. Holmes." Billy Burke had met Ransford on several occasions. They'd even worked together at times when cooperation between funeral directors was called for. "Good to see you Ransford. How's your family?"

"Just fine, Billy. When are you going to start one of your own?" said Ransford, who was fond of the young man.

After several trips to the wagon the two men had toted an impressive assortment of equipment and supplies into the parlor. Tubes, mason jars, pumps, odd looking steel tools, and numerous dark brown glass bottles filled with various chemicals used in the embalming arts were assembled on another table next to some bookshelves in the corner.

They went out to the wagon and, with the help of two soldiers, carried the "box"—an incredibly bulky wooden crate that had been lined with lead—into the room. They packed the box full of ice that had been transported separately and transferred General Grant's body into the frigid cavity where he could be kept cool prior to embalming. They would spend the next day and a half preparing Grant's ravaged body for travel and viewing, applying the best of the mortician's arts to what many considered a fool's errand.

Once the body had been embalmed, touched up with cosmetics to hide places where his skin had become discolored, and dressed in a suit tailored to more closely fit General Grant's diminished frame, viewing hours for family and close staff commenced in the living room of the cottage. A short time later, a company of soldiers, former aides, elected officials, and members of the press left the cottage for the Saratoga Train Station and the beginning of General Grant's final tour of duty.

On the way, Ransford took his leave of the entourage at a nearby cross road, returning to South Corinth after more than two days. He was drained by the experience and looked forward to returning to his settled life in the mountains. The encounter with General Grant and Ely Parker had revived bitter recollections, but also fond memories of his short, vivid adventure with the men of the 44th. More than ever he yearned to learn more about their experiences after he'd been wounded, where they were now.

XVI: Gettysburg

Over the next several years, Ransford would strive to connect to the men he'd grown close to in the regiment. Some, like his dear friend Solomon Hickok, had died during the war. But many had survived the war and the many bloody battles that had followed their first major encounter with the Confederate Army at Hanover Court House, where Ransford nearly died. The 44th had distinguished itself in some of the war's most significant battles. They'd fought at Malvern Hill, Second Manassas, Antietam, Fredericksburg, Chancellorsville, Gettysburg, Wilderness, Cold Harbor, and Petersburg. And somehow, despite all the unrelenting carnage, many of his compatriots had survived. Perhaps it was training or perhaps it was luck, or then again, perhaps it was providence of a sort he did not understand. Ransford, now comfortably along with his life, longed to understand and reconnect with the men he had served with so long ago.

Whenever possible—between his growing responsibilities in business, family, and civic affairs—Ransford would write letters to members of his former platoon. And they, for the most part, would comply, keeping him abreast of their lives. Of course, he'd see Elijah Earls quite regularly around town at church or the general store and he would, on occasion, meet with Whitney for an ale at a tavern on Broadway in Saratoga. Jack Finnegan's whereabouts were less easy to ascertain; letters from Jack would occasionally appear postmarked from exotic corners of the world.

> *"Dearest Ransford,*
>
> *I find myself in Istanbul (that's in Turkey bumpkin) wearing a strange hat. Barely dressed women are bringing me beverages that bubble. I long to return to the States one of these days and I will, upon returning, promptly look you up. Happy to hear that you have settled with your sweetheart and have brought young Ranfords into the world. We are all the better for it.*

Your Humble Servant,

Jack

Ps. Please give my regards to your family . . . tell them you saved me."

Ransford was always amused and mystified by Jack's letters, this one in particular. He longed to see his friend again but accepted that he probably never would.

The years began to speed by as Ranford's children grew up to have families and children of their own. He and his son, Isaac, moved the funeral and furniture business into the heart of Corinth, opening the three-story storefront on Main Street just up the hill from the Methodist Church.

Before long, his grandson, James Harrison Densmore, joined them in business. A new century arrived with announcement after announcement of mind-boggling new technologies. The simple folk of Corinth were soon grappling with the implications of telephones, electric power, manned flights, and automobiles. As the world sped up, Ransford's life slowed down. His role in day to day matters of family and business lessened as he proudly watched his offspring carry on his legacy.

However, the memories of the great war and his brief role in it never abated. Now in his 70s and a lonely widower (Amy had passed a few years earlier), Ranford was part of a rapidly diminishing number of veterans who were largely tolerated by younger generations that knew little of the war, save for the exaggerated exploits of generals. When announcement came of a reunion to celebrate the 50th anniversary of the battle of Gettysburg, Ransford felt pulled to it and what could be his last opportunity to see members of his old regiment.

Accompanied by his son, Isaac, the two men made their way to the sprawling battlefield in the rolling green hills of southern Pennsylvania. By the time they arrived the town was teaming with 100,000 visitors, more than half of them aged veterans looking for one last glimpse of their former lives and the great struggle that defined them. Recognizing that Gettysburg could not nearly accommodate the influx, federal authorities stepped in to establish an enormous tent city on 280 acres of farmland that had hosted a great slaughter half a century earlier. Ransford and Isaac found themselves sharing a tent on a sweltering July night, each with a cot and a bucket of cold water.

The sparse accommodations did little to dampen the air of enthusiasm as the sun set over 50,000 aged veterans. A strange festiveness permeated the camp as fiddlers and harmonica players played familiar tunes around a thousand camp fires. Laughter, jigs, pipe smoke, and tall tales filled the night, transporting old men back to their youth. Isaac saw the light return to his father's eyes—relieving the melancholy that had taken root after Amy's death—as he shared memories with comrades from the 83rd Pennsylvania, the 20th Maine, and a few of the boys from the 44th.

Their sleep was short that night as dawn and the need for a latrine brought men out of their tents in droves; soon they were dressed, many in replicas of their former uniforms, bright badges and medals dangling from their chests, and venturing out to giant makeshift cafeterias in search of coffee and sustenance. Later that morning, oddly harkening back to a time when sergeants and captains barked commands and soldiers complied without thought, organizers rode through the camps announcing that "battle lines" would soon form for the long-awaited reenactment of Pickett's Charge. Like the parting of a blue-gray sea, great swaths of old men made their way to the positions many of them had occupied on the sprawling hay field between Cemetery Ridge and Seminary Ridge on that pivotal bloody day that marked the high tide of the Confederacy.

With the firing of a distant cannon from Little Round Top, several rag tag southern "regiments" bearing various Confederate battle flags and banners, appeared out of the western woods almost a half mile away. They waved their gray and butternut caps and let out howls and other noises meant to approximate the rebel yell as they proceeded slowly, deliberately across the great field between the two armies. The ragged line was marked by men on crutches, patches over eyes, or missing arms, all determined to make what was, for them, a difficult journey. As they drew closer, Ransford recognized in their faces a hard resolve, a fierce commitment to see the thing through no matter the consequences. Their jaws set and their shoulders leaning forward toward the distant ridge where tens of thousands of Union defenders stood, they appeared transfixed upon an unattainable goal. It was a look he remembered seeing on nearly every soldier he encountered on real battlefields long ago.

Union veterans, Ransford among them, stood in rough versions of their former regiments atop Cemetery Ridge, surveying the scene, patiently awaiting the onslaught. It was a warm, blue skied day, and the sound of drums and flutes added drama to the scene unfolding before more than 100,000 curious people, who had come to witness one of the greatest and most tragic events in American history. No one really knew what to expect. After all, there were no rifles or cannon fire or smoke to make the battle real in the minds of veterans.

Fifty years earlier, relentless cannon fire from Little Round Top rained down upon the rebel forces as they advanced gloriously across the field, leaving gaping holes in their ranks. Halfway across the field, Pickett's diminished regiments had to stop and dismantle a wooden fence in order to proceed, leaving them vulnerable to ten thousand Union rifles and cannon fire. Still they had proceeded, their lines shattered, up the gentle slope toward the stone wall at the top of the ridge. Blindly believing in their commanding general's invincibility, they continued to advance when half their ranks were dead or wounded, leaning hard into the hot lead that was tearing them to pieces. As the sea of elderly men slowly made their way up the hill, Ransford could see that same look in their eyes. There was no smoke, no sounds of battle, and no gore, but for the men in both lines, the battle still raged.

"My lord, Dad, I'm worried some of them won't make it," Isaac remarked, marveling at the thousands of elderly former Confederates laboring to cross the field.

"Oh, they'll make it, son," Ransford replied. "They always make it."

After quite some time, the rebel lines reached a scant 20 yards from the Union veterans and paused as if collectively wondering what on earth to do next. Tense moments in the Union veterans' lines followed with an odd anticipation hanging over the battlefield. Just then a series of yells—tired but noble facsimiles of the once terrifying rebel yell—rose up among the former Confederate soldiers as they began to run, as best they could, toward the Union vets' line. Flags and caps waving, canes extended over their heads, they closed the gap and descended upon the blue-clad warriors behind the stone wall. Upon reaching them a great spontaneous cheer erupted from both lines as the veterans embraced at the top of the wall. Many laughed and howled joyfully. Many wept.

Ransford hugged a Confederate veteran from a North Carolina regiment and they traded tales, even learning that they had both been at Hanover Court House in May, 1862. Surprised at the affection he felt for someone he'd tried to kill a half century earlier, Ransford and the man spoke of their trials and exploits in service of different armies as if discussing a sporting match. It was now a distant, detached thing to both of them. Ransford didn't feel angry at southern soldiers anymore, they were just like him, pulled into that horrible nightmare by the failures of their leaders.

Celebrations broke out spontaneously throughout the great campsite and the nearby town as if both former armies were experiencing the weight-relieving joy that can follow a good cathartic cry.

"Thank you, son," Ransford said to Isaac at one point. "I couldn't have made it here without you."

"Why on earth are you thanking me, father? I should be thanking you for your incredible sacrifice," Isaac said and then laughed, pointing to the top of Ransford's head. "I really couldn't have made here it without you!"

Ransford chuckled. "I suppose not, son."

After the joyous mayhem of the reenactment of Pickett's Charge had subsided and groups dissipated to other attractions, Ransford and Isaac procured a ride in a carriage that was shuttling visitors to various popular sites on the massive battlefield. They asked to be taken to Little Round Top, where, long after Ransford had left the service, the 44th had joined with the 83rd Pennsylvania, 12th Michigan, and the 20th Maine to repulse a furious attack on the second day of the great battle. While the 20th Maine and their valiant commander Colonel Chamberlain received much of the credit for his brilliant bayonet charge to blunt an assault that threatened to flank the entire Union army, the other three regiments had been holding off wave after wave of similar assaults by several Texan and Alabaman regiments upon their positions in the rocky crags and boulders along the mountain's western face. Many would credit the brigade's stubborn defense of Little Round Top that crucial second day of Gettysburg with not only winning the battle, but ultimately turning the tide of the war in the Union's favor.

On the little mountain's peak, a granite monument, the largest on the battlefield, had been erected by the patrons of the 12th and 44th New York Infantry Regiments to serve as a lasting reminder of the units' service during the war. Ransford and Isaac entered the darkened chamber of the battle monument, whose dimensions—12 feet in diameter and 44 feet tall—had been designed to symbolically represent the 12th and 44th Regiments. As their eyes acclimated to the dimness inside the chamber, they saw small groups of visitors scouring the bronze plaques lining the room for the names of long-lost loved ones. Ransford and Isaac made their way to a section containing the names of all who had served in the 44th. A family, comprised of two women and two children, a small boy and a girl, were huddled around a place on the wall, searching.

"Gramma Aura Lea! Gramma Aura Lea! Looky here! Isn't this Uncle Jack's name?"

A slender woman with braided golden hair and delicate features turned to look down at the boy, who was dressed in a replica of a Union military uniform, little gold epithets adorning his shoulders, and pointing upward toward a name carved into the plaque.

"Why, yes, my darling boy, that's Uncle Jack's name! What good eyes you have!"

Ransford turned instinctively toward the lyrical name he hadn't heard in many decades. *It couldn't be*, he thought. But she did appear to be about the correct age, mature but not old, like him. *Could she be?*

"Pardon me, Ma'am." Ransford tipped his cap politely, smiling at the petite, pretty woman. "Did I hear your name correctly? Would Aura Lea be your name?"

"Why yes, sir. Aura Lea is my name," she said smiling up at him, an almost other worldly glow emanating from her face. Ransford, clearly taken aback, looked at her with wonder.

"Could you, by any chance, have been from Yorktown, Virginia? Were you possibly orphaned during the war?" He asked incredulously, anxious to hear her reply.

"Why yes, sir. How would you know such things about me? I don't believe we've ever met, have we?" she said, still smiling.

Ransford stared at the woman in amazement, her family gathering around in rapt curiosity. He shook his head while reaching out to shake her hand.

"My name is Ransford Densmore and, while I was a soldier in the 44th New York Infantry Regiment, another soldier and I

279

brought an orphan baby to a church in Yorktown. A pastor there introduced us to a fine young woman who took her out of my arms. We called her Aura Lea . . . .. Was that baby you?"

A tear welled in the woman's eye, and then another. She smiled at Ransford with a strange and wonderful familiarity.

"So you're one of my uncles!" She instantly embraced Ransford, hugging him sincerely. "I wanted to bring my family here, my daughter and her children, to visit this monument. They've been told about the 44th their entire lives and, well, this just seemed like a good time . . . .. I'm so, so happy to meet you!"

Ransford gazed in awe at the middle-aged woman in front of him and her daughter, a handsome young woman in her 20s, and the two lovely, exuberant children who were clinging to their mother's dress and staring upward at him. Their husbands, who would eventually join them, were outside touring Little Round Top with scores of other tourists, most of whom had read about the battles in history classes.

"I heard the lad say 'Uncle Jack;' Did you have kin in the 44th?" Ransford asked.

"Why no, Ransford. My grandchild was referring to Jack Finnegan. He's Uncle Jack. He's always been Uncle Jack to my family," she said laughing.

"How could that be?"

"As my momma tells it: A short time after the army left Virginia for the first time, a letter arrived from Private Jack Finnegan to the church explaining that he and my 'uncles' from the 44th wanted to provide for my care and eventually my education. I don't think a month went by without a letter from Jack and his friends in the 44th and it always contained money, not southern money, mind you, but Union money. Sometimes more, sometimes less, but he always provided. And back then, in Virginia, money was so hard to come by. So many suffered, especially after the war. But then Uncle Jack would send money

280

and ask my mother to put it in an account for my schooling, some day . . .. He's been our guardian angel, all these years."

"I am truly flabbergasted," said Ransford. "My dear, it is one of the greatest joys of my life to see you here, alive and grown into such a healthy and happy woman with children of her own. I was wounded the next day and sent home. Jack never told me in his letters. Kept it to himself, like he did a lot of things."

"Well, Ransford, he and you will always hold a dear place in our hearts. We owe you our lives!"

The sincerity of the statement had an impact on the old man, especially while looking at all of the wonderful lives standing before him. "It would've been truly wonderful if Uncle Jack could've lived to see this day."

Ransford again felt a wave of surprise overtake him. He hadn't known.

"Has Jack passed?"

"Why, yes, I'm sorry to say. His wife, Sophie, sent me a letter several months ago informing us of his passing. We were so distraught."

Aura Lea explained that Jack had married late in life to a woman he'd fallen for in Paris. They'd lived happily together in a villa just outside of the City of Light and would often travel to European cities and northern Africa. Jack had apparently found his fortune once again, but had never lost track of Aura Lea.

"We would often sit out on the porch and wonder aloud: Where could Uncle Jack be tonight? Strolling down the *Champs-Élysées*? Riding a camel with Sophie in Egypt? Climbing the steps of the Acropolis? He was always such a wonderful mystery to us," Aura Lea smiled at the memories. "But I wish I could have met him. Just once."

"He was just as charming and mysterious a fellow as you've imagined. I'm sure he was as proud of you and your family as I am here and now, Aura Lea," he said, choking up as he spoke. "I don't think you could ever understand how happy you've made me. So much death and sadness was born out of that war. But there was hope in the ashes. You all have shown me that. Thank you!"

The family converged around Ransford, bestowing a group hug that brought the old soldier to tears. Isaac, silently taking in the entire scene with a newfound admiration for his father, added himself to the loving gaggle that seemed to suspend time in the dusky war memorial. After a while, the entourage ventured out into the light, where they were greeted by Aura Lea's husband, a friendly, quiet man who showered his wife with attention and appreciation. After exchanging addresses and vows to remain in touch the two families made their farewells, Ransford shaking hands with the men, Aura Lea's daughter and granddaughter, and embracing Aura Lea heartily. But when he turned to the little soldier and reached out his hand, the boy straightened his back, adopted a serious military aspect, and snapped a resolute salute, staring straightaway at Ransford. For his part, Ransford stood at attention and followed suit, holding his salute.

"Permission to be dismissed, Captain?"

"Permission granted, Private!" the miniature officer chirped with great sincerity. "At ease, Soldier."

It wasn't long before Ransford and Isaac boarded a train and left Gettysburg. As they chugged away from the site of the greatest and most terrible battle in American history, Isaac recalled thinking that his elderly father appeared surprisingly refreshed, fulfilled by the trip. It was, he thought, the best thing they could have done together. Ransford had found himself again.

The remaining years of Ransford's life were unremarkable, the days peeling by rapidly, largely undifferentiated from one another. His children had grown and had families of their own. His eldest son, Isaac, was now grooming his son, James, to assume ownership of the funeral home and furniture business. Meanwhile, James' son, Irving, was enrolled in medical school at Union College in Schenectady. Known as a bit of a rabble rouser, young Irving liked tooling around in one of the community's first automobiles, a spiffy convertible Ford Roadster that popped and growled as it rolled down the country roads around town.

Unlike Ransford's later life, the world was reeling from industrial and political upheavals that had followed World War I. The carnage of that foreign struggle had shocked the world, much in the same way that the Civil War had surprised military historians for its application of more lethal technology. Air power to strafe and bomb, armored vehicles, machine guns, cannon that could launch projectiles many miles, and even chemical warfare were used with impunity on European battlefields to deadly effect. As they had during previous wars, Corinth boys returned from the first World War dead, wounded and damaged, but not to the extent of the Civil War.

Improvements in industrial technology, however, made the International Paper Company Mill in Corinth one of the grandest and most productive in the nation. Three shifts kept the great mill humming round the clock as the men of town, almost all of them, toiled in the massive machines that churned out miles and miles of coated paper daily. By 1929, the industrial world and the capitalism that fueled it was exploding, while hungry investors remained largely oblivious to the risks that lurked in the bloated stock market.

Back in Corinth, a lingering cold had taken a toll on Ranford's 90-year-old body and, sensing the worst, his doctor had sent for the family. Lying in his bed at the family's home on Main Street, four generations of Densmores gathered around Ransford, who seemed to take longer and longer between each labored breath. Looking up, his blue eyes squinting, he could see the faces of his children and grandchildren and even Irving, his great grandchild, gathered around him.

"Very proud," he whispered. "Time for me to go."

Ransford slipped away, this time for good. The demons of his dreams, perhaps quenched by so much blood, were gone. He saw light and went toward it.

XVII: My Mother's Couch

I wake one bleak February morning on my mother's red couch. It's been a long uncomfortable slumber, marked by occasional calls from the dark bedroom where my 89-year-old mom slept fitfully last night. Since a hospital visit, followed by a short convalescence at a Saratoga nursing home, my mother had, with some arm twisting, convinced medical professionals to let her return home, but only under round the clock care. My six brothers and sisters and I had devised this plan—"Seven Nights for Seven Siblings," we dubbed it—in order to provide the overnight care she needed without incurring enormous medical bills. It was supposed to have been a temporary commitment on our part, only while she either recovered strength, proving her ability to live independently once again, or realized that an assisted living facility might be the most appropriate place for her.

The sounds emanating from the bedroom indicate my mother has risen, imparting a sense of relief in me. She's come a long way over the last several weeks, reducing the weight she had gained from fluid in her torso and extremities, leaving her able to get up and down and move around the house much more freely. The slow clunk and roll, clunk and roll of her walker announces her arrival in the living room where I sit on the couch. Her jaw set, stoic and resolved, Mom pushes herself slowly forward toward the dining room table where she has established a daily beachhead, surrounded by her papers, phone, address book, and various salves, drops and pills.

"Good morning, honey," she says, followed by a report on various pains and ailments she'd experienced in the night.

"Morning, Mom. Can I get you some coffee?"

"Yes, dear, that would be nice. I'll take my pills with some of that peach yogurt and a tall glass of water, please."

"You got it, Ma."

"What I'd really like are some of those blueberry muffins from the bakery. They're so good . . .. But you have to get up there early before they sell out."

"Not a problem, Ma. I'll head out in a minute."

"Maybe you'd better call ahead, Stephen. They sell out you know."

"Will do, Mom."

I call and the nice lady at the bakery assures me they've got plenty of muffins, but they'll set some aside for me. With Mom established at the dining room table, I don my jacket and head out into the brisk morning air. It's colder here in the Adirondacks than down in Montgomery, where I live with my wife, Jackie, in a nice suburban home off a quiet cul-de-sac tucked in the middle of Orange County horse farms.

"I'll be back in little while, Mom," I call to her as I leave.

Instead of going directly to the bakery though, I divert down Main Street to take in the town of my youth. The memories flood back. Everywhere I look I can vividly recall an event or people that I shared an experience with.

Traveling through the heart of the little village it's clear that Corinth is still reeling from the loss of International Paper Company, which had closed almost two decades earlier. Its taxes and employment had gone with it and my home town, like many that lose the goose that lays the golden egg, is still searching for ways to reinvent itself.

A hole in the downtown streetscape remains from the devastating fire that wiped out some of the key commercial buildings along lower Main, including my brother's furniture store. Through the vacant lot I can see Sherman Avenue and the Densmore Funeral Home, the large white compound where we grew up in a sprawling five-bedroom flat over the parlor. I can still hear my father calling to us from the hallway in the middle of some nighttime service: "You kids be quiet, there's business downstairs!" My younger brother Robert took over as funeral director many years ago, as was my father's greatest wish, becoming the fifth generation to run the family business.

Sherman Avenue, a tiny residential street that runs from Main Street to the Hudson River, was always teeming with children. Several families on the street, most my relatives, had packs of children (Densmores, 7; Towers, 9; Saunders, 11) and on any given day 20-30 kids of all ages would be outside in the street or backyards playing pick-up kickball games, tag football, balloon fights, and riding bikes hither and yon. There was always, in a manner of speaking, a lot of life around the funeral home.

Today, fewer families congregate in the village center, which now boasts a couple gas stations, a market, some restaurants, a liquor store, and several vacant storefronts. And there's my cousin Debbie's ice cream and gift shop. It is a harbinger of optimism in an otherwise gloomy streetscape, offering soft ice cream, snacks, locally made products and crafts to seasonal visitors and locals. Deb and her husband Craig represent the future, what Corinth could become if it just found the right way forward.

I turn right onto River Road and the entrance to the Irving H. Densmore Memorial Bridge, a name given to the bridge over the Hudson a few years after Dad's death. He'd given much of his later life to civic affairs and served as its mayor for over a decade. Local papers had dubbed him the "Walking Mayor" after learning of his daily early morning walks across the bridge and into the woods on the other side. Every day, regardless of rain, snow or heat, he would take a lengthy trek to help him prepare mentally and physically for the rigors of administering to village affairs, the funeral home, and his enormous brood. Often, I'd hear him say to my mother with all sincerity: "Pauline, I just need a little peace and quiet."

But, as much as he craved solitude to balance his rambunctious life, I'm convinced he also adopted his daily walks and marathon swims in the family pool as a way of girding himself from the pain and discomfort that came from the broken back he'd suffered in a car accident as a young man. Doctors had told him that the injury to his lower back would limit him physically and probably shorten his life. He refused to surrender to those admonitions though. Throughout his long life, Dad was a picture of fortitude: he hunted deep into the mountains with his friends at the Hadley Hunting Club, he hiked the logging trails, and he swam effortlessly far past the breakers during our family trips to Maine.

When his back "acted up" he'd sit for hours in his bedroom under a contraption with a strap under his chin attached to a heavily-weighted pulley. This "traction" system was designed to pull his spine upward and give him relief from the shivering pains that occasionally shot through his lumbar region. When he knew he'd be walking or standing for long periods of time he'd affix an elaborate customized brace that looked much like a corset around his waist, my mother cinching the laces up tight so he could withstand hunting trips and long village board meetings. He never complained about any of this.

Irv Densmore had been brought into the funeral business after the untimely death of his father, James Harrison Densmore, who was felled by a heart attack in his forties. With his grandfather Isaac aging and not wanting to sell the otherwise thriving family business, Dad left medical school to return to Corinth and help Isaac with the numerous daily responsibilities that came with the operation. My father never complained about this either. He would just say to each of us, over and over, in a mantra we would hear throughout our childhood: "All I want is for you kids to graduate from college."

I continue north along the Hudson, over a lazy five-mile stretch between Corinth and Lake Luzerne. It's a pretty part of the river, deep and slow, dotted with summer camps and with docks jutting into the cool water. I pass the base of Antone Mountain, which stands like a sentinel guarding the gateway to the southern Adirondacks. We would ride bikes along this road to visit Luzerne and swim below the rapids where the Sacandaga and the Upper Hudson join in the village. Sometimes we'd grab some inflated inner tubes and hitch a ride in a pickup truck to that same spot where we would launch our little fleet and float down the river back to Corinth. It would take hours, just lazing in the summer sun, getting burned on our bellies. That, by God, was the life.

Just before I pull into the village of Lake Luzerne, I pass Waterhouse Restaurant, one of my father's favorite places to eat. Years before he passed, I'd return home on break from college sometimes and Dad and I would steal away for dinner there. Good comfort fare—pot roast and potatoes, spaghetti and meatballs—and walls lined with knotty pine paneling. They were some of the few times I could talk with my father uninterrupted. In large families like ours few conversations are ever really finished, just a series of interruptions from various factions voicing support or disapproval for this statement or that. I relished these times of quiet conversation with my father.

Sometimes I would gently goad him about his many affiliations, such as his lifelong membership in the Masons. A budding journalism student whose skepticism at times came across as arrogance, I inquired about the activities of the club, knowing full well that it was a "secret society."

"So, Dad, what do you guys do over at the Masonic Temple every other Wednesday night?"

"Well, Stephen, we do good things for the community."

"What sort of good things do the Masons do for the community?"

"I can't tell you that."

"Why not?"

"Because we've taken vows to never discuss our activities with non-members."

"Oh c'mon, Dad! You guys just drink beer and watch stag films over there."

"We certainly do not! And I don't think I care for your insolence, young man."

"I'm sorry, Pop. I'm just kidding around. I'm sure you do some very nice things . . . and maybe drink a little beer."

He would chuckle. "Well, maybe one or two."

My father passed a few years later. As you might expect, his wake was an epic affair for our little town, drawing hundreds of people and leading to an hours-long receiving line that was inspiring and exhausting all at the same time. So many relatives and family friends, interspersed with folks whose lives had intersected with my father in myriad ways unbeknownst to me, all lined up to pay their respects. Some were perfunctory and proper while others expressed heartfelt sincerity, even a curious twinkle in their eyes, that made me yearn to understand their connection to my father further. But they moved on, shuffling past my father's casket and into the night, lost to me. I was left wanting to know more about my father and his long and layered life. The next day at the Densmore Funeral Home, a special ceremony was arranged by the Corinth Masonic Temple to honor of one of their lifelong members.

At an appointed time, more than 20 Masons, all dressed sharply in neatly-fitted black outfits, abbreviated aprons, and pure white gloves, filed into the funeral home and stood at attention to render a service in front of grieving friends and family. After nearly two days of mourning and familial grief, it was a poignant reminder of my father's commitment to civic affairs, even if that commitment had been at times secretive. The sincerity and solemnity of the men, many of whom were strangers to me, was intriguing, since I knew almost everyone in Corinth.

The Masonic service began with a series of prayers, spiritual and appropriate to the Masonic creed, expressing the belief that their brethren would flourish in a world beyond this one, acknowledging a higher power but espousing no particular dogma. After the prayer, a thin elderly gentleman, again, unknown to me, recited without benefit of any written prompt a lyric Celtic poem lasting several minutes about a passing warrior that had many of us weeping by its end. I did not write it down and can't remember a line of it, but it moved me like few other things I've heard. Perhaps it was the circumstance. I don't know, but I was touched by the sincerity of these men and their commitment to their experience with my father and I regretted, from that point forward, ever questioning the Masons or my father's involvement with them.

Another night out with my father, I recall asking Dad about his experiences with the hereafter. As was my custom, I would occasionally inject odd questions into otherwise mundane conversations about school or girlfriends or the Yankees. Over an appealing plate of ziti and meatballs, I bluntly confronted my father with a particularly sensitive subject that I had never explored before.

"Dad, if there's anyone in the whole world who might know whether ghosts really exist, it would be you. I mean, hell, you're around dead people all the time. So Dad, I'm asking you: Do ghosts exist?"

My father suddenly took on the aspect of a Mafia witness being interrogated by an FBI agent. He leaned over his plate of pasta and adopted a familiar look, one that told me he'd rather not be heard by those dining around us.

"Well, yes Stephen, there is something there . . . after death."

"What do you mean, Dad? What's there after death?" I leaned instinctively inward over the small table, acknowledging that what he was saying was somehow privileged, like it was off the record for fledgling journalists like me.

"Well, it's not like there's things floating around in front of you. It's not like that," he said, looking concerned that he'd said too much. "It's like they speak to you . . . in your mind, while you're around them. The dead, I mean."

"Really?" I said in unguarded amazement. "What do they say?"

"That everything is going to be alright. That they're okay and not to worry."

I remember thinking how raw and simple it was. It took me by surprise; but I never forgot it. After interviewing a thousand people in my career, I'd rarely encountered anyone more sincere and convicted than my father that night. And I guess that explained why he was so comfortable around the dead with no one around. He had no fear of the dead and, by extension, I don't believe he feared death. But he did love to live, and he held onto life as long as he possibly could.

Which brings me back to my mother, who'd been waiting patiently for her muffins for quite some time now. I turn the car around and drive back down the Hudson to Corinth. I take River Road past the bridge and the paved recreational trail connecting the village beach to Pagenstecher Park. When she was head of the village's recreation committee, Mom worked to get the funds to build the pathway that clings to the southern edge of the river affording beautiful views of the rapids below Curtis Mill and the great sheer cliffs that dominate that stretch of the river before it reaches Palmer Falls, the magnificent cataracts that made Corinth home to many mills and factories in its early history. Whenever I visit Corinth I love to drive the loop into Pagenstecher Park and take in the wondrous view from the cliffs looking north up the Hudson. Standing beneath the barrel straight hemlocks that keep the park about ten degrees cooler than elsewhere, I can see the rapids below where intrepid teenage boys used to swim naked on hot summer days, past Curtis Mill to the picturesque village, with its cozy little beach and the bridge named after my father, up the lazy part of the river to the foot of Antone Mountain, the rest of the

Adirondacks looming in the distance. I've been to Alaska, Montana, and New Mexico; hiked the Green Mountains; and biked in Acadia National Park in Maine; but, to me, those glorious places have nothing on certain spots in the Adirondacks and this is one of them.

I left here after college to find work and adventure. For awhile I worked at a paper in Saratoga and then I took a reporting job far down river in Dutchess County. There my life took root, leading to partnerships and marriages that some would call failures. But I view them as necessary steps leading to the good things in my life now: my wife, my children, my business. But through it all I have always returned to Corinth, it seems to always draw me back up the river to my ancestral home.

Mom greets me as I enter the house.

"Is that you, Stephen? You've been gone quite some time."

"Yes, Ma, I'm sorry. Took a little drive around town."

"That's nice, son. When you get your coat off, could you bring me some more coffee and one of those muffins?"

"Of course."

As I comply with her request, I hear her approaching, pushing her walker forward into the kitchen. She has an earnest look on her face, that stoic look that I've seen before, not just on her face but on the faces of soldiers in paintings as they assault an impregnable position. She is noble in her struggle, I think to myself.

"Stephen I've been thinking about my 90th birthday this summer. I'd like to share some ideas about how we're going to celebrate."

"Sure, Mom." This catches me off guard. Not long ago we were counting each day and week as a blessing. But now she's planning her party.

"I want to have it here, not at any restaurant," she states. "I'll warn you right now, Stephen, it's going to be big . . . and expensive."

I can't help but laugh. "Then we better start planning, Mom."

Unlike me, my mother never left Corinth. She is rooted here, as strong and as beautiful as the mountains beneath her feet, as relentless as the river.

Works Cited

Atwater, D. & Barton. C. *A List of the Union Soldiers Buried at Andersonville*, New York, The Tribune Association, 1866.

Bisbess, M. C., lyrics. "Always Stand on the Union Side," 1863.

Bowen, J. "Drill for Dummies." *1ˢᵗ US Infantry*. http://www.1stusinfantry.org/articles/drilling_dummies.html

Davis, D. & Sauers, R. *The Civil War Chronicle*, Lincolnwood, Publications International Ltd., 2004.

Eggleston, A. "A History of Corinth 1997-2000," Corinth.

Faust, D. *This Republic of Suffering—Death and the American Civil War*, New York, Vintage Books, 2008.

George-Kanentiio, D. "Passing into the Spirit World: The Mohawk Rituals of Death." *Manataka American Indian Council*. www.manataka.org/page735.html.

Hardy, M. *The Battle of Hanover Court House: Turning Point of the Peninsula Campaign, May 27, 1862,* Jefferson, McFarland & Company, 2006.

Hess, P. "The First Days of the Civil War in Albany." *The New York History Blog: Historical News & Views From the Empire State.* 23 June 2015. newyorkhistoryblog.org/2015/06/23/the-first-days-of-the-civil-war-in-albany/#sthash.

History of Herkimer County, New York. New York, F.W. Beers & Co., 1879.

History of the Town of Corinth/History of Saratoga County.

Jordan, B. *Marching Home—Union Veterans and Their Unending Civil War,* New York, Liveright Publishing Corporation, 2014.

Kellison, J. H. "Baseball During the Civil War & Reconstruction Era." Academia, 9 December 2013. www.academia.edu/5405666/Baseball_During_the_Civil_War_and_Reconstruction_Era

Lincoln, A. "Second Inaugural Address." United States

    Capitol, Washington D.C. 4 March 1895.

McFeeley, M. & W. *Grant*, New York, Literary Classics of the

    United States, 1990.

Nash, E. A. *A History of the Forty-Fourth Regiment New York*

    Volunteer Infantry, Chicago, R. E. Donnelly & Sons

    Company, 1911.

Robertson, J. *The Untold Civil War—Exploring the Human Side of*

    War, Washington D. C., National Geographic, 2011.

Stanley, J. "The Death and Embalming of U.S. Grant." *History*

    in the Raw (The bare facts of history that you don't get to read

    very often). 2 July 2011.

    http://edisoneffect.blogspot.com/2011/07/death-

    and-embalming-of-us-grant-1885.html.

Tooker, E. *Native North American Spirituality of the Eastern*

    Woodlands, Mahwah, Paulist Press, 1979.

Wright, J.D. *The Timeline of the Civil War*, San Diego, Thunder

    Bay Press, 2007.

Acknowledgements

This book would not have been possible without the talent, contributions and sacrifice of many, including:

Cover Design by Dee Densmore Studio

Editing by Briana Maloney

The dedicated historians, librarians and record keepers of Corinth and Saratoga County.

Colonel Elmer Ellsworth of Mechanicville, NY

The Densmore Family

The 70 young men from Corinth who went off to war on behalf of the Union cause and the 20 who gave the ultimate sacrifice in that struggle